GENA SHOWALTER

The Darkest Whisper

"[Showalter] infuses her stories with plenty
of passion, hope and love. If you like your
paranormal dark and passionately flavored,
this is the series for you."
—*RT Book Reviews*, 4 stars

The Vampire's Bride

"Thanks to Showalter's great writing and
imagination, this story, reminiscent of a reality
show with all-powerful gods pulling everyone's
strings, will really appeal."
—*RT Book Reviews*, 4 stars

The Darkest Pleasure

"Showalter's darkly dangerous Lords of the
Underworld trilogy, with its tortured characters,
comes to a very satisfactory conclusion."
—*RT Book Reviews*, 4 stars

The Darkest Kiss

"In this new chapter the Lords of the Underworld
engage in a deadly dance. Anya is a fascinating
blend of spunk, arrogance and vulnerability—
a perfect match for the tormented Lucien."
—*RT Book Reviews*, 4½ stars

"If there is one book you must read this year,
pick up *The Darkest Kiss*...a Gena Showalter book
is the best of the best."
—*Romance Junkies*

The Darkest Night

"A fascinating premise, a sexy hero and nonstop
action, *The Darkest Night* is Showalter at her finest,
and a fabulous start to an imaginative new series."
—*New York Times* bestselling author
Karen Marie Moning

GENA SHOWALTER

TWICE as HOT

Tales of an extra-ordinary girl

HQN™

Recycling programs
for this product may
not exist in your area.

ISBN-13: 978-0-373-77437-1

TWICE AS HOT

Copyright © 2010 by Gena Showalter

Dear Reader,

What could be more fun than a woman developing unexpected superpowers? That same woman trying to plan her wedding to a sexy government agent, of course! *Wedding dress* is suddenly synonymous with *bonfire*, and a paraster—paranormal disaster—waits around every corner.

But I had to write this story. In *Playing with Fire*, the first novel in the TALES OF AN *EXTRAORDINARY GIRL* series, there was one narrative thread that I did not tie up (and *could* not tie up at the time). One thread that stuck with me all these years.

Was Belle Jamison the one and only woman for Rome Masters?

Rome's ex, the world's best psychic, doesn't seem to think so. And when Rome returns from a mission, minus only his memories of Belle, Belle begins to wonder, as well. Are they or aren't they? Can they or can't they? I hope you enjoy discovering the answers as much as I did.

Wishing you all the best,

Gena Showalter

Other sexy, steamy reads from
GENA SHOWALTER
and HQN Books

To Super Sisters:
Shonna Hurt and Michelle Quine

To Authors FantasticO:
Jill Monroe, Kresley Cole, P.C. Cast
and Candace Havens

To Team Amazing:
Margo Lipschultz, Tracy Farrell,
Margaret Marbury and Tara Parsons

To Web Weavers:
Matthew and Jennifer

To Beyondcallofduty Girl:
Elaine Spencer

To Wonder Boy:
Max

May the force be with you all!

Acknowledgments

To you, my readers.
Thank you!

extraordinary:—*adj* **1.** beyond what is usual, ordinary, regular or established: *Belle Jamison* **2.** exceptional in character, amount, extent, degree; noteworthy; remarkable: *an extraordinary woman named Belle Jamison* **3.** (of an official, employee, etc.) outside of or additional to the ordinary staff; having a special, often temporary task or responsibility: *minister extraordinary and plenipotentiary. Superhero extraordinary Belle Jamison.* [Origin: 1425–75; late ME *extraordinarie,* fr. L *extraordinarius*]

To Do List

—Find out what's bugging your BFF Sherridan even if you have to freeze her ass to a wall. Literally! Her mood swings are worse than yours.

—Buy (another) wedding dress. And for God's sake, don't set this one on fire.

—Order the wedding napkins—without soaking them in torrents of your deadly rain (again). Remember to insist your initials go *before* Rome's this time and maybe even call him "Mr. Belle Jamison." He deserves it for continuing to call you Homicidal Tendencies Wench. You warned him!

—Order the invitations—finally! Oh, and maybe call Rome "Mr. Belle Jamison" on those, too. Or "Cat Man."

—Buy Tanner a ~~hooker~~ blow-up doll to help him get over his breakup with Lexis. Poor kid. Maybe let him pinch your butt.

—Kick some scrim ass (it's your job)! Try to make sure that be-yatch Desert Gal is first up. She's wily, that one.

—Set Rome's body on fire—without actual flames this time! If you can find him, that is, the missing bastard jackass jerk.

CHAPTER ONE

OKAY. Here's the lowdown. My name is Belle Jamison. I'm twenty-five, happy, engaged and smart depending on who—whom?—you're asking. (Sadly, my teddy bear of a dad is the only one who would pipe up with an affirmative *She's brilliant!*) I'm a former coffee wench (plus former bus driver, used-car salesman, factory worker, maid and a thousand other menial jobs), now employed by the mysterious and shadowy government agency known as PSI: Paranormal Studies and Investigations.

Oh, and I happen to control the four elements with my emotions. (If you ask my ultra-hot fiancé, Rome, he'll tell you that control is relative.) *Anyway.*

Before, I was an everyday, average, *normal* girl. Normal and wishing for more. I should have known better. Sometimes you actually get what you wish for, and the results are *not* what you expected. I'd wanted excitement. And yeah, I'd gotten it. But that excitement came with a death warrant.

See, a few months ago a crazy scientist secretly dropped a chemical into my grande mocha latte and that chemical…changed me. Belle Jamison, average no longer. Suddenly I could shoot fireballs from my eyes, freeze an entire room with a brush of my fingertips against a wall, cause a tempestuous rainstorm with my tears and start a level-five tornado with only a thought.

At first, I was upset. I mean, really. The ability to destroy the entire world and everyone in it is a huge burden to carry. But that burden also brought the sexy and insatiable Rome Masters into my life, so I don't begrudge it too much. Anymore. Plus, now that I have a little influence over my gift—yeah, that's a better word for it. Gift—people who piss me off "accidentally" get their eyebrows singed and that's pretty damn fun.

Sure, Rome once tried to kill me. Or, as he'd say, "neutralize" the threat I'd become, as I'd had yet to perfect my new powers. Sure, I later accidentally-on-purpose Tasered the hell out of him. But now we can't live without each other.

That might seem weird, but hey. Some people held hands to show their love; we drew blood. Or we would, if Rome was anywhere to be found.

"I swear, he has five seconds to call me or I'm going to torch his entire gun collection and use the melted metal to make a few necklaces. Maybe some earrings."

My best friend Sherridan looked up from the romance novel propped against her upraised legs. She lounged on the couch, a vision of curly blond hair, big blue eyes more often than not filled with sadness nowadays and curves that went on for miles. I wasn't jealous. Really. "He's called you, like, four times in the past week. And seriously, you should be embarrassed. I've never met anyone who has as much phone sex as you two."

My eyes narrowed on her. "How do you know about the phone sex?"

"Duh. I pick up the phone and listen."

I gaped at her.

Sherridan laughed. "Kidding, I was only kidding. But you should see your face. Hi-lar-ious! The problem is, you're, like, freakishly loud. Seriously, earplugs don't help.

Cranking up my iPod to full blast doesn't work. Despite myself, I've been really impressed with your skills."

Color flooded my cheeks. *This* was the problem with roommates. But better Sherridan and Tanner, my other BFF, lived here where Rome and I could protect them from scrims—supernatural criminals—wanting to hurt us by hurting our loved ones. "Never mind my incredible phone sex. Rome was supposed to call me again last night. He didn't. He hasn't. That's not like him. Do you think something's wrong?"

"Stop worrying," she said with a wave of dismissal. "That he-man can morph into a jaguar, for God's sake. He's fine. He's probably planning a surprise homecoming or something."

Yes, Rome could morph into a jaguar—a sleek and sexy jaguar I loved to pet—all because of experiments he'd volunteered for, hoping to make himself stronger to better guard his loved ones. He *could* defend himself and he *did* like to please me, so a surprise arrival wasn't a stretch, but... My hand fluttered over the pulse hammering in my throat. "Really? You think that's what's going on?" Was that neediness really mine?

"Of course."

She sounded confident. But then, she hadn't battled people more monster than human. People who could walk through walls, shift into creatures of the night and leap at you with fangs and claws bared—or simply materialize in front of you with a knife in hand.

I had. Rome had. And I had no idea what he was up against this time.

Heart thundering in my chest, I stood in the middle of the living room and studied the home I now shared with him. I'd decorated it, so of course it was made of awesome. From the bright red velvet chairs to the beaded blue pillows tossed haphazardly about to the purple lace hanging from the windows, the place was a veritable rainbow. Rome hadn't complained. First time he'd seen it, he had walked in, looked around and shaken his head with a wry smile.

"Should have expected it," he'd said, before pouncing on me for a few hours of undercover fun.

"He's never *not* called me when he said he was going to call me, Sherridan." I didn't dare refer to her as Sherri. I was the one with superpowers, but she would have found a way to peel the skin from my bones and wear it as a victory coat. "He has one of the most dangerous jobs in the world. He could be a pile of ash for all I know." *Oh, God.* Another thought like that, and I was likely to flood my beautiful rainbow living room.

Sighing, she shut the book with a snap. "All right. You need to vent, so I'll listen to you vent. But do it quickly, because Rydstorm was about to plunder Sabine with his thick, hard—"

"Sherridan Smith! Tanner's in the next room and from what I've been able to get out of him, he's still mourning Lexis." Lexis was Rome's still-infatuated ex-wife. When she'd realized Rome loved me—and would always love me, I added for my own benefit— she had turned to Tanner for comfort. The now twenty-year-old kid-boy-*man* had been all too willing to console her. Virgin that he was—is?—I think he'd even fallen in love with her. But then, about a week ago, she'd kicked him out of her house, claiming she didn't want to see him again.

Tanner had been a mess ever since.

Lexis was the most powerful psychic I'd ever encountered, so I was willing to bet she'd had a negative vision about Tanner and had cut him loose because of it. While

I (sometimes) liked her, though, we weren't on friendly enough terms for me to phone her and ask.

Sherridan's lips lifted in a slow, wicked smile. Her first in days, and that warmed me up inside. Between her and Tanner, I'd gotten my fill of doom and gloom. "If I know that pervert, he's watching porn."

I couldn't refute that. Tanner did like his porn.

"Besides," Sherridan said, "it's not like his superpower is supersonic hearing." She was grumbling now.

No, Tanner was an empath. A human lie detector. He could sense emotions, which was why he was the perfect partner for me. He let me know when my feelings—and thereby the world—were about to explode so that I could calm myself down.

"Call your boss, whatshisname," Sherridan suggested. "Bob…or Jim. John!" She clapped, clearly proud of herself. "Yes. Call John. He'll know where Rome is."

"I've already spoken to John. I had my mandatory testing twice this week, and he was there to watch the poking and the prodding." Because of the chemical I'd ingested and its lingering effects, John liked to monitor me. To our mutual consternation, his tests were totally screwing with my restraint. Every time he had his vampire—you think I'm kidding?—withdraw a vial of my blood, I lost a little more control and my powers went a little wonky. Yesterday I'd turned a potted plant into a treecicle simply by glancing at it.

Or maybe the problem was this distance from Rome. I needed my man. He kept me grounded, centered. He was also able to filter out the worst of my emotions. Yeah, it was probably this temporary separation that was screwing with me. It was screwing with everything else. My peace of mind, my hormones, my appetite.

Was such dependence dangerous? And did I care?

Where the hell was he? My shoulders slumped. "John wouldn't tell me a damn thing about Rome. Even when I threatened to quit."

Sherridan rolled her eyes. "You threaten to quit every day, so that's no big deal. I told you that if you didn't save the big gun for a big battle, you'd have no ammunition when the big battle finally arrived. Didn't I? Didn't I tell you that? You're like the boy who cried wolf—or jaguar in this case—and I told you not to do it. I told you."

I kicked into motion, pacing over to frown down at her. "Do you *want* to be deep-fried?"

"Please. I'm the only person brave enough to be the maid of honor at a wedding guaranteed to be a Who's Who of Superheroes and Supervillains, so you need me. We both know I'm not in any danger from your fury-fire."

No, she wasn't. She was more likely to drown in my tears or freeze from my touch. I was depressed and scared, and my fear always summoned ice, my sadness rain. My anger summoned fire, of course, and my jealousy summoned earth. Yes, I could make dirt pies. Calling the wind required an emotional cocktail of both negative and positive, so it was the hardest to manipulate. It was hard to be happy and sad, loving and hateful at the same time.

Once, for a short window of time, I'd been able to use my powers without relying on my emotions. No longer. For whatever reason—cough John's tests and Rome's absence cough—that was now nothing more than a pipe dream.

"What if he's…" I couldn't say it. I just couldn't finish that sentence. Suddenly my chin was trembling too badly. God, I was a wreck lately! And no, I wasn't pregnant. (I'd already taken a test.)

"He's not. Who was Rome battling, anyway? And why didn't you go with him?"

"Run-of-the-mill armed guards, most likely, and I'm an idiot. Besides, Cody went with him." Cody could manipulate electricity, so he was a good partner to have. Better than me, for sure. "I've been planning a wedding, babysitting yo—uh, Tanner, researching Desert Gal and—"

"Desert Gal, huh." Sherridan sat up straighter. "You mean the psycho-bitch who drains the water out of everything she touches?"

"Yes. That's her." Unfortunately—or fortunately?—I hadn't had a face-to-face with the sadistic woman yet. One, she'd managed to elude me and two, I'd been too busy getting nailed by other scrims who'd started coming after me the moment I joined PSI. Their mission: recruit me to OASS—Observation and Application of Supernatural Studies, a nongovernment agency whose methods sometimes bordered on criminal and sometimes straight up *were* criminal. Or, if they couldn't recruit me, plan B was to kill me.

Eight had tried so far, and I'd managed to beat them all. Okay, okay, Rome had ensured victory most of the time. I was still new at the whole shadow-game thing.

"What's she look like?" Sherridan asked.

That was the kicker. No one had a picture of her. Well, not that they'd shown me. Secret agents were so…secretive. But still. I'd already proven I was trustworthy, and why not share something that would help me? "I don't know, but I'm envisioning a dried-up prune with teeth."

"Okay. I've got a visual on her now. Continue."

"One of Rome's contacts intercepted a communication between her and some as yet unknown man and learned some stuff we didn't know. Like how Pretty Boy, her former boss—you know, the evil guy Rome and I had to kill during our courtship—had several warehouses filled with people he'd locked up and experimented on. Desert Gal moved them to a central location to test them and weed out the weaklings, and Rome went to save them. But knowing Pretty Boy, and having studied Desert Gal, there were a few booby traps along the way." Just saying those two words—Pretty Boy—caused me to shudder. And I'd said them twice. Double shudder.

He'd been the most beautiful man I'd ever seen, lushly sensual, darkly erotic, yet he'd possessed a black, monstrous heart. He'd tried to experiment on me, too, as well as attempting to kill Rome. He *had* experimented on others—the ones we'd known about before his death— replacing their skin with impenetrable metal, adding animal glands to their brains so they'd have beastlike instincts. He'd done other stuff, too. Stuff I couldn't even consider without gagging. All to build an army. An army that would bring him money and (more) power.

Très cliché if you asked me.

Sherridan leaned forward, clearly intrigued. The book fell to her feet, a warrior's bright eyes staring up at me. "There were survivors?" she asked. "I thought all the people Pretty Boy tampered with ended up dying. Even the ones you guys rescued from those cages."

"They did. Well, those did. Like I said, he had other warehouses, more people. Apparently these groups not only survived, they've begun to thrive. Rome was to bring them to PSI for questioning and testing. John wants to do a little recruiting of his own, I'm sure."

"Wow, experiments that actually worked," she said reverently, her blue eyes glazing over. Then her features softened, and her mouth parted on a dreamy sigh.

Her mind was wandering.

What, she wanted to be experimented on? I shook my head and had to hook several strands of my honey-colored hair behind my ears to keep them from slapping my cheeks. "Sherridan."

No response.

I rubbed my temples and closed my eyes for a moment. If I knew my friend, and I think I did, since we'd been friends for years, she'd just entered her Happy Place. She would be there for half an hour, at least. Trying to engage her now would be pointless.

Ever since Sherridan had learned about my abilities, she'd been acting strangely, retreating more and more into her mind. Oh, she still loved me. That wasn't in question. And I knew she didn't fear me. If she asked me to blow-dry her hair from fifty paces one more time, I was going to strangle her. But there was something almost…depressed about her, as though her life now lacked excitement and adventure.

I knew that feeling.

There were people in the world with beauty, riches, power. Their every step seemed blessed; failure and rejection were not things they'd ever experienced. Excitement greeted them everywhere they went, danger was something to be laughed at and anything they desired, they could have. In their hands, they held the power to change the world. At one time, I would have killed for such a life. Now, I *have* killed for it, but it wasn't the charmed existence I'd once thought it would be.

Perhaps I should have known such gifts would come with a price. But all I'd seen was the glitz, the glamour. The exhilaration. I hadn't known that there would always be a thousand others willing to rip me apart to possess what I have.

I prayed Sherridan didn't desire what I had desired— what I had gotten. This power beyond imagining. I prayed she was smarter.

Behind me, I heard a door creak open. Close. Footsteps.
I twisted. A slump-shouldered Tanner was strolling
down the hall. I worried over the change in his appearance. He wore black as usual, but in the past his clothes
had always been clean. Now his dark attire was dirty and
wrinkled, his azure hair unwashed and in spikes around
his head. He looked terrible. There were bruises under
his eyes and lines of tension around his mouth. He'd
even taken out his signature eyebrow ring and Eight
Ball contacts.

I'd known and loved him for several months, and I
hated seeing him like this. He was tall and when I'd first
met him he'd been extremely lean, more boy than man.
But he'd begun to fill out and muscle up, coming into his
own in both command and confidence. This past week,
though, he'd started to slim down again, as if he didn't
have the will to eat.

"Hey, Crazy Bones," I said. It was my pet name for him.

Usually he grinned. Now he stopped a few feet away
from me and peered down at Sherridan as if I hadn't
spoken. "Happy Place?" he asked.

I nodded, my heart lurching at the sadness in his tone.

"She's weird."

"Tanner," I said, then stopped when he faced me. My
heart gave another lurch. God, his eyes. Once a bright blue
(when he didn't disguise them with those crazily patterned
contact lenses), they were now dull and listless and swim-
ming with misery. They were dark and dismal. Hopeless.

In that moment, I hated Lexis. Tanner was the brother
I'd never had, hadn't known I'd wanted and needed, and
couldn't live without. I couldn't stand seeing him like this.

"Don't," he said. His jaw tightened. "Just don't."

"Don't what?" I asked, even though I knew what he
meant. I just wanted to draw him out of his miserable shell.

"Don't feel sorry for me." He moved forward, brushing me aside with his shoulder.

I remained in place, a little stunned. He hadn't made a single derogatory comment about my breasts or tried to cop a feel. Even when death had been breathing down our necks, he'd been unable to go five minutes without talking about my nipples.

Okay, so maybe "brother" wasn't the best word to describe him. He was the boyfriend I adored but wouldn't sleep with. Wait. No, that didn't work, either. Whatever he was, I loved him. Plain and simple.

"Tanner, I don't feel sorry for you," I called, bypassing our air purifier and following him into the kitchen. Because my abilities were so attuned to nature, toxins were my greatest enemy now, so there was another air purifier in the kitchen. Another in my bedroom. Another in the hallway.

Tanner was digging inside the fridge. Bottles clinked together; something thumped from the top shelf. "Doesn't matter. I don't want to talk about her."

"You need to, because it's festering inside you. You're falling apart and—"

"Hey, which of us is the master of emotions here? Besides, I know what you're going to say. You've been here, done that. Yeah, I know. Only difference is, you got a happily ever after. I won't."

"She was your first love, but there will be others. You'll see. Just give it time. You'll get over her and someone else will catch your eye."

Every muscle in his body stiffened, but he didn't face me. "So what you're telling me is that if Rome didn't want you, you'd be okay with finding someone else?"

No. Never. Rome was it for me. The one and only. My man. I couldn't even imagine myself with someone else. Poor Tanner, I thought again. Had he really loved Lexis like that?

"Why did she end things?" I asked softly.

Silent, he straightened. He was holding a beer, staring down at it.

"Uh, you're not twenty-one," I pointed out, just to break the quiet tension.

Finally he flicked me a glance. "Feel free to turn me in." He popped the cap and leaned back, the rim suddenly at his lips. In record time, he drained the contents of the bottle, tossed it into the trash and reached for another.

"No, I meant, you're not twenty-one so you shouldn't be drinking without a responsible adult drinking with you. Toss me one."

That earned me a grin. Swift, but there for that brief moment all the same. I felt as if I'd conquered the world. And I hadn't even had to use my powers! "Like you're responsible," he said.

"Well, I am an adult."

"That's debatable, too." He tossed me a beer.

My reflexes were not as defined as my paranormal abilities, and I almost dropped it, the condensation making it slick. I had to clasp it with two hands to maintain a firm enough grip.

"Already had one?" he asked.

I looked drunk? This early in the morning? "I'm not belting out show tunes, so no."

With a flick of his wrist, Tanner closed the fridge and faced me fully. I settled atop one of the bar stools, sipping at the beer. Ick. Not my alcoholic beverage of choice, especially for breakfast, but it would do. Anything for Tanner. "Talk to me. Please. I'm worried about you."

He shrugged, his eyes once again swirling with more misery than any one person should have to deal with.

"Nothing to tell, really. We got together because she needed someone to comfort her and I needed a willing body to lose my virginity to."

"And did you?"

One of his black brows arched. "None of your business."

Did that mean no? The Tanner I knew liked to kiss and tell and besides that, they'd seemed so hot and heavy. PDA was not something they'd eschewed.

He drained the second beer as quickly as the first, then closed his eyes and pressed the dripping bottle against his chest. Once, twice, he banged his head against the refrigerator, saying, "She told me she knew we weren't meant to be together. That something was going to happen, and one day I'd realize it." He laughed bitterly. "She said I'd even thank her."

Oh, crap. Lexis's predictions were never wrong. That didn't lessen the sting of the here and now, though. I knew that well. Long ago, Lexis had dumped Rome because she'd known deep down she wasn't the woman of his heart, wasn't his one and only. She'd known he would stay with her anyway because he was the father of their child. She'd known, and it had broken her. So she'd cut him loose. Just like she'd cut Tanner loose.

Was Tanner destined to love someone else?

Suddenly I didn't hate Lexis quite so much.

She'd told me once that she didn't know if I was Rome's one and only, either, that she'd had a vision of that girl but had never seen her face. A lot of days I could pretend that didn't bother me. Most days, in fact. Sometimes in the early morning, though, when I was alone in bed, too sleepy to block my fears, I would wonder if some girl was out there, soon to meet Rome—soon to enthrall him, steal his affections.

But then I would wake up and remind myself that

Rome was not a man easily swayed. He loved me. He wanted forever with me or he wouldn't have asked me to marry him.

Tanner's eyelids cracked open, his features now covered with an expressionless mask, his gaze empty and his jaw relaxed. "She also said her true love would be coming back into her life." His voice was devoid of emotion, as well.

Okay. I hated her again. *Her* true love? Her true love would be coming *back* to her? Last time I'd spoken with her, she had (mistakenly) thought her true love was Rome. So what the hell had she meant by *true love?* There had better be someone else she considered her true love, someone else from her past, or I would extract her intestines and use them to choke her.

A knock sounded at the door.

I didn't move, too keyed up from my rush of anger. Rome and Tanner were more important to me than breathing, and that bitch had better—

Another knock, this one harder, more insistent.

"You should get that, 'cause damn," Tanner said, "you're about to light the house on fire and I don't need to add homelessness to my plate-o-shit. Besides, your visitor might be John with the lowdown on Rome."

The one thing sure to push me into action. My fury drained. "Don't move. I'll get the 411, get rid of whoever it is—" hopefully without too much of an emotional outburst, whatever the news, which had better be good "—and we'll finish our discussion. You matter to me, and we're going to figure this thing with Lexis out." *And then I'm going to hunt her down and demand some answers Belle-style.*

Uh-oh. There was my anger again.

Tanner shrugged, but I could see the spark of hope suddenly lighting his eyes. He trusted me to help make things better, and that made me doubly determined to do so.

As yet another knock echoed, I rushed to him and hugged him tight. Then I raced out of the kitchen and past the still-entranced Shcrridan, not stopping until I reached the door.

I glanced through the peephole. The moment I saw who waited on the porch, my hands curled into fists, plumes of dark smoke suddenly wafting from my nose. Red dotted my vision like fireworks on the Fourth of July. Well, well, well.

Speak of the devil and she would appear.

CHAPTER TWO

MY JAW WAS LIKE STONE as I punched in the security code to disable the alarm and opened the door.

Lexis stood before me, a vision of feminine beauty as always. Long dark hair, straight as a pin. Hypnotic green eyes, pretty pink lips. Golden skin that defined the word *perfection*. Sunlight bathed her, seeping from the sky as if compelled to caress her.

Behind her, cars meandered through the pristine neighborhood. Birds chirped from the blue sky and locusts rattled in a surprisingly sensual beat. Intense humidity and heat wafted my way. I, of course, began to sweat like a construction worker while Lexis continued to appear unaffected, her silky emerald suit completely dry.

"What are you doing here?" I demanded, thinking, *Somehow, someway, I'm taking you down.*

Smelling like an ancient garden, all flowers and magic, she tried to stride past me. My arm and leg whipped out, blocking her path. After an indelicate *humph,* she glared up at me. I was taller than she was, nah nah nah. A girl had to find joy where she could.

"Let me in, Belle," she snapped.

Usually she was poised, nothing able to ruffle her. Score one for me. "No," I snapped back. A tiny flame flickered at the end of my index finger, and I whisked it behind my back. Wouldn't be good form to fry her up before I'd obtained answers. "What do you want?"

She squared her delicate shoulders, looked away from me. "I need to talk to you."

"Uh, that would be a no. Tanner's here. Which means you're not welcome anymore."

Her features softened and her eyes widened, regret churning in their depths. "This is important."

"He's more important than anything you've got to say," I said, still not allowing her inside. "By the way, where's Sunny?"

"My brother-in-law has her."

"*Former* brother-in-law." Bitch. "You're divorced." Sunny was Rome's little girl, his pride and joy, and we watched (and pampered) her every weekend. Today was a weekday, but anytime Lexis was called away to work we happily took over Sunny's care early. I loved that child like she was my own.

Lexis's gaze met mine in a heated clash. "I'm here about Rome. Something's happened."

Magic words. I moved aside. Fear instantly cascaded through me, dousing the heat of my anger, freezing and thickening every drop of blood in my veins. Mist formed in front of my nose with every exhalation I made.

Lexis strode inside. I had to fight past the tightness in my joints to follow her. My movements were slow, forced. *Something's happened, but that doesn't mean Rome's hurt. Calm down!*

She stopped in the center of the living room, breathed deeply—to catch Rome's lingering wild scent?—and glanced at Sherridan, who was still sitting on the couch with a blank expression. "Happy Place?" she asked, turning to face me.

I nodded. There was a hard lump in my throat, and I was having trouble swallowing. *He's fine.*

Lexis returned her attention to my friend, shock flashing over her features, there one moment, gone the next. Then she was shaking her head, a little sad. "Her greatest wish is going to come true, and she's going to hate herself for it."

"What do you mean?" I asked, finally finding my voice. "What wish?" As I spoke, I prayed it wasn't what I'd suspected earlier. Sherridan had a thriving real estate business, a date with a new, sexy man every weekend and me as a best bud. She didn't need anything else.

From the corner of my eye, I saw a flash of black. Oh, no. Everything else was forgotten as I focused on Tanner. He stood in the doorway between the kitchen and the living room. He leaned against the wall, his arms crossed over his chest, his eyes anywhere but Lexis.

Lexis noticed him, too, and gulped, sadness skating over her expression a second time only to be replaced by determination. "Tanner," she acknowledged softly.

He gave a stiff nod and said, "S'up," as if he hadn't a care.

"I just… I—" Sighing, she turned away from him, giving him her back.

Hurt flashed over Tanner's face, and then his jaw hardened, his eyelids narrowed. So badly I wanted to shake Little Miss Know-It-All until she passed out.

"What's wrong with Rome?" I asked. "Tell me and get out."

"Something's wrong with Rome?" Tanner was at my side, his arm around my waist and offering support within seconds.

Needing every ounce of strength he could give me, I rested my head on his shoulder.

He shivered. "Damn, you're cold," he said, and I knew he meant it literally. "Deep breaths, Viper." Viper, *his* pet name for *me*. "Good, that's good, but you're not calming."

Lexis watched us with a hint of longing. Exactly what was she longing for? A partnership like Tanner and I had? Well, she'd destroyed her chance. More than that, Team TannaBelle wasn't accepting new members. Except for Rome. I needed him, too. Like I'd said, he was my filter. He could take my emotions and cage them inside his body, removing the edge, the danger.

Was he okay? Had he been hurt?

A crystallized raindrop dripped from the ceiling, my fear and sadness too much. It spilled out of me and would soon consume the entire house if I wasn't careful.

"Tell me what's going on," I managed to croak.

That emerald gaze slid from my face to the hands twisting at my T-shirt—to the engagement ring glittering on my finger, a flat, fire-retardant titanium band with diamonds encrusted in the center. It was exactly what I would have picked for myself. Rome knew my likes, my dislikes and had known that anything similar to the five-carat rock he'd given Lexis would have irritated me.

Delicate mist formed in front of Lexis's face as she breathed. "Something went wrong. I— He—"

Oh my God. "What! Just say it!"

Tanner squeezed my side as another crystallized droplet fell, shattering when it hit the wooden floor.

In, out, I breathed. In, out. I was shaking uncontrollably.

"He and Cody made it into the warehouse and fought the guards posted there. It was more of a battle than they'd anticipated. Desert Gal, who wasn't there at the time, had taken over OASS, as we suspected, and had already fortified all their defenses, as we did not. Still, they managed to beat the guards and free the prisoners." Her voice shook. "Then one of those prisoners…attacked Rome."

"Is he okay? Is he—" I still couldn't bring myself to say it. Tanner began shaking, too.

"He's alive," Lexis said.

Thank God. Relief poured through me, palpable, heady. My eyelids closed, and my knees would have buckled if Tanner hadn't been holding me up. The ice inside me started to melt and the ceiling ceased its weeping. "I should kill you for scaring me like that."

"You didn't let me finish," was the hard reply.

My eyelids popped open, and the ice immediately returned. "Finish, then! Tell me everything. Right. Now! I'm fighting for control here, and you're only making it worse."

She nodded, grim, and that quick acquiescence made me all the more uneasy. "During the fight, his opponent disappeared. Inside him," she added grimly. "The man disappeared *inside him*. It did something to him, something bad."

I shook my head, hair slapping my cheeks but not managing to abate my confusion. "How is that possible? That's not—"

She laughed bitterly, cutting me off. "Anything is possible. You should know that by now."

I did. Oh, God, I did. "Is the man still…" And if so, what did that mean? I'd only known about this supernatural side of life a few months. I'd been thrust into it unexpectedly, utterly unprepared and, at first, disbelieving. In so many ways, I was still a baby.

"No. He only stayed inside of Rome a few minutes, and then he exited Rome's body as if nothing strange had happened. Cody tried to capture him, but the man stepped inside of him, too, before escaping. Both Cody and Rome collapsed, but Cody was the first to awaken. He gathered

Rome and the remaining experiment victims and re- turned to PSI headquarters. They arrived this morning. Rome is still unconscious."

Shock was once again beating through me. I should have been there. I could have helped him, could have erected an air shield while he worked and kept him safe. But I hadn't gone; I'd been too preoccupied with planning my wedding. Guilt joined the shock, followed quickly by shame.

"John should have told me," I said softly. Why hadn't he? He'd had the opportunity. Knowing him, though, he'd probably wanted concrete answers—how, why, last- ing effects—before freaking me out.

"He didn't even call me. I only know because I saw it…last night in my…dreams."

Why the hesitation? "You see the future, not the past." Hope filled me. "Maybe it hasn't happened yet. Maybe we can stop—"

She was shaking her head, grimmer than I'd ever seen her, dashing every bit of my hope. "I know my visions. This has already happened."

That struck me as odd, but I was too crazed at the moment to reason it out.

Tanner gave me a little shove toward the hallway. "He's going to be fine. Change out of your pj's and get your stuff. I'll take you up there."

AN HOUR LATER, I found myself standing outside of Rome's recovery room in PSI headquarters. I'd been beside his bed, but my grief had gotten the better of me and ice tears had once again begun falling from the ceiling, so I'd been asked to leave. Now I was looking at the love of my life through a glass partition.

He lay motionless, his dark hair in disarray. His

features were smooth, as if he were merely sleeping, at peace and healthy and dreaming of love and heart-pounding sex. Perhaps the last was wishful thinking. Long black lashes feathered over his sharp cheekbones. I wanted to trace the shadows they cast, the slope of his nose. His lips were soft and parted. I'd kissed those lips. Those lips had kissed every inch of me.

He hadn't lost any weight. His body was still tanned, primed and roped. Pure strength, total vitality. The only evidence that something was wrong was the electrodes scattered all over his torso. On the monitor, his heartbeat appeared steady and sure.

Lexis stood beside the bed, clasping his hand. Tears were sliding down her cheeks and dripping onto his bare chest. They should have been *my* tears. *I* should have been the one holding his hand.

Right then, I hated my powers.

Tanner was in the waiting room with Sherridan, who had yet to exit her Happy Place. How I envied her. Rome was my Happy Place, but I couldn't get to him. And I couldn't leave to give them an update. Approaching Rome was too dangerous, but I refused to move from this spot. When he awoke, he would need me. By then, I would be calm.

Really? Several ice crystals splattered atop my head. Hand shaky, I brushed them off. Stupid fear. Several more instantly took their place, but I didn't bother with them. Until I did that pesky calming thing, they wouldn't stop falling.

"Belle."

I felt the heat and zap of Cody's body as he approached me, and then I caught the scent of a wild storm. Familiar, but not as comforting as it should have been. I didn't turn. My gaze was still locked on Rome. My

Rome. Lying there, so helpless. Even with all my powers, there was nothing I could do to help him right now. None of the doctors knew what was wrong or why they couldn't rouse him.

"What happened?" I asked Cody softly. He and Rome were friends. They worked together, trusted each other. He would tell me the truth—no matter how much it hurt.

"I honestly don't know."

Or maybe not. "If you're saying that because you think the truth will cause me to break down—"

"Nothing like that, believe me." He laughed, but there was a hard edge to the sound. "If I knew, I'd tell you. But it's like a piece of my brain is missing, my memories of the event gone. All I know is that I saw Rome open one of the cages and then he was unconscious on the ground. Next thing I knew, I was on the ground myself and crawling to get to him. Had Lexis not told me about the man entering our bodies, I would have no knowledge of it whatsoever."

"He's going to be okay," I said, more for my benefit than his.

"Yes. He's strong. A fighter. Remember when our old friend Pretty Boy plugged him full of poisoned bullets? He lived through that, thanks to you, and even helped end the son of a bitch, so he can live through anything."

My hands fisted at my sides, tongues of fire suddenly licking at my skin and melting the ice. "I'm going to capture the bastard who hurt him."

"It will be my pleasure to help you."

"Thank you." I'd take any help I could get. "I doubt John will balk. The guy who attacked you and Rome is linked to Desert Gal, since she's the one who rounded up all of Pretty Boy's experiments, so technically his case should be mine, anyway." God. This might not have happened if I'd taken care of her already. She wouldn't have gathered those people, that horrible body-entering man, and Rome wouldn't have gone to that warehouse. "As soon as Rome wakes up, I'm hunting them both." No longer would I be lax in my duties.

"I'll be ready," Cody said. "From what I hear, Desert Gal is worse than Pretty Boy. More coldhearted, hungrier for power, with no perceivable weakness."

Didn't matter. I would not fail. Not again. "I'm going to request Tanner and Lexis as backup." The two might not get along, and Lexis might not be my favorite person right now, but they were amazing agents. If anyone could help me find and destroy my fiancé's tormentors, they could.

"The bastard is going to suffer," I said with determination.

"Belle," Cody said gently.

"Yes?"

"Look at me."

And away from Rome? "No, I—"

"Please."

When a strong, dominant man said please, it was best to give in unless you wanted six-foot-four of solid muscle breathing down your neck. Something I knew firsthand from Rome. I'd delighted in refusing him, and he'd delighted in changing my mind.

Eyes welling, I slowly turned to face Cody. He was almost as beautiful as Pretty Boy had been. Like a fallen angel or a glamorized devil. He had silvery-blond hair and silver eyes with a hint of violet that actually sparked with the electricity he contained inside himself, allowing him to shift into nothing but energy particles.

But he wasn't Rome, wasn't my Cat Man, and he'd never made my heart pound or my skin tighten with anticipation. I wiped at the droplets splattering my cheeks and arms.

He stepped away from me, clearly not wanting any of that water to hit, and perhaps electrocute, him. "Don't do anything rash, okay," he said, gaze sharp. "Rome would have my ass if something happened to you."

Yes, he would. Rome was wonderfully protective, one of the many things I loved about him. "He'd have mine, too."

Softening, Cody covered his fingers with his shirt and skimmed his hand over my brow, mopping up the moisture. "John doesn't want the man who did this killed. He wants him brought in for testing."

I should have known, I thought, looking back at Rome. John had wanted me for the same reason. Testing. Like an animal. Rome was supposed to be the one to bring me in; instead, he'd been the one to shelter me, teach me how to use my powers, how to love. He'd helped me escape. In the end, though, I'd turned myself in to save him, and I've never regretted it.

"Some scrims aren't meant to be saved," I said.

"That's not for you to decide." There was an edge to his tone, an edge I did not like.

I stiffened, gave him my full attention. "Who's to decide, then? John? What gives him the right? The guy who attacked you and Rome attacked agents who were there to help him. He lost his right to live."

The flickering lights in Cody's eyes brightened, spreading and deepening, becoming an electric storm that reminded me of lightning in black velvet. "Lexis told me the man was crazed. He'd been locked in one cage after another for God knows how long. Who knows if he'd been fed. Who knows what kind of torture he'd endured. He wasn't in his right mind."

I popped my jaw, refusing to soften. "I still plan to find him."

"Just…promise me you won't kill him. I ask this for your own good."

"I can't promise that. If Rome…if Rome doesn't…"

Stop! Just stop.

"He'll wake up. He'll survive this."

He would. He had to. I wouldn't allow anything else. And just like that, the rage left me and the sadness returned. I wouldn't allow? I was *powerless*. Another droplet hit me. "We don't even know exactly what's been done to him."

"We'll learn. Give it time."

My gaze skidded back to Rome. Still unmoving, still unconscious. "No one hurts my loved ones, Cody. No one. It's a message the paranormal community needs to understand. Touch them and suffer."

His hands settled atop my shoulders and he shook my attention back to him. One of his brows was arched in exasperation. "If John hears you talking like this, he'll take the Desert Gal case away from you. And if he takes the Desert Gal case, you can forget getting a chance at this new target. I don't care what threats you issue, he'll toss you in Chateau Villain."

Ugh. Chateau Villain. An underground prison where superpowers were neutralized in whatever way necessary.

Sadly, he was right. John put the interest of science—and understanding the scrims we fought—above all else.

I nodded as if Cody had convinced me to play by the rules. He hadn't. I'd just be more careful with my words from now on, I thought as I once again turned back to Rome. Or rather, the window that allowed me to see him.

Desperation flooded me, more potent than ever before. I had to touch him, had to feel his skin against mine. To do so, I had to be able to keep myself under control. *You can do it.* I just needed a few cheerful thoughts. Like? I wondered with a bitter laugh.

Well, your dad is safe in his assisted-living center and dating several of the female residents. Excellent. *Rome is still alive.* Even better. The storm inside me finally began to calm. *My best friends are with me.*

Oh, yeah. My best friends. They were still waiting.

"Will you give Tanner and Sherridan a progress report?" I asked. Not that there'd been any. Progress, that is.

"Sherridan is the rockin' blonde?"

"Yes."

"I tried to talk to her before I found you. She just stared at me blankly, like I was invisible or something."

I waved a hand in dismissal. "She wasn't doing it to be rude, I swear. She was just in her Happy Place."

"Uh, Happy Place? Can you be more specific? She have the power to transport her spirit or something?"

Of course he'd think that. He'd worked for PSI a lot longer than I had, and had seen countless different abilities. I'd have to choose my descriptions more carefully. "She had lousy parents and learned to retreat into her head when things got too rough. Lately, she practically lives there." Though I still didn't know why, exactly.

I inhaled deeply, having lost some of my cheeriness with the direction of the conversation. Cheerful thoughts, cheerful thoughts. *You can do it.* Me, walking down the aisle. A grin lifted the corners of my lips. *Good. Keep going.* My dad, healthy enough to escort me. Rome, smiling at me from the altar and glowing with love.

The ice inside me melted, leaving a cold shell that gradually thawed. Deep breath in, out. No mist formed. Thank God. I waited several minutes, but still the cold did not return.

"I'm going back in the room," I said. I wrapped my

arm around my middle and as I moved forward, my gaze snagged on Rome's left hand, where a ring—a symbol of our union—would one day rest.

His fingers were twitching.

I stilled, gasped.

"What?" Cody asked.

"He moved!" Eyes widening, I raced around Cody and into the hospital room. I shoved a nurse out of my way and barreled in front of Lexis. She snapped a curse as she stumbled backward.

After righting herself, she quickly made her way to my side. "You're too dangerous to be around him. Get out!"

"His hand moved," I said, the excitement in my voice ringing like a bell.

"What?" She grabbed his hand and lifted his fingers into the light.

"He really moved! I saw it." I tugged his hand from her grip. He was mine, and I didn't share. But as I held him, time ticking away, the muscles remained relaxed. I tried not to weep with disappointment.

So clearly I remembered the morning he'd left for this last mission. A morning I'd taken for granted, thinking countless more like it were on the way. We'd been in bed, naked, sweating from a wild pleasure-fest.

"I don't want to leave you," he'd said. His fingers had traced the ridges of my spine.

"I don't want you to leave me, either. Maybe I'll hold you prisoner."

He'd chuckled. "God, I love you. I'm even addicted to you. Get twitchy without you."

"Good, 'cause I tend to get homicidal without you."

Another chuckle. "Too bad that happens while I'm gone. You know I love to exhaust you into calmness. For world safety, and all that, because I'm such a giver."

"Well, I feel a hot rush of fury suddenly sweeping through me…"

"Do you, now? Let's see what I can do about that." He'd kissed me then, a hot, breath-stealing kiss that had rocked me to my soul.

"Come back to me, baby," I whispered now. "I need you."

His fingers twitched.

I uttered another of those shocked but happy gasps. "Rome?"

His eyelids began to flicker open.

"I think…I think he's waking up," Lexis said excitedly.

My heart nearly burst from my chest when his eyelids finally remained open. Thank God. Thank God, thank God, thank God. Rome really was awake. He was going to be okay. I twined our fingers so we were holding hands like we did every night after making love. His skin was callused and hot, so amazingly hot. So wonderfully familiar.

I breathed deeply, taking in his warmth, his deliciously feral scent. My heart kicked back into gear and fluttered wildly. I was so energized—and had been so upset—I could feel a wind swirling inside my head, a blend of the negative and positive. Maybe that wind blustered even outside my body, since my hair was dancing around my shoulders. I didn't care, though. One of my tornados could gust through the room, and I wouldn't have budged from Rome's side.

I wanted to be the first person he noticed, truly noticed. In my mind, I could already visualize him smiling warmly, love and lust gleaming at me.

Then, finally, blessedly, his eyes lost their glaze of sleep, gradually becoming alert. He glanced around the room and frowned in confusion.

"Hey, Cat Man," I said softly. "You were out in the

field and got hurt, but you're going to be fine. You're back with PSI now." *You're back with me.* "You're safe."

His gaze locked on me. His frown deepened and his brow furrowed. "Who are you?"

CHAPTER THREE

"OKAY, WHAT THE HELL is going on?" I shouted, trying to tamp down the flames already leaping inside me.

"Keep your voice down," John, my boss, said, shaking his head in exasperation.

"Your walls are soundproof so there's no need for quiet." We were inside his office at PSI headquarters, Lexis, Cody and Tanner with us. Everyone was seated. Except me. I was pounding from one wall to another, too agitated to stay still. "If I don't get some answers, I'll do more than shout!" And they all knew it was true.

So far, I'd managed to keep a tight leash on my super-reactions. Maybe because I was numb. A numbness that was due to shattering disbelief. I was a freaking stranger to my own fiancé.

I kept replaying his rejection through my mind, trying to make sense of things.

"Stop kidding and give me a hug," I'd said to him after his "Who are you?" crack. Lexis had already taken off to find John, so it was just the two of us. We should have been making out by then.

"I don't want to hurt you, lady, but if you don't move away from me I'm going to snap you in half." He'd ripped free of my grip and gritted out, "John." He looked past me to the door, searching for any sign of our commander.

"Rome," I'd said shakily.

He ignored me. "John! Get in here. What's going on?"

"Rome, you're scaring me." Even when he'd planned to neutralize me, he hadn't spoken so coldly.

His irritated gaze swung back to me. "Is this a joke? Who the hell *are* you?"

"I'm Belle." My chin quivered, the words emerging as a horrified whisper. "Your Belle."

"You aren't *my* anything."

He meant it. More than his voice, there was a coldness in his eyes I'd never seen before. Well, not directed at me. Scrims, yes, but never me.

Icy tears ran down my face. "How can you not know who I am? We're getting married!"

He stared over at me, the coldness finally melting— only to spark into anger. "The joke is now officially old. You can leave."

At last, John entered the room, an annoyingly triumphant Lexis beside him. "You rang?" he asked drily. "Must say, I'm glad to see you're awake, but your timing stinks. I was in the middle of an interrogation."

"Why is this—" When Rome noticed Lexis, he smiled slowly, happily, his question clearly forgotten. It was the kind of smile I'd dreamed of receiving. "There you are," he said. He even held out his arm for her, and she rushed over to twine their fingers. "I've been worried about you."

Nausea churned in my stomach as they cooed at each other, doing all the things Rome and I should be doing. What was happening? I almost couldn't process it.

"You were worried about Lexis?" John asked, as confused as I was.

"Of course." Rome's gaze never left his ex as they continued to coo.

John cleared his throat. "Okay, you two. That's enough. Do you know who you are, Rome?"

"Telling him his name kind of defeats the question," I muttered. I wasn't in a good mood.

"Of course I do." He cast a pointed make-her-leave glance at me. "And I'd like to talk to you. Privately."

Me, leave? I wanted to die.

"She's one of us." John pursed his lips. "She stays. Now tell us who you think you are."

"It's okay, darling," Lexis said, petting his bare shoulder. "You can speak freely."

I wanted to kill.

Rome nodded stiffly. "Who am I, you asked. I'm Agent Rome Masters, PSI elite."

"Excellent." John clasped his hands behind his back. "And you remember Lexis."

That earned another earth-shattering, "Of course," which caused Lexis to exhale with relief. And smug satisfaction, if I wasn't mistaken.

"But you don't remember Belle?"

"Who?"

Oh, God, oh, God, oh, God.

"I'll explain later. First tell me if you remember Tanner Bradshaw," John said.

Again, "Who?"

Clearly not.

As John continued to question Rome, it became all too apparent that the only things he'd forgotten were me and all things pertaining to me. It was as if I'd never entered his life. As if he'd never loved me.

Why? It made no sense.

John propped his elbows on his desk, the ensuing *thud* jolting me from my terrible thoughts. He rested his chin in his flattened palms. He had thinning gray hair, wore thick bifocals when he forgot to apply his contacts and had a slightly rotund belly. Despite all of that, he managed to radiate intense power.

He probably had a superpower, but I didn't know what it was. And yeah, I'd pestered him for the info about a million times, but he was the most secretive man I'd ever met. Which was smart, I guess. If you didn't know what he could do, you couldn't guard yourself against it.

"I've talked to Rome some more, explained who you are to him," John said. "At first he thought I was doing some sort of test, trying to gauge his reactions. But there at the end he accepted what I was saying as truth. That didn't change his mind about you, though. You're a stranger to him. A…nothing, much as I hate to say it. I'd lock you guys in a room, force you to talk it out, but a simple conversation or even a knock-down-drag-out fight isn't going to fix this. His memory of you is gone, which means his feelings for you are, too."

I nodded for him to continue, though I hated his every word. Sadly, everything he'd said I had already figured out.

"The man Lexis saw jump inside Rome's body, well, we think he was a memory eraser."

"That would explain why I lost some of my memories, too," Cody said.

I stopped pacing for a moment and gaped at him. "You don't remember the man, but you do remember me."

Two damn days had passed since Rome had woken up and looked at me like I was a strange horned alien. Two damn days of John promising to learn more, to provide me with new information but getting nothing. Finally, I'd called this meeting because—my hands fisted at my sides—Rome had been released. Physically, he was fine and yeah, he'd been quite vocal about getting back to work. But had he come home to the woman he was supposed to cherish for eternity? No! He'd remained on the premises to be close to Lexis. God Almighty, that still hurt.

"Besides that," I added through clenched teeth, "Rome remembers Lexis." The way they'd comforted each other those first few moments after he'd woken up…my hurt sharpened around the edges, slicing me so deeply I knew I'd bear the internal scars for eternity. "Why doesn't he remember *me*?"

From the corner of my eye, I saw Lexis peer down at the floor, perhaps hoping to hide her smugness. Lately, she wore it like a cloak.

Tanner, bless his heart, looked ready to bitchslap her.

"Belle, listen to me." John's eyes were like lasers as they pinned me in place. "I've spoken with him at length. I think the memories of you were somehow tangled with his memories of the man who attacked him and when one was taken, the other was dragged along for the ride."

My stomach twisted into itself, squeezing, churning. "No way. No damn way that's what happened. One, there's no reason good enough to make me believe every single memory he had of me was tied to that case. Two, memories or not, Rome should feel *something* when he looks at me. Something besides disdain, that is." More than not remembering me, he seemed to hate me and I didn't know why. If I was a stranger to him, why show me such hostility?

John splayed his arms. "Fine. You're right. I was grasping, trying to buy time to sort this out before you cause some kind of disaster."

"You want to avert a disaster? Give me something helpful!"

A moment passed before he said pointedly, "There's only one sure way to find out what really happened."

I knew that. All I had to do was find the man responsible and ask him—before I burned him alive. Or froze him. Or buried him in a mound of dirt. Maybe a combo of all three. The nice thing about having power over the four elements was that I had a smorgasbord of choices when it came to torture.

Rome would not like these thoughts, young lady. They're violent, and that isn't like my sweet baby Belle.

Uh, what was my dad doing inside my head?

Didn't matter, I supposed. *I need you, Daddy.* I wanted to crawl into his lap and rest my head on his shoulder like I'd done every time a boy had broken up with me in junior high (not that I'd had many boyfriends back then, ugly duckling that I'd been). He was a big teddy bear and when his arms were wrapped around me, I felt invincible. Not helpless and alone and tormented.

"I'm sure you've already done this, but if not, send a team back into the warehouse," I told John. "Have them search every inch and bring us everything they find. A scrap of paper, a twig, doesn't matter. We need everything." Dr. Roberts, the scientist who had infected me with my superpowers, had hidden his "magic" formula on wooden floor planks, the ink invisible until I'd frozen them, causing some sort of chemical reaction. If he'd taught me anything, it was to dig beneath the surface. I'd use my powers on every grain of dirt brought to me if necessary. Anything to help Rome.

John glared at me. "What am I? An idiot? Of course I've already sent a team to the warehouse. They're bagging and tagging every speck of dust as we speak."

"Good."

"I wasn't done. Furthermore," he continued, "we'll see if I allow you to go through the evidence. You're not objective where Rome is concerned, and let's face it, your abilities have been more unstable than usual lately."

"That's because—"

A hard rap suddenly reverberated throughout the room, saving me from having to defend myself. I whipped around, my heart stuttering to a stop. Maybe Rome had remembered me. Maybe he was here, searching for me. I licked my lips, once again barely able to stand still.

Behind me, I heard a rustle of clothes. John must have pressed the enter button, because the door slid open.

A uniformed guard stepped inside, a protesting Sherridan dragged behind him. My hope burned to ash, leaving a hollow chasm of disappointment in its wake.

"I caught her wandering the halls, sir," the guard said. "What would you like me to do with her?"

"She's with me," I said on a sigh. "Let her go."

She spotted me and stilled, her anger fading to relief. "Oh, thank God I found you. I can't believe you left me sleeping at home."

No, I'd left her wallowing in her Happy Place. Again.

"I got tired of waiting for you to return, so thought I'd do you a solid, hunt you down and allow you to give me some answers. *Most* of the security guards here are nice, by the way. They recognized me and wanted to help. Which isn't asking too much," she threw at the one still holding her. Before I could comment on how sweet she was to "allow" me to give her answers, her eyes scanned the room, and she added, "Hey, Tanner. You look as tense as those Marines we saw on those commercials. It's hawt."

"Thanks," Tanner replied.

Her gaze continued to shift before stopping abruptly and narrowing. "Lexis, I wish I could say you look hawt, as well, but you don't. Actually, the sight of you sickens me."

That made two of us.

Lexis brushed an invisible piece of lint from her shirt as if she hadn't a care.

"Let her go," I repeated to the guard.

Bastard waited for John's nod before releasing his charge.

"Yeah, that's right." Scowling at him, Sherridan rubbed her arm. "You better release me or you'll feel the wrath of Wonder Girl."

Wonder Girl, another of Rome's nicknames for me. My chin trembled.

Before John could tell me to tell her to beat feet, I said, "She's now a member of my team. Let her stay. Please," I added to placate him.

He opened his mouth to protest.

"I need her. She'll keep me calm since Rome can't." Or wouldn't. "And don't tell me Tanner can do it. Like you said, I'm more unstable than usual. I need all the help I can get."

Rome had once told me I had hair-trigger emotions. And he'd said it with affection, the sweetie, as if it was part of my charm. *Oh, God. Rome.* Tears burned my eyes, and a raindrop splashed from the ceiling.

"See!" I croaked to John. "I need help." I had to stop reacting like this, charming to Rome or not. It wasn't healthy for me, and it wasn't good for the case.

"We need her, John," Tanner said. What he meant was, *I* needed her. But he loved me enough to fight for me. I wanted to hug him.

Several minutes ticked by in silence as John mulled things over. He was a pros and cons man; in this case there were probably more cons. Sherridan wasn't trained for covert missions or even combat (to be honest, neither was I) and would therefore be in danger. Everywhere we went. She might even place *us* in danger. But keeping me composed *was* important.

"Lexis?" he finally said.

"She'll survive, she'll even aid," was all Lexis said, though her tone was curt.

John nodded, satisfied. "Fine. She stays."

As happy as I was that John had just relented, I refused to be grateful to Lexis for her part in it.

"Have a seat, Miss Smith. Nothing you hear goes beyond this room. Understand?"

"Yeah, hello. I've seen this movie."

Such disrespect. She'd learn. As for John, I wasn't surprised he knew her name, even though I'd never introduced them before. John knew everything. Everything except why the love of my life no longer knew who I was.

"Wow. The inner sanctum. Never thought I'd be allowed here." Sherridan's shoulders were squared proudly as she scanned the spacious office, probably noting the expensive oak desk, the plaques on the walls and the massive bookshelves. "Hey, there's not a chair for me."

"You can sit in my lap," Tanner said. "You know you're always welcome there."

I blinked in surprise. That had sounded like the old Tanner, the Tanner I knew and adored. Was he finally healing? Or was this an act for Lexis's benefit? Either way, I was proud of him.

Lexis stiffened. Cody frowned.

"Best seat in the house." Sherridan grinned and plopped herself on Tanner's lap. "Someone catch me up."

I did, and her expression of sympathy nearly undid me, thereby completely obliterating my claim to John that she calmed me down. Somehow, I maintained a neutral facade, my tears drying. *I'll do whatever it takes to remind Rome of our love. This is just a minor setback.*

"Here's the game plan," John said, taking over. "There are twelve victims of Pretty Boy and Desert Gal's cruelty currently in lockup. Divide them up, interview them and compare notes. And be careful. The guy who hurt Rome may not be the only scrim found in those cages. It was wrong of us to assume they were all innocent. No telling who the bastard had in there."

"I'll interview Rome," I said firmly. He wasn't in lockup, but he was a victim of cruelty.

"*I* will interview Rome," Lexis countered, her determination clear.

Uh, what now?

"I will," she repeated. "He'd want me to, I know it."

Oh, no, no, no. Hell, no. She still loved him, the truth was there in her emerald eyes, and she hoped to win him back—which was the real reason she'd dumped Tanner, I realized.

Ho. Ly. Shit.

The truth slammed into me, and I sputtered for air. God, I was stupid. I should have seen this. I wasn't a psychic, but I damn well should have seen this. All along, she'd known this would happen. Not because she'd dreamed it; she hadn't. Despite her earlier assertion, she couldn't see the past. She only saw the future. She'd simply wanted to cover her tracks. She'd known this would happen and she hadn't warned me. She hadn't warned Rome. She'd let him walk into that warehouse completely unaware. Just to win him back.

That…that… There wasn't a name vile enough for what she was. How was that for love?

I opened my mouth to scream at her, maybe shoot a little fire.

"He remembers me," she said, cutting off any tirade I'd planned. Her chin lifted a notch. "He's more likely to tell me what he knows."

True. And the knowledge destroyed me. Well, more than I already was. "You're not going near him. You knew this would happen, you bitch, and you did nothing to stop it."

"No," she said, violently shaking her head. "That's not true. John, you have to believe me."

A muscle ticked below his eye, but he remained silent. He needed both of us, couldn't afford to anger either of us, so he was taking the coward's way out.

Not me. To help Lexis understand the depths of my determination to keep her away from Rome, I braced my legs apart and spread my fingers at my sides. Unleashing the hot tongues of my fury just then was not a problem. They swam in my blood and licked down my arms, catching fire at my fingernails. My eyes narrowed on her, red spots forming. "Just try to keep me away from him and see what happens."

She was shaking a little, but she jumped to her feet in challenge. We faced off.

"Viper," Tanner said. A warning. "You're edging too close to total meltdown. Not that I mind your target, but still."

Lexis's expression hardened.

"Calm down, Belle," Cody said. "Please."

The "please" didn't faze me this time.

"Kick her ass!" Sherridan whooped. "Send her back to hell."

Out of the corner of my eye, I saw Cody focus on my friend, who was looking anywhere but at him. Why? Whatever was going on in her head, I'd find out later.

I blocked all of them from my mind, focusing on Lexis even though my next words were not for her. "John. What's it going to be? I talk to Rome, and everyone walks out of this room alive. Or she does, and everyone says hello to third-degree burns."

"Or," Lexis gritted out, "Belle, who has worked for

you for only a few months, goes to lockup, where she belongs for threatening us. I've been with you for years. I've proved myself and my capabilities over and over again, and I've never questioned your leadership. More than that, Rome now responds to me. *Me.*"

One more word, and she would be eating fire. I wasn't even going to try to control myself. Even now, steam curled from my mouth, wafting toward the ceiling.

There was a long, protracted silence. Heavy, tension-filled. Lexis and I never turned away from each other, not even to face John. Our gazes were linked by invisible chains. We were panting. Ready to leap at each other.

"Belle," John said with resolve, "you're up. I'm putting you in charge. Of the case, of our new prisoners. Maybe your lack of objectivity will actually help. I've never seen you so determined. Just don't let me down."

Maybe he wasn't a coward, after all.

Lexis gasped.

"I won't," I said, and now it was my turn to be smug. "You have my word."

"Good. But for the record, you need to go in there, forget this love nonsense and be professional. Do your job. Be the agent I know you're capable of being."

Forget this love "nonsense"? I knew John was married because Cody had once made a reference to his wife, but wow. The poor woman, to be saddled with a husband who eschewed love.

"But if you fail," John added, "I'm sending Lexis in and placing her in charge. That means *she'll* be your boss."

"Not gonna happen," I said with a confidence I didn't feel. Still. There was a chance I'd say something to strike a memory match in Rome's brain, and he would tell Lexis to go fuck herself.

I left the room smiling.

Rome was prowling the length of the small interrogation room when I stepped inside. Immediately I smelled the earthy fragrance that always emanated from him. Immediately I reacted, my legs trembling, my blood heating.

Part of me expected him to stride to me and mesh his lips against mine, his tongue plundering deep, his hands all over me. That's how it would have been if he'd remembered me. But he spotted me, stopped and scowled.

"You," he said, and I could have sworn there was disgust in his voice.

Don't be hurt, don't be hurt, don't you freaking be hurt. He couldn't help it, I assured myself. As John had said, his memories had most likely been wiped. This in no way meant Lexis's former prediction that I might not be Rome's true love was coming to fruition.

Oh, ouch. I hadn't considered that angle until now.

"Yeah. It's me." I was surprised at how calm and assured I sounded. Maybe it was because Rome was on his feet, looking healthy and as strong as ever. Big and muscled, tanned and breathtakingly sexy.

The walls were plain gray, and yet, for Rome, they were a complementary backdrop. Even in his anger— what the hell had I done to make him mad?—his black-framed eyes glowed like magical sapphires and promised untold sexual delight. His teeth were sharp and white, ready to sink into me, to nip and nibble.

I shivered.

His nostrils flared. "Stop that. Now."

"Stop what?" I asked, confused. I hadn't done anything.

"Whatever it is you're thinking. Stop."

Was he kidding? "Why? You have no idea what I'm thinking."

"I can guess. You want me, and I don't like it. Yeah, I know we were engaged. I don't remember, but I've been told, seen pictures. That doesn't mean anything to me right now."

Were engaged, he'd said. *Don't be hurt!* "You're awfully full of yourself, aren't you?" My pride spoke for me, and I was helpless to stop it. "Maybe I'm looking at you but thinking of another man. One who actually remembers me."

"Fuck this. John," he shouted. He even banged a fist into the two-way mirror, rattling the walls. "Get her out of here."

My jaw clenched, but I managed to say, "Sit down, Agent Masters." *Remember me. Please.* "John asked me to speak with you and he's our boss, so we'll speak. Whether you like it or not. The sooner we get started, the sooner we can part."

Sadly, that propelled him into instant motion. He stomped to the table and sat, then waved his hand for me to do the same.

Pretending indifference, I tossed my notebook and pen on the surface. Eyes narrowed on him, I smoothed my jeans and sat across from him. "This interview isn't about us. It's about what happened to you that night at the warehouse. Have you remembered anything since waking up?" I asked, getting down to business. Surely *something* would trigger his memory as I hoped.

Ever the stubborn male, he said, "I've already answered that question. Several times."

"Not for me."

For a long while, he simply peered over at me, expression blank. I shifted left, right, realized I appeared nervous (I was) and commanded my body to still. Then Rome surprised me by saying, "I broke into the laboratory with a fellow agent and helped neutralize the eighteen on-duty guards—a few with a syringe full of night-night cocktail, a few with sleeper holds and a few with gunshots. Then we freed the prisoners."

When he offered no more, I arched a brow. "That's it?"

"Yes."

Nothing new. "Well, then, you can just start over. This time, break it down for me minute by minute."

He scowled again, but did what I'd asked. I learned how he'd taken the guards by surprise, tracking them through the vents and dropping onto them without them ever being aware. I learned how he'd copied data from the computer system, though the disks he'd stored that data on were now missing, gone like his memories. But I learned nothing that would help me.

"Okay, then." I tried another avenue. "What do you remember doing *before* that last mission?"

"Talking to John."

"Before that? And think hard." Because he'd been with me.

He propped his elbows on the table and leaned forward. There was a wicked glint in his eyes, one I knew well. He was about to provoke my fury. Before, that would have excited me because I would have known we'd make love for hours afterward. Now… "I kissed my daughter goodbye and left my wife sleeping in bed. Very, very satisfied."

A blazing mound of dirt suddenly and unexpectedly appeared in the palm of my hand. Rage and jealousy, all blended into one fiery ball. I wanted to jerk my hand under the table so he wouldn't see, but I didn't. It was better he learned what happened when people upset me.

"You're not married," I said stiffly. "You're divorced."

"I know that," he growled. "I left my ex-wife satisfied, then. But it's only a matter of time before she agrees to marry me again." His focus never strayed from the fiery mound of dirt, and before I could start sobbing over his claim, he added, "Impressive."

"Thank you." So badly I wanted to remind him of all the (naughty) things we'd done together, but this conversation was being recorded. Others were listening. My colleagues did not need to know the things I allowed—okay, begged—Rome to do to me. Then again, maybe Lexis needed to hear all about it. "Now why don't you tell me why you're so angry with me?" I tossed the crackling mound from hand to hand in a mesmerizing rhythm. "If you have no memory of me, you would treat me as a stranger. Polite, but distant. Instead, you treat me as an enemy. Why?"

One of his brows arched, a slash of black topping a barely tolerant expression. "Is that an official question?"

"Why not? I'm the official in this meeting, and I asked it."

"You're not going to like the answer." His gaze returned to the scorching dirt. "And I definitely won't like the consequences."

"Tell me anyway."

A muscle ticked in his jaw. "I read your file and it wasn't pretty. My wife told me—"

"Uh, we've already established that she's your ex-wife." And if he called her by that title one more time, something bad was going to happen. I didn't need Miss Know-It-All to verify that, either. Already the flaming dirt ball in my hand was snapping, smoke billowing through it as it prepared to welcome another stream of fire. A fire that would not be so easily contained.

Careful. Any more smoke, and I would soon be coughing for hours, since pollutants were my Achilles' heel. Apparently, so were gorgeous cat men.

"Wife, ex-wife. It's just semantics," he said. "Lexis

told me you were trouble, that you burned down her entire building. Do you deny it?"

One point in his favor: he referred to the building as hers, not theirs. Some of the flames flickered, then died. "No, I don't deny it. I was trying to save your life." I'm sure Lexis had left that part out, though. Bitch. "Did she also tell you that we made out on her couch?" So much for keeping our private life private. "You had your tongue down my throat and your hands...oh, about right here." I cupped my breast with my free hand. The girls weren't big, but they were perky and I knew Rome loved them.

His pupils dilated and he licked his lips, but he said nothing.

My cheeks were red as I released myself. It had been worth a shot. "Your ex may not like me, but your daughter does. Are you aware of that?"

He nodded stiffly. "I've talked to her, yes, and she asked about you."

"What'd you tell her?"

"That you were busy and would call her later," he said through gritted teeth.

Finally! Progress. "Clearly, you're missing a big chunk of your life. Maybe, just maybe, I was a *good* part of it."

"Like I told you a little while ago, Weather Wench, I don't deny that. That doesn't mean I want you to be a part of it now."

"That doesn't mean you should go running back to your ex, either. And just a word of warning." Glaring, I tossed the ball into the air, caught it. Several grains of dirt scattered over the tabletop between us. "If you go near Lexis again, you'll soon find her wearing one of these. And my name is not Weather Wench. Call me that again and *you'll* be wearing one of these."

Rather than upset him, my boast seemed to amuse him. His lips twitched.

That twitch looked good on him; maybe because it was so Rome. The old Rome. My stomach quivered in delight. Could he be losing his animosity toward me? I decided to push a little more. What could it hurt?

With a backward-forward swing of my wrist, I launched the ball over his shoulder. It crashed into the far wall, instantly covering the entire surface in steaming mud.

At the whoosh of air, Rome's head had whipped around to survey the damage. When he faced me again, shock and admiration bathed his features.

More. Push more. "After that," I said, "I'll seek comfort from your friend Cody. You remember him, right? Dressed, he's sexy as hell. Undressed, I'm sure he's every woman's downfall." Okay, now I was lying. Only one man could tempt me to fall, and that was Rome. *But what if Rome goes back to Lexis?* Bile rose in my throat. *Just finish this.* "I hear he's an amazing lover, that he won't let his partner leave until she's so sated she can't even speak. It's been a while since I had that kind of experience." Low blow—and untrue—but he deserved it.

If Cody was listening, he was probably patting himself on the back and smiling smugly.

Rome's nostrils did that flare thing again.

Was he…could he be jealous at the thought of me with another man? Even though he didn't remember me? Please, please, please.

"Do it," he said, his voice low, gravelly. "Go to him."

O-kay. Maybe not. I tried not to wallow in crushing disappointment. "I will," I lied. Damn him. "You'll see."

He leaned back in his seat and rubbed two fingers over his jaw. "Answer a few questions for me first."

"Sure. Unlike you, some agents are actually happy to

help a coworker in need." My heart skipped a beat. What did he want to know?

"I brought you into PSI, correct?"

"Yes." He'd done a whole lot more to me, but whatever.

"Because you ingested some sort of chemical, you now control the four elements. Earth, wind, fire and water."

I shrugged. "Sometimes yes. Sometimes no."

"What does that mean?" He glanced again at the mud-caked wall behind him. "That sometimes they control you?"

A nod. "You call me Four Elements Girl. Or Homicidal Tendencies Wench." What I would have given to hear either of those stupid monikers again. Spoken with affection, that is. He'd made "Weather Wench" sound like "Heartless Bitch." "Sometimes you even call me Wonder Girl because, well, I'm wonderful. And in return I call you Cat Man, and you like it."

His teeth ground together. In irritation? "I would never allow a woman to call me Cat Man and I would damn well never like it. You're lying."

Oh, yes. He was irritated. Why? "Why would I lie about something like that? What would I have to gain? What would *anyone* have to gain?"

"My secrets."

I rolled my eyes. "I already know your secrets." He cried during romantic comedies when the couple had their black moment (if only he'd cry during this one! I only prayed it wasn't a tragedy). He was a cheap drunk. And he'd once told me that he couldn't sleep when I wasn't in the bed with him. "Besides, we're on the same team."

"Are we? The others, yes. I know them, know they wouldn't hurt me. You? Not so much. You're a blank canvas in my mind. You could have all of them fooled. You could be a mind manipulator and have tricked them all."

"Do you seriously think *anyone* could do that to so many people at once? Especially when the people in question are trained government agents?"

A pause. He ran his tongue over his teeth. "No."

"Okay, then. It's safe to say I'm not a mind manipulator."

In the blink of an eye, his arm snapped out and he latched onto my wrist. I gasped in shock. In delight. His skin was warm and callused and abraded mine deliciously. He turned my palm over, inspecting every inch of dirt that smudged the crevices. My engagement band gleamed in the light.

He was quick to look away from it, I noticed.

"What are you doing?" Did I sound as breathless to him as I did to myself?

"If we were lovers, I would know this hand. I would recall having it on my body."

The words had been growled, as if he wanted desperately to remember and hated that he couldn't. I chewed on my bottom lip, not knowing what to say or what to do to turn this situation around. *Recall* something. *Please.*

"But there's nothing." Disgusted, he dropped my hand. "Not even a glimmer."

Slowly I drew my arm back and placed it in my lap. My normally olive skin appeared washed out, completely devoid of color as it rested against the blue of my jeans. "We were more than lovers," I said softly. "We were engaged, as you were already told. I've been planning our wedding."

He laughed, but it was an ugly sound and made me cringe. "You can just un-plan it," he said. "Maybe even sell the ring, 'cause I don't want it back. Like I said, I'll soon be marrying someone else."

CHAPTER FOUR

"BITCH! TRAITOR! Liar!" I slammed my fist into Lexis's cheekbone. Usually my first instinct was not to fight but to say something bitchy and run. However, these past few days my anger levels had been so spiked it was almost a relief to let go like this. At least physically. I felt I'd been waiting for this moment forever.

Her head snapped to the side and she stumbled backward a few steps, righted herself and glared over at me. Her gaze never falling from me, she used the back of her hand to wipe at the soot my blazing skin had left and the blood trickling from the cut my engagement ring had caused. Rome might not remember me, but Lexis wouldn't be forgetting who I was to him anytime soon. I wasn't taking the ring off, and I damn sure wasn't selling it. Hell, no.

"Nothing to say?" I was panting, barely able to contain the flames working through me. Any moment they might burst free, charring everything and everyone around me.

Good, I thought. Let them.

"Get out of my face, Belle. I'm better at this game than you are. Trust me, you don't want to mess with me."

"Oh, but I do. And I don't care if you grind me into powder, I'm not letting you get away with this."

Lexis and I were standing inches apart inside the workout room John kept for his agents. After leaving

Rome, I'd searched the entire building and had found her in here, running on the treadmill. She'd taken one look at me and had jumped down, clearly prepared to deal with nothing more than a heated conversation.

That's when I'd punched her.

She might be a powerful psychic, but she'd never been able to predict the things that would happen to her. As I now planned to do with all my enemies, I had used her weaknesses against her and I wasn't sorry.

"And anyway, why are you here? Why aren't you interviewing one of the prisoners like you were told?" I already knew the answer. She'd been waiting for me. Or rather, for a chance to pounce on Rome, to see if he'd remembered me.

Sweat dripped from her chest, past her vivid red sports bra and down the planes of her flat belly. "Had no luck with him, I take it?" she asked in that smug tone I so hated.

Bingo. I'd been right. "No thanks to you."

Guilt flashed, quickly gone. "You're not right for him. It's time you both realized it."

"Is that so?" Before his last mission, Rome had been teaching me to fight. And fight dirty. Without warning, I kicked out my leg and nailed her in the stomach. Breath whooshed from her mouth as she skidded backward, instinctively hunching over. Other agents were in the room, and I heard them muttering:

"Hundred on Lexis. Girl has skill!"

"Dude, you haven't seen The Mighty Water Hose in a temper. You're on."

"Is anyone else as turned-on by this as I am?"

"You don't want to do this," Lexis repeated, straightening. Even sweaty and winded, she was a beautiful sight. The shiny length of her black hair was pulled back in a ponytail, her green eyes flashed brightly and pink flushed the exotic slope of her cheeks.

"What you've done to me, Rome and Tanner is underhanded and wrong, and you know it. Someone needs to punish you, and I happily volunteer."

"I don't care if it's wrong. I don't care if it hurts you. I can't!" Righteous fervor poured from her, a deluge that only strengthened my anger. "I love him."

I sputtered for a moment, dumbfounded by her logic. "And that makes your behavior okay? If you truly loved him, you would have warned him about the danger he faced. Had the situation been reversed, had I known I would lose him, I still would have warned him to save him. *That's* real love. But guess what? None of that matters. You had your chance with him. You blew it, cut him loose and he moved on. He wants me now."

Her chin lifted, and hell, she'd never appeared more superior. "*Wanted* you. He wanted you. As of two days ago, he wants me. He wants to be a family for Sunny, the kind of family we were before."

I ran my tongue over my teeth, fire inside my mouth, burning, blistering. Surely there was something I could say to make her understand the depths of her betrayal. Surely there was something I could do. Surely…*please*. "Once you said you knew he wasn't the man for you, that he would love another. What's changed?"

"Everything," she shouted, tossing up her arms. "The world offered me a second chance and I took it. I won't make the same mistake twice. He and I can—will—make things work this time."

Oh, that burned. In more ways than one. "Let's forget about Rome for a minute. How could you do this to Tanner? He treated you like a queen. Worshipped you, would have done anything for you."

Again guilt curtained her expression, but as before, she quickly masked it. "He's young, and I'm not the girl for him."

Damn her! "Again, that doesn't excuse your cruelty. He's a good guy, and you broke his heart as if he meant nothing to you. As if *he* was nothing."

"Trust me, he'll get over it. Sooner than you think, too."

What did that mean? That Tanner was about to meet the love of his life? I'd wondered that very thing a few days ago and had even felt sorry for Lexis. Not an ounce of my pity remained. "Knowing that doesn't make what you've done okay, either. You're ruining people's lives."

"No," she insisted. "I'm making things right. Finally."

Clearly, I'd made her understand nothing. I braced my feet apart, my hands at my sides, preparing for the battle soon to come. "Just so you know, Miss Know-It-All, you're not the girl for Rome, either."

"I will be. Just watch and see."

I swung my arm and, though I'd been aiming for her nose, I nailed her in the cheek again. She gasped, straightened, another trickle of blood joining the first. "That's for what you've done to Rome." My other arm whipped out, connecting with her other cheek. "That's for Tanner." Now, for me. I clasped both hands together, ready to slam my joined knuckles into her nose.

She sucker punched me in the face before I could move an inch. In fact, her arm flew up so quickly, I had no idea she was moving until my brain slammed into my skull.

Several seconds passed during which I saw nothing but stars. But when I realized what had happened, my anger ratcheted yet another degree, a flame sparking from my eye and catching on my eyelash. *Control. No fire.* If I burned her to a crisp, I'd be incarcerated, considered a scrim even though *she* was the criminal here.

"I warned you," she said. "Rome taught me to play dirty, too."

I blew out the flame, though my attention never left her. "That's all right. I've learned a few tricks on my own."

She waved her hand at me. "Bring it."

So I did. Silent as a cat—*my* cat—I launched at her. Amid the chorus of male laughter and insincere pleas to stop, we slammed together and tumbled backward. Lexis hit the floor, and my weight smacked into her. Any air she'd managed to suck in previously was expelled in a gust.

While she struggled to breathe, I straddled her, my knees pinning her shoulders. There would be no hair-pulling and scratching in this fight. We'd settle this like men. Superstrong, paranormally-enhanced men, but whatever. With my left fist—oops, a flame—I popped her in the nose. She yelped. With my right—what do you know, another flame—I nailed her in the jaw. Snarling, she wiggled for freedom. Blood dribbled down her lip and chin, and black soot smudged her too-perfect face.

The laughter faded, the muttered "Stops" becoming real, concerned. No one dared approach us, though, fearing for *their* lives.

As I reached back to introduce her eye socket to my knuckles, one of her legs worked between us and kicked. Next thing I knew, I was flying backward. I landed on my ass but swiftly jumped up. She was already on her feet. Both of us were panting, glaring.

"What's the matter? Can't stand a little competition?" she taunted.

"Can't win a man without cheating?" My fingers caught fire completely. Several of the men decided to brave our ire and approached. I threw a fireball, causing a wall of flames to form in front of them, keeping them away. While they scrambled for an extinguisher, I said,

"You knew this would happen to him, and yet you did nothing. He's suffering because of you. His life is a mess because of you."

She shook her head viciously, as though she could block my words with the back-and-forth flap of her ponytail. "I'm making things right. But you know what? If he really loves you, he'll pick you this go-round, too." Her legs widened and her hands fisted in a classic ready-for-war pose. The same one I'd adopted twice already. "Now, enough talking. Let's finish this."

Hardly willing to obey her, I held my ground. Smoke billowed toward the ceiling, curling, stretching fingers out to me. I coughed until the sudden tickle in my throat eased. "If you touch him, I'll forget killing a fellow PSI agent is a no-no." Truth and determination dripped from my every word. "And then, when Rome's memory returns, he'll hate you for what you've done and ask me to kill you all over again."

Her cheeks leached of color, and a tremor worked through her. "Maybe his memory is forever lost. Besides, hating me is not the future I see for him," she said, voice softening.

Everything inside me stilled. My lungs. My heart. My blood. Cold washed over me, ice crystallizing on my fingers and causing every flame to sizzle, die. "What do you see?"

Her mouth opened and closed, but no sound emerged.

I inhaled sharply, and another round of coughing ensued. "What the hell do you see, Lexis?"

Again, she remained silent. To be cruel? I was in her face a heartbeat later, scared, angry again, coughing even harder, frost and fire battling for supremacy inside me. Wind whipped between us as I hooked my foot around her ankle and shoved. Down, down she fell. On the mat, she used her elbows to crab-walk backward, away from me.

"What the hell do you see?" The cold began to leave me, my fury eating away at it and leaving a burning trail. Jealousy was there, images of Rome and Lexis living happily ever after with Sunny flashing through my mind. A muddy fireball formed in my palm. "Tell me!"

The agents finally doused the flames in front of them and moved around us in a circle, probably meaning to close in until they rendered us completely immobile. Instead, their positions aided my cause. Lexis hit a pair of boots and stopped.

Gasping, she rolled to the side just as I tossed my bounty. It barely missed her, yellow-orange flickers crackling where she'd been, smoke billowing from the foam. The men jumped back with a collective gasp as another muddy fireball formed. I threw it, too. Again, Lexis rolled, escaping harm, causing more of the mat to hiss and the men to step farther away, widening the circle rather than closing it.

"You really want to know?" she shouted. "Fine, I'll tell you. But you'll wish I'd kept quiet. You're going to continue to plan your wedding, but he'll want nothing to do with it. Another man will court you, but Rome won't care. Do you hear me? He won't care! You're going to date this other man. It's *him* you'll marry. Him. Not Rome. Him."

She was lying. She had to be lying. Anything to shred my confidence, my hope. Anything to give herself an edge. I wouldn't, couldn't believe otherwise. No way I'd marry any man but Rome. No way I'd love any man but Rome. "Too bad you won't live long enough to find out if your predictions are true." I advanced toward her, stalking my prey with every intention of destroying it. I hadn't lied to her earlier; I no longer cared about consequences.

But then, panting as I was, the black plumes still wafting

from the mat enveloped me, soaked into me and filled me up, and I started coughing again. My steps slowed, then stopped altogether. As the seconds dragged by, those coughs became gut racking, shaking my entire body. Damn it! Not now. Any time but now.

While I gasped for breath, someone tackled me, tossing me to the ground and pinning me. What the— three male bodies weighed me down. I struggled and kicked and screamed.

Lexis, who was being patted on the back and asked if she were harmed, sprang for me. Through wide eyes I watched as she closed the distance, fist drawn back. One of the men dove for her, knocking her down just before she reached me. She scrambled to her knees just as I worked my way free of my own captors. Determination like ours couldn't be contained.

Even as I coughed, a raging fireball formed in my hand. Attack me while I was unable to defend myself, would she? Try and steal my man, would she? Hurt my friend, would she? Not without paying a very dear price. I pulled my elbow back, wrist relaxing…preparing…

"Stop!" a masculine voice shouted.

Rome.

I twisted, my heart pounding, nearly cracking my ribs. He was clearly angry but all the more magnificent for it. Too bad I didn't have time to drink him in. Lexis's foot connected with my back and sent me flying forward. Forever I seemed to trip, the fireball falling from my hand and catching a corner of the mat in a blazing inferno.

As I righted myself, someone rushed over and saturated the flames with liquid nitrogen.

With a quick glance, I rasped, "Low blow, Lexis." I wouldn't be foolish enough to give her my back again. But damn it. *Well played, Miss Know-It-All. Well played.* I should have been smart enough to do something similar to her.

She was standing, shoulders squared, expression once again smug. "There's more where that came from."

How could I ever have trusted this woman? Even a little?

At least I'd gotten in a few good blows. Her lips were cracked and bleeding, and a bruise had already begun to form under one of her eyes. No telling what I looked like, though. Without the rush of adrenaline, without the glacial blast of fear and the conflagration of rage, my knuckles throbbed and my facial muscles ached.

"What the hell is going on?" Rome demanded.

I strode to Lexis's side, though I remained out of striking distance, and returned my focus to him. This time, I *was* able to drink him in—but oh, I was sorry for it. Quite simply, he scrambled my brain. He was tall, dark, dangerous. Exotic, sensual. Mine. He was the fantasy I'd always craved, the reality I thought I'd never achieve, but had. Only to lose it.

This isn't over.

His eyes strayed from Lexis to me, from me to Lexis. I wasn't sure which one of us caused his pupils to dilate, his nostrils to flare. Sure signs of arousal. At one time, I would have known who that arousal was for. It would have been me, no question. He would have stalked to me, grabbed my hand and jerked me into the hallway—coworkers be damned—where he would have pinned me against the wall, unable to exist a second more without my taste in his mouth. One of his hands would have cupped my breast, and the other would have worked at my jeans.

"Out," he snapped.

Both Lexis and I jolted in response, though neither of us obeyed. We knew he wasn't speaking to us.

"Out!" he repeated, harsher this time.

There were scampering footsteps behind us as our fellow agents fled.

When there was silence, Rome crossed his arms over his chest. "There will be no more fighting between the two of you. Understand?"

"Yes," Lexis said, clearly wanting to please him. "But I was only defending myself. She attacked me."

Perhaps I should have followed her lead, should have tried to placate him. That had never been my style, though, and I wouldn't change now. "Fuck you," I told him. "I'll do what I want, when I want, and there's not a thing you can do about it. You lost the chance to order me around. And besides that, she's a heartless bitch who deserved every punch I landed. Next time I'm not going to stop until she's unconscious."

Lexis gasped.

Rome blinked over at me, shock forming in those electric blues.

Someone whooped behind me. I turned—and it was one of the hardest things I'd ever done, looking away from Rome. But I had to. Any longer and I would have run to him and jumped into his arms. He was just so familiar to me, so…necessary. More than that, shock was a look I received from him quite often. Every time I said something he didn't expect but liked, he would blink, grab me and kiss the breath right out of me. Yes, he kissed me for a lot of different reasons.

"Hello, everyone." Grinning, Cody leaned a muscled shoulder against the door frame, so beautiful he could have been a painting come to life. Hell, in this supernatural world of ours, I wouldn't doubt if that were the case. "Hello, gorgeous," he added, gaze on me.

My brow puckered in confusion. Was he talking to me? Surely not. He'd never spoken to me like that before.

The only women Cody wouldn't seduce were those that belonged to his friends or those who were looking to get married. I was both, so I was definitely off-limits.

Or had been, I thought sadly. This sucked.

"I need a moment with the women," Rome said stiffly.

"Well, I need a moment with Belle."

"No."

Cody laughed now. "So you're saying you're her man? If that's the case, I'll leave."

Rome's jaw clenched. He remained silent.

"Fine, then. You're no longer her man," Cody said, "so you can't speak for her anymore. Not that you could have before," he added with another laugh.

"Get lost," Rome retorted.

"I believe the little lady told you to fuck yourself. Rather than tell you the same, I'll just ask Belle what she'd prefer to do. Stay here and receive a lecture about giving naughty girls the spankings they deserve, or come with me and have fun."

My head lashed back and forth between them as they spoke. Rome bared his extra-sharp teeth in a scowl, but Cody never lost his grin. These two men were friends, colleagues, yet here they were, locked in some sort of tug-of-war. Not over me, but over power. Surely. Why?

"Miss Jamison…Belle," Rome said, and hearing my name on his lips was heaven. Nearly my undoing. "Tell Cody you want to stay. We need to talk."

Giving in to him now would have undermined my take-no-crap stance. Besides, as Cody predicted, he probably wanted to yell at me for hurting his previous and future wife. Ugh. No way. I'd seriously vomit. Then I'd burn something. That didn't mean I wanted him to spend time alone with Little Miss Know-It-All, though.

Hating myself, I faced Rome. "I think we've said all

we need to say to each other. Unless you've remembered something?"

He gave an abrupt shake of his head.

Not one to miss an opportunity, Lexis rushed to his side before I could latch onto her arm and petted his shoulder. "Let her go. She's caused enough trouble today." Next she whispered something in his ear.

A muscle began ticking under his eye, his gaze never leaving me.

My insides twisted in disgust. What the hell was she telling him? That I was the devil and I'd attacked her for no reason? That she'd begged for mercy but I didn't possess any?

"Belle," Cody prompted.

Do it. Spin. I spun. Each step measured, I walked to Cody, knowing the distance between me and Rome was growing. I was shaking, my eyes a bit watery. Any minute now, raindrops would pour from the ceiling. *You are such a baby. Hold your head high.* My chin lifted.

When I reached Cody, he wrapped one of his arms around my waist and tugged me into the hard length of his body. I would have gasped, but he smothered the sound by pressing my mouth into his chest.

Then *he* whispered to *me,* "I'd be willing to bet Rome's eaten up with jealousy right now and it's killing him."

Looking up at Cody, not daring to hope, I freed my mouth enough to say, "Really?"

"I'd place my substantial savings on it."

"I thought you wanted to speak with her, not eat her whole," Rome sniped.

Dear God. Cat Man was indeed in a snit. I grinned up at Cody, happier than I'd been in days. "He can do both," I said without looking over my shoulder. "I've always loved a man who could multitask."

"My kind of woman," Cody said, grin widening. "And why do you care, anyway, Masters? You're done with her." To me, but just as loudly, he said, "I was listening to your earlier convo with Kitty over there and wanted you to know you were right. I leave my women so sated they can't even speak. I'm willing to let you find out for yourself."

I had to bite my lip to keep from laughing.

"I told you. I need to speak with her. About the Desert Gal case," Rome added tersely, "and how it connects with our last mission."

"Don't worry," Cody said. "I've already talked to her about that."

"Rome," Lexis said. "Take me home. Please. My head is throbbing and I need to get cleaned up. You heard Cody. He's got things under control."

I pictured the two of them alone. Perhaps showering together, as Rome and I liked to do. My stomach clenched painfully, amusement forgotten. "Cody, will you take me to the nearest clinic? I need someone to dig the knife out of my back. Lexis might need it again. And the good doctor might want to give me a tetanus shot. I think she bled on me."

Stunned silence.

I often had that effect.

"Rome," Lexis said, and this time her tone was pure *I'm-pissed*.

Not wanting to hear his response, I whirled on them and said, "Actually, it doesn't matter if Cody has things under control or not. I've been placed in charge of this case, which makes me your boss. *Both* of your bosses. And I expect both of you to begin interviewing Desert Gal's victims in the morning. Then I expect you to report to John's office at noon. We'll compare notes and decide what to do next. Oh, and a word of warning. Fail to show, and I'll introduce you to Mean Belle."

No longer appearing stunned, but rather braced for whatever slipped out of my mouth next, Rome snorted. "You mean we haven't met her yet?"

"Not even close."

CHAPTER FIVE

CODY DROVE ME HOME, though we didn't speak. We sat in silence, the radio switched off. I wasn't ready to talk or listen—to anything—and he probably sensed it. What were Rome and Lexis doing? Not knowing was killing me. It was like having a knife in my chest, the blade slowly inching deeper while the hilt was twisted round and round.

He parked in the driveway, and we made our way up the porch. Mine and Rome's. Not that he'd remember. Jerk.

A tiny flicker of anger popped up and said hello. At least my hands didn't catch fire again. In fact, I wasn't producing ice, wind or dirt, either, though my emotions were in turmoil. Jealousy, love, hate, sadness, hope and helplessness were all storming through me. Odd. Maybe my powers were on a break. Maybe they were on the fritz again. I mean, I'd never been further away from Rome's love than I was now.

I sighed. Maybe I shouldn't have walked away from him. Maybe I should have stayed on his ass and reminded him of why he adored me. My eyes widened with the thought. Of course! Of course that's what I should have done. Constant visual and auditory reminders were the best ways to trigger his memory.

I clapped my hands, a plan already forming. I was going to glue myself to Rome's side. Simple. Easy. "But probably painful, all things considered."

"What is?" Cody asked.

Oops. I hadn't meant to say that aloud. "Never mind." Up the steps I climbed—and stopped abruptly. A vase of pink, violet and azure orchids waited beside my door, an emerald bow circling the amber glass. A rainbow of colors, just as I liked. To match my living room?

I rushed forward and crouched beside them, my eyelids closing as I inhaled deeply. A sweet summer's breeze wafted through me, transporting me from my doldrums for a moment.

"Who are those from?" Cody asked.

Rome? A girl could hope. "Let's see." My hand shook as I reached for the card. Shook even more as I unfolded the paper. "Beautiful flowers for a beautiful woman," I read. "I hope you enjoy them as much as I'm enjoying you. Yours forever." Rocked by the force of my disappointment—Rome was *not* currently enjoying me—I glanced up at Cody. "There's no name."

"Hey, Rome could have—"

"No. He couldn't have. Rome would have signed his name."

Cody shrugged, an *I-tried* gesture. "Yeah. He's not much for allowing others to take credit for his work. This I know from experience."

Part of me had hoped Cody would lie and disagree with me. "So who could it be? The only man I know who likes me, or rather, used to like me, was Rome." It was sad, really, that I couldn't stop foolish hope from forming once more and mixing with my disappointment. "Do you think he maybe could have remembered all about me in the last hour and called from PSI and had these rushed over but there wasn't time to add his name so he—"

Cody shook his head, his eyes kind. "Not to rain on your parade, Weather Wench, but Rome didn't send those. He would have been here with them. Probably naked. You two really were disgusting."

His words shredded my hope to ribbons and left only that crushing despair. Rome took what he wanted, when he wanted it. Something I loved about him. Cody was right; if he'd had flowers to give me, he would have thrust them into my hands, cupped my chin and raised my mouth for a bruising kiss.

At least, that's how I imagined it would go down. No one but my dad had ever sent me flowers. Despite my imaginings, I knew Rome considered them "too easy." He liked the challenge of picking a gift that had personal meaning for the one receiving it.

"You, then?" I asked.

Cody's lips curled sweetly. "Sorry, but not me, either. One, I'm not that thoughtful. And two, you're not my type."

Ouch. Even though I'd already known, the words stung—so much rejection in so little time. "What type am I?"

"Taken."

Once, that would have been accurate. Now…I know I'd thought this earlier, but some things were worth repeating. This sucked. "Tanner could have sent them, I guess."

Cody barked out a laugh. "Have you met the boy? He would have complimented you on your pretty nipples somewhere on that card."

True again. Confusion growing, I gathered the vase and pushed to a stand. "My hands are otherwise occupied, and my keys are in my purse. Can you get them?"

"My pleasure." After rooting through the contents of my purse for God knows how long, muttering, "What the hell do you keep in here?" Cody finally found my keys and opened the door.

I sailed inside.

"You ready to talk now?" he asked.

"Depends on what you want to talk about." I didn't stop until I reached the kitchen. Seriously, who had sent me such a lovely gift? The vase made the perfect center-piece for my table—was even flecked with the same cerulean crystals that decorated my countertop.

I stood there, admiring them for a moment. The flowers seemed to perk up as sunlight streamed in from the windows.

My cell phone was a few inches from the vase, I noticed. Shit. I'd left it home again. I picked it up, flipped through the caller ID and saw that my dad had called. So had the caterer and so had the dress shop, probably hoping to confirm my marathon "trying on" session set for tomor-row. I sighed. I'd call them all back later. Right now, I didn't even know if my wedding was going to happen.

According to Lexis, it was. With a different man. The one who'd sent me flowers? *Don't think like that!* Rome and I belonged together. We'd work this out. We had to.

"What do you think they're doing right now?" There. I'd asked. Gotten it out in the open.

Cody didn't have to inquire as to who I meant. "Rome and Lexis are talking. That's all."

Good. That was good. Was he lying? My hands fisted as I choked out, "About?"

"The weather. Definitely about the weather."

Now I knew he was lying. Forcing myself to relax, I toyed with one of the flower petals, letting the velvety softness tickle my fingertips. Maybe I didn't know my own strength, because several of those petals tore from their base and fell to the table. "Think they're kissing?"

"If they are, Rome's not liking it. Guaranteed. He's a one-woman guy and you're his woman. He'll figure it out sooner or later."

I prayed that was true, sooner rather than later. I didn't know what I'd do if he and Lexis made lo—had sex. Didn't know if I could forgive, even with these screwed-up circumstances.

"If I were a gentleman," Cody said, taking my hand and kissing my knuckles, "I'd try and steal a ten-minute Frencher, make out with you a little and, if you insisted—which I know you would, because it was clear from your interview with Rome that you're begging to be so sated you can't talk—take you to bed. You wouldn't regret it, and it'd be great fodder for making Rome jealous."

I snorted, pulling my hand from his clasp. He was never going to let me live down my comments in that interrogation room. "All that if you were a gentleman?" What would he do if he weren't?

Another curl of his lips. "But I'm not, so no reason for us to discuss it and get your hopes up. Why don't we discuss your friend Sherridan instead?"

After the way he'd looked at her in John's office, part of me had seen this coming. I faced him, crossing my arms over my chest, prepared to do what was necessary. "Do you like high-maintenance women?"

"No."

I'd known that. In the months since I'd met him, I'd watched Cody interact with the opposite sex. Those who enjoyed a good time—and nothing more—he charmed. Those who preferred hearth and home, he avoided. "Then stay away from Sherridan. She's as high as they come."

His head tilted, and he studied me intently. Even propped his hip against the counter as though he were settling in for a long conversation. "What makes her high-maintenance?"

I shrugged. "I told you she had a crappy childhood. I wasn't lying. And that's all I'm going to tell you about her." *Crappy* wasn't the half of it. She'd been ignored and neglected most of her life, and that had made her a needy adult. Nothing wrong with that, I adored her, but some men couldn't tolerate it for long.

Cody didn't look properly horrified, though.

"Fine," I continued. "I'll tell you something else. I can guess how a relationship between the two of you would go down. You'd sleep with her, then walk away from her because you can't commit, and she'd come running to me and ask me to kill you. Friend that I am, I wouldn't be able to say no. Don't try and deny it."

His brow furrowed. "Did I look like I was going to deny it? One, most girls want to kill me when I'm done with them because I'm taking away their chance of being pleasured into speechlessness again and two, I don't even have a house because I can't make myself stay in one location long enough. And as for girls, I have a three-date min-max rule."

"Min-max?"

"No less, no more."

O-kay. I'd dated a few commitment-phobes over the years, but that…wow. "Why?"

"One date, you're left wanting more. Don't see the girl again, and she becomes an obsession. The one who got away. Two dates, you begin to notice little annoyances, but not enough to stop the sex from happening. Three dates, the little annoyances become big annoyances and the attraction fades completely. You can walk away a free man."

I stared at him for several long, drawn-out moments, then shook my head in wonder. "God, you're a mess."

"But I'm cute, so…"

Yeah. So. I rolled my eyes. "*Anyway,* you break up with Sherridan and she'll think it's because of something she did." Normally I wouldn't have discussed my friend's problems without permission from the friend herself. In this case, I realized there wasn't time to gain permission. I had to murder this little attraction right away. Couldn't have Cody veering into Obsession Land. And any more of Sherridan's Happy Place, and *I'd* need a vacation mind-spot. "She won't be able to help herself. Everything was her fault as a kid. A plant died, and she must have overwatered it. A bad grade on her report card, and she must not have tried hard enough. Her dad had an affair, so her attitude must have driven him away."

Cody's features softened with understanding, the silver in his eyes liquefying. "Poor kid."

"Ugh. You sound *more* intrigued by her. I mean it," I added, jabbing a fingertip into his chest. "She's not for you. Stay away."

Cody held up his hands, palms up, and laughed. "Fine. I'll avoid her like she's a married nun looking for another husband to keep out of her bed. Scout's honor."

I eyed him suspiciously. "Were you even a Scout?"

He gave a mock shudder. "Hell, no. I was too busy talking the girls into playing Show Me Yours, and I'll Show You Mine."

Now I laughed. "I think Scouts do that, too. Anyway, was Sherridan the only thing you wanted to talk to me about, you pervert? If so, I need to—"

"Nope," he interjected. "There's more."

When he said nothing else, I prompted, "Well?"

A sigh parted his lips. "Maybe you should sit down for this."

No. No, no, no. No more bad news. Instantly my affinity with the four elements made itself known. Mist formed in front of my nose, dancing over my face like fairy glitter. Or rather, demon dust. I plopped into the nearest seat, accidentally slid out and thumped onto the kitchen floor. Dumb ice crystals. Why couldn't they have remained hidden?

"So melodramatic." He *tsked* under his tongue.

I righted myself, disconcerted to realize my lungs were beginning to freeze. "Tell me!"

"Okay, here goes. So…while you interviewed Rome, one of our agents finally decoded a few of the papers John's recovery team found. Papers that were hidden in the wallpaper, of all places. Maybe Dr. Roberts did it, since that's his style. Anyway, they were records of some of OASS's prisoners. I decided not to wait for our meeting tomorrow to inform you because I wanted you to thank me with Sherridan's phone number, but never mind."

"You're babbling! Get on with it."

"Right. So the guy who stole Rome's and my memories is known by other scrims as, big surprise, Memory Man. Pretty Boy captured him and when PB died, Desert Gal took over Memory Man's *care*. You know what I mean by care, right? I mean—"

"I'm not stupid. Continue."

"Okay, okay. To our knowledge, MM wasn't part of the experiments but actually alternated between being a prisoner and an employee. I'm guessing he didn't like working for them, but they threatened him in some way and got him to do things. Then PB died, of course, and DG moved MM. We found him soon after that."

So far, not too bad. For Rome, I mean. Poor Memory Man. To be a prisoner all these years, somehow forced to comply with his captors' wishes. *Are you really feeling sorry for the man who helped ruin your life?* Plus, none of that was truly verified.

"Go on."

Cody nodded. "There was a mention of his *stealing* memories rather than erasing them, as John thought."

"Stealing?" I blinked. "As in, see a pretty diamond ring in a store window, smash the window, grab the ring and run?"

"You nailed it."

"I see," I said, but I didn't. Not really. That just didn't make sense. There was no reason for Memory Man, or M-Squared, as I'd begun to think of him during Cody's rundown, to steal memories from Rome and Cody. Unless he'd wanted PSI secrets? That made sense but didn't fit. Both men remembered their time at PSI, so those memories were intact. M-Squared had only taken memories of himself, probably to keep his identity hidden, and me—well, and those specifically associated with me.

My brow furrowed in confusion. Why me? And why had M-Squared not taken Cody's memories of me? Why had he only taken Rome's? What had made Rome's memories of me so special that he'd snatched them up rather than state secrets? Wasn't like I was a knockout. I was cute (or so I'd been told), with light brown hair, hazel eyes and a trim physique running away from bad guys had given me. But I was a B-cup on good days, didn't usually wear anything besides jeans and T-shirts and had a smart mouth. Oftentimes, people wanted to *forget* me. (For proof, see every mention of Rome.) And speaking of Rome, how was I going to remind him of why he loved me, even if I was glued to his side, when I suddenly couldn't think of a single redeemable thing about me?

What a depressing day.

"I think Pretty Boy, and then Desert Gal, planned to send Memory Man into PSI headquarters, maybe let us capture and try and recruit him, all so he could steal some of our memories," Cody continued. "John's specifically. But who knows? Even with whatever they used to control him, they must not have fully trusted him. He was locked up, after all."

Dear Lord. "Having him inside PSI, willing or not, would be a nightmare."

"You have no idea," he muttered.

Yeah, I did. John carried some of the biggest secrets in the world. Where scrims were imprisoned, who worked undercover in the paranormal underground, where agents—and their family members—lived. In the wrong hands, that kind of information could place everyone I loved on some scrim's kill list.

"So why didn't Memory Man take Rome's PSI knowledge when he had the chance?" I asked. "He left those memories alone."

"Only he knows the answer to that." Pensive, Cody rubbed at his scalp. "With Desert Gal now at the helm of the OASS empire, Pretty Boy's plan to destroy us is alive and well, even if Pretty Boy himself isn't. We need to follow every lead, not just focus on Memory Man. In those papers I mentioned, there was a reference to Big Rocky Spring Water."

"What reference?"

"Some sort of coded message, I think. 'You'll never be thirsty at Big Rocky.'"

Hard to argue with that statement, no matter what secret message it might contain. I loved me some Big Rocky. Fresh and crisp with no chemical aftertaste. "What does a major water company have to do with those disgusting scrims? Could one of the employees be a potential target? Or maybe an asset of some kind?"

"I don't know, but I plan to fly to their headquarters in Colorado and find out."

I didn't have to ask how he'd get answers. His usual

method was to sleep his way through a company until he learned all he could about it and its employees.

Yet another reason he shouldn't be allowed near Sherridan. Even if he were dating my friend, he wouldn't walk away from a target's bed if sleeping with her was necessary.

"All right. Hop a flight, but stay in contact with me. I want to know what you know, when you know it. I'll expect daily updates," I added so that he couldn't feign ignorance later.

He saluted me, the smart-ass. "Aye-aye, Captain. That was my plan, anyway. John and I already talked."

Of course they had. John might have told me I was in charge of this case—to keep me from threatening to quit, *again,* I'm sure—but I knew the truth. Even though I held the title of Special Agent in Charge, Cody and Rome were the ones calling the shots. In John's eyes, at least. Still, I planned to do things my way.

"Give me your list of prisoners to interview," I said. "I'll do it for you." Well, Tanner and I would. Tanner, my human lie detector, would find the answers that I, novice that I was, couldn't hope to find with written, detailed instructions and a GPS tracker.

"I'm a few steps ahead of you, Wonder Girl. While you were arranging your flowers, I stuffed the list in your purse."

As he spoke, a wicked gleam entered his eyes. What else had he done to my purse? With Cody, a girl never knew.

The front door creaked open, preventing me from asking. Footsteps echoed, and then the door banged closed. Voices drifted into the kitchen.

"I can't believe you'd nail Lexis over Jessica Alba. Jessica's hot!" Sherridan said. "I'm not a lesbian, but even I'd do her."

"Yeah, but—wait. What? Details, woman," Tanner

said. "I need details. Start with how you'd strip her and end with her smiling and saying thank you."

Cody groaned as though he were in pain. "Are you sure I can't take her out? Girl-on-girl crushes are my favorite, and I'd like to hear more about hers."

Men! "I'm sure," I told him. More loudly, I called, "We're in here."

The footsteps quickened. Then, "Oh, look at the pretties!" Sherridan cooed as she brushed past me to smell the orchids. "Who sent? Rome? Has he finally come to his senses, the jackass? Or maybe his amnesia has a silver lining. It wasn't like he was this considerate when he was using half his brain rather than none of it."

"I wish, but no." Bastard. "They're from a secret admirer."

"Maybe Sherridan sent them," Tanner said, leaning against the entry frame. Did my heart good, seeing him so relaxed. "Since she's into girls and all."

Cody gave another of those groans.

Both Tanner and Sherridan faced him. Tanner nodded in acknowledgment. Sherridan puckered her brow in confusion.

"Hey," she said in greeting. "I'm Sherridan, Belle's friend. And you are…?"

Was she serious? "Uh, Sherridan. You've met him. In John's office. Even a few times in passing before that." I glanced from her to Cody, Cody to her. Her features registered disbelief. His registered embarrassed irritation. "Remember?"

She frowned, bit her bottom lip. "I'm drawing a blank. Are you sure he was in the office?"

Was everyone in my life destined to suddenly forget pieces of their own?

"I was there," Cody answered for me.

Ouch. He sounded pissed.

"Sure, sure, I, uh, recall now." Sherridan laughed, probably to cover her lie, and damn if it wasn't a good look for her. Her cheeks glowed a rosy shade of pink, and her blue eyes sparkled. Tall and curved as she was, she could have been a goddess or an Amazon come to passionate life. Had to make her total disregard hurt Cody's ego.

He turned to me. "I see we didn't need to have this conversation after all."

"What conversation?" Tanner asked.

I patted Cody's cheek as I said, "I'll tell you later, Crazy Bones."

"Belle." It was a warning unlike any I'd heard from Cody before. "I thought we were speaking in confidence."

"When did I ever give you that impression?" I said, all innocence. "I tell Tanner everything."

"Some things a man likes to keep private."

"Like what?" Sherridan asked.

Cody gritted his teeth. "I'm out of here. I'll call you tomorrow, Belle. Maybe." He didn't wait for my reply, but stalked from the kitchen, then the house, the door slamming behind him.

"You are such a liar," Tanner said.

I gasped in affront. "I told the truth! I *do* tell you everything."

"Not you. Her." His gaze slid to Sherridan, who was squirming in place.

"What?" she asked, projecting the same innocence I had.

"You can't fool Mr. Sensitive." He'd chosen the name himself, and it always made me laugh. "You totally remembered him."

"You did?" I stared at her, wide-eyed. How dumb was I, not to have known that? "You sly little hooker, why'd you pretend you hadn't? And don't get me wrong. I'm not complaining. I'm impressed."

She crossed her arms over her ample chest and grinned. "Clearly he's a player. I mean, I remember you told me he even romanced the silver foxes at your dad's assisted-living center when he was on guard duty."

That was true. When I first acquired my powers, Pretty Boy had used my family to try and force me to work for him. Cody had been sent in as protection. But now that PB was dead and my dad in an undisclosed location, no longer in need of round-the-clock security, Cody had come back to PSI.

Thinking of those dark days had me wondering if Pretty Boy had done something similar to Memory Man, held his family over his head like the sword of Damocles. And if Desert Gal had done—or would do—the same in PB's place. Could that be the reason M-Squared had taken Rome's memories of me? At her behest, to save someone he loved? Had she just wanted to torture me?

Maybe. But Cody had said M-Squared hadn't done what PB or DG had wanted most of the time, which was why they'd kept him locked up for so long. So why would he suddenly start obeying them? More than that, I doubted DG knew about me. We'd never encountered each other, and I was new to this game. Unless she'd somehow heard that I was working her case.

God, this was confusing. I didn't know what to believe. And really, when had I become such a text-happy teenybopper? With all these acronyms, I was going to need that Who's Who reference guide Sherridan had mentioned.

"Are you listening to me?" Sherridan asked. "Cody was romancing silver foxes, Belle. Silver foxes. That clearly shows that as long as a woman is breathing, he's interested. So when I saw him checking me out in John's office, well…I decided to push him away before anything could get started. I know I date a lot of men, but I'm looking for Mr. Right. He is *not* that person."

Maybe I hadn't needed to warn Cody away, after all. I'd never seen Sherridan so strong; she could have sent him away on her own, no problem. And had. Still. I was grateful Cody was on his way out of town and her newfound strength wouldn't be tested daily. "I'm proud of you."

She beamed over at me, curls bouncing. "Thanks."

"And hey. Life's gonna be nothing but roses for you. Lexis—"

"Bitch," Sherridan said at the same time as Tanner scowled.

"Yes, well, that bitch said you're going to get your greatest desire soon."

Sherridan's eyes widened slowly, her mouth falling open in sync. Strangest expression change I'd ever seen. "She's never wrong about these things."

"I know," I grumbled. "And I hate that that man-stealing tramp knows your greatest desire but I don't."

She didn't take the hint. She placed her hands over her heart and twirled. "It's going to happen for me. It's really going to happen."

"What is?" I asked outright. So much for subtlety.

Sherridan stopped and grinned over at me. "I'm going to develop a superpower!"

CHAPTER SIX

SHERRIDAN'S WORDS HAUNTED ME all night. She knew how careful I had to be not to fry the entire world. She knew my name was at the top of many agency hit lists. She knew I had to undergo twice-weekly—sometimes daily—mandatory blood tests. She knew there was nothing I could do about any of it unless I abandoned everyone I loved, ran off and spent the rest of my life in hiding.

Having powers was more a burden than a blessing. Why would she want that for herself? And how could I stop it from happening?

Simple fact was, I couldn't. Never wrong, bitchy Lexis had assured us Sherridan would acquire them and I'd never been able to stop Lexis's visions from coming true before. If I tried this time, I might destroy Sherridan's newfound sense of happiness and thereby her strength, dash her "greatest desire" and ruin our friendship forever.

What a freaking mess.

Was Lexis right this time, though? Maybe her future-seeing ability was on the fritz. I mean, I still couldn't picture another man winning my heart. Or me marrying said man.

Those thoughts led to the flowers. Did the sender truly admire me or was it some kind of joke? Maybe even a Trojan horse. Like maybe there was a camera in the vase, so the bad guys would know when to attack.

See! This was what being a superhero did to a person. Made them question everything. Even flowers. And Sherridan wanted that?

Muttering under my breath, I stumbled into the kitchen, grabbed the vase, stumbled outside and chucked it, flowers and all, into the garbage. I went back to bed but once again, my mind was too active to allow me to sleep.

Finally sunlight pushed its way into my room. I lumbered from the cocoon of covers, showered and dressed in Rome's second-favorite outfit of mine: a pair of stone-washed jeans and an emerald-green cotton shirt that buttoned all the way to the hem. He liked to undo the buttons, one at a time. Sometimes at different times throughout the day, as though it was a prolonged peep show.

I couldn't wear his number-one favorite: skin and a smile. Not to work, at least. So I made do with second string. I only hoped he'd appreciate it.

Once I was dressed, I anchored my hair into a ponytail and went in search of Tanner and Sherridan. Before I found them, my cell phone rang and I rushed back into my room to swipe it off the dresser, where I'd thrown it last night. Hoping…

"Hello," I said, huffing for oxygen.

"Belle Jamison, please," a pleasant feminine voice said.

My heart sank. "This is she. Her. Me." I could never remember what was correct. "I'm Belle."

"Oh, good. I'm Martha Hobbs from Let's Get Together and I'm calling about your upcoming wedding. We've got you scheduled to come in today at noon to look over our invitation selection, and I just wanted to confirm with you."

I closed my eyes and rubbed my temples with my free hand. "I'm sorry. I forgot, and something's come up."

"All right. Twenty-four hours' notice would have been

appreciated, but we can work with this." Professional that she obviously was, there was only the slightest hint of irritation in her voice. "Would you like to reschedule?"

I wish. "I'll have to call you back. I really am sorry. My fiancé, he's—well, things are up in the air right now."

"Oh. I'm sorry. I do understand." And she did, it seemed. Her tone had gentled. "I hope you'll call us if things…work out."

"Sure. Yes." I gulped, hung up, threw the cell on my bed and jumped back into my search for my friends before I burst into tears. This was the first time I'd voiced out loud that the wedding might not happen, and well, it hurt. Like that damn knife was back in my chest, twisting.

I found Tanner in the living room, lounging on the couch. There was no sign of Sherridan. Most likely, she still lazed in bed, avoiding me. She knew I wanted to talk to her about the power thing. Last night I'd tried to find out what kind of ability she wanted, what she thought she'd gain from it and if she was willing to be chased by bad guys for the rest of her life, but she'd made her announcement and then popped open a celebratory bottle of champagne. Only, she had the bottle pressed to her mouth before Tanner could grab a glass. Always a quick and easy drunk, she'd been a goner five minutes later, none of my questions answered.

Tanner groaned when he spotted me. "Not the button-up shirt."

Perhaps I wore it a little too much. But damn it, I liked when Rome unbuttoned me.

"If I know Lexis, and unfortunately, I do," Tanner said drily, pushing to his feet, "she'll be wearing a dress. A sexy, I-want-your-hands-all-over-me dress. Your jeans and T-shirt won't compare. You'll resemble her poor frumpy cousin from Hick Town."

Ouch. Honest friends were not as wonderful as I'd always assumed. "Yeah, but he split with Lexis. Remember?" Hopefully someone did. "A glamazon is not what he wants for himself."

"At one time, he did. And that one time is the state of mind he's in right now."

Shit. Tanner was right. My shoulders slumped as I said, "I need five minutes."

"Do everyone a favor and take ten."

Rolling my eyes, I stomped off. I rifled through my closet, but didn't have anything that could compete with the ever-fashionable Lexis's wardrobe. *Just pick something already.* I had people to interview and a meeting to attend.

Finally I stripped to my underwear and jerked on a too-fancy-for-work chocolate dress that boasted thin straps, an empire waist and a flowing skirt. Very Greek-chic, I hoped. I couldn't wear a bra because I didn't own a strapless and the straps of my comfortable white cotton would have showed. And not in the oh, so sexy you're-seeing-something-you-shouldn't way, but in the granny-got-dressed-in-the-dark way.

On my feet I wore shiny brown sandals that ribboned up my calves. I removed the band in my hair and let the (silky, I liked to think) mass fall. It was straight and hit the middle of my back. Rome liked to sift his fingers through it. Or rather, he used to. Bastard. Lexis had long hair, too, so I was probably okay in that arena.

I straightened my shoulders and studied myself in the full-length mirror. Not bad. Kind of pretty. Definitely elegant.

"This is war," I told my reflection. "Lexis is going down."

I dumped the contents of my purse into a nicer one with one quick shake—a girl had to match—and sailed from the room, ready for the battle to begin. Tanner now stood in the entryway, once more leaning against the wall.

He nodded in approval. "Nice. Your nipples are hard."

I punched him in the stomach, but I was grinning. From Tanner, that was the highest of compliments. Besides that, he'd sounded like his old self. The happy, perverted boy I knew and loved, not the sad wounded puppy he'd been.

"I need my cell," I muttered, rushing back into my bedroom. The little black device flashed red in the upper right-hand corner, which meant that I'd somehow missed a call. A search of the ID showed that it had come from the caterer. Not another one, I thought with a groan. I should call them back, but damn it, if I called I'd have to cancel and I didn't want to cancel them. They served chocolate cake that tasted like it had fallen straight from a rainbow in heaven and booked up fast. Two seconds after I canceled, someone else would already be lined up.

As I joined Tanner in the foyer, I made a mental note to call them, as well as the dress shop, later today and beg a new date.

He opened the door and I sailed past him. Or tried to. Instead, I tripped over a box of…chocolates, I realized, righting myself. Three tiered boxes, one stacked on top of the other like the cake I'd just been imagining, and all wrapped in gold foil. A card was taped underneath a bow.

"Are you seriously that clumsy?" Tanner asked.

"Yes." Warm, humid air beat around me, sunshine hot against my bare arms as I peered down at the boxes, motionless. *Idiot! Check them out.* Heart racing, I tore open the card and read, "There's nothing as sweet as you, though I do hope you enjoy these. Your admirer." Again, no name.

They weren't from Rome, then. My secret hope that he'd suddenly remembered me and now thought to romance me back was once again dashed. I could have drop-kicked those chocolates into a new dimension.

"First the flowers and now candy," Tanner said. "This guy's serious about getting you into bed."

"Shut up. Not all men have sex on the brain."

"If they don't, they're dead."

Or maybe their intentions were nefarious, I thought, reminded of my fears last night.

Tanner crossed his arms over his chest. "So what I want to know is who the hell admires you?"

"Like it's impossible," I replied, ignoring the fact that I'd wondered the same thing. I grabbed the box and clutched it to my chest, determined to find answers. Was there a camera strapped to the outside, someone watching my every move? Were the little treats poisoned? "Some men do think I'm cool."

"That's not what I meant, so sheathe the claws, Viper. You're an engaged woman and the only guys you meet are scrims."

Though our minds were on the same track, I said, "Maybe my banker or my grocer finds me irresistible." We headed toward his car. A sleek red Viper—the very vehicle he'd named me after. Okay, fine. First time we met, I'd told him Viper was my name.

"Yeah, well, maybe your banker and your grocer need a beat down. My bet is the chocolates are from a rival agency. You know, to lure you to the dark side. Or maybe even kill you."

This wouldn't be the first time someone tried to soften me up before attacking. Once, a scrim had jumped behind my car as I was backing out of a parking lot—I hadn't known she'd jumped at the time—and I'd slammed into her. She'd known how to absorb the impact without truly damaging herself, but again, I hadn't known that. Concerned, I'd thrown the car in Park and rushed to her, only to watch in horror as she pulled a gun on me. Only problem with her plan was that she'd already engaged my emotions. My fear froze the bullets inside the gun's chamber and her ass to the pavement.

"And to think, this is the life Sherridan craves for herself," I said. "I can't even enjoy a box of chocolates." A fate far worse than being shot at.

We reached the car, but Tanner didn't open my door. He slid into the driver's side and waited for me to let myself in, the turd. Once I settled beside him in the plush leather seat, my dress tucked daintily around my legs, the candy resting in my lap, I said, "I'm in silk." A lie. I'm sure it was a poly-blend. "At the very least, you could treat me like a lady."

He snorted. "You. A lady. Funny."

"Just drive us to PSI, Mr. Sensitive." As I spoke, I popped open the lid to the top box and gazed in amazement at the assortment of truffles, chocolate squares and cookies. How innocent they appeared…how delicious. My mouth watered, and my stomach rumbled.

Tanner backed out of the driveway at Mach one, his preferred speed. "Don't eat them. They could be poisoned."

"I'd already thought of that. I just wanted a peek at what I'm not going to enjoy."

He glanced at them and whistled. "Those suckers are expensive."

One of my brows arched as I faced him. "How do you know?"

"My dad used to buy that brand for his girlfriends."

His dad had died not too long ago, and I patted his arm in sympathy. His mother, an alcoholic, had left on his eighth birthday—some present, right?—and his dad had been all he'd had left. The loss had devastated him.

I knew that sense of loss intimately.

I'd just started learning to walk when my mother died in a car accident. Though I couldn't remember her features without looking at a photograph, sometimes I would swear there was a hole in my heart. A hole her death had caused.

But I still had a parent, still had someone to lean on. My dad had always taken care of me. He'd bought me tampons for my first period and talked to me about sex, even though he'd been uncomfortable, his face as red as a lobster. Those things had made me love him even more, but they'd also made the pang of not having a mother worse.

"You're staring at the chocolates like you've spotted Jesus," Tanner said. "Just…toss them on the floorboard. John can dust the box and the candy itself for prints."

I replaced the lid, but left them in my lap. "If we're dealing with a rival agency, there won't be any prints." It saddened me that I wasn't more upset someone might want to kill me. But then, been there, done that. A lot.

"Better safe than sorry."

"Since when? Your motto is 'bad shit draws chicks.'"

He nodded. "True. Maybe I should eat one. Being poisoned is a good war story."

My lips twitched into a grin. As good a mood as Tanner was in, now might be the perfect time to talk about his ex. My nemesis. The world's biggest bitch. "So Lexis—"

"Still isn't up for discussion," he said firmly, his good mood melting away in the blink of an eye.

Grrr! Men. "I think you guys need private time. You know, to talk."

"Yeah." He rolled his eyes, the good mood returning. "Translation—you want private time with Rome. You're willing to throw me to the wolves just to play a little game of suck face. You are such a bad friend."

I didn't try to deny it. "But you love me anyway."

"That just proves I'm the dumb one of the friendship."

I snorted. "I can't really refute that, which is sad for you. And me, I guess, since my friends are so dumb."

"Why have we never hooked up?" he asked with a little laugh.

"Because I'm so smart."

Another laugh. "Funny."

A few minutes later, we arrived at PSI headquarters in the heart of the city. Outside, we had to check in at security and flash our badges (even though we were recognizable at this point—I guess unlike Sherridan, we weren't cute enough to make the guards overlook procedure). Inside, we had to sign in at another security booth, ride an elevator to the fifteenth floor and sign in at yet another security booth. We even had to do fingerprint and retinal scans.

John liked things as protected as possible.

Finally deemed acceptable, we strode out of the comfortable lobby, with its brown leather couches and lush green plants, and down a long, plain hallway. From there we turned left, left, right, and hit the laboratory encased by tall glass windows. We left the box of chocolates with forensics—Tanner had to pry them from my Kung Fu grip—and headed to the hall of interview rooms. Along the way, we ran into other agents, but no one stopped to talk. At PSI, everyone had a mission and idle chatter was discouraged.

"Who we interviewing first?" Tanner asked me.

I dug Cody's list out of my purse, glad it had survived the transfer of belongings from one bag to another, and unfolded it. Something untangled from the middle of the paper and fell to the floor. I stopped, grabbed it and—barked out a laugh. Cody had taken a Polaroid of himself, blowing me a kiss. At the bottom, he'd written: You're welcome.

Who used Polaroids these days? Men who wanted to take dirty pictures of their bed partners, that's who, I thought, barking out another laugh.

"You coming?" Tanner asked, ignoring my outburst. He was used to my swift mood changes.

"Yeah." I kicked back into motion and shook my head in wonder at Cody's antics. No wonder he'd looked so wicked when he'd informed me the list was in my purse. As I stuffed the photo back in my bag, I passed an agent staring into one of the interrogation rooms. Before I realized what I was doing, I was peeking inside the room myself. I spied Rome. I stopped abruptly, breath snagging in my throat.

Tanner cursed, backtracked and pressed into my side. "What?" he asked. Then, "Oh."

Inside, Rome sat in the corner, looking casual in a slatted wooden chair. He wore black pants and a black T-shirt that hugged every inch of his muscled forearms. His hair was unruly, as though he'd plowed his hands through it a few thousand times. There were dark circles under his eyes and lines of tension around his mouth.

Thank God he didn't look like a satisfied man. So where exactly had he slept last night?

In front of him, Lexis sat at a metal table, facing one of the people Rome and Cody had rescued from the warehouse. That damn Lexis. How was I supposed to glue myself to Rome if she was always there, right in his face? The nerve of her!

My gaze raked her, and I gasped when I saw what she was wearing. Stone-washed jeans and a green button-up shirt. My teeth ground together.

"That bitch is wearing my outfit." And she rocked it

hard-core. She'd even pulled her glossy dark hair into a ponytail, highlighting the perfection of her exotic features.

A moment passed as Tanner studied her. "My bad. You should have gone with your instincts."

No shit. Now here I was, stuck in a dress when I'd known, deep down, that Rome preferred me in jeans.

"I think you look nice," the agent beside me said. If I was remembering correctly, his name was Edward and he worked in the labs. He had a folder tucked under his arm.

"What's Rome doing in there, anyway?" Tanner asked. "He's supposed to be interviewing his own set of people."

"He's protecting her," I practically snarled, knowing without having to be told.

"The guy she's talking to is the one in need of protection," he replied drily.

At least he didn't sound pissed or sad about seeing the ex-husband and wife together as said ex-wife blatantly attempted to lure said ex-husband under her evil spell.

"Who are they interrogating?" Tanner asked.

"That's Tobin McAldrin." I knew because I was the one who'd picked the people Lexis was to interview. It was pure coincidence that everyone on her list either resembled a beefed-up Arnold in his prime (having the strength to kill her) or seemed as gentle as a lamb and was amazingly good-looking (to romance her). Really.

Tobin was of the beefy variety. Plus, his eyes were cold, empty. My guess, he wasn't some innocent victim of experimentation. Like Memory Man, he was probably a scrim Pretty Boy and then Desert Gal had hoped to recruit and use against us.

"What's his power?" Tanner asked. "Do we know if he even has one?"

"Sadly, no," I muttered.

Edward handed me the folder. "Actually, we do. I've

been testing McAldrin for the last two days. The guy has inhuman strength, and it's like nothing I've ever seen before. Not all of it is his own, though. Someone surrounded his bones with metal Wolverine-style, which caused his strength to increase exponentially."

As he spoke, I flipped through the pages. There were X-rays, graphs I couldn't decipher and anatomy charts covered with arrows.

"Why's he still here, then?" Tanner asked. "I mean, if I had that kind of strength I'd have busted my way free, like, yesterday."

I closed the folder with a snap and handed it back to Edward. "Maybe a few of Desert Gal's victims aren't really victims at all, but plants. Plants someone plans to use to take us down." Of course, Desert Gal would have had to know—or at least hope—PSI would break into her warehouse. For that to happen, she would have had to leak the information herself. That would explain why she'd moved all Pretty Boy's "innocent victims" to a new location and why Rome's contact was only then able to obtain the info.

"I'm sure we'll find out soon enough," I said, my gaze landing on Rome and giving me a jolt.

He shifted ever so slightly in his chair, angling his face toward the two-way mirror, suddenly staring straight at me. He couldn't see me, I knew that, but God, those electric blues singed me all the way to the soul.

Tanner must have pressed the speaker, because suddenly I could hear Lexis coaxing Tobin.

"—here to help you. That's why we freed you. Cooperate, and we'll let you go as soon as this investigation closes."

I hoped she realized that was a lie; I hoped he didn't.

"Now, I'll ask again. How long did Vincent have you locked up?"

Vincent Jones. Street name Pretty Boy.

"I told you," came the cranky, raspy reply. "I don't know. Wasn't like I was given a calendar. Now, are we done here?" He made to stand, his massive body looming like a storm cloud over the petite Lexis.

"Sit down," Rome barked.

Barked. I rolled my eyes at the irony. Rome, a jaguar shape-shifter, and dogs did not get along, a lesson I'd learned just a few weeks ago when I dog-sat our neighbor's golden retriever. The gentle giant had foamed at the mouth for a piece of Rome, and had nearly chewed through my man's thigh. Needless to say, there had gone any chance I'd had of ever getting a dog of my own.

Tobin sat.

"God, I wish I was like that," Edward said. Then he shook his head, cheeks reddening as he realized he'd spoken aloud. I had forgotten he was beside me. Poor, unassuming man. He was probably forgotten a lot. Then again, I could relate. "Well, uh, I'd better get back to work." He rushed off without another word.

"Bye," I called.

No reply.

Through the rest of the interview, Rome kept his gaze glued to me. Or rather, the window. I gulped. *Could* he see me?

"When did Desert Gal take over your care?" Lexis asked.

"About a month or so ago," Tobin mumbled.

So he wasn't so bad with time, after all.

"Did she use any name besides Desert Gal?"

"Nope."

We'd check that with the others, see if he—

"Truth," Tanner said before the thought could fully form in my head.

So we still didn't know her real name. Crap.

"Describe her to me," Lexis said.

For the first time, Tobin grinned. "I can't. She never came to see us herself. She sent someone else to take care of us."

"Who?"

"Don't know her name, only that she's young, hot and has red hair. Girl had a mouth on her, though. Damn did she have a mouth."

Red hair narrowed things down a little. It would make her easier to spot, if nothing else. Well, if the red hair was real. It could have been a wig, or temporarily dyed.

Lexis leaned back in her seat, the very picture of resolute agent. "Did she ask you to do anything for her or Desert Gal?"

"Nope." He wasn't a bad-looking guy, with brown hair and big brown eyes. No tattoos, was even clean-cut. Those steroid muscles, though…someone should have told him there was such a thing as too much. "Not a thing."

"Lie," Tanner said.

The guy had delivered his lies with a straight face and no telltale signs. Without Tanner, I would have believed him. "We'll have to keep him incarcerated, then, because we can't risk letting him wander around, trying to hurt us. Or maybe not," I added after a moment's reflection. "Like you said, he's probably strong enough to bust out of here. But he hasn't. Which means, as I suspected, Desert Gal and her cohort might have asked him to stay and spy on us. If we let him go, we can follow him. Maybe he'll lead us to them."

Tanner slapped me on the back. "Damn, Viper. Now you're thinking like an agent. I like it. Come on. We've got our own people to interview."

I nodded reluctantly and turned, keeping my attention

on Rome as long as possible. Because of that, I saw that he'd pushed to his feet, his chair skidding behind him.

I stopped. Both Lexis and Tobin glanced over at him questioningly.

He didn't say anything, just headed straight for the door. My eyes widened and my heart thumped in my chest. Was he coming for…me?

CHAPTER SEVEN

THE INTERROGATION ROOM DOOR swung open, the hinges squeaking, and Rome stepped into the hall. He didn't glance around. No, he instantly pinned me with a hard stare, as if he'd known exactly where I was standing all along.

I gulped. Had he?

Beside me, Tanner muttered, "Shit. Cat Man's pi—issed."

That he was. His eyes were narrowed, his pupils a thin, feral line. I licked my lips, a nervous gesture I couldn't have stopped had my life depended on it. Here he was, my most primal fantasy in the flesh. Dark, dangerous and untamable.

Rather than smile and tug me into his arms for a kiss, he snarled, "Can you two keep it down? You're distracting us."

Us? When neither Lexis nor Tobin had even glanced at the window since Tanner and I had stepped up to it? "Uh, I could scream the national anthem and no one inside that room would be able to hear me."

His lips pursed, and he remained silent. Stubborn man.

"Just…go back in there and finish the interview." I gestured to the window. Lexis, too, had gone silent the moment Rome had exited, and she and Tobin were listening through the still-open door. "Well, no one can hear us when the door is properly…clo…sed." I had trouble getting out the last word.

Rome's gaze was in the process of raking over me, heating from cold ocean to azure fire. He lingered on my calves, where the chocolate ribbons x-ed a path to my knees, and ran his tongue over the seam of his lips. "What are you wearing?"

It was a question laced with some sort of husky promise. I gulped again, this time for an entirely different reason. Maybe the dress hadn't been such a bad idea, after all. Maybe Rome liked me no matter what I wore.

"This old thing? Oh, it's just something I threw on."

Tanner snorted. Thankfully, he kept his mouth shut.

"You look very…pretty." Rome's voice was low, raspy now.

Clearly, his first choice had not been "pretty." Maybe I'm an idiot. "Thank you," I said, raising my chin. Whether he'd meant to say "amazing" or "wretched" I didn't care. Really. He'd either like me or he wouldn't, and there was nothing I could do about it.

Now, that is. There was nothing I could do *now*. When his memories returned—and they would, I refused to believe otherwise—he would pay for all of this and assuage my stinging pride.

I stretched my arm around him, careful not to touch him, and closed the door. "How did you see us through the glass?" I asked. I had to keep the conversation rolling or I'd find myself sidling up to Rome and resting my head on his shoulder out of habit. No telling how he'd react.

"I told you. Eye enhancements. Two-ways are not a problem for me."

"You never told me—" Wait. Yes. Yes, he had. I gasped as the implications hit me, hope infusing my every cell. While we were "dating," a.k.a. while he chased me so that PSI could neutralize me, he'd told me all about the voluntary procedures he'd undergone to increase his physical strength and scrim-hunting skills. "You remember telling me about the procedure?"

Confusion settled over his gorgeous features. "I—I—"

Right on cue—because she'd known how close we were to a breakthrough, the bitch—Lexis opened the door and stepped into the hall.

"What's going on?" she asked in a snotty tone far worse than her usual smugness.

Beside me, Tanner went rigid.

"Do you remember?" I insisted, keeping my attention centered on Rome. "We were in a car, being chased by Pretty Boy. I was snuggled into your side and you were trying to distract me from my fears so I wouldn't ice the car. My head was resting on your shoulder, my hand on your chest, so I could feel your heart drumming and—"

"Great story." Lexis ran her palm up and down Rome's arm, petting him. "But it isn't as though it can possibly be verified."

"I can verify it," Tanner told her, the words more a growl than anything. "I was in the backseat listening."

Damn, I loved him. "Rome," I said. "Do. You. Remember?"

The confusion faded from his face and anger returned. He shook his head. "No. I don't. I don't know why I said what I did."

Still, my hope remained. My fiancé was in that head somewhere. Whether his memories had been erased or borrowed didn't matter. Somehow, a part of him *did* remember me.

He placed an arm around Lexis's waist—my hope blended with a fiery prong of rage—and tugged her closer to him. For comfort? My hands burned. Then he released her to close the door behind her. He'd only meant to move her out of the way. The burning subsided.

"What's going on?" Miss Know-It-All repeated. She focused on me, blinked when she spotted my outfit, then smirked. She ran a fingertip along the buttons of her shirt. "Nice dress, Belle."

My cheeks heated with embarrassment. "I'd tell you those jeans look nice on you, but they make your ass look fat."

"Truth," Tanner said with a grin.

Lexis paled but didn't offer a retort.

Tanner reached for me and squeezed my hand in comfort, and I noticed he was trembling. Not by word or deed did he betray it, though. With his neutral expression, he appeared every bit the confident man. I'd never been prouder of him.

Suddenly Rome's lips pulled back from his teeth in a show of aggression.

"Sweetheart?" Lexis said.

His gaze never left me.

"What?" I demanded.

"Nothing," he snapped, though his eyes were glued to Tanner's and my joined hands.

Wait. Was he jealous, as he'd been with Cody? Or did his anger stem from the insult I'd dealt his precious Lexis? I opened my mouth to say something—what, I might never know—when Rome's voice lashed out.

"Where's Cody?"

"I sent him out on assignment." He'd sent himself, but whatever. "So what'd you guys learn from Tobin?"

Lexis rested her head on Rome's shoulder, as I'd wanted to do earlier and as I'd just told him I'd once done in his car, and patted his chest. To his credit, he shifted uncomfortably. Even disengaged from her to peer inside the interrogation room at Tobin, who had not moved from his chair.

Lexis couldn't mask the hitch of her breath.

I suddenly couldn't stop smiling.

Her eyes homed in on my smile like a missile just before impact. "He stayed at my house last night."

"We slept in separate rooms," Rome said before I could react. He turned back to her, frowning. Upset by what she'd insinuated? "I asked you to stop that."

Stop trying to distress me? And they'd stayed in separate rooms? Thank God! I'd tried not to worry about it, had managed to suppress any mental images of the two of them together, naked, but the worry *had* been there, deep in my heart.

"You did?" I asked, then cursed myself for how needy I'd come across.

"We're working on the emotional aspects of our marriage before we get physical," Lexis retorted, defensive.

"You're working on your marriage?" I'd known that. He'd implied it before, but still. Knife…twisting…

Rome shifted uncomfortably from one foot to the other and tangled his fingers through his hair. "Yes. No. I don't know. I told you I was going to remarry her." This time, at least, he didn't sound so sure.

"God, I can't believe I ever dated you." Tanner, too, tangled a hand through his hair, dislodging the blue locks and causing them to stand on end as he scowled at Lexis. "Every day, hell, every hour, I get over you a little more. Were you always this manipulative and nasty? And how the hell did I miss it?"

As he spoke, I studied Rome's face, watching for any sign of acceptance, any sign that he realized the truth of Tanner's claim, that he was being manipulated in the worst possible way. But while he appeared hard and uncompromising, he did not appear enlightened.

"Watch how you talk to her," he said.

"Why? I've said worse to her," Tanner replied. "While we were in bed."

Rome surprised me; he didn't lash out over that "in bed" remark.

"I'm just looking out for my family, Tanner," Lexis said softly, no longer smirking or smug. "For my daughter."

Tanner pushed out a disgusted breath. "No, you're looking out for yourself."

Rome's head tilted to the side. In thought? "Wait a second. You truly dated him?" He faced Lexis. He didn't appear upset by the knowledge that his ex-wife had dated a much younger man. Maybe because he knew, on some level, that he didn't love this woman any longer.

"For a little while," she said, rubbing the back of her neck. "Now isn't the time to discuss it, though."

Now was as good a time as any, so Lexis could suck it. "Don't you think you should rediscover your past before you work on your future?" I asked him.

Rome scrubbed a hand down his face. "Yes. No." Once again, anger hardened his features. "I don't know what to think about anything anymore. Okay?"

"He's about to blow," Tanner muttered. He probably meant the words for me alone, but they echoed through our little circle. "So, uh, why don't we change the subject as The Great Puppeteer suggested. Tell us what you learned from that Tobin guy."

A long while passed in silence, time Rome used to clear his expression and soften his body language to give nothing of his emotions away. From seething statue of granite to average citizen with not a care. Well, as average as a guy like him could look.

"We'll give you our report at the lunch meeting," he said. "We've got a few more people to talk to first, and I want to confirm a few things before they're bandied about."

"All right." I nodded. That had always been Rome's style. "Tanner and I should go. We've got a few people to interview ourselves."

Rome frowned again, a hint of concern pushing through that blank mask. "Who? And why together?"

Was that concern for me? And maybe more of the jealousy I'd sensed earlier? "Elaine Daringer, for starters. And because we work well together."

"Rome." Lexis tugged at his arm impatiently. "We really should finish speaking with Tobin. He's growing restless."

Rome ignored her. "Elaine is an energy vampire," he told me.

"I know. I read her file." I flicked Lexis a glance. She pinched one of her shirt's buttons and rolled it back and forth, the motions agitated. Didn't like the attention I was getting, I supposed.

"Have you ever dealt with an energy vampire before?" Rome asked.

Still talking to me, I realized happily. "No, but I've studied the PSI manual and know what to do. She'll be strapped down and I won't touch her."

"Besides," Tanner said, his chest puffing up, "Belle will have me. She'll be fine. Better than fine."

That frown grew in intensity. "Let me talk—"

Boom!

Plumes of plaster and rock suddenly bathed the air, debris flying in every direction. Tanner was knocked flat on his ass, part of the wall and window that had exploded pinning him down. Lexis and Rome were propelled to the ground, as well.

Me, well, I was knocked backward and scooped into a viselike grip before I could kiss the tiles.

Tobin had broken through the wall.

A high-pitched alarm screeched to life, echoing all

around. When I realized what had happened—and what *was* happening—I kicked and punched with every ounce of strength I possessed. When that failed to gain my freedom, I jabbed Tobin's trachea and poked his eyes just like Rome had taught me.

Nothing slowed him; nothing relaxed his grip. He barreled down the halls, past shocked agents, shoving them to the floor and going straight through walls. He didn't mist, though, a form of teleporting. No, he simply shattered the plaster and wood. The agents would jump to their feet, use their powers or human abilities—a lightning bolt whizzed past, a slew of knives and throwing stars, even a thick, choking smoke that clouded the air— but Tobin dodged everything effortlessly, as though he'd trained for just such a thing.

"Let me go!" Every time he slammed through those planks, I felt as if a thousand fists were punching me. The impact was compounded as his heavy feet slammed into the floor one after the other, bouncing me up and down. At least I was able to cough some of the smoke out of my lungs. "You're killing me!"

"Be still," he snarled.

"I will when you tell me where you're taking me!"

"My friend wants to chat with you, okay, and my friend gets what she wants."

She. Desert Gal? Desert Gal's friend? I increased my struggles. "For God's sake, if she wanted to talk to me, she could have called me!"

Another wall. More fists, more vibrations. "This way, she can ensure you answer her questions properly."

Great. Torture was on the horizon.

By the sixth wall, I was cut, bleeding and coughing from more than smoke inhalation. I wouldn't be able to stop him through regular means, I realized. I'd have to use my powers. What should I use, then? Rain? No, he'd slip but keep running. Fire? No, I might burn the entire building down. Ice?

Yes! Ice. I could freeze him in place. And maybe, just maybe, since Rome, my filter, was in the building, I wouldn't mess this up and refrigerate the entire city of Atlanta. *Come on, Belle. You can do it.*

Fear, I needed fear to create ice. I was scared right now, but it was a numbing fear, which meant the emotion was there, it just wasn't accessible, as though this was simply a dream and I wasn't really involved. I needed to break through that numbness just like Tobin had broken through those walls.

Okay, so. What scared me so much I couldn't pretend everything would work out in my favor? The thought of the upcoming torture, for sure. Knives under my nails, fingers removed, ears bitten off. As I thought them, I pictured them happening. A cold mist began to drift through my veins. It was a good start, but not nearly enough to immobilize my captor.

"Don't kill me," I shouted, hoping that would help. I'd read somewhere that hearing oneself beg for mercy could start a domino effect inside one's body. Supposedly the sound sparked a terrified tremor and that tremor unleashed a torrent of endorphins. Wait. Endorphins numbed fear. I think. Argh! Things weren't supposed to be this complicated. I *was* going to screw this up.

With that last thought, my fear kicked up a notch, the mist solidifying into an icy rain. Oh, excellent! Failure must frighten me stupid.

"I'm such a failure," I wailed. Another notch.

"Shut up, woman."

"I can't do anything right." Another notch. Sadly, I couldn't refute the words. Not only was I facing potential death, but there was a very real possibility that Rome was going to stay with Lexis forever, that I'd lose him, never hold him again.

Ice spread over the floor, and Tobin lost his footing. As he slammed into an office, people screaming, debris raining, an animalistic roar suddenly ripped through the air. Both Tobin and I were propelled forward at a faster velocity. When we hit something solid—a desk—Tobin grunted and released me. I went skidding across the floor, once again losing my hold on the ice-inducing fear.

What the hell?

I jumped to shaky legs, scanning the area. Rome had morphed into his jaguar form, sleek and black and deadly, and had tackled Tobin from behind. The wild black cat tore a chunk from the struggling man's neck. Not enough to kill him, but enough to slow him down.

Tobin raised a meaty fist and batted him across the room—at me. Rome and I were knocked together, oxygen gusting from my lungs on impact. But when we landed, the cat was somehow underneath me. He must have twisted us midair. He rolled me to my back.

There was a warm lick across my face and then the weight lifted and the two men were facing off again, Tobin bleeding, Rome snarling. I gagged, seeing the blood on both of them.

There was no manufacturing fear this time. As I lay there, laboring for every breath, the emotion flooded me. Inhumanly strong as Tobin was, he could snap Rome's neck. Or punch him in the head and crack his skull into a thousand pieces. Perhaps, though, that would be a good thing. Perhaps it would knock some sense into him, as my dad always says.

Wait. Finding a silver lining was not good in a situation like this. Tobin could—

Scream, "Son of a bitch," and launch at Rome. The two clashed together, twisting to the ground, rolling and fighting. Tobin, punching. Rome, biting.

"I didn't take your woman," the strong man growled. "No reason to react like this."

Rome gave another of those ear-piercing roars, sharp teeth flashing white.

Okay, okay, okay. I had to concentrate. I hated doing things like this, worrying I'd somehow think them into actually happening, but sometimes it was the only way to work my emotions in the direction I needed them. To jump-start things, I closed my eyes and pictured Lexis walking down the aisle to marry Rome. That brought anger, not fear, melting the ice. Scratch that.

I drummed up an image of Tanner, warring with the boys. Every day he trained in self-defense and combat, but he wouldn't stand a chance against Tobin. A tendril of fear swept through me, cool but not cold.

In my mind, I threw Sherridan into the fight. Pretty, don't-like-to-sweat Sherridan, and my fear increased. I would have considered my own torture again, but my fear for the others was greater. Quite simply, they were my everything.

Next I planted my dad. Weak as his heart was, he wouldn't survive any kind of physical fight—especially not one where I could hear grunting, groaning and bones snapping. Once more, my fear increased and finally, blessedly I achieved the glacial temperature I desired. My blood thickened and my palms iced over, a crystallized ball forming in the center.

"Rome," I shouted, eyelids popping open. "Duck."

The large cat dove out of the way, and I tossed the ice ball with a shaky arm. My aim was true. The ball slammed into Tobin's chest, frost instantly spreading and coating his entire body. He'd been in the process of swinging his massive fist at Rome's head, but froze in place just before contact.

At that point, everything seemed to still.

Agents had gathered around the area, I noted, each staring down at us, silent. They hadn't jumped into the mix, either too afraid the volatile cat would come at them next or afraid they would hit and kill Rome while trying to slay Tobin. Tanner and Lexis, I noticed, were both absent. Shit. My fear increased, though I no longer needed it, and another ice ball formed in my hand. Were they okay?

Rome remained on the ground, fur slowly falling from him, naked sun-kissed skin taking its place. Panting, I stood and lumbered to him, keeping the ice ball cradled safely against my chest. Were I to drop it, the ground would be covered in seconds. I fell to his side and stroked his hair with my free hand. Bruises were already developing on his chest and legs, but his eyes were open and he was breathing.

Just as relief drifted through me, the ice around Tobin began to crack. He was fighting his way free, I realized.

Everyone reacted at once.

With Rome out of the way and Tobin an easy mark, a lightning bolt sailed, a throwing star embedded and that thick smoke billowed. A gunshot even rang out, cracking the ice and leaving a gaping hole. Blood trickled from it, but I wasn't taking any chances. I tossed the second ball of ice at him. Once again, frost spread.

Everyone waited, time seemingly suspended, but the second layer held firm and kept the beast in place.

"Rome!" Lexis shouted, suddenly pushing her way into the room. Blood dripped from her temple and onto her shirt as she knelt in front of him.

Tanner limped in behind her. He, too, was bleeding.

But he was alive, and that was all that mattered. He searched the room until he found me. "You good?"

I nodded, incapable of speech at the moment. My chin was trembling too violently.

"What the hell happened? And why is everyone standing around?" John's voice rang with authority, kicking everyone into motion. Scanning the room, I found him looming in the middle of a giant hole in the wall. "Get that scrim locked in the freezer so he remains immobilized, and get Jamison, Bradshaw and the Masterses to medical. Now!"

Several agents rushed to the block of ice and hauled it out together. Several more helped Rome and me to our feet. Our eyes were locked together during it all. Whatever thoughts drifted through his mind, I might never know. Lexis elbowed one of the agents out of the way and stepped in front of me, winding an arm around Rome's waist and finally blocking him from my view.

CHAPTER EIGHT

"I DON'T WANT to do this," I grumbled. Again.

"Don't care," John told me. "You used your powers, and I want to test your blood against the blood samples taken when you hadn't."

"You've done that before."

He held his ground. "The more I do it, the more I can find the consistencies and differences."

"You're a blood monger, you know that?" I was still at PSI headquarters, but I was now sprawled out on a gurney, my beautiful dress replaced by an ugly, paper-thin, unflattering hospital gown. I should have been alone—this was a private room, after all—but John and his blood-testing goon refused to leave my side. I covered the vein the goon wanted with my hand. "Enough is enough."

"Wrong," John replied. "It's never enough until I say it's enough."

Such a man thing to say. "Can't we at least do this the normal way? You know, with needles? No offense," I told the guy waiting to drain a pint or so out of me with his teeth. No lie. His teeth.

"None taken," he said with a grin. He hadn't removed his hand from my wrist, though.

"No, we can't," John said, then prompted the goon, "Reese. Sometime today."

Reese, a tall man with a handsome yet innocent face

and a dimpled smile, gently lifted my hand closer and closer to his mouth. His teeth were white, straight and a lot longer than the average human's. And sharper. God, were they sharper. "Don't worry, Belle. I'll treat you the same way I'd treat my girlfriend. If I had one."

There was something so hypnotic about his voice. Something wicked and wanton that belied the sweet purity of his face. He'd worked for the agency for several years, and had taken my blood many times before this. He'd always been tender with me, even the times Rome had stood over his shoulder, snapping at him to hurry.

Rome. Was he in a room similar to this? Maybe even the room across from mine? Was Lexis with him? Tending to his wounds like a loving girlfriend? Bitch.

"Wait," I told Reese just before he started chomping. He stilled. "I'll let him test my blood, but you need to leave," I said, pinning John with a fierce stare. "I don't want an audience. It makes me nervous. Besides, I want you to check on Rome." Ensuring he *did* have an audience.

John waved a hand in dismissal. "Rome's fine."

"Make sure." *Or rather, play chaperone.* "I won't be able to settle down until I know for sure he's racer-ready."

"Belle—"

I arched a brow at him, hoping I looked as stubborn as Rome did when he used the expression. "This is not a negotiation. Go, before I change my mind about the bloodletting and roast Reese alive."

Reese chuckled, a lock of blond hair falling onto his forehead. I liked the way his eyes sparkled with his amusement. I mean, I might love Rome, but I wasn't dead.

"So feisty," he said, and there was a ring of affection in his tone.

"One day I'm going to start docking your pay for trying to act like the boss." John stomped from the sickroom, as I called it, and slammed the door shut behind him.

"Alone at last," Reese said, his thumb tracing over my pulse. "I've been hoping for a chance to talk to you."

Every muscle in my body stiffened. Oh my God, was he hitting on me? Was he my secret admirer, perhaps? "Uh, Reese. As you know, I'm kind of engage—uh—" wrong "—I'm kind of seeing someone."

"Like I could forget the way Rome used to hover. But, uh, I don't want to date you, and please don't be hurt by that. You're just too scary for me. I want to date your friend Sherridan. I saw her yesterday, when she was looking for you, and thought she had a nice pair of… legs." He looked away from me, suddenly…shy? "Does she have a boyfriend?"

Somehow, I'd become the resident matchmaker. Ironic, considering the state of my own love life. "She's single. But…" I pressed my lips together. As it turned out, I didn't need to finish the sentence for him to understand my meaning.

His gaze lifted, a little tortured but not offended. "You want to know if she'll become a vampire like me if we get hot and heavy."

I gave a reluctant nod.

"That would be a big fat no. *You* haven't, and I've bitten you countless times."

Reese was John's preferred method of blood testing. Said the vampire was more reliable than any machine, his taste buds sharper than any piece of equipment, and that he could tell anything and everything about a person's body simply by ingesting the life-giving fluid.

In the beginning, I'd worried that exposure to my blood would make Reese turn out like me. I think perhaps John had hoped for such a thing—two powerful element-wielders for the price of one—and that was the real reason he'd had Reese perform the tests on me. But the agent had never sickened like I had when first infected. He'd never shot uncontrollable fire beams out of his eyes or accidentally frozen PSI headquarters so that the entire operation had to be moved. And as unstable as the powers were at first, he would have done something.

"Yeah," I said, "but we weren't caught up in passion. What if she bites you back? What if—?"

"Wouldn't matter. I'm not a virus. No one can catch what I've got. Besides, I would never allow anything bad to happen to her. Or you," he added fiercely. "I hope you know that."

I settled more deeply against the bed pad. Unlike Cody, Reese didn't strike me as a player, therefore he might just be acceptable. "Before I give you my seal of approval, I have some questions for you." While I admired his zeal, the BF in me needed to know more. "Have you ever cheated on a girl?"

"No," he said, and this time he *was* offended.

I wished Tanner, my lie detector, were here. How was Tanner, anyway? He'd been bleeding, but on his feet, yet John had insisted on a CAT scan. "Are you looking for a long-term relationship or just a friend with benefits?" Either way, Reese was a much better choice than Cody, I decided. To my knowledge, he didn't have a river of broken hearts running behind him.

Reese eyed me for a long, silent moment. "Are you her dad or something, and I just didn't know it?"

"Think of me as her guardian angel. Her very powerful, fry-you-like-battered-shrimp guardian angel. So answer the question before I give you an eight-hundred-degree suntan."

He rolled his eyes but said, "I'm looking for a date.

To get to know her, see if we're compatible. Anything that happens afterward is private, suntan or not. If you'd like, we could even make it a double date. Sherridan and me, you and Cody. I, uh, hear you two are a couple now. That true?"

"No, it's not true," I grumbled. Exactly how had such a rumor gotten around so quickly? I studied him. *You can trust me not to hurt you,* those green eyes said. But could I? I no longer trusted my instincts when it came to men. Damn, but I wished I'd paid more attention to office gossip. I might have learned why Reese and his girlfriend, someone he'd been with for over a year, had broken things off last month. A sigh slipped from me. "Feel free to ask her out," I said, "but know that if you make her cry, I really will ash you."

He shuddered, though there was an amused glint in his eyes. "First time I've ever been issued a threat like that and known it could actually happen." His gaze flicked to my wrist. "So…are you ready?"

Reluctantly I nodded.

Slowly he raised my hand to his mouth. His warm tongue laved my pulse point, massaging the skin. Nothing sexual about it, but I found myself wondering if he perhaps lingered a little too long. Then I tensed slightly, expecting the coming sting. It arrived a second later, his sharp teeth sinking into my vein, his mouth giving a gentle suction.

"How'd you become a vampire, anyway?" I asked, though I knew he couldn't talk with a mouth full of, well, me. "Experiments, I bet. Blink once if I'm right, twice if I'm wrong."

He blinked once.

That's how Rome had acquired his abilities. That's how I had acquired *my* ability. Tanner and Lexis were the only legitimate superheroes in the bunch (though I hated to think of Lexis as either super or heroic), having been born with their gifts.

Even Rome's daughter, who could mist through walls and come out the other side, was the product of science. Lexis hadn't known she was pregnant when she'd signed up to "enhance" her already powerful intuition.

"Enjoying yourself?" a hard voice suddenly asked.

My attention whipped to the now-open door, where Rome towered like an ancient god, glaring over at me. He'd dressed in another black T-shirt and matching pants. Between him and Tanner, can you blame me for having decorated our house in the brightest possible color scheme? His hair was combed, his face clean. Always a supernaturally fast healer, he had no injuries that I could see.

"Yes," I said defensively. Had he just come from seeing Lexis? Had she showered with him? Bitch, I thought again. I'd probably think it a thousand times more. "So?"

Reese pulled his teeth from me and straightened. There was an odd sheen in his eyes, a sheen of some dark emotion I'd never seen him project before. Anger, maybe? Then he leaned his head back, eyelids closing as though he was savoring the flow of my blood through his veins. He wasn't, I knew. He was processing, scanning my blood as John wished.

"Reese," Rome said.

Reese's lids cracked open. "Can't a guy work in peace? Jeez. But fine, whatever. I know my cue to leave. I'll step into the hall and analyze the blood out there."

"Stay," I commanded, just to be contrary.

"Leave or die," Rome said.

Reese winked at me and stood, covertly patting my arm. "I'm certainly raking in the death threats today. At serious risk to my health, I just have to say your blood gets sweeter every time I taste it." With his free hand, he kissed the tips of his fingers. Then he turned on his heel and marched past a grim-faced Rome.

Rome kicked the door shut with his foot, the sound of the knob clicking into place almost deafening in the sudden silence.

The old Rome would have tripped Reese for saying such a romantic thing. The new Rome hadn't even glanced at him as he stalked out. I couldn't complain, though. Finally, I was alone with my kind-of/kind-of-not fiancé, no one looking in through a two-way mirror, no one recording our every word.

Rome tossed a small square at me. "This yours?"

I looked down, saw Cody's smiling face in my lap. "Yeah. So?"

"So. It was found in your purse. You guys really dating?"

Rather than answer him, I said, "How's Lexis?" Let him stew, I thought, feeling a little mean.

His jaw tensed for a moment. Then he shrugged, as if the answer hadn't mattered to him. "She's good."

Too bad. On both counts. "And Tanner?"

"The kid? A little cut up, but he claims he needs the scars. He's a little…out there."

A polite way of saying he was weird. "No, he's not. Chicks dig scars, therefore he likes scars. It's perfectly logical. And just so you know, if I hadn't decided to marry you, I would have married him." If he would have had me. Right now, only my admirer—who may or may not want to kill me—seemed interested.

Rome blinked over at me. "You're lying."

I was, and I didn't feel guilty. I raised my chin. "How do you know? You don't know anything about me."

He couldn't refute that, and he clearly didn't like the

reminder. His expression darkened. "Isn't that child a little young for you?"

"I'm twenty-five. He's twenty. Hardly a big difference."

"Yes, but when you were learning to drive he was telling girls they had cooties."

"Yeah, well, that turns me on." Apparently it *had* turned Lexis on, because she had dated him and she was older than I was.

Rome's tongue flicked out, tracing the seam of his lips, as if the picture in his mind made him hungry. So very hungry. For what? "What else turns— Never mind." He stuffed his hands into his pockets, his skin flushing. "It's better if I don't know."

Me. Hungry for me.

How close we were to actually flirting. How far would he take it, this man who had no idea who I was? *Let's see, shall we?* "So...you came in here because you wanted me?" I asked, knowing very well how suggestive my words were.

His pupils dilated, the only sign he'd noticed. "Yes." He cleared his throat. "I wanted to...thank you for helping me back there. You didn't have to, and hell, everyone would have understood if you hadn't, considering how shitty I've been to you. And on that note, I'm also here to apologize."

My eyes widened, and I sat up straighter in the bed. I would have stood, or thrown my legs over the side and sat up completely, just to be closer to him, but that would have revealed the hospital gown in all its ugly glory. Right now my legs and stomach—and thereby my modesty—were covered only by a light blue blanket. "Well, I wanted to thank you, too, for coming to my rescue. But if you're going to apologize to me, I'd rather it be for forgetting me when you said you'd love me forever. Oh, and for treating your ex like a freaking queen."

"Good. Because I'm apologizing for all of it," he said, his jaw clenched. "Everyone knows we were a couple, and until a few days ago you thought so, too. You didn't know this would happen to me, and you didn't—*don't* deserve my cruelty."

Were, he'd said. Everyone knew we *were* a couple. Past tense. I fingered the engagement ring I still wore and tried not to sink under a wave of depression. "*Why* did you treat me like that?"

"Because I—" He shifted uncomfortably from one foot to the other. His gaze remained fixed on me, even though it was obvious he wanted to glance away. "Because I woke up thinking I was supposed to be working things out with my ex-wife, but I took one look at you and—"

Once again he stopped, but this time he didn't continue. He'd taken one look at me and had…wanted me? Craved me like the air he breathed? The way I did him?

"Yes," he said, clearly shamed. "Whatever you're thinking, yes. I wanted you when I should have wanted her. And every time you looked at me, that wanting just got worse. I thought if I pushed you away, made you angry, *something,* you'd stop looking at me and the wanting would go away. It…didn't."

My skin heated, burning, blistering, the thought of his desire sparking my own. But that desire was underscored with a jubilation so complete, tears filled my eyes. Even without his memories of me, he couldn't deny his body's reaction to me. That was a start. A very promising start.

"Don't cry," he croaked. "Please don't."

"I'm not." Shaking, I swiped my eyes with the back of my wrist. At least I didn't have to worry about rain falling from the ceiling. These were tears of hope, not sadness. Not that I was crying, I reminded myself. "Really. It's dusty in here, that's all."

His gaze zeroed in on the puncture wounds, and he bared his teeth in a scowl. "John should use a needle on you."

So we were off the subject of his desire for me, were we? "You've said that before. About the needle."

He ran his tongue over his teeth, a sure sign of irritation. With me? Or himself? "I wish I remembered. I wish my memories hadn't been taken."

Himself, then. "Me, too. So…are you still trying to work things out with your ex?" The question tumbled from my mouth before I could stop it, needy and whiny. That embarrassed me, but I didn't try to take back the words.

"No. Yes. No. I don't know." He strode forward and claimed the seat Reese had formerly occupied. He propped his elbows on his knees and scrubbed his face with his upraised hands. "This is such a mess."

"I know," I said softly.

There was a beat of silence, heavy, uncomfortable.

When he faced me, his eyes were tortured. "I want you to know, I haven't slept with Lexis. She wanted to, but I just couldn't do it. I couldn't even bring myself to kiss her. And I won't. Not until this…thing between us is resolved. Okay? All right?"

Those damn tears burned my eyes again. Relief was like a separate entity inside me, rushing me, tackling me. I wasn't sure what I would have done if he'd slept with her. Could I have forgiven him? I'd wondered before, but hadn't known the answer. Still didn't.

Even though I'd despised my ex, the Prince of Darkness and my last boyfriend before Rome, at the time of our breakup, learning that he'd cheated had destroyed my pride, my self-esteem, my every feminine instinct. I'd felt disposable and worthless.

In Rome's mind, it wouldn't have been cheating. I knew that. But in my mind, it would have. He was still my man. Still my heart, my one and only. "Why are you telling me that? Don't get me wrong, I'm grateful. I'm just curious about your thought process." To him, we were strangers. He didn't owe me anything.

"Because in your mind, we're engaged," he said. "I owe you that much."

He owed me a lot more, but whatever. We'd get to that, one step at a time. And for the first time, the familiar thought didn't seem like a pep talk meant to get me through the day. It felt true. Like it would happen. Like everything really would be okay.

"And...I don't want you to be with anyone else, either," he finished suddenly.

I blinked over at him. Even choked, and he had to pat my back to help clear my airway. But instead, I lost my ability to breathe. Dear God, his hands were on me, hot and callused and shiver-inducing. I would have pretended to choke for an hour, just to keep those hands on my body, but all too soon he settled back on his chair and crossed his arms over his chest. Lines of strain branched from his eyes, though, as if he hadn't wanted to pull away.

"I think I misheard you," I said. "Or maybe you were kidding. Because I know you didn't just tell me, a person who currently means nothing to you, that you—"

"I did, all right? I don't want you seeing anyone else."

One, I would never consider seeing one man while engaged to another. I wish he knew that about me. Two, Rome was the only one I wanted, period. "Until?"

"Until we work this out."

"And just how long do you think that will be? I won't wait for you forever, you know." Another lie. I'd wait however long was necessary, and I knew it. I just didn't want him dawdling. A man could not have his cake and eat it, too—unless that man was Chuck Norris.

I'd been watching Chuck Norris movies lately to improve my roundhouse kick.

Rome scowled at me. "You're being difficult, Belle."

"So give me a severe tongue-lashing. That will shut me up. Or make me scream for mercy. It's a toss-up." I didn't give him the chance to scold me or tell me to stop. "So what do we do now?" I asked. "About us?"

Rome's jaw was tight. "I want to remember you. I do." He leaned back in the chair, eyes hot on me, boring deep. "Tell me about us."

Where to start, where to start? "Well, the sex was amazing. The best you'd ever had. Top five for me."

His lips twitched into the semblance of a smile, another reminder of the Rome I so loved. "I figured that out on my own. The part about it being amazing, I mean."

My heart skipped a beat, leaving me winded and shaking. "You remember?"

"No. I…guessed."

"Oh." My shoulders sagged. "How?"

His gaze perused me slowly, lingering in all the right places, making me tingle like a woman who'd just experienced a total body caress. "Let's just say a man can look at a woman and know how it'll be between them."

"And you know it'll be, was, amazing…with me?"

"Yes." No hesitation.

Wow. Of all the wonderful things he'd said during this conversation, that little tidbit gave me the most hope that we'd end up back together. A man who desired a woman couldn't resist her for long. Could he?

"You probably burned me alive," he added softly. Wistfully.

I had. Literally. At first, I'd been unable to control my powers and had caught him—and whatever room we'd been in at the time—on fire. That wasn't what he'd meant, but I couldn't help but reminisce and ache and crave those days again. "We had fun together. I made you laugh, even when I didn't mean to, and you made me feel like the most important thing in the world to you."

His gaze whipped from me, as if he were suddenly afraid to face me. "Belle, I—"

Whatever he was going to say, I didn't want to hear it. I didn't have to be psychic like Lexis to know he would ruin this happy buzz I had going. "Look, if you don't need anything else, I'd kind of like to be alone. I need to dress, and then round everyone up for our meeting. So…"

He didn't stand. His expression went flat and hard as he faced me again. Determination pulsed from him. "You can dress. After."

"After?" I managed to croak out, suddenly having trouble breathing again. Surely he didn't mean what I thought he meant. But he'd gone so serious, so quickly. Just the way he did when he—

"After you kiss me."

CHAPTER NINE

ROME DIDN'T GIVE ME a chance to consider his words. He leaned forward, grabbed the base of my neck and jerked me onto his lap, my blanket falling to the floor in a forgotten heap. Completely caught off guard by the aggressive display, I flailed for a moment, unsure what was happening as I searched for a solid anchor. Then his hot body met mine and his equally hot tongue thrust deep into my mouth.

He kept his fingers firm on the back of my neck, angling my head for even deeper contact. His familiar flavor filled my mouth, primitive and spicy. The muscles in his back were clenched, rock hard under my hands—hands I allowed to roam, kneading with abandon.

Over and over his tongue rolled against mine, shooting little sparks of ecstasy directly into my bloodstream. His free hand settled on my breast, the nipple beading immediately. The thin gown I wore was no kind of barrier, so it was as if he caressed me skin to skin.

My stomach quivered as heat speared me. Heat I had not thought ever to feel again. "Rome," I moaned.

"Wrap your legs around me," he commanded huskily.

My legs? Lost in the pleasure as I was, it took me a moment to one, remember what legs were, and two, figure out what mine were doing. When I realized they were hanging over the edge of his chair, I shimmied until they were anchored around his waist, my core pressed against his erection. Sweet heaven!

Never once did I break the kiss.

"You taste good," he said. "Like fire and ice. I didn't expect *that*."

"What'd you expect?" I managed to gasp out between licks inside his mouth.

"Amazing. Just not…perfection."

See? This was how he'd gotten me to fall in love with him. At times like this he made me feel like the most treasured woman in the world. "So you don't remember doing this to me? Naked? In the shower? On the bed? On the floor?" *With Matt Damon?* Okay, how had the Sarah Silverman video gotten in my head, now of all times?

The hard length of his shaft throbbed against my heat. "No." It was a tortured cry.

"I do. I remember every…delicious…detail."

He pulled away to stare into my eyes. He was panting, sweat trickling from his temples. He didn't release me, though. No, he held me more tightly. "Tell me. Help me remember." His thumb played with the pulse at the base of my neck.

I shivered. "More kissing first." I had him where I wanted him. Talking could come later.

Needing no more encouragement, he dove in for another taste. Every time his tongue rolled over mine, it was like white lightning shot through me, molten flashes branching and spreading. I couldn't catch my breath, didn't want to catch my breath. This was nirvana, a place I could die without regrets.

"I want to touch you," Rome said.

"Yes." I tangled my hands in his silky hair, fisting. "Touch me."

He groaned. "I shouldn't."

"You should." Please, please, please, I almost added, but managed to hold the pleas inside.

"We shouldn't."

Pull away and I'll kill you. "We're dumb if we don't."

Another groan. "How do you do this to me?"

I nipped at his lips, so desperate, so needy for more. I wanted his hands all over me, caressing every inch. I wanted his naughty tongue to follow, to lave me deep and forever. "Do what?"

"Make me so…crazed."

Now *I* groaned. I made this strong, drool-worthy man crazed? Still? "Touch me, like you want," I urged. "Please," I allowed myself to add this time. Pride was foolish in the face of passion, I realized.

His palm was under my gown a second later, his fingers kneading my breast. Just like that, the kiss turned savage. He snarled, pressing into me with so much force our teeth banged together. I writhed against him, the friction delicious. Consuming. My nails sank into his scalp, probably drawing blood.

He didn't complain.

He nipped at my bottom lip, his teeth sharper than normal, his fingers slipping around me and clamping onto my ass, urging me to rub against his erection, harder. Faster. I did, rocking with complete abandon, feeding him kiss after fervent kiss. He was in my nose, my mouth, on my skin, inside my cells, deep in the marrow of my bones. Just then, he was everything to me. But strangely, that did not reduce me to nothing. It made me…more.

He hissed at me. "We keep this up, and I'm going to come."

I was, too. Was so close, needed only another brush… it had been too long, too long without him…another taste and I'd—yes, yes, yes, right there! With a scream,

I erupted into a million pieces. And as the earth-shattering orgasm ripped through me, I also erupted into flames. Not just a fireball sprouting in my hand, and not simply fire spraying from my eyes.

My entire body burst into a crackling, orange-gold inferno.

Rome yelped and jerked to his feet. I slid off him, slapping into the cold floor. I couldn't see him through the flames, and whimpered. Crackling and hissing filled my ears, roaring through my head.

"Belle," he shouted, reaching for me, probably meaning to pat me out.

Panting, I scrambled backward before he could touch me. I wasn't in pain, could feel the heat but not the burn, and knew the same would not be true for him. He would blister. Perhaps worse.

Stubborn man that he was, Rome chased after me.

I continued to scramble away until my back hit the bed, and the flames leaped onto *it*. No. No, no, no.

Calm down, I had to calm down. Passion and anger were both volatile emotions and ignited my body like matches (literally). But never, not even when I first underwent the change from human to superhuman and my abilities had been horribly unstable, had I experienced *this*.

"I don't know what to do," I cried. Was this happening because of the blood Reese had taken or the fact that Rome wasn't filtering for me as he'd done in the past? Probably the latter. I was a mess without him, our passion as out of control as the fire.

"Don't move," Rome said. I still couldn't see him, but I heard the pound of his footsteps amid the chaos inside my head.

I was too frightened to move, yet that fear failed to

produce ice. What. The. Hell. Deep breath in, deep breath out. Happy thoughts might work, I thought. Or hoped. 'Cause I couldn't think of anything else that had worked in the past. Happy thoughts were hard to conjure, though, when I was a freaking human BBQ. *Try. Try, try, try.* Kissing Rome—that had been nice. And sexy. Shit! A flame shot from the top of my head, making sparks fall in every direction.

No thoughts of the kiss. That only inflamed me—on every level.

My heart drummed erratically in my chest, visions of agents catching fire and burning to death, their screams in my ears, filling my brain. If only Rome could remember how to filter for me! He could take the hottest thrums of my emotions and cage them inside himself, calming me inside and out.

Happy thoughts, my mind screamed. My dad. Sherridan. Tanner. My mom, when she'd been alive. Not that I remembered her. I felt a wisp of sadness stir inside me, felt a raindrop land on top my head, the fire crackling, and realized I was going about this the wrong way. Ice might be beyond me at the moment, but rain wasn't. Besides, happy thoughts might stop the fire from blazing from my body, but they wouldn't stop it from spreading throughout the room—and the building— and the city.

I needed more rain. Which meant I needed more sadness.

Before I could work up a good reason to cry, though, another round of footsteps echoed. Ice-cold foam was suddenly sprayed at me, dousing me completely. I closed my eyes and pressed my lips together, even stopped breathing so I wouldn't inhale the frigid stuff. Since employing me, John had made sure a fire extinguisher waited in every hallway.

When the spray stopped, several moments ticked by in silence.

"It's okay," Rome said, panting. "The fire's out."

Slowly I cracked open my eyes. I had to wipe my face with my hand to clear my line of vision. Rome hovered in front of me, his face concerned.

"You're covered in soot and your clothing has holes," I told him, shivering as the cold seeped into my bones. And I had done that to him. Me. I had placed him in danger. Hurt him. Could have killed him. "I'm sorry. So sorry."

"Well, you're naked." There was no anger in his tone, no accusation about what I'd done. He was genuinely amused. "Nothing to be sorry about. I like the end result."

Still. Tears burned my eyes as I surveyed the damage to myself. I gasped. My gown had indeed burned away. The only thing that saved me from a complete, full-body flash was the white foam. I looked like a snow queen, covered as I was with it.

Rome scooped me up, and I yelped in surprise. "I've got you." He latched onto the blanket before settling back on the chair with me on his lap and draping the material over me. "You okay?"

"Yes." Embarrassed to my soul, but fine physically.

"Does that kind of thing happen—"

"Belle Jamison. Want to tell me why—" John, who'd charged into the room, stopped abruptly. His expression didn't change when he spotted me sprawled on Rome's lap, but his voice did calm. "I don't even want to know what kind of kinky sex games the two of you have been playing this time, but it's nice to have you and your memories back, Rome. I'll want an EEG, of course, to compare your brain waves then and now."

Rome lost his air of relaxation. "My memories haven't returned."

John's gaze flew to me, confusion registering. "Oh. Then why… Never mind."

My cheeks heated and I scrambled off Rome and back onto the bed, taking the blanket with me. I covered myself as best I could. Cold as I was, I couldn't hide the two little pearls saluting anyone who glanced my way.

"Fine. I have to know. Something happened between the two of you." Both of John's brows arched, and he sighed. "What?"

"You already know, you pervert," I snapped.

He didn't back down. "Reese says the components that make your blood different from the average human's increase every time he tests you. This time, they were off the charts."

I'd suspected that before, that the bloodletting was making my powers wonky, but had decided that was wrong. I still thought so. Being without my filter was the issue. Had to be. Because every time Rome left me, I had problems. I didn't tell that to John, however. Not now. He might try to find me another filter, someone who didn't mind being with me, and that wouldn't do. Not when the only person I wanted that close to me was Rome.

"Well, something's off," I said, which wasn't a lie. "I managed to set myself on fire."

John's eyes widened and he looked to Rome for confirmation.

Rome gave an ominous nod.

"I wonder what's different. Is the formula strengthening as time passes?" Silent, John tilted his head to the side. He tapped his chin. He looked from me to Rome, Rome to me, and his eyes widened further. "Ah, of course. You hinted, I think, but I didn't understand. Something's different about you every time he leaves, yes?"

"What's different?" Rome asked.

Crap. John had figured out the truth on his own.

"Should we put her in lockup?" he asked, surprising me, the question clearly aimed at himself. He continued to tap that finger against his chin as he studied me.

"I'm right here! And no, we shouldn't. I'm not a scrim. And before you say it, I do not want another filter."

Dark eyes leveled on me with unerring intensity. "I do what's necessary to protect both my agents and the world, no matter what's required. You know that. If your powers are that unstable…"

"I can handle it," I told him. "I'd already figured out the problem, but hadn't realized how bad it could get. I know now and I'll take precautions." Though the only precaution I could think of was staying away from Rome until his memories returned, and that wasn't acceptable. "Just back off."

"Listen hard, Miss Jamison," John said through clenched teeth. "You are not my boss. You do not issue commands. I, however, do. From now on, you are to inform me of every change that occurs, not just hint about them. You could have killed someone today! Understand?"

"I understand." And I did. He wanted the best for everyone. So *I* backed off instead, remorseful.

"New tests need to be run."

"Of course." I'd known that would happen, which was part of the reason I'd kept quiet. John liked to test *everything*. In ways that were sometimes painful, sometimes humiliating, but always a nuisance. He meant well, I knew that, but it didn't lessen the aggravation.

Dr. Roberts, the scientist who had secretly placed that

formula in my grande mocha latte, had also given it to several other people. I was the only one who survived—and still, months later, no one knew why—so I was the only living vessel John had, which made me the only source for answers.

"If I let you stay in the field," he said, "you'll have to be monitored."

I shook my head, my hair slapping my cheeks. "No way." *Monitored* equaled *babysat*. Reports would be made, detailing my every mistake. Any sense of privacy I had would evaporate.

He didn't back down. "No exceptions. No negotiations."

Rome watched the entire exchange, attention volleying back and forth between us. Blank as his expression was, I had no idea what thoughts he entertained. Perhaps it was better that way. He'd just kissed me to climax, watched me catch on fire and had nearly lost his life—not to mention his eyebrows—because of me.

"Fine." A tremor raked my spine, vibrating into each of my limbs. Damn cold. "Tanner can—"

"I'll do it." Rome's voice echoed in the sudden silence.

"Which will cause you and Lexis to fight, and fighting isn't good for our cause," John said. "With your memory loss—"

"I haven't forgotten how to do my job," he snapped.

Nope, he'd just forgotten me.

"I'm damn good at what I do," Rome continued, "and I have more experience than anyone else you've got. You want to win this one, you'll send me out there. Whether Lexis and I fight or not, we would never compromise a mission."

"Fine," John said after a long pause, in which he'd probably been weighing each of his options. "Rome, you will monitor Belle. I'll expect daily reports."

Yep. I'd been right about those reports.

Rome nodded, anger defused since he'd gotten his way. "You'll get them."

With their every word, the illusion that I was in charge of this mission was shattered, and it was beyond annoying. I had the most to win—and lose—if this thing went— Hey. Wait. If Rome acted as my "monitor," he would have to spend all his time with me, and that's exactly what I'd wanted to happen. I almost smiled— until a new thought occurred to me. No longer did Rome observe me through rose-colored lenses. What if I irritated him so much he decided he didn't *want* to remember me?

"Lexis might not compromise a mission, but she'll compromise me," I muttered. It was the only argument I could think of.

Rome shrugged those strong shoulders. "No, she'll deal."

"And you'll keep your hands to yourself," John stated matter-of-factly, pointing at me, then Rome. "I won't have any more fires like this."

Outrage blustered through me. "You have no right—"

"No more fires," Rome interjected. "Nothing like this will happen again."

It wouldn't, would it? I narrowed my gaze on him. He'd liked my kisses, I knew that. But he hadn't liked the consequences. Was I no longer worth the danger, then?

I could feel a hot poker jabbing at my chest, wanting out. Maybe he hadn't liked my kisses, after all. Maybe he'd lied; maybe he hadn't been near climax. He wasn't panting, wasn't strained and desperate for release. His erection was gone.

If I wanted to keep the blanket draped over me rather than burn it away, I had to calm down. Again. "Listen,

Tobin mentioned that he had a friend who wanted to talk to me." Anything to change the subject. "In fact, he said *she* wanted to talk. She. A woman. Tanner and I were listening in on his interrogation and Tobin said he'd never spoken with Desert Gal. Tanner verified that was a truth. Maybe this mystery woman is one of the women pulled from the warehouse. Or maybe she's on the outside, working with Desert Gal or even secretly against her. Maybe she was the one taking care of the prisoners. Either way, we now know someone else is involved."

John sighed. "We really didn't need another needle in our already massive haystack. I'll have all the women from the warehouse who have already been questioned interrogated again, this time in regards to Tobin. Hopefully, our mystery girl is here. I don't like the thought of someone else being out there, gunning for you."

Me, either. I glanced at Rome to gauge his reaction. His expression was blank again.

God, I hated this. How could he dismiss me so easily? Would he really act as if the kiss had never happened? Would he run back to Lexis because she was the safe choice?

Another flicker inside my chest. I had to stop this. Thinking about Rome rather than my case was what had gotten me in trouble in the first place.

I raised my chin. "I'll do whatever you need me to do, John, to figure this out. Even dangle myself out there as bait." Determination seeped from my voice. One way or another, I wanted this case closed. As soon as possible. Until it was, I couldn't concentrate fully on Rome. Or destroy Lexis.

"Good girl. I'm not sure we need to do something so extreme just yet, but I'll keep it in mind. Now get cleaned up and dressed," John told us. "It's time to get back to work, and you two have people to interview and a meeting to attend."

With that, he left us alone. And this time, when I told Rome I needed some privacy, he didn't ignore me. He left.

CHAPTER TEN

BEFORE MY SHOWER, I decided to get a little personal business out of the way so that I would better focus on the case the rest of the day. Rome had brought me my purse, and I'd blessedly remembered to pack my cell, so as I made my way to a room John kept for agents who had to pull all-nighters, I called the dress shop and printer to reschedule, then called the caterer and pretended everything was fine. I even scheduled a day to come in and sample some of their main dishes. I cursed myself the entire time, but damn it, I'd pay for that food (with Rome's credit card) even if the wedding didn't happen.

It will.

But would it?

Yes! Stop arguing with yourself.

No way grilled cheese sandwiches and bowls of tomato soup—the extent of my culinary prowess—were going to be served to my guests. (Hey. Some of us were too busy saving the world to learn how to cook.)

When I hung up with The Golden Swan, I called Sherridan and asked her to bring a change of clothes. Something better than my beautiful but ruined dress. Then I did something else that made me ashamed. I finally called my dad back and lied. *Everything's fine. Rome and I are great,* I told him. Uttering that delightful gem made me nauseous, but he had a weak heart and I didn't want him worrying about me.

We talked for fifteen minutes before one of his silver foxes hollered for him in the background. Seemed he'd kissed Maggie in the garden while dating Kate. Judging from the tone of Kate's voice, there was going to be hell to pay. I smiled. It was good to know some things never changed, especially when so much else had.

"Take care of yourself, Dad."

"Always. Love you, baby Belle."

"And I love you." We disconnected, and I threw the cell into my purse. "Time for my shower," I muttered, padding into the small but clean bathroom. Maybe I could wash the guilt and the anger and the sadness away.

Halfway through my shower, soap in my eyes, Sherridan arrived with that change of clothes. As she held her choice up for my inspection, I slid the stall door open a crack and shook my head in wonder. Shouldn't be surprised, I supposed. Part of me had known she'd interpret my "something better" to mean "something as slutty as possible." It was her warped way of helping me win Rome back.

"Hurry it up, will you? I want to see you all dolled up."

"You see me dolled up every day." I rinsed off and stepped from the stall.

She had a towel extended. "More like hoboed up, if you want to get technical. You're the worst dresser I know, always wearing the same lame outfits."

I grabbed the fluffy white terry cloth and wrapped it around myself. "Have I ever told you how amazing you are for my self-esteem?"

She blew me a kiss and breezed from the bathroom.

Sighing, I donned the tiny skirt, bright blue halter top and knee-high boots. Cool air stroked my too-bare, damp skin as I stepped into the room, a thick mist floating out behind me. I did not want to know where she'd gotten this stuff.

Tanner was there, saying something to Sherridan, but he stopped midsentence and whistled. "Look at the delicious piece of candy that just walked in."

He was looking pretty tasty himself. Injured yet strong, just the way he liked.

"Oh, you look so hot!" Sherridan said, clapping excitedly. "Do I know how to dress a girl or what?"

"I'm still waiting to hear how you *un*dress one," Tanner muttered. Clearly Jessica Alba was still on his mind.

I held out my arms in exasperation. "I have to do interviews in this, I hope you know."

"Interview the men," Tanner suggested. "'Cause they'll take one look and answer anything you ask."

I rubbed my temple, knowing a headache was imminent. How I longed to sink into that dark leather couch and snooze the rest of the day away. Or maybe I'd recline in the matching leather chair. Hell, I'd even splay myself on the worktable in the center of the room. "Unfortunately for me, our first meeting is with a woman. Elaine Daringer, the energy vampire—not to be mistaken with the blood-drinking kind like Reese, and—"

A buzz sounded. "Subject is waiting in interrogation room three." John's voice echoed through the room. "She's *been* waiting for half an hour. Do you need a second monitor to watch the clock for you?"

"We're on our way," I said with a sigh. It'd be a miracle if I survived the rest of the day.

ELAINE DARINGER WAS NOT what I expected.

When Tanner and I had entered the interrogation room, I'd actually gasped. She was young—probably in her early twenties—with a short crop of blond hair and an angel face. Big brown eyes, a pert nose and dimpled cheeks. Seriously, she could have fallen straight from a copy of *Heaven's Gates Weekly*.

The only thing menacing about her was her outfit. A black cloth covered her from neck to toe, and not even her fingers were visible. Had to be that way, I knew. One touch of her skin, and she could drain every ounce of our energy.

As a further precaution, she was cuffed to an inflexible, uncomfortable-looking chair.

"Hello," I said.

Instantly her eyes glared pure hatred at me. "Go to hell," she snapped.

O-kay. Not so angelic, after all. "Welcome to PSI. We have a few questions for you, and you have my word we're not going to hurt you. All right?" I watched her, waited for a response, but didn't get one. "I'm sorry about the accommodations, but they're regulation for someone with your abilities."

"Please." She snorted. "Sorry? Ha! You're grateful for the accommodations. You're too scared to face me, girl to girl."

"Actually, no. I've—"

"Save it and feed the lies to someone else. I want to go back to my cell. I'm done here," she shouted to the two-way. "Do you hear me? I'm done!"

I stepped into her line of vision. "Look, I've been where you are. Well, not exactly. But close." She might be working for Desert Gal, she might not. She might be Tobin's mystery friend, she might not. But I wasn't going to treat her as a hated enemy during this interview. Not without cause, and her crappy attitude wasn't exactly cause. She was cuffed, for God's sake. Probably sweating underneath all that fabric. I'd be pissed, too.

She pushed out a forceful breath to blow the hair from her brow. "Is this the part where you sympathize with me and I tell you all my secrets?"

Tanner choked out a laugh. "Someone's been watching B movies, I see."

Those puppy-dog browns strayed to him as though noticing him for the first time, and she stilled. For several seconds, she even managed to keep all hints of emotion from her features. But after a while, the effort drained her and she sagged, fascination consuming her expression.

Hello, attraction.

I couldn't blame her. Tanner was a heartstoppingly good-looking guy when he wasn't wasting away from heartbreak.

"Who the hell are you?" she demanded shakily.

He inclined his head in greeting. "They call me Mr. Sensitive."

"Really? I'd have pegged you for Blueberry Lollipop."

She'd meant it as an insult, I think, but predictably, Tanner took it as a sexual innuendo. "God, I wish. It would let girls know up front that I'm okay with being licked."

Red spread over her cheeks like the wildfire had spread over my body.

"I just realized I forgot to make introductions, and I'm sorry for that," I said. "I'm Belle Jamison and this is my friend and associate, whose real name is Tanner Bradshaw."

"Feel free to call me Lollipop, though."

Elaine cleared her throat and tried to shift in the chair, as if that tiny movement could somehow save her from Tanner's penetrating stare. "Yes, well, everyone calls me Draino."

"Seriously?"

Yeah, seriously? And I'd thought Homicidal Tendencies Wench was bad.

"Yes" was the sniffed and clearly offended reply.

"Sorry," Tanner said, "but that name sucks a big juicy one. You need something new."

Not exactly the way to win the girl to our side. Actually, at this rate, Tanner would guarantee Elaine joined the other team. If she wasn't already part of it. Time for me to take over and at least pretend I knew how to conduct an interview. "Listen, we're getting off track. What I was starting to say before Mr. Sensitive here interrupted is that a few months ago this doctor came rushing into the café where I worked and spiked my drink with a formula that gave me power over the four elements. Earth, wind, fire and water."

Her eyes swung back to me, the anger returning. "So?"

"So," Tanner piped up before I could say anything else, "she's trying to prove to you that she's been where you are, just like she said. Two agencies marked her for extermination, one of them being the group that was keeping you prisoner in that warehouse, and began chasing her. I helped her get away. It could even be said that I saved her from certain death, but I'm not one to brag so I'll leave that part out."

Elaine looked between us, a spark of jealousy stealing over her features. Jealousy she couldn't hide, even when she cast her gaze to the gray tiled floor.

"He's like my brother," I explained, palms up. Did I ever understand what she was feeling. "Swear to God."

"Like I care," she said, but slowly she relaxed, her body seeming to melt into that slatted wood. "If I'm going to talk to you, I need proof that your intentions are good. Something more than just your word. I've learned to be cautious."

"All right. How?"

"First up is proving you can do what you say you can

do. You have control over the elements? Well, make it rain inside this room. Here, now."

Uh, not just no but hell, no. "I'm afraid not." I shook my head to emphasize my refusal. "Sometimes I can't stop it once it starts."

"Then you're a danger and need to be neutralized."

For a moment, her comment returned me to the good old days. Rome might have been trying to kill me back then, but at least he'd known exactly who I was. "Same could be said of you."

"Yes, and that's why I'm tied down."

I sighed. For her to trust me, I had to be willing to trust her. So I said, "Would you feel better if I told you pollutants are my downfall? I can't work my magic around them. I become too weak." OASS already knew my weakness, so I wasn't revealing so much John would have an aneurysm.

Her eyes locked on me and for a moment I thought I'd reached her. Then she shrugged. "Nope, I wouldn't feel better. You could be lying about that, too."

"True. You don't know us. But think about what we're asking from you, what we're not. How we're treating you, how we're not." Tanner and I hadn't hurt her in any way. We hadn't degraded her, or demanded world-crumbling secrets.

There was a long pause. Then, "So what happened to you? After you drank the formula?" There was a twinge in her voice, as if she were finally softening.

"Well, I got sick. So sick I almost died. And for several weeks, my new powers were unstable. More unstable than they are now. Remember the freak ice that covered several buildings?"

"When?"

"About a month ago." Or was it two months ago? I really was bad with time.

"I was in those cells your agents 'rescued' me from, so no."

Poor thing. "Well, that was me." I gave her a moment to digest that. "So what about you? Were you born with your ability or was it thrust upon you?"

She shifted in the chair again, grimaced when the cuffs pushed into her bones, and glanced between me and Tanner. Little angel couldn't get comfortable. "The information isn't going to do you any good."

"Tell us anyway. We're curious about you."

"Why?"

Still so distrustful. Had the situation been reversed, I wasn't sure I would have believed anything my captors said, either. She was alone, vulnerable, helpless, her wits her only weapon. "Because I see a lot of myself in you."

Elaine snorted. "You look like a hooker and I look like a nun. I doubt we're similar."

Sherridan and her damn outfit choice! "I didn't mean in appearance, smart-ass."

Tanner laughed. "Well, I can see the similarities now."

I punched him in the shoulder. "Funny."

Elaine watched the byplay with something akin to longing. "Just forget it," she said. "None of it matters, anyway. You can't help me, and I can't help you."

"Give us a chance," Tanner said, expression growing serious.

"Look," I added. "We're all you've got right now. We know that. And you know we need to pick your brain. So what will it take to get some answers? You want a lobster dinner brought to your cell? Done. You want an iPod? Done. Anything you want is yours. Except freedom."

"What about a pony?" she asked sarcastically, but the pessimism didn't quite reach her eyes, and she was having trouble controlling her breathing.

"If you're willing to clean up after it, why not?"

She licked her lips, and then words were suddenly tumbling from them without pause. "I want a meat loaf. With mashed potatoes and gravy. White. Homemade rolls and dressing. And broccoli and rice casserole. Do you know what that is? I also want a chocolate cake. Do *not* scrimp on the icing. And I do want that iPod. I'll make you a playlist."

She paused to inhale and Tanner whipped out a tiny notebook from his back pocket to write everything down.

"We'll get it to you as fast as we can," I said. If John complained—or flat-out refused—to meet these demands, I'd see to them myself. Again with Rome's credit card. He owed us all. "That it?"

There was another round of silence before her shoulders slumped. "You asked how I came to be in that warehouse. Well, a bastard named Gordon Jones read a newspaper article about a mother and father who weakened every time they held their little girl. Parents who were looking to give said girl up for adoption because they couldn't deal with her." Her chin rose defiantly, probably in an attempt to hide its trembling. "He bought me from them, experimented on me, and suddenly I didn't just weaken people, I killed them. Gordon used me to keep his agents in line. 'Refuse me, and watch Draino work her way through your family,' that kind of thing."

"Truth," Tanner whispered, and the single word possessed an edge of…fury? Affront?

My hand fluttered over my heart. "I'm so sorry, Elaine. Truly sorry." Gordon Jones. Father to Vincent Jones, no doubt.

Surprise filled those beautiful brown eyes. But that surprise soon morphed into anger. "Yeah, I'm sure you're real sorry. Here I am, another agent to recruit, huh?

Another subject for your agency to experiment on. Maybe you'll even control me the way he did, huh? Promise to fix me if I just *do one more thing* for you."

"I don't want to recruit you," I said, "and I sure as hell don't want to experiment on you. And I know beyond any doubt that I'll never be able to fix you."

Outside the room, someone rapped on the window.

All three of us turned, but we couldn't see who it was. Probably John, issuing a warning, I thought. With him, it was always business first, the people that business affected second. I flipped him off and turned back to Elaine.

"Like I was saying, *I* don't want to recruit you," I assured her. "Other people might, but I don't. If you don't want to be an agent, no one should force you to be one."

Once again surprise lit her eyes, turning the dark brown to a bright amber.

"Look," Tanner said. "You deserve to be free. No one can deny that."

Another knock.

"Stop that," I shouted. "We're not going to lie to her or tell her only what you want us to. You left me in charge of interviews, so I'm doing this my way."

Bang, bang, bang.

Well, this was getting us nowhere. "Since you're here, uncuff her," I called without looking back at the window. "I want her to finish the interview unfettered."

Now her mouth fell open.

"Do it!" I shouted. "Or I'll walk out of here and—"

"Me, too," Tanner interjected.

"And we can guarantee she won't talk to anyone else. Right?"

"R-right," she said, clearly confused. Most likely, no one had ever trusted her not to use her superior abilities and attack. Because all it would take was a single brush of her hand to send us to our knees.

Finally, the door swung open. I expected John's short, stocky legs to stomp inside. Expected John's dark eyes to bore into me. Instead, it was Rome. He strode to Elaine, bent down and carefully unlatched the metal bands. They fell to the floor with a clank.

She drew her arms into her lap and rubbed at her wrists.

Rome straightened, looked me up and down and said, "That is not appropriate," in a tight voice.

Whether he meant freeing Elaine or my outrageous clothes, I didn't know.

"If you hurt them," he told Elaine, "I will personally kill you." He left then, slamming the door shut behind him—but his gaze remained on me until the last possible second. I could only stare at the door in wonder. He'd been watching me…protecting me? My heart began an erratic drum in my chest. Or was this part of his monitoring duties? My heart now slowed.

"Your boyfriend?" Elaine asked. No longer was there even a hint of disdain or unhappiness. Perhaps I'd finally earned her trust.

"No," I said for Rome's benefit. Let him take that as he would: that I no longer wanted him, that we were over forever, or that we were over right now but there was hope for the future. Whatever. Right now, it didn't matter. It couldn't. But later… "Maybe once."

Tanner patted my shoulder, forcing my attention from the door, from Rome. "How long had you been locked in this last prison?" he asked Elaine.

Once more, her gaze dropped to her feet, and she shrugged. "I realize you're being nice to get the information you want, but I don't like it. We already came to terms. So you can stop the act. Okay? All right?" She didn't give us time to reply. "I was in that particular prison for a few months."

"Months!" Tanner shouted, clearly outraged on her behalf. "That's barbaric. And just so you know, we aren't just being nice to get what we want. Time will prove that."

She gave another of those falsely negligent shrugs, though there was a spark of hope in her eyes. "I'd started resisting Vincent's commands—he's the guy who took over after his dad died. I knew he would never help me, so I even tried to escape. Again. He'd warned me what would happen."

I eased into the chair across from her. "You were incarcerated with a man named Tobin McAldrin. Do you know who I'm talking about?"

"Yes," she said with a nod. "The meathead."

That was the guy. "He told me he had a friend, someone who wanted to talk with me."

"That would be Candace Bright."

Tanner wrote the name in his notebook. If Elaine was telling the truth—and I thought that she was, since Tanner hadn't called her a liar—we now had a lead. I wanted to grin.

"Tell me about her," I said.

"She's pretty, a redhead, but the color isn't natural. It's just *too* red. She brought us food and water, made sure our cages were cleaned. For the most part, she wasn't bad, as far as jailers go. I don't know a lot about her, just her name really. And I only know that because she used to work for Vincent."

"Maybe she worked for him because her family was being threatened, too," Tanner speculated.

Elaine shook her head. "I doubt that. She talked about Desert Gal like the woman was God. And trust me, that kind of affection has nothing to do with force.

Anyway, Tobin, a.k.a. Brick, and a prisoner called Memory Man were her favorites and the only ones she spoke to. Me, she stayed away from. I think she was afraid of me."

Memory Man. Or M-Squared. This was the first time one of our interviewees had brought him up. Now, he was verified. Rather than excitement, I experienced a wave of anger. Enough to cause little tendrils of steam to waft from my nostrils. He had been one of Desert Gal's favorites? Did that mean he had willingly aided her and hadn't been forced as we'd begun to think? Oops. There went more steam.

It would probably be best for everyone to keep him out of the conversation for now.

"Where did Vincent—who we not-so-affectionately call 'Pretty Boy,' by the way—keep you?" Tanner asked. "Before the escape attempt? And did you do any jobs with Ms. Bright? Can you tell us her fighting style?"

If Elaine was fazed by the barrage of questions, she didn't show it. "He has—had—a house in every corner of the world, it seemed. He moved me around a lot. I didn't even know I was in Georgia until I arrived at PSI. But no, I didn't work directly with Candace."

"What about Desert Gal? Have you ever met her?" I asked.

"No. Sorry. My social life as an OASS agent was... limited."

Limited. Sadly, the description was probably generous. I felt so bad for this girl, wanted to take her under my wing, protect her. Maybe she and Tanner could—no, I thought sadly. They couldn't. One touch of her skin, and she'd kill the boy. That, I couldn't allow.

I couldn't even give her a hug unless we both wore full-body condoms.

"Tell us about the jobs he had you work." Tanner plopped into the chair next to mine.

"I was his killer, just as I was his father's." Shame dripped from her. Shame and regret and horror. "It was easy for me. Quick. No one ever suspected, never realized they'd welcomed death, until it was too late. All I had to do was walk past them, brush my hand against theirs. And I know what you're thinking. I should have touched Vincent and killed him. I would have loved to do that, but he made sure he was never in striking distance."

My chest constricted, and I wondered again if that's what had happened with M-Squared. Which caused me to soften. Again. Pretty Boy had issued commands from a remote location, so there had never been anything M-Squared could do to stop the man. Except, he'd been Desert Gal's favorite. Why would he have been her favorite if he hadn't helped her? Oops again. There was more steam. Apparently, I was a yo-yo when it came to that man.

"Who did he want you to kill?"

"People who disagreed with his business practices, PSI employees who wouldn't join him, no matter the incentive. Innocents who had something he wanted."

And that had clearly torn her up inside. Even after everything she'd already endured. Okay. I didn't care if she could drain me. I didn't care if one touch of her skin could destroy me. I stood to shaky legs and strode forward, closing the distance between us. There was another rap on the window, but I didn't slow. I knelt in front of her and placed my palms on her gloved arms. There was no buzz of sensation, no zap of my strength.

She stiffened.

That didn't deter me, either. This lonely girl had not known the kindness or love of even a single parent, as I had. Hers had sold her, as if she were a car or a boat. They hadn't contacted her afterward, I'm sure. Hadn't visited her on her birthdays or called her when she was sick. No one should have to endure such a travesty.

"Wh-what are you doing?" she asked.

"Giving you a hug." Slowly, so I wouldn't startle her, I leaned my head into her chest, my shoulder into her middle.

Her eyes widened the closer I came. "You could be hurt. Something bad could happen to you and I wouldn't— I—"

She didn't tell me to stop, I noticed, and that was more telling than she probably realized. I wrapped my arms around her and pressed my cheek just above her breast, heard her heart pound as if it wanted to beat its way out.

A tremor moved through her, shaking us both. I think a teardrop even splashed atop my hair.

I held on to her for a long while. Finally, her arms reached around me, tentative at first, then squeezing tight. "Why are you doing this?" she whispered, the words broken.

"Because no one should have to endure the things you've endured. Because I hate that you can't be touched. Because you deserve better." I wanted to absorb all of that pain inside myself, take it away from her and show her just how precious and wonderful life could be.

A hand suddenly patted my back and I turned slightly, seeing Tanner kneel behind Elaine. His arms wrapped around her, too, but had to slide around me to make contact. That's when the flood of tears came, no mere trickle, not anymore.

We held her through it all. I didn't care what I looked like, didn't care that Rome saw me this way rather than as a badass agent who beat the crap out of "subjects" for answers.

When she quieted, I pulled back but Tanner held on, his hands flat on her stomach. I think he needed the contact as much as she did, because there were tears in his eyes, as well. Perhaps *Elaine* was somehow absorbing the pain Lexis had caused in him.

I swallowed the hard lump in my throat as Elaine gripped his wrists, holding him to her.

Then her gaze lifted and clashed with mine. "I may not have met Desert Gal, but I know that she wants you," she told me quietly.

Me? I hadn't challenged her yet. Not really. "For what?"

"I'm not sure, exactly. I overheard Candace tell Tobin that PSI would be rescuing us soon, and he would get a fat reward from Desert Gal if he brought you in."

I'd been right. Some of the "victims" were plants. So many pieces were falling into place, and soon the puzzle would be complete. I was more excited than I'd been in a long time. The excitement was blended with fear, though. Desert Gal was after me, yet my powers were wonky and my filter a stubborn shithead. *Tamp down both emotions before you summon wind.*

"Any idea where Desert Gal is?" I asked.

"I wish. I'd like to shove my foot up her ass."

"Me, too," Tanner and I said in unison.

Elaine nibbled on her bottom lip, dropped her gaze again. Her gloved fingertips traced Tanner's arm, and she watched the movements as though mesmerized. "Wh-what are you going to do with me?"

"We'll take care of your food requests and iPod as promised, that much I know," Tanner said and released her. "The rest, I'm sad to say, is up to our boss."

A little whimper escaped her lips, but she didn't ask him to touch her again.

The cell I'd hooked to my waist started buzzing. I

reached for it, saying, "For now, I'm going to have Tanner take you to—"

The rap on the window was harder than ever.

"To my house," I finished determinedly. Bringing her there was a risk, but I couldn't have her thrown back into some dank cell. I just couldn't. "You might have to go to lockup for a little while first, though. And as Tanner said, we've got to talk to my boss, convince him of the wisdom of my plan."

Hope had been blooming in her expression, but it quickly died. "Hey, don't worry about it." She laughed, but there was no humor in the sound. "I'm used to cells like the one here and we both know he's not going to allow me to leave."

I threw a glare over my shoulder, hopefully pinning Rome with my anger. "We are not like Vincent. We are not cruel. And if you were my daughter, I would never allow such a thing to be done to you." I knew the remark would hit its target. Because Sunny, Rome's daughter, could mist through walls, Rome feared PSI—or some other agency—would one day try to use her.

Tanner pushed to his feet and squeezed Elaine's shoulder. "When Belle puts her mind to something, it gets done. Don't worry."

Slowly a smile curled the corners of Elaine's lush pink mouth, and she angled her head up to him adoringly. "Thank you."

He returned her grin, even reached up and caressed a fingertip over her cheek. "My pl—"

Immediately she lost her smile.

He did, too. His knees gave out and he crumpled to the ground in a motionless heap.

CHAPTER ELEVEN

I SPENT THE REST OF THE DAY and night glued to Tanner's side, trying to hold myself together. Maybe Rome, Lexis and John met to discuss the Desert Gal/M-Squared case at lunch, maybe they didn't. I didn't particularly care. I had only one concern right now. Tanner. And I refused to leave him.

So far, he hadn't even twitched. At least he was now breathing on his own, which was a big improvement from a mere hour earlier.

Cody had called me a few times, but I'd been too focused on remaining calm to pick up. If my emotions overtook me, I'd have to leave. The room, the building. Because I couldn't risk hurting Tanner further.

"Gonna stay here another day?"

The question came from behind me. I didn't turn, even though a warm flutter started in my belly and spread to my heart. Rome. I hadn't allowed myself to think of him, hadn't allowed myself to wonder what he was doing and who he was doing it with while I'd been here. "However long it takes."

Rome had come rushing into the room the moment Tanner had fallen. Without a word, he'd scooped him up and carried him to the medical wing of the building. If he hadn't been there, I would have broken down, would have floundered, lost, not knowing what to do.

Tanner and I might not be blood-related, but he was my brother in every way that counted. I needed him.

"Is he…okay?"

The question came from Lexis, soft, hesitant.

I straightened as if I'd been jolted with lightning, but still I didn't turn. Seeing Lexis pretend to care might unleash a fury so potent, so *alive,* the small tether I had on my control would be severed. "Get out of here. Now!" My fingers curled around the bedrail, knuckles leaching of color. "You have no right to come near him. No right to upset him *again.*"

Silence. Footsteps.

"She's gone," Rome said. "You shouldn't have chastised her, Belle. She's worried about Tanner, too. And by the way, you look like hell. Even in that skirt."

Finally I turned. I couldn't help myself. He was indeed alone, leaning against the door frame the same way Tanner liked to do. Actually, Tanner had picked up the action from him. To emulate him, I think. "You should probably leave, too. We'll fight, and that won't do anyone any good."

He remained in place. His dark hair was in disarray, stress lines around his mouth. His lips were red and moist, as if he'd chewed on them. Or maybe they were still red from the blistering kiss I'd given him. "Quite a few days we've had."

Fine. He wanted to stay, he could stay. But small talk? Not gonna happen. "Make yourself useful and go convince John to sign Elaine's custody over to me."

Expression hardening, he shook his head. "Not a chance. We've got her back in lockup and that's where she's going to stay. She took down an agent, Belle. You're just lucky we're gathering everything you promised her."

"It was an accident, Rome." I ran my tongue over my teeth and gave him my back again. I'd expected the refusal, just not that it would be delivered with such iron-clad determination. "I want her out."

"Why? Were you lying and don't really care about the boy on that bed? You said he was your best friend and there he is, practically comatose. Don't you want to punish the one who put him there?"

"Like I said, she didn't do it on purpose."

"You don't know that."

"*He* touched *her*. Not the other way around."

"Doesn't matter. She's a danger to—"

"*I'm* a danger. Okay? That's what you once said about me. But here I am, fighting for your team. So let. Her. Out. I'll take full responsibility for her. Actually, let her out and bring her here. She can keep me company. Anyone is better than the man I'm currently dealing with." A man who had defended his ex to me. Again.

"I questioned her about her past victims." Rome's tone was flat, empty.

Had my words hurt him? Surely not. He would have to care about me, about my opinion. "And?"

"Many died within the first hour of touching her, their lungs too weak to fill on their own. Some survived for a day. A few, for good. Tanner's already past the first hour, as well as the first day, and he's now breathing on his own. I think he's going to be all right."

I wanted to believe him. I wanted to hope. It was hard, though, when Tanner looked so pale, so still.

"So…while I had Draino's attention, I asked her some other questions. Specifically about Memory Man. She said they spent some time together in the cages and that he hated Desert Gal. Fought her every step of the way."

My brow puckered in confusion. "If he hated her, why'd he help her and take your memories? Why was he one of her favorites?"

"Maybe she was simply trying to win him to her side. We'll have to ask him to know for sure."

"Which means we'll have to find him," I muttered, scrubbing a hand down my tired face.

"Draino said—"

"She has a name," I interjected, my irritation clear. Paranormal nicknames were important; they were the drumroll before an entrance, a defining factor of our identity. I wouldn't allow Elaine to be degraded by hers. So until we thought of a new one, Elaine would have to do.

A pause. Then, "*Elaine* said that a few times, when they'd both caved to Pretty Boy's demands, she and Memory Man were sent on missions together. She's seen him steal memories and said he only takes the ones he likes. That he often talked about how he wished he could have visited the places he saw in those memories, or met the people in them for real. Apparently he swore that one day, he'd make that wish a reality." Another pause, this one heavy. "Since he took all my memories of you, I can only guess he liked you."

I traced my fingers over Tanner's arm. His skin was cool, his blood flow too sluggish to warm him. "What are you trying to tell me, Rome?"

"That he's here because you are. That he wants to meet *you* for real. That he might even try to win you."

I laughed, but there was no humor in the sound. "Win *me*?" Surely not. "That's…that's…" Preposterous. "Can't be right. I haven't met anyone new. And why me? I'm sure he had an abundance of choices. I mean, really. He could have chosen Lexis."

"But he didn't."

"Why?" I insisted. This honestly made no sense.

"I wish I knew," Rome said sharply, as if he really did

want to remember. More than anything else in the world. "Maybe if I knew, I could make sense of this…obsession I seem to have with you."

My hand stilled on Tanner, that sweet proclamation ringing in my ears. Where had this determined man been when he'd first awakened? When he'd gone home with Lexis? Yeah, he'd assured me nothing had happened between them. But it had still hurt. Unlike M-Squared, he'd chosen her over me.

"If he has my memories of you, I'm not sure if he thinks he's me or he's still himself, but either way he's most likely…developing…feelings for you." His voice deepened, became more steely, with every word spoken. "I called Cody to talk some of this out, and he mentioned someone sent you flowers."

"That same someone also gave me candy." *Could* Memory Man have sent them?

"Candy?" An outraged hiss. "If he thinks he's me, he's going about this all wrong. I'd never send candy. It's too cliché. When did you get candy? And if you ate a single piece, I'll—"

I traced a finger along the line of Tanner's IV. "I took them to the lab to be dusted for prints and tested for poison."

A blur of movement, and then Rome's heat was radiating beside me. "Smart girl. When I leave here, I'll check on them for you, see what was found."

"Thanks. Now, smart girl that I am, you know I wouldn't ask this next question without reason."

"If you say so."

So suspicious. "Will you bring Elaine to me?"

"Sorry, but you're not getting anywhere near her, Belle."

I pushed a breath out between my clenched teeth. "Look, we both know you don't give a shit about me. You're just fixated right now because you're frustrated at not being able to remember. That's understandable. But you lost the right to protect me when you went home to your ex-wife."

His hand settled atop my shoulder, hot and firm. "I told you. Nothing happened. And I *do* give a shit."

I shrugged from his hold, saying, "Not enough." Not nearly enough. "I need you to leave now, Rome. Please." I just didn't have the stamina to deal with him right now.

"Guess who called me—" Sherridan's voice ground to a halt as she entered the room. She must have spotted Rome. "Oh, it's you." Yep. "What are you doing here, you traitor?"

"Hello, Sherridan. It's nice to see you, too."

"So you know *me?*" she asked, some of her outrage falling away and pride taking its place.

He sighed. "I've done my homework."

"Oh."

I twisted in the chair, and our gazes met. My exhausted hazel against her determined blue. She breezed to me, as warm and pretty as a summer day, and kissed me on the cheek. "How's our boy holding up?"

"He's the same." Tears suddenly burned my eyes, threatening to spill over. "Damn it!"

Her eyes raked over me and she *tsked* under her tongue. "Well, *you're* worse, no doubt about it. You need a shower and another change of clothes. Which, amazing friend that I am, I brought you."

The boast had the desired results: I laughed, my tears gradually drying. I was still wearing the halter top and could-only-be-seen-under-a-microscope skirt. "You brought me something a little less slutty, I hope."

"I don't," Rome muttered.

We both ignored him. I was positive I'd misheard, anyway. "Better," Sherridan said. "I figure my role on this kick-ass team is to make sure we'll all look stylish, and I take that role seriously. That's why I brought you something très superheroey."

I cut off a groan.

"Can I see?" Rome asked.

He was fighting a grin, the bastard. I could hear the smile in his voice.

"No," Sherridan said, but she pulled a black leather catsuit from her overlarge purse, anyway, and held it up for my inspection.

I couldn't help peeking at Rome to gauge his reaction. He nodded in approval, his eyes heating as if he were picturing me wearing it. "I think that's perfect."

So the Cat Man liked the catsuit. This time, I couldn't stop my groan. I grabbed the dangling material from her fingers and stood. "What were you saying when you came in? Someone called you?"

"What?" Confusion furrowed her brow before her eyes widened and she clapped. "Oh. Yeah. Cody called me. Said he couldn't get hold of you, and hadn't been able to make Rome stop talking about you long enough to listen to him. Oh, and if you're wondering how he got my number, he said he borrowed your cell before he left and copied it." She bit her bottom lip, running it through her teeth. "You know, he's actually pretty nice. Once you get to know him."

I studied her, saw the color blooming in her cheeks, watched the way she danced from one foot to the other in agitation. "Dear God, you're already falling for him. After one phone conversation, you're ready to have his babies." But amid my growing concern, one thought echoed in my head: Rome hadn't been able to stop talking about me?

"No. No, no, no." She wagged her head back and forth for emphasis, even held up her hands. "He was nice, that's all. But weird. He told me to tell you to answer your phone once in a while and that he'd tracked down some rodent at the very top of an ocean and was going off the road...no, that isn't right...off the grid, yes, that's it! Off the grid to keep the little critter from sniffing his cheese, so you probably wouldn't be able to get hold of him and..." She tapped a fingertip to her chin. "There was something else, but I'm drawing a blank."

Rome stepped forward, tension in every muscle in his body. He gripped her shoulders, shook her. "What?"

"I'm thinking! Don't pressure me. And really, you of all people have no right to complain about someone else's faulty memory."

I threw the catsuit over my shoulder, pried Rome's arms from her and replaced them with mine, forcing her to face me. *Calm, stay calm.* How many times would I have to tell myself that in the coming minutes? "This is very important. I need to know exactly what he said."

Sherridan closed her eyes, intense in her concentration and sickeningly adorable. "It didn't make much sense. It was something along the lines of candy being bright and unexpectedly merging with the...desert that splits? Oh, and he'd like you and Rome to join him for cocktails, but wants you to wear your dinner jackets because the nights are cold."

My stomach twisted into a million little knots. "I think you've just been promoted from stylist to interpreter, Sherridan," I managed to work out. Of its own accord, my gaze lifted, seeking Rome's. I could see the wheels turning in his head as he tried to decipher my friend's words. I did it for him, too impatient to wait for him to catch up.

"Cody was sending us a message. Because of some papers PSI found at the warehouse, we thought there might be someone in Desert Gal's employ working at Big

Rocky Spring Water. The rodent must be code for our suspect, and the ocean means Big Rocky, so the lead was right. Only, it's bigger than we realized. Cody's going off the grid means, I think, that he's going undercover. The fact that it's cold at night and we need protection means it's dangerous and he needs our help. The bright candy is—shocker—Candace Bright, and Cody thinks she's Big Rocky's president or owner—the rodent at the very top of the ocean could mean either one."

I paused for breath, my gaze becoming pointed. "And last but not least, he also thinks Candace Bright and Desert Gal are one and the same."

THOUGH I HATED LEAVING Tanner, I did it. His condition was stable, his vitals better than they'd been. I had his doctor's phone number in my pocket and had insisted I be called if anything changed: good or bad.

Right now, I had a trip to prepare for.

"I'm going with you, and that's that," Sherridan said as we strode up the porch to our house. I half expected a present to be waiting for me, but no. Not today. Was M-Squared really my admirer? And like Rome, had he decided I wasn't worth the effort? I desperately wanted to talk to him, beg him to return Rome's memories.

I was no longer quite so mad at him now that I knew he wasn't helping Desert Gal, that he'd taken those memories simply because he liked me. Yeah, I'd softened. Again. *Definitely* a yo-yo.

But why did he like me? The question still plagued me. I'd already decided it wasn't because of my cuteness. So what did that leave? I wasn't the brightest bulb in the lamp, had been called flaky more times than I could count, apparently needed my friends to dress me (see? not the brightest bulb), and for the last few years hadn't been able to hold down a job for more than a few months (PSI excluded—maybe).

I was an ordinary girl dealing with extraordinary things. That's all.

"Belle. I'm talking to you."

"It's a nice day," I said, hoping Sherridan wouldn't notice the change of subjects and the fact that I hadn't responded to her *I'm going* statement.

She mopped at her cheeks and neck with her free hand as she unlocked the door. "Nice day, my ass. It's hot as hell. Thank God for air-conditioning."

We sailed inside, and a cool breeze instantly caressed me. In the living room, Sherridan stopped, faced me and crossed her arms over her chest, clearly prepared for battle. "Don't think I failed to realize you avoided responding to my vow to go with you. It's Colorado, for God's sake. Nothing bad happens there."

"Hello. Do you recall being in the room when you were relaying Cody's message to us? Bad stuff happens there all the time. Case in point—we'll be hunting and *fighting* Desert Gal." Who was most likely the alter ego of Candace Bright. Or vice versa. Did they know about each other? Was Candace Bright like Clark Kent to Desert Gal's Superman, one persona used to interact with normal people, the other to fight crime? Only Desert Gal didn't fight crime, she created it. Okay, so maybe that made her more like Jekyll and Hyde. Why had she shown the prisoners her human side, though? So they'd feel less threatened by her? Trust her more? "She's the prune with teeth, remember?"

"Of course I remember. Do I look like Rome Masters to you? But got it. Check. We're going to hunt ourselves a prune. Sounds fun."

Well, crap. "Why do you—" I pressed my lips together. Maybe she *should* go with me, I mused. Unstable though my powers were, I would be a better guard than anyone else because I loved her and would place her safety above my own. I'd take a bullet for her if necessary. And hopefully, somehow, someway, I could protect her from whatever doom Lexis thought was headed her way in the form of her greatest wish coming true.

I pushed my hair out of my face, surprised to see my hand was shaking. What the hell? "You can come. I *want* you to come."

"Oh." Bit by bit, she relaxed. "Well, good. 'Cause I am."

I tossed my purse on the side table. "I just want you to reconsider the superpowers thing. Okay? I caught myself on fire yesterday." My knees were shaking, too, I realized as I walked forward. I had to stop and lean against the wall to keep myself upright. Something was wrong with me; I was losing energy fast. "We're going after a woman who can suck the water straight out of our bodies and we have a friend on an IV because he touched a girl I was interrogating. Simply *touched* her."

Hey, wait. Was I having a delayed reaction to Elaine? Was that why I was weakening so quickly? I hadn't touched her skin, but I *had* hugged her.

Sherridan stared down at her sandaled feet. "Yeah, but people admire you, look to you for help."

Was *that* what this was about? "Sherridan, people admire you, too. You're beautiful, successful and highly intelligent. Proof—who helped me get this beautiful home? And in two days, two men have asked me for your number. Cody, of course, and Reese, a very sexy vampire I've been meaning to tell you about."

"Who cares about dating when we're on the verge of a mission?" She kicked at the carpet. "And yeah, I helped you get this house, but I can't blow-dry your hair from fifty paces."

Again with the blow-drying? "You're wonderful the way you are. In fact, *I* want to be *you.*"

Her expression hardened, her narrowed gaze lifting. "No, you don't, you liar. You can't. You're special."

"So are you—"

"Rome really liked the suit," she interjected, clearly done with that line of conversation. She tossed her purse on top of mine and collapsed in the recliner. "I think he was imagining peeling it off you."

I sighed, unsure of just how to convince her of her fabulousness. "No, he didn't and no, he wasn't. I casually mentioned changing into it before heading home, which I didn't do, I might add, and he couldn't get away from me fast enough."

She kicked up her legs. "Because he had a hard-on he didn't want you to see."

A girl could hope. We'd left Rome at headquarters, and he hadn't cared enough to say goodbye. Hadn't tried to follow me, protect me. Monitor me. He was probably with Lexis again. Okay, no probably about it. He was. In a few hours, they were meeting us at a private airstrip, and then we were all flying to Colorado, where Big Rocky headquarters was located.

They were probably making arrangements for their daughter. Sweet little Sunny. My chest constricted as her image filled my head. Petite, dark-haired, with the face of a heartbreaker. When I returned, I was going to visit her. Her dad and I may not be getting along, but I loved that little girl.

Hold me, Belly, she was fond of saying, and I would laugh and scoop her up.

She was five years old and as mischievous as the devil.

You couldn't turn your back on her without severe consequences, but she loved as fiercely as her daddy.

"Speaking of hard-ons, I bet Cody's screwing the brains out of Little Miss Pruneface and that's why he's so determined to go undercover," Sherridan said sulkily, pulling me from my thoughts. "*Really* undercover."

The man *was* fond of seducing for information. Poor Sherridan. I could tell she was intrigued by and attracted to Cody. I'd known he would hurt her, though. He'd expressed interest in her one day but might have given himself to the enemy the next. Typical.

If he'd really wanted Sherridan, he wouldn't have cared about my warning to stay away. He would have fought for her. Women deserved to be fought over, after all. We were a prize to be earned and treasured. At least, we should be, I thought darkly. I couldn't imagine Rome fighting for me in his current condition.

Hopefully, Cody would return in one piece and I could freeze his ass to the wall for intriguing my friend. Rome could fry beside him. Fire and ice. A nice contrast.

"Since I am *not* a liar, I will just say that yeah, you're probably right."

"Bastard. Think he'll be okay?" Sherridan asked despite her obvious irritation with him.

"He'll be fine." I hoped. Cody had power over electricity and could disappear inside a light socket—talk about freaky—but what if Desert Gal drained him of water the way Elaine had drained Tanner of energy before he could get away?

Before leaving PSI, I had tried to talk John into allowing Elaine to go with us to Colorado, but he had firmly refused. Taking a maybe-kinda-sorta enemy into a known enemy camp was not an intelligent strategy, he'd said. Men. Such idiots sometimes.

"All right. Enough of that. We've got two hours," I said, forcing myself to push from the wall. My knees almost buckled. "Be ready."

"Yes, ma'am." She saluted me and popped to her feet, then we went our separate ways in the hall.

There were five bedrooms in the house, and Rome and I had the master suite. I lumbered inside, my legs still strangely heavy, and shut myself in. The trek from PSI to the house had left me sweaty, so I hurried through a shower, mentally cataloging everything else I needed to do: dress in something less ridiculous than my previous few outfits had been, pack and weapon up. I should probably grab some food, too. I hadn't eaten since yesterday, I realized, and I hadn't gotten any sleep last night. *Aaah,* no wonder I was shaky. Elaine had nothing to do with it.

When I finished, I wrapped myself in a towel, padded into the bedroom and—

Stopped dead.

Rome sat at the edge of my bed, dark, dangerous and glaring.

CHAPTER TWELVE

I CLUTCHED THE TERRY-CLOTH TOWEL so tightly my knuckles creaked. My hair was dripping down my back. My skin was damp, flushed from the steam and, now that I'd seen Rome, tingling. Any other time, I would have dropped the cloth and beckoned this man over. Any other time, we would have laughed and loved, and I would have marveled at the bliss that was my life.

Fine, I would have taken it for granted. Now, however, I knew better. Knew how quickly something prized could be stolen.

"What are you doing here?" I asked, the question emerging shakily. "Did something happen?" Nothing but bad news could have parted him from his precious Lexis, the hateful side of me thought. Just call me Bitch McBitcherson, the paranormal name I currently deserved.

"No, nothing happened." Rome pushed to his feet, unfolding his big, strong body from its semicrouch. I was used to his height, loved it even, but just then he appeared intimidating. Menacing. A scowl darkened his features, and I could hear the rumble in his throat.

His cat wanted free. To fight or to play? Sadly, I couldn't tell anymore. But I still reacted.

Suddenly trembling, I backed up a step. My heart skidded out of control, beating so hard it was like a hammer in my chest. *He's not affecting you. You're just hungry, remember? Hungry for food,* I hastily added.

"Rome, you have to tell me what you're doing here."

Remaining silent, he stalked to me. There was lethal power in every step, and for a moment I could have sworn I was transported to a jungle, the swish of trees and the howls of the monkeys in my ears.

This time I backed up until I hit the wall.

Only when he was a whisper away did he stop, his body threatening to press into mine. His wild scent filled my nose, a decadent reminder of what I didn't have… what I might never have again. Oh, I loathed those kinds of depressing thoughts. Where was my determination? Still, I tried to hold my breath. When that didn't work, I tried to move around him. But he had me completely pinned, surrounded by his strength and heat.

"Belle," he said softly.

I had to strain my neck to look up…up…at him—and found those crystalline irises swirling with fury.

He was mad at *me?* "How'd you get in here, Mr. Break In?" I demanded, pointing out his sin before he could point out mine, whatever it was. "This is private property and you no longer belong."

"Hardly. This is the address on my driver's license, so I knew I'd have a key. I used the only one I didn't recognize, and what do you know, the door opened."

"Well, you can just give the key back. You don't live here anymore."

He arched a brow, his fury fading to…amusement? Still he didn't back away from me. "Says who?"

"Says me." My head tilted to the side. "Says Lexis, I'm sure."

The fury returned, stronger than before, nearly sparking. "I'll come over any time I damn well please."

"Why?" I asked—again—then cursed under my breath as the answer popped into my head. He was here to monitor me, as he'd told John he would. I would have been happy about that if I didn't so easily recall the way he'd sworn never to kiss me again. "Never mind. I'm buying a vicious dog. He'll chew you up and spit out your bones."

"I'm sure he'll *try.*"

Infuriating, conceited man. Did he know what a turn-on that was? Probably. I tried another approach. "As you can see, I'm fine. I'm not causing any trouble or using any of the elements irresponsibly. You can go."

The rumbling started up again. "I'm not going anywhere. There was a box on your porch when I arrived. I took the liberty of opening it," he added, not even pretending to be ashamed.

Another present? And he had dared to open what was clearly meant for me? "You had no right!"

Rather than defend his actions, he continued throwing words at me as if they were weapons. "It was from your secret admirer."

Deep breath in, deep breath out. *Calm is your friend.* "Well, what was it?"

"Lingerie. With the words *Wonder Girl* sewn onto the ass of the panties."

Totally not what I'd expected him to say, and my lips curled into a slow grin.

His eyes rounded like saucers. "You think this is funny?"

"Well, yeah." I probably should have been offended. I mean, really. Lingerie most likely given to me by a man I'd never even met. A man who'd stolen my fiancé's memories, no less. But part of me realized that if it *was* M-Squared doing the sending, he was finally tapping into Rome's psyche and *learning* about me. What I liked, what I didn't. That was just the sort of gift I would have swooned over had Rome given it to me.

"Where's the box?" I asked.

His mouth straightened into a mulish line as he braced his hands beside my temples. "Don't worry about that. I'm taking care of it."

If I inhaled deeply, my nipples would brush his chest. "I'm not worried, I just want to see them."

"Too bad. Now listen. I stopped by the lab on my way here. There were no prints on those chocolates, but they were a very expensive brand, so we've got agents hacking into the distributor's database to see who made the order and from where."

Mmm, chocolate. Was that my stomach rumbling? "Sounds like a plan." I flattened my palms on him to push him away, but his heart beat faster and harder than I had imagined, and I could only stand there in wonder, savoring the feeling. And though his shirt kept me from actual skin-to-skin contact, the heat of him enthralled me. "Now back off?" It was a question when it should have been a demand.

Rome didn't. Rather, he pressed closer. So close my hardened nipples finally, blessedly brushed his chest. I gasped; he hissed in a breath.

"Memory Man," he said, voice strained, "has probably been in this house. With my memories, he'd know the best ways inside."

"So we're one hundred percent sure it's him? And really, you fortified the place with all kinds of security."

"Not one hundred percent, no, but we're pretty damn confident. And he'd know exactly what security measures I used and how to bypass them."

"Oh." How easy it would be to slide my hands up and around Rome's neck. How easy to draw his head down for a kiss… "Well, he hasn't hurt me. *If* it's him." Was that breathless temptress *me?*

"Not yet. But let's say that he wants you to fall in love with him the way you fell in love with me. I mean, we know he liked my memories of you. And if we're right, he's trying to romance you, win your heart. When you fail to react the way he wants, he could become angry."

"First, for all we know, whoever it is leaving me these gifts just wants to sex me up." I spread my fingers, felt his nipple harden underneath my palm. "Second, who says I can't fall in love with Memory Man?"

Rome stiffened. He gripped my arms and shook me, forcing my attention to his face. "Don't kid."

I snapped out of the sensual fog, and my hands fell to my sides. "Who's kidding? He's now in possession of your memories of me, which means he's the closest thing I've got to the real *you.*"

"He's dangerous, Belle."

"So are you, and we made things work. For a while."

His grip tightened and he leaned down, placing us nose to nose, his choppy breath trekking over my lips. "You like taunting me, don't you? Well, guess what? It works. I can't fucking get you out of my mind." He released me long enough to slam a fist into the plaster just beside my temple. "That kiss was a goddamn mistake. It was supposed to purge you from my thoughts, make me stop wondering what you taste like."

He'd wanted to forget me entirely? To never think of me again? Suddenly I felt as if I'd been strapped down and cut open, salt poured into the wound. "I think I hate you right now," I said honestly.

He pulled back, studied my face before shaking his head. "You don't hate me." His gaze dropped to my mouth, lingered. "You want me."

He could have been saying *get naked,* as huskily as he'd uttered the words, but that kind of assurance about my capitulation irritated me. A man that confident would feel comfortable doing something destructive to a relationship—like going home to his ex-wife—and think an apology was all that was needed to patch things up.

"Look, Rome. I love you. I do. And I want you." God, did I want him. Maybe it was my hunger making me admit these things, but I couldn't hold the words back. "The thing is, I won't let myself have you." Not now. Not after he'd rejected me. Again.

His gaze jerked up and clashed with mine, confusion darkening those gorgeous irises. "Why not?"

Was he…pouting? Surely not. "You should be totally on board with my refusal. I thought we'd already decided to keep things platonic. That's what you told John, isn't it?"

His eyelids slit dangerously. "I only promised him you wouldn't catch on fire again. *Not* that I wouldn't kiss you again."

Hope, such silly hope. "I don't believe you. And you can't just change your mind like that. I'm not a piece of chocolate—" hmm, chocolate "—you can drool over one moment, then forget about the next, and then think about eating again later." Okay, perhaps that wasn't the best analogy. Rome, eating, teeth and tongue moving, working… I shivered. "I know what it feels like to be made love to by a man who loves me, and I won't settle for anything less. Now, you need to leave."

The very teeth I was imagining all over my body suddenly flashed in a show of aggression. "I can't stay away. That's the problem. What the hell have you done to me?"

Anger gave me strength. I fisted the fabric of his

shirt, bones so taut they could have snapped. "What are you implying?"

"Does your saliva have an addictive agent in it? Is that another of your powers?"

So. He thought I'd somehow tricked him into desiring me, that he couldn't possibly want me because he had loved me, because we'd had something special. *Had,* I thought. Key word.

My love life was going up in flames around me, and there was nothing I could do but watch it burn.

"Maybe it does," I said sadly. Then, with more force, "Maybe, when I find Memory Man, I'll kiss the hell out of him. Maybe *he'll* ask me to marry him and actually go through with it." Though I'd meant to sound flippant there at the end, my hurt rang through loud and clear.

The more I spoke, the more Rome's pupils narrowed until there was nothing left but a thin black line. He cupped my chin, forcing my face to his. "When I was a boy, I saved my money for months because I wanted to buy a pet lizard. Have I told you this before?"

"No, but what does that have to do with anything?" I asked, even though I was desperate to hear the story. I loved him, but I didn't know much about his childhood.

"Just listen. Like I said, I saved for months. Finally, I'd saved enough. I went to the pet store, bought everything I needed for its care and took little Bone Crusher home."

"You named him *Bone Crusher?*"

He acted as if I hadn't spoken. "I owned him for three weeks before my mom noticed him. By that time, I loved him, couldn't imagine my life without him."

I swallowed the lump forming in my throat. "Bone Crusher, though?"

"My mom saw him and freaked. She made me let him go out back, held me against her so I couldn't run after him. I cried for days."

"I—I—" Wanted to hug him. The little boy he'd been, the man he'd become. Both were precious to me. I coughed to cover my softening. "What does Bone Crusher have to do with me?"

Once more, Rome got in my face. He was fury and he was hurt; he was longing and he was determination. He was…everything. "I've regretted that I didn't fight for him ever since."

"I don't understand." Was afraid to hope.

His jaw hardened, so firm and stubborn my heart swelled. "I'm going to kiss you, Belle. And I'm going to touch you."

I lost my breath. Or rather, it caught in my throat, hanging there, suspended. "We're not supposed to do this," I whispered, because I couldn't say no. But maybe I could talk us out of this.

"So?"

"So." I licked my lips. "I'm not going to let myself have you until your memory returns." If I could find the strength to continue to resist him. Right now, that seemed more impossible than Desert Gal deciding to turn herself in.

His gaze had followed the movement of my tongue. "I remember our last kiss." The hoarse statement dripped with desire.

Oh, God. Already my resistance was crumbling. "I could burn you." Again. Could burn this house.

"Could?" He chuckled without humor. "You already have."

Fight his appeal. "It's dangerous." A reminder for me, for him.

"Doesn't have to be. John told me I caged your abilities once, kept us both safe from them."

"Key word *once*."

"I want to try again. And I will." He didn't give me time to utter another protest. He simply smothered my lips with his own, his tongue thrusting deep and hard and hot.

My hands were in his hair before I could stop them, fisting, nails digging into his scalp just as his were in mine. Our tongues took and gave and fought, but I finally allowed him to conquer. His lips were soft, his body a hard press.

One of his hands kneaded my breast through the towel, and the nipple pearled to a sharp little point. He moaned into my mouth. I swallowed the sound, the flavor adding a new level of passion.

As I arched into him—*yes, God yes, so good*—his erection rubbing against me, common sense tried to rear its ugly head. *Stay in control. Don't give him everything. Hold a part of yourself back.*

But why? my heart cried.

Without his memory, he'll hurt you once the loving is over. And, as you tried to remind him, you could kill him with your fire. He might not be able to cage your abilities like he used to, even though he thinks he can.

True, so true. I'd have to be careful, stay in command. Enjoy him, yes. For a little while. Because I simply could not resist him anymore. And I needed to forget, if only for a bit, the bleak abyss my life had become.

But as common sense demanded, I'd have to hold a part of myself back. That was the only safe way I could allow myself this kiss. And I had to have this kiss, for he was devouring me as if he needed me to survive. He was here, in my arms, craving more of me. He was the man I loved, the man I would—hopefully—marry.

"I want to touch you," he said, releasing my hair and tugging at my towel.

"No. Too much," I replied between nips and licks.

"Want to touch you. Want you to touch me."

I was working his shirt over his head before he'd finished the sentence. I tossed the material to the floor in a forgotten heap. Then I flattened my palms against his chest and gasped. He was hot, both hard and soft, as though fire flowed in his veins, as though silk covered stone.

"You're so beautiful." I'd missed this contact with him. This connection.

"Not as beautiful as you." He licked his way down my throat, then licked his way back up. "Touch me more, but kiss me, too. Your mouth is killing me, and I want to die."

"Like this?" I kissed a path down his neck just as he'd done mine, my nails lightly scraping at his back. All the while, fire flowed through *my* veins. I could feel the first tendrils waking up, sparking to life. I tamped them down, using every ounce of strength I possessed.

"You were made for me, weren't you? My sweetest temptation." His fingers traced the bottom of my towel, slowing drawing it up...up...revealing inch after inch of thigh. When he reached the curve of my butt, he stopped and played, massaging. "Perfection."

I bit the cord at the base of his throat, just the way I knew he liked, and he hissed in a breath. "Careful, Rome darling, or you'll fall in love with me again."

For a moment, he didn't reply, and the bedroom echoed with the sound of our panting. "I'll love you in and out of that catsuit. I know that." So Sherridan was right about the catsuit after all, both the wearing of and the peeling off. Score! I didn't have time to gloat about— uh, dwell on it, though, because he arched his hips, rubbing his erection between my legs.

I cried out at the pleasure, had to fortify my grip on my inner fire. "What about the dress? Did you love me in that?"

He chuckled softly, darkly. "In that dress you almost gave me heart failure. Then, in nothing but the foam, you were like a fantasy come to life. *Then,* in that halter and miniskirt, you had me drooling. Now, in the towel, you're a dream come true."

"Don't—don't talk like that." Already the fire inside me churned to be released. Any more of his sweet talk, and I'd lose my grip on it.

"How're you doing?" he asked, as if sensing my struggle.

"Burning," I said truthfully, and then licked one of his nipples. I just couldn't help myself. A shiver stole through me and flowed into him. "But I'm okay. Got it under control as long as we keep things physical. No emotions."

The muscles in his stomach quivered and he tangled one hand in my wet hair, pulling tight. The other remained on my ass, squeezing. "Give me the heat, baby."

I froze in shock, in joy. *Baby.* He'd just called me baby. That's what he'd called me BML—before memory loss. Part of me had thought never to hear him speak the endearment again. Hearing it now, while I was in his arms…there was no stopping my surge of emotion, which was like adding kindling to the fire inside me.

"What?" he asked, grip loosening on my hair but not my ass.

"N-nothing." *Mind blank, Belle. Mind blank. Only desire is welcome right now.* I kissed and nipped my way to his other nipple and gave it the same treatment. He was hard against me, hard and thick and long. I knew just how magnificent it would feel to ease him inside me, pushing deep, all the way to the hilt. He would stretch me, and I would love it. We'd both become mindless, lost, and the pleasure would be extraordinary. We'd explode like rockets.

But what would happen afterward? I found myself wondering again. So much for a blank mind.

Again, as if he sensed my internal struggle, he rubbed against me, once, twice, and I moaned, once more losing myself. The pleasure was just too damn good.

Higher and higher my fire raged. Tighter and tighter I gripped it, holding it captive. But for how much longer? "I—I need a moment," I panted. I jerked my hips backward, out of touching range. Several deep, shuddering breaths later and I still wasn't in as much control as I would have liked.

Rome traced a fingertip along the curve of my cheek. "What's wrong, baby?"

Baby again. "Just have to catch my breath."

"Yeah. Right. Give me your heat," he commanded again. "No."

When his fingers began inching down my throat to the edge of the towel, tracing as if he meant to push it away and caress my nipples skin to skin, perhaps bending down and kissing my belly before laving at the desire between my legs, the fire inside me grew, spread, soon demanding release.

I needed to push him away. I settled for dropping my hands to my sides. I straightened, but couldn't look him in the eyes. Not yet. Those eyes always enslaved me. "We—we have to stop. For now."

"We just got started," he said, but his fingers ceased their movement.

God, do I know it, I thought, already mourning what could have been. There was so much more we could do, so much more I yearned to do. "I'm sorry."

He sighed. "Either you changed your mind about

wanting me, which I doubt is the case since I can smell the sweetness of your arousal, or you're afraid to give me your fire."

My legs were trembling so much I expected to topple at any moment, and this time the trembling came from something besides hunger, something besides anger. He was right, it came from fear. "Doesn't matter which sup-position is correct. Tell me you remember something about our life together." Something, anything. Only then could I trust him to properly filter me.

Silence.

I cut off the surge of hurt before it could bombard me. "*That's* why we're stopping. You don't remember me, and until you do, you get nothing from me. Like I said, I won't let you screw me as if I'm a stranger. I want your love or nothing at all." I'd have to remember that myself, as easily and as quickly as I gave in to him.

"Fair enough," Rome said evenly. He held up his hands, palms out, and stepped backward, no longer crowding me.

I sagged against the wall to keep myself in a standing position, despising the loss of contact. *Stupid girl,* my hormones cried.

"But I hope you understand that I do plan to change your mind," he added, then strolled out of my bedroom and out of the house, the door clicking shut behind him.

CHAPTER THIRTEEN

I DIDN'T ALLOW MYSELF to ponder Rome's threat/delicious promise as I ate three protein bars and packed my bags. Toothbrush, fire-resistant change of clothes, raincoat, snow boots and a photo of me, Tanner, Rome, Sherridan and my dad, taken a few weeks ago when Tanner had prepared a dinner of his "famous" booby sandwiches— bread and meats cut in a circle and topped with olives.

Still I didn't allow myself to dwell on Rome's parting words as Sherridan and I loaded our stuff in the car. I couldn't. I'd lose all focus on the case. Again. I'd have to think about it later—and decide what to do if Rome actually attempted to seduce me.

I couldn't think about Tanner, either. My sweet Tanner, who was stuck on a gurney, hooked to an IV and missing all the action. No one loved action more than Tanner.

My cell rang as I shut the trunk. "Hello," I answered, leaning against the sedan. *Please don't be about the wedding.* After everything I'd been through, saying my marriage vows was the last thing I wanted to worry about.

"Hello, Belle." The speaker possessed a warm, masculine voice I'd never heard before.

I frowned. "Who is this?"

"Did you like the flowers? The candy? The…panties?"

My jaw nearly dropped. Could it really be… "Who is this?" I demanded again.

"You probably know me as Memory Man."

I froze. So it *was* him, and he *did* want me. My first reaction was anger, the slight softening I'd had when I'd heard about his torture, then learned of his dislike for Desert Gal, forgotten. Yo. Yo. "Listen, you. I—"

"I know you're mad," he interjected. "And I understand the reasons for it. I do. But all I'm asking for is a little of your time so you have the chance to get to know me. I'm not such a bad guy. Let me—"

"No. Whatever you're going to say, no. You have a lot of nerve calling me. You took something that doesn't belong to you and we want it back."

Sherridan motioned to the phone with a wave of her hand.

"Memory Man," I mouthed, and she scowled.

"I'll give you anything you want," he said stubbornly. "Anything but that."

Oh, really? "You just wait until I find you. The memory you have of me Tasering Rome will seem like a spa visit compared to what I have planned."

"You have so much spirit." He chuckled softly. "I love that about you. I love so many things about you."

"No, you don't. Rome does." Or did. I wish I had a tracer on my phone. I'd find out where M-Squared was and blast him as promised. He had no right to say that kind of thing to me.

"Doesn't matter whose memories they are." His voice had veered from sweet and amused to hard and stubborn. "They're in *my* head, which means *I* lived them. Kind of," he added on a wistful sigh.

"They don't belong to you, and you know it. You have to give them back to Rome."

"Not going to happen. I like them too much." There was that stubbornness again.

Damn him. "Why me?" I asked, still dumbfounded by that fact. I had to know. "You could have had Lexis. She's grade A."

"Actually, she's kind of a snob. But you…you're beautiful, always make the people around you laugh, and… and you know what it's like to have a powerful gift the world wants to use you for." There at the end, sadness had dripped from his words.

So he hated his ability. He felt used, probably didn't know whom he could trust. And his own memories were no doubt tainted from his days—weeks, months, *years?*— of captivity. Some of my anger drained as I once again found myself softening—what was wrong with me? But I would not feel sorry for him, I vowed. "None of that matters," I said, more gently than I would have liked. "You had no right to do what you did. If you don't—"

"You didn't let me finish. You're also kindhearted and passionate and—"

"Stop right there. Not another word about my passion. But thank you." What kind of moron was I? Compliment me and I'd melt like ice cream in the sun. "The truth is, I'm cranky, flaky and borderline homicidal."

"No. You're loyal, dependable and you stand up for what you believe in. You nearly worked yourself to death just to pay for your dad's health care. You gave yourself to PSI to save that man and his little girl. You're the only person I know who is truly selfless."

"That man has a name. And I promise you, I'm far from selfless."

He expelled a frustrated breath. "I know I can make you happy, Belle. If you'll just give me a chance."

Sherridan crooked her fingers expectantly, silently demanding an update. I motioned that I needed a minute and turned away from her, resting my elbows on the hood of the car. Had the sun always been this hot and stifling? "Why don't you tell me where you are and we'll discuss this face-to-face?"

He laughed. "How adorable are you, trying to lay a trap for me. You're taking to agenting very nicely. Look, I just want to be with you. I want you to look at me the way you looked at *him*. And like I said, I want to make you happy. I know I can. Is that a crime?"

"When you steal from others, yes," I said through gritted teeth. His devotion was just so damn nice. It wasn't fair that I was getting it from him.

A sigh crackled over the line. "I'm sorry if I hurt you. I am. I just couldn't help myself. You're everything I've ever wanted in a woman and for the first time in my life, watching you, I actually felt…alive. You're worth living for, Belle Jamison. You're also worth dying for."

Damn him, damn him, damn him. "If I promise not to lay a trap, would you please consider meeting with me?" Somehow, someway, I had to make him understand the horror of what he'd done. *My* life depended on it. "Think about it. We can make new memories. Memories of our own." Sure, those memories would involve me holding him in a wind lock until he gave me what I wanted, but he didn't need to know that.

"One day soon, we will. I promise. For now…just be careful out there, Wonder Girl. I don't know what I'd do if anything happened to you." *Click.*

I stared at the phone for a long while, shaking my head, wondering if I'd imagined what had just happened. With the week I'd had, I wouldn't doubt it. Hallucinations had to be par for the course. But no. I couldn't fool myself for long. It had happened, I just hadn't gotten the results I'd wanted. I'd gotten the opposite, actually. The wrong man was determined to win my affections.

"HE'S GOING TO BE FINE, Belle," Sherridan said as we settled into the Honda.

I took the wheel. Bad a driver as I was, I was still better than There's-No-Such-Thing-As-A-Brake Sherridan. "Who is?" I asked, inserting the key and twisting. The engine roared to life. Though only an hour and a half had passed since I'd last stepped outside, it was far more humid. Humid enough to melt the Wicked Witch of the West. Which, to some people, I probably was. I cranked the air-conditioning as high as it would go, but sadly, that didn't help. "Memory Man?" I hoped he'd be anything but fine. Kind of. Damn him. I didn't wish him ill. For the most part. Damn him, damn him, damn him, I thought again.

My emotions were all tangled up where he was concerned. He'd said he wasn't a bad guy, and he hadn't seemed like one. And yeah, somewhere during that conversation, I think I'd even stopped hating him. For real, not just for a few seconds while my dumb little heart softened. I was still pissed as hell, but I no longer wanted to cut off his balls and wear them as earrings. At all. Proof: I was thinking about him but steam wasn't coming out of my nose. He'd just been too sweet. Too devoted. To me. The dummy.

I guess Rome's hypothesis had been right. M-Squared wanted me to love him. I couldn't, and that made me wonder if I should indeed fear what would happen. Would he become desperate? Start hurting the people I did love?

To be honest, he hadn't seemed the type to go down that violent road. He wanted me happy, he'd said. He wanted me safe. I mean, he'd called me to tell me to be careful. Not the actions of a man who would next try and off me.

"Hello. Are you listening? You know who I was

talking about," Sherridan said. "Mr. Sensitive. Your sidekick. Our horny roommate."

Ah. "I can't talk about him." Not without crying. I hated leaving him, felt guilty, like a horrible friend.

"Let's talk about me, then." Her favorite subject. One of mine, too, truth be told. "What superpower do you think I'll get?" she asked as I maneuvered the car out of the driveway.

To my surprise, a dark sedan with tinted windows started forward, too, maintaining a perfect distance. When I'd first come home, it had been parked a few houses away. I'd noticed it because it had been the only other car currently on the road. And because sedans gave me the creeps. All agents—good and bad—seemed to use them. You'd think they'd come up with something more original, but no. Was I being followed? *So suspicious.* Well, I had reason.

I made a left turn. Waited. The sedan turned left, as well. Next I turned right. Waited, again. Again, the sedan turned right. No doubt about it. I had a tail.

Rome? was my first thought. I glanced into the rear-view mirror. The windows were too dark to see inside the car. Not Rome, I decided anyway. Love me or not, he wouldn't have wanted to scare me.

Was this courtesy of John? Had he sent someone besides Rome to monitor my abilities? That theory was more plausible. As my vehicle eased through the neighborhood, taking turns I didn't need, I kept an eye on the sedan. I couldn't head toward my destination until I knew who was behind the wheel.

"All right, Grandma," Sherridan said, drumming her coral-colored fingernails into the console between us. "It's okay to put a little pressure on the gas. You have my word you won't skid out of control if you pump it up to ten miles per hour."

"Very funny. Don't look, but I think we're being followed."

"What! By whom?" She immediately twisted in her seat, peering out the back window.

"I said don't look. Jeez!"

She turned, facing front and going stiff as a poker. "What should I do?" she asked, her voice shaking. With fear? Excitement?

"Just…I don't know." Nervousness rushed through me. "Get my cell out of my purse."

Bending down, she dug through the contents. Finally, she pulled out the little black device. "Rome's on speed dial. Press one."

She did. Then, "What next? Should I talk to him?"

"Press speaker," I said. I didn't want whoever was behind me to know I had someone on the line.

Bring, bring. Pause. *Bring, bring.* He had better answer!

"Miss me already?" Rome asked huskily.

I shivered, then cursed under my breath. There was no time for that. "Did John put a tail on me? And be honest. This could be a life-and-death situation."

"Shit." His voice lost all hint of husky entreaty. "Someone's following you?"

Okay. That answered *that* question. "What should I do?" Always before when we'd been chased, Rome had been the driver. Now, everything hinged on me. Had I been alone, I wouldn't have been quite as frightened. But Sherridan's life rested in my hands.

"Give me two minutes," Rome said. "I'm on my way to you."

"I'm headed south on Cedar, and I'll keep going straight."

"Good. I'm calling John. Don't answer your phone for any number but mine." *Click.*

Sherridan dropped the phone in her lap. "Could be nothing," she said, rubbing her hand against her jeans. "Just a regular Joe on the way to the private airport no one knows about but us."

She was reaching, but man, I wanted to agree.

"No one would follow you so blatantly. Right?"

"I wouldn't think so." Unless...was this Memory Man? Trying to keep me safe?

But why scare me like this? Fear hadn't been the emotion he'd wanted to incite in me.

My hands were shaking on the steering wheel, my knuckles so tight they'd already leached of color. The bones felt brittle with cold. *God, do not let me freeze our car.* We'd be immobile. Even, dare I say it, helpless. I had powers, sure, but as unstable as they were without my filter, I couldn't use them and risk destroying the entire neighborhood.

I kept my attention riveted to the rearview mirror. The sedan maintained a steady pace behind us, the driver not the least bit concerned with my slow speed, it seemed. I pressed the gas, increasing to about twenty miles per hour.

The sedan sped up, as well.

Up to twenty-five.

The sedan preserved the same, short distance between us.

Thirty.

Yep. Once again, there was an increase.

Why would the driver be so blithe about this? He—she?—didn't seem to care that I knew what was going on.

"Parked car approaching," Sherridan said, gaining my attention.

I switched my gaze to the road and swerved to avoid impact with a pickup. "Thank you."

"Anytime."

My cell phone beeped, and Sherridan quickly pressed speaker again.

"I'm almost there," Rome said without preamble. "And John did not put a tail on you. You okay?"

"Yeah. Thankfully, they aren't doing anything menacing. They're just keeping pace with us."

"Could be Memory Man," he said, voicing my earlier thought. "Can you see the driver?"

"Not even a hint. The windows are too dark."

He cursed. "A man who can make you forget that you've seen him wouldn't worry about keeping his identity hidden, so I doubt it's him."

Good point. So who was it? "If they wanted to talk to me, why not do it while I was loading my supplies in my car? I would have been a captive audience."

"The security there. The cameras. We'll find out. Later. Right now I only care about your emotions. How are they?" Rome asked.

"Fine, they're fine." I turned the wheel to avoid another parked car, then eased back to my side of the road. "No freezing or—"

Something shattered my back window. Startled, I accidentally swerved, my right front tire popping a curve.

Sherridan screamed.

"Duck," I shouted, hammering my foot on the gas and revving us to sixty in just a few seconds. Fear swam through me.

Thankfully she obeyed, throwing herself on the floorboard. Her eyes were wide as saucers as she panted, "What about you?"

"What the hell happened?" Rome demanded before I could reply.

"They freaking shot at us!" Sweat broke out over my

skin, but the fear still surging through me instantly froze it, leaving me covered in a fine sheen of ice.

There was a loud *pop,* then a bang, something slamming into the back of the car, causing us to jerk forward and back. Sherridan belted out another scream.

"Belle!" Rome. "Talk to me. Are you hit?"

"They just rammed us, and I think they flattened a tire, but we're good." But for how long? I was coming to a dead end. "I'm going left on…Maple," I said. I didn't let my foot off the gas, so the tires (or what was left of them) squealed.

"I see them," Rome growled. "Go left on Pine and then keep going straight. There's an exit to the main road about three blocks down."

At the next turn, I spiked the wheel. Once again the tires squealed and Sherridan and I were thrown to the side as the car veered sharply. "What are you going to do to them? I don't want to leave you to—"

"Do what I told you." *Click.*

From the rearview, I watched as Rome's sedan approached. (See? A sedan.) Closer to them…closer. He slammed his car into theirs. Both pivoted, and Rome rammed forward again. This time, the bad guy's vehicle turned a full circle.

I lifted my foot from the pedal, cracking the ice that had bloomed from me and bound me to it, and the car slowed. I took another turn, then another, wanting Sherridan as far away from the action as I could get her. Unfortunately, the cold sweat had solidified all over me, making my motions stiff, my clothing uncompromising. The ice had even slithered to the car's dash, freezing the gauges. Much more, and the car itself would be useless.

Glancing around, I found a shadowed alcove in the back of a house. Sure, I didn't know who the house belonged to and the owners didn't know me or Sherridan, but I pulled into the garage and parked anyway.

"Rome said to head to the main road."

"Yes, well, I haven't pledged to love, honor and obey him yet. Stay with the car," I told Sherridan as I unbuckled. Rome would need help, so help he would get.

"No. I—"

"If you don't, the home owners might try to have it towed. Don't let anyone inside. Oh, and there's a gun in the glove box. If you feel threatened, start shooting and ask questions later." I didn't give her time to refuse me. I just hopped out of the car and booked it to the street where I'd left Rome. Along the way, I allowed my fear to grow and fester. Soon, even the street beneath me possessed a patina of ice. My agency-regulated boots slipped and slid, and twice I almost fell. Somehow, though, I managed to maintain my balance.

What would I find? Rome—shot to death? God, I hated thinking like that, but right now it was to my benefit. Even as I thought it, ice balls formed in both of my hands. I clutched them tightly, keeping them at the ready.

Finally, the two combatants came into view. No one had emerged from their cars. Instead, the vehicles were still ramming together, metal crunching against metal. In the distance, I could hear sirens. Much longer, and the police would arrive. PSI would have to do cleanup, and that would piss John off royally. The world could not learn about the paranormal underground cohabiting with them. They'd panic. They'd probably try and hunt us down, kill us all. Melodramatic? I didn't think so. I'd watched all four X-Men movies.

I had to get Rome out of here before someone attempted to arrest him. But how?

I inched closer to the action, doing my best to remain

hidden by bushes. Rome finally managed to pin the bad guy's car into a tree. He threw open his door, staying low to the ground. His assailant got out, too, but I couldn't see him because he was low to the ground. Through the slit between road and car I could see his feet, though. Boots. Big boots. Definitely a man.

"State your business," Rome demanded.

"We just want the girl."

We?

Another pair of feet hit the ground. Then another. Dear God. There were three men—all training their weapons on Rome, most likely. Teeth grinding together, I sharpened my focus to the man closest to me, the one who made the mistake of straightening to try and ferret out Rome's location, and let one of my burdens fly. I missed. The ice ball slammed into their car, spreading quickly and lethally.

"Get back!" Rome shouted at me.

A *pop*. A *whiz*.

I dove for the ground. I didn't feel the bullet sail overhead but I knew that one had, the air above me blistering. *Move! You're out in the open.* I rolled as swiftly as I could, hiding behind a fence of bushes.

Another *pop*. Another *whiz*. The dirt just in front of the bushes exploded, spraying in every direction.

"Why?" Rome asked, drawing their attention away from me. "Why do you want her?"

Damn him! I didn't want them shooting at him, either. *Pop. Bang. Pop. Bang.*

I knew that sound well. As I'd feared, they were shooting at Rome, their bullets slamming into the car's metal frame. What should I do? What the hell should I do?

"Why else?" an unfamiliar voice said. "Money."

"Who wants her?" Rome. "Maybe we can work something out."

There was a snort.

I couldn't see anyone through the thick green foliage, and perhaps that was for the best. The grass underneath me turned to ice, the bushes wilting under the weight of the crystals. I crouched lower. What would Rome do if he were in my position? Just stand up and start tossing ice?

"You're all right," a voice suddenly whispered from behind me.

I almost screamed in shock and fear. My gaze jerked left and right, up and down, searching, but I found no one. "Who's there?" I whispered back.

"I won't let anything happen to you, Belle." Another *pop* rent the air, this one so close my eardrums almost burst. "I swear it."

A howl of pain echoed from behind the smashed cars. Not Rome's, thank God. Then a round of bullets was pumped my way—until Rome and my guardian angel began pumping out rounds of their own.

Another howl.

"Two down," the husky voice behind me said. A male voice. Warm. Somehow familiar.

Dear Lord. Memory Man. And I had an ice ball with his name on it. "Where are you?"

"To your left, behind the wall of the house."

Slowly, so as not to draw attention to myself, I turned. A man peeked out from behind the wall, exactly where he'd said he was, smiling over at me, there one moment, gone the next. There was no time to toss the ice, which was why he'd probably hidden so quickly. I'd caught the barest glimpse of sandy hair, thirtyish features and a tall, perhaps a little lean body. He'd been too far away to tell what color his eyes were, though I thought they were dark. He was handsome, that much I had seen.

"I thought I told you to be careful," he said.

Like this was my fault. "I was driving, minding my own business," I replied, scanning the area for another sign of him.

He let out a long-suffering sigh. "You can't help it, I suppose. You're a magnet for trouble."

"Tell me something I don't know," I muttered. "But can you see why it would be a good idea to return Rome's memories to him? This is the kinda thing I'm always embroiling my boyfriends in."

"You misunderstood me, darling Belle. I happen to love trouble."

"You'd be wise to let me take her," someone snarled from the cars, drawing my attention away from Memory Man and saving me from thinking up a response. "Otherwise, more and more men like us are going to be coming after her."

Like them—a.k.a. assassins, I thought, stomach churning with sickness. I'd been marked for death, then. Again. When would it end?

"Why?" Rome repeated.

Footsteps echoed. Theirs? Rome's? I lifted my fist, the one that still contained an ice ball, and prepared. But my ears began ringing before I could launch it, startling me. No, wait. The *sirens* were ringing, impossibly loud.

The authorities had arrived.

Shit! Before I could panic, Rome was at my side, panting, beautiful. Clearly furious. I didn't know who he was at first—only that someone had snuck up on me— and threw the ice. He'd been expecting it, though, and ducked. It sailed over his shoulder, hit the front door of the house and turned it into a large popsicle.

He scowled down at me, keeping an inch between us so that he didn't freeze like the door. "Foolish woman. I could have gone after them, found out what they wanted with you, rather than scramble after you on guard duty."

"And you could have died. You can't do everything on your own. Trying will only get you killed." I searched once again for M-Squared, but didn't catch another glimpse of him. "If you hurt him," I called to Memory Man, "I will hate you forever."

No response.

Rome eyed me strangely. "Hit your head?"

I didn't reply. He ignored my questions at times. I'd ignore his. "Where is he? The survivor, I mean? And should we, like, make a getaway?"

"He ran. And yes. First, where's your gun? Nice aim, by the way."

"I don't have a gun."

"How'd you shoot at the men, then?" In the distance, policemen shouted commands at each other. Footsteps pounded. "Never mind. Tell me later. Right now, you've got to calm down and we've got to get out of here before we're arrested."

CHAPTER FOURTEEN

WE BACKED AWAY from the house, staying low to the ground. Only when we were hidden by brick did we stand. And for the next fifteen minutes, we hiked silently through the neighborhood, always careful to hide when someone emerged from their home or a car drove past. Finally we reached Sherridan. She was in the process of backing our Honda out of the garage where I'd parked it as the owner of said garage yelled and waved his hands at her.

"What—" I began, only to be cut off.

"Get in," Rome commanded.

He threw open one door, and I threw open another. Sherridan screeched as we settled inside. Me in back. Rome in front. The driver's seat, to be exact, shoving Sherridan out of the way.

"You scared the pee out of me." Her hand fluttered over her heart. "What the hell's been going on? I heard multiple gunshots."

Rome floored it, lurching out of the driveway and onto the street. "Get down and stay down, ladies."

Both of us ducked without protest.

"The gauges are wet," he said, confused.

"They're thawing. I, uh, accidentally froze them." Thankfully, I'd managed to get my emotions—and thereby my powers—under control with thoughts of M-Squared. He was out there, watching. Protecting. Best of all, I knew deep down he'd approach me again. He'd enjoyed our interactions; that much was obvious. More than that, he was still determined to prove to me we could be happy together.

Maybe-perhaps-hopefully I'd finally convince him to return to Rome what was rightfully his. Because, and surely he would realize this, that was the only way to make me truly happy.

Rome withdrew his cell and pressed a single button. He was speaking to…John? a moment later. "We need cleanup on Pine." Pause. "Two dead, one escapee and civilians all over the place." Another pause. "Yeah, we're good. On our way to the airstrip now. I'll need someone to pick up my clothes and equipment."

He disconnected.

Over and over the car whipped me to the side, Rome taking the turns at an alarming rate.

"Ever get a good look at your attackers?" he asked me.

I wrapped my arms around my middle. My ice had melted on me, too, leaving me damp, so the air-conditioning was colder than it should have been. "No. Did you?"

"Not really. They pulled on masks as they got out of the car. So where'd you learn to shoot like that and where'd you store your gun? You didn't leave it behind, did you? Because I know it's not currently in your possession."

"I told you. I never had a gun. Well, not on me."

He flicked me a quick glance over his shoulder. "No, you said you *didn't* have a gun. What do you mean, you *never* had one? You fired at the bad guys."

"No. I didn't shoot those men. Someone else did."

The car jerked—I think Rome's foot flexed on the pedal. He turned his head to flick me another glance, this one through narrowed lids. Not wanting to admit to the rest just yet, I looked away from him and focused on

Sherridan, who was curled on the floorboard of the passenger seat and staring at me through the slit between the bucket chairs.

You okay? she mouthed.

I nodded. *You?*

So far.

In unison we reached for each other and twined our fingers.

"Shit. They've already started to block off the exits," Rome muttered. The car slowed, eased into another driveway, then backed out and headed in the opposite direction. "We're going to have to brave an interrogation. Belle, Sherridan, switch places."

Switch— "What? Why?"

"Do it. Now." No compromise.

Sherridan and I shared a wide-eyed, confused look before squishing together, shimmying around each other and changing locations. The bright sun was suddenly glaring at me, spotlighting me.

"Good. Now sit up and buckle."

My heart was currently in the process of racing our car. My heart was winning, and my blood was chilling. "I thought we needed to hide."

"I doubt the bad guys will try anything with this much fuzz on location."

Fair enough. I buckled, my hand shaking, and the moisture on the gauges crystallized again. I wanted to reach out, touch Rome in some way, absorb his strength, his heat, but didn't.

"What are you going to tell the police?"

"I'll get to that. First, tell me about the gun you don't have."

Was he trying to distract me? Well, it was working. That didn't mean I was ready to give him the truth, though. I swallowed, searching my brain for the least incriminating excuse. "Guardian angel?" I said weakly. I'd meant it as a statement, not a question. How many times had I done something similar in the past few days? I had to gain better control of my voice inflections.

A muscle ticked in his jaw. "Try again."

No matter how I laid this out, Rome was going to hate it. He would shout, maybe lecture me. "Someone was there, all right?" I tossed the words like a weapon. "Someone was there, helping me. Shooting the bastards to protect me."

"Someone—a man?"

"Yes."

"Was he cute?" Sherridan asked.

"Yes, but you're not dating him." *You're not going near him,* I silently added. I didn't know what I'd do if Memory Man decided he wanted Sherridan's memories of me, too.

"And you didn't think to tell me he was there?" Rome asked quietly. "I could have talked to the man, learned more about his purpose."

"He took off when you arrived." I think. M-Squared was wily, I'd give him that.

"Or so you think," was the harsh reply, as though he'd read my mind.

"I'm sensing anger, Rome," Sherridan said. "The guy saved her. You should kiss his ass in thanks, not yell at Belle because you failed her."

I loved Sherridan.

Rome ran his tongue over his teeth. "I can drop you off here, you know."

"All right, kiddies," I said, clapping to gain their attention. "That's enough. Rome didn't let me down, and Sherridan's staying right where she is." Who would ever have thought I'd be placed in the role of moderator? Usually, I had to be moderated.

"What'd the guy say to you?" Rome demanded, not allowing the subject to drop.

"Nothing." I rolled up the ends of my jeans, removed my shoes and tugged off my socks. They were too wet, having collected most of the water that had dripped from my skin. "Well, he told me not to be afraid of him and that he'd help me."

"That's something. But who was…he. Oh, hell, no." The steering wheel whined as it bent backward. "Tell me it wasn't Memory Man, Belle."

Sometimes it sucked to love a man who was good at putting clues together. "So you want me to lie?"

Crack. The top half of the steering wheel detached from the bottom half.

"He called me, too," I added. Might as well disclose the full truth, now that our channels of communication were so open.

Like a child who'd just been told he couldn't play with his favorite toy anymore, Rome tossed the decimated piece on the floor.

"Jealous?" I asked hopefully.

"Hardly."

He was, I thought, trying not to grin. He really was. His breath was sawing in and out and his teeth were grinding together. That was more than just anger, and what sweet progress it was! This was the Rome I knew and loved. A man who wanted me all to himself, who hated for other men to even glance in my direction. Sounded Neanderthal, but I loved it.

In the past, boyfriends hadn't cared who looked at me or even what I did with the person doing the looking. I'd been a kind of backup plan for them, easily discarded when something better came along. To Rome, I'd always been that something better, and he'd wanted to cherish me.

"We're being pulled over, ladies," he suddenly said. "Let me do the talking."

"What!" Sherridan shouted. "Why? You weren't speeding. At least, not that much."

I rubbed my palm over my chest, my heart once again fluttering wildly. "Think they know we—"

Rome gave a single shake of his head. "They'd have guns trained on us if they suspected. They're just taking names, finding out who was out and about in this area during the shootout." The car slowed, then came to a halt altogether at a curb in front of a sprawling two-story house.

Once again I found myself watching a scene play out through a rearview mirror. The black-and-white car door swung open. Booted feet hit the ground, and then a short, stocky male was unfolding himself from the car and standing.

I groaned when his rough, weathered features came into view.

"What?" Sherridan and Rome demanded in unison.

"I know him." And that was not a good thing! "I bet he's trying to catch us riding dirty."

"Wait. You know the policeman?" Rome asked, brow furrowing.

"Yeah. A girl never forgets her first arresting officer."

Sherridan snapped her fingers, anger flaring in her navy eyes. "So we're about to have a face-to-face with K. Parton?"

"You know him, too?" Rome demanded.

"Well, Belle was driving my car, and I had to bail her out. Get ready to meet the antichrist, my friend. This guy likes to treat innocent women like hardened criminals."

"You were arrested?" Rome turned the mirror so that he could have a better look at the man approaching. "For what?"

Rome had once done a background check on me, so he already had this info at his fingertips. Rehashing it did not equal fun. "I had an expired license. No big deal."

Now he blinked over at me. "You're kidding. There are violent felons out there, and he booked you for a damn license violation?"

"Yep. I was on my way to a job interview. Of course, I never made it so I didn't get the job. And I would have nailed that interview, I just know it. I've always been good at those." I should be, anyway. I'd sat through what seemed like thousands of them.

"Kill him," Sherridan commanded of Rome.

Officer Bastard, a.k.a. Officer Parton, advanced on the car with strong, sure strides. What were the chances I'd run into the devil twice in a lifetime?

Who knows? Maybe he'd changed. Maybe he'd—

He stopped in front of Rome's window and I was given a full, unobstructed view of him. Oh, no. Little Partie Wartie hadn't stopped loving himself, that much was obvious by the proud tilt of his chin and the superior gleam in his eyes as he lifted his sunglasses. Clearly, he still considered himself God in that dark blue uniform.

Funny, but just then he reminded me of Lexis.

Don't get me wrong. I had nothing against cops in general. We worked in a similar field, so of course I respected what they did. But people who were so in love with their own power drove me batty.

I had the power to destroy families, armies. I mean, I could fry this man with a fireball. He'd scream and he'd suffer and he'd die. But while the thought morbidly pleased me, I wouldn't act on it. I didn't think myself better than him—well, than *everyone*—because of what I could do.

That was the difference between us.

Rome opened the driver-side window and rested his elbow on the rim. "What's the problem, Officer? Was I speeding?"

Parton tapped a pen against the pad of paper he held. "License and registration." His gaze traveled over me, but it was clear he didn't recognize me. Unlike last time, his lips did not curl in distaste.

At this rate, I was going to develop a complex. Was I *that* forgettable?

He looked Sherridan over next, paused to admire her for a bit, then studied the jacked-up steering wheel. He didn't ask, to my surprise, but he had to wonder.

Rome gave him both with a nervous laugh. I knew that laugh was faked. Nothing made Rome nervous. Look how he'd handled those shooters. Not even a moment of hesitation.

"You live in the area," Officer Parton said, looking over Rome's information. "Where you headed?"

"What does that matter?" I found myself asking.

Rome pinched the bridge of his nose. "Sweetheart," he said through clenched teeth, "just because you have a headache doesn't mean you should inflict your bad mood on the rest of us. Let the man do his job."

Parton wanted to slap Rome on the shoulder in a way-to-keep-your-woman-in-her-place gesture, I could tell. "You'd do best to listen to your husband, ma'am."

"He's not my husband," I grumbled.

Rome stiffened.

Parton's head tilted to the side as he considered me a second time. "Do I know you?"

"No," I lied. If only Rome had recovered his memory that quickly. "I'm sure I'd remember—"

"We're actually in something of a rush," Rome interjected before I could finish with *an upstanding law enforcer such as yourself.* Really. "Doctor's appointment. For her headache. So if you're through with us…"

Parton slid his sunglasses back into place, and a dark brow arched over the top of them. I had the feeling he was still looking at me, trying to place me, not really listening to Rome. There was a cold brush of ickiness all the way to my soul.

I glanced down at myself. My T-shirt and jeans were still damp, my nipples hard and peeking through my bra. I appeared every inch the aroused vagrant. Rome was no better (minus the aroused part, alas). He had a few cuts on his face and bruises already forming on his hands, all of which would be healed by the end of the day. Grass stains and soot clung to his clothing.

"Officer?" Rome said.

Parton's attention whipped to him. Oh, gag. He *had* been sizing me up. Maybe even perving on me. I was going to need a hose rammed down my throat to wash out the vomit.

His pen started tapping against his notepad again. "You guys hear or see anything unusual since leaving your house?"

"Why?" Rome asked, acting like any other morbidly curious person. "Like what?"

Parton shrugged. "Gunshots? Yelling? Cars crashing together?"

"There was a shootout? In this neighborhood? Oh, man. What's the world coming to? I mean, nowhere is safe nowadays. I wish I could help you, Detective, but I didn't see anything."

"It's officer."

Rome glanced at me. "Did you see anything, honey?"

"No."

"Me, either," Sherridan said, shifting in her seat.

Parton frowned and eyed our car. "How'd your car get so beat up in the back, the windshield shattered? Why is half your steering wheel missing?"

"Fender-bender," Rome said, glancing irritably at his wristwatch. I wasn't sure if he was pretending now or if he had unintentionally unleashed a bit of his anger. "We were rammed from behind and the impact caused all kinds of damage. Cars aren't as durable as they used to be."

"Do you have a case number?" he said easily, but he started writing in his notepad. Taking our names? Making us suspects? Pretty soon, he'd probably be radioing for backup.

"Don't remember it."

"That's all right. Your name will be enough to find the report."

I nearly groaned. Should I freeze him? Most likely he'd thaw and go on to live a long life—unfortunately. Or would dousing him in ice bring too much attention to us? Were people watching us from inside their homes, peeking out through the windows?

Either way, I couldn't allow him to detain us longer than he already had. We had a flight to catch. An agent to…save? No telling with Cody.

"Were you the one driving?" Parton continued. "Or was your girlfriend? I seem to recall cuffing her and taking her in for some sort of vehicular violation. Your name, though… We called you Foul Mouth James, or something like that."

"Enough of this." In a motion so swift I saw only a blur, Rome reached out and grabbed the officer by the neck, squeezing his carotid tight. First Parton turned red, then blue, and then his knees gave out and he collapsed. He never once fought.

"A quick lesson for you girls. Block the blood to your opponent's brain, not their airway. They go down faster and won't struggle." Rome let the man fall, not even trying to catch him as he emerged from the car. "Stay here," he said, scooping Parton into his arms.

I unbuckled, leaning out the window to watch him place Parton in the backseat of his squad car. Moments passed, the job done, but Rome remained bent over in the car. What was he doing?

Finally he strode back to our car, settled inside and threw it into gear. He tossed the notes Parton had written into a heap on the floorboard.

"What'd you do to him?" I asked.

"Left him naked for his buddies to find. You're welcome. I also radioed that one of the men from the shootout was found about a mile from here. Hopefully, all available officers will head that way, allowing us an easy escape. Now let's get the hell out of here."

His plan worked. We made it out of the neighborhood with no other incidents. We even reached the airstrip unimpeded.

Rome parked and killed the engine, and everyone released a sigh of relief.

"Thank you," I told him. "For everything."

Sherridan emerged to get her bags from the trunk, and I attempted to do the same. But Rome reached out and grabbed my arm, stopping me. His expression gave nothing away.

"I thought I'd lost you back there," he said, and even his voice was devoid of emotion.

I couldn't help but wonder how my loss would have affected him. "But you didn't."

"I'm glad." He released my arm only to reach up and caress my cheek. "And I'm sorry about this."

Tingling, heating up, I gulped. "About what?" The question emerged breathless, needy.

"I can't let you fly. You nearly froze the car before I reached you and then again while I was driving. If that were to happen in the plane…"

My growing desire morphed into anger. "I'm not afraid of planes, so there won't be any chance of sudden sky-frost."

"What about turbulence? What if one of the engines blows?"

"What if I grow bunny ears and a tail?"

His eyes narrowed. "You're not flying like this, and that's that."

Oh, really? "You can't leave me behind. I'm the agent in charge." On paper, at least. "I'm on this case whether you like it or not."

"No, I mean, I can't let you fly awake. Your emotions are too volatile, which means your powers are too volatile. So once again, I'm sorry."

A second later, something sharp dug into my shoulder. Having distracted me successfully, he'd reached over with his free hand and injected me with something. His night-night cocktail, I suspected. That was why he'd wanted me and Sherridan to switch places, the diabolical bastard. He'd been planning it all along.

"Sweet dreams, Belle."

"I can't…believe…" Lethargy beat through me, spreading and consuming me. Black winked over my eyes and rocks settled over my lids, pressing them down. "Payback will be hell," I managed to gasp out before sinking into oblivion.

CHAPTER FIFTEEN

MY EYELIDS FLUTTERED OPEN, my brain thrusting into gear as a haze of voices filled my ears. *We're lucky, folks. It's gonna be cool and misty today, with a high of sixty-one.*

Perfect weather for shopping. Right, Helen?

Laughter.

Any weather's perfect for shopping, Jane.

Weights seemed to pin me into the—bed, I realized, the mattress soft and smooth against my back. At least I wasn't on cold, hard ground, chained and forgotten.

I scanned myself through sleep-rimmed eyes. I was still wearing the same clothes I'd left Georgia in: plain black shirt, jeans. My gaze lifted, taking in my surroundings. The room was small but clean. The twin-size beds were pushed against the wall and draped by soft, thick comforters of dusky rose. There were a nightstand, desk, TV— ah, the conversation about the weather made sense now—and a closet, but not much else. Hotel room, I realized.

With the sun streaming in through a crack in the curtains, it was clearly a new day. Which meant the plane ride had started and ended without my ever being aware. Which meant someone had had to carry me in and out of the plane, then into this room. My jaw clenched tightly. Rome, of course. The very person responsible for my impromptu snooze. Where was that bastard? I was going to kill him.

As if my thoughts had conjured him, he strode from

the bathroom, Lexis and Sherridan trailing at his heels. What had they been doing in there? And where had everyone slept last night? None of them looked in my direction; they were too busy, the women trying to get Rome's attention, Rome ignoring them. They stopped in front of the room's only window. The drapes were drawn.

"So what's the long black tube thingy do?" Sherridan asked.

Rome threw her an irritated scowl, then shifted his attention to a black duffel bag. He dug inside, saying, "We're across from Big Rocky's corporate offices, and this is going to help me keep an eye on everything. Now listen. We got here, we were supposed to rest before kicking things off this morning, yet you talked all damn night."

That answered one question. We'd all slept in this room. Maybe I wouldn't kill him, after all.

"You promised you'd give me peace and quiet while I worked," he continued.

"I lied. So what are you looking for?"

He sighed, defeated. "I want to know when Candace Bright arrives, how long she stays and what direction she heads when she leaves. I want to know what she drives, if she has guards and who they are. I want to know if Cody is now supposedly working for her and if so, what he's doing. I want to know why he thought it was so important to get in there, rather than simply take Desert Gal down."

"And before you ask how he can watch for all of this if he's not here 24/7, he can plug into the camera's feed from his phone. Now give him some space to work," Lexis said, her irritation showing, as well.

"I will if you will," Sherridan retorted.

God, I loved my friend.

The two women shared a scowl before backing away from Rome and plopping onto the bed I did not occupy to watch TV. Rome continued to work, hooking cords into outlets, pounding on the keyboards and adjusting lenses. Every so often, he inched the drapes farther apart and looked through an eyepiece. He would grunt in satisfaction, utterly absorbed with his task.

I couldn't deny such concentration was sexy as hell. Once, not so long ago, all of that focus had been directed on me. I knew how amazingly intense and erotic it could be. The man hadn't let me out of bed until I'd climaxed (no less than) three times.

I wanted to sigh dreamily, but didn't. I wasn't ready to announce my wakefulness. Yet. What if Rome decided I couldn't handle the situation and needed more rest? My hands curled into fists as anger sparked through me. *Uh, can you handle the situation? Continue down this anger-path and you'll set the room on fire.*

True. I forced my thoughts away from Rome and his actions. My crack team had already erected a tripod and had several computer monitors set up at the desk. How could I have missed all of that, drugged or not? How embarrassing, that I was such a liability. Worse—depending on how you looked at it—pretty Lexis was an asset.

Jealousy summoned the earth, and I didn't want to find myself buried in a mound of dirt, so I forced my thoughts away from Lexis, too. Had there been any sign of Desert Gal? Cody?

"When are we going to see some action?" Sherridan grumbled, reminding me of Tanner.

Tanner. My heart lurched in my chest. How was he? Hopefully awake and raising hell. Had his doctor called me? Maybe there was a voice mail waiting for me.

"Soon," Lexis said. "I feel it. There's something… menacing in the air."

Rome stopped and eyed her. "You don't know what?"

She shook her head, dark hair swinging over her lovely face. Her emerald eyes were slightly dulled.

"Means it's going to happen to you," Rome said. He pinched the bridge of his nose, a sure sign of his exasperation. Good. I wasn't the only one who antagonized him. "Fucking great. One more worry is just fucking great."

Yep, was he in a mood.

"Maybe not." Lexis brushed a piece of lint from her shoulder. "The fact that I know something bad is going to happen suggests that it can't be me who's the target."

More danger. Wonderful. I wanted to curse as Rome had done.

"Belle, do you think?" Sherridan's hand fluttered over her heart.

"Belle will be fine. I'll make sure of it." Rome straightened, features blank. "I'm going to check the perimeter, place some cameras in the hall, lobby. That way, if we're found out, we'll know someone's coming for us before they reach us. I want you to stay here, keep an eye on things."

"I will," both women said in unison.

Rome rolled his eyes. "You, too, Belle."

So much for my career as a spy. Gingerly I sat up and frowned over at him. My hair fell around my shoulders in complete disarray. "You take the fun out of everything."

"Not everything." He crossed his arms over his chest and stared down at me. "You gonna stay here and be a good girl like the others, Wrinkles?"

Wrinkles? I gave myself another inspection. Sure enough, my clothing was a mass of creases, and still stained from the car chase. No telling what kind of grass and dirt smudges I had on my face.

All three of them were staring at me. Lexis through narrowed eyes. Sherridan with a relieved grin. Rome expectantly.

"Yeah," I grumbled. "I'll be a good girl."

He nodded. "Good. Then you can remain awake."

"Come at me with another syringe, and I'll add your balls to my trophy case," I told him with a sugar-sweet smile. Hey, being a good girl wasn't the same as being a doormat.

His lips twitched. "I won't be gone more than a few hours."

He made it sound like a few hours equaled a few minutes and nothing bad could possibly happen, yet I had a vision of me, Lexis and Sherridan trying to kill one another amid the endless ticking of the clock. We needed Rome to act as referee.

"Shower and change into the outfit I brought you," he added.

One of my brows lifted. "Outfit?"

"Outfit?" Lexis parroted, paling.

He nodded. "When I'm done with surveillance, the two of us will be attending a party."

Oh, a party! What kind of party? And why? "Who put you in charge?" I said, barely stopping myself from clapping with excitement.

"I did. While you were napping."

I flipped him off.

He chuckled, a delicious sound of amusement.

Lexis ground her teeth together. "Why does she get to go?"

His gaze never left me. "Her powers might come in handy. Besides, you and Sherridan will be watching the monitors and calling me if you catch sight of Desert Gal or Cody."

"Like I told *Sherri,* you can check the monitors from your phone."

"Oh, no, you didn't just call me that," Sherridan said, baring her nails at Lexis. "If you did, you would be dead."

"This way," Rome continued as if my best friend hadn't spoken, "I won't have to and I can keep my attention where it needs to be."

Where did it need to be and why?

There was no time to ask. "Tell Belle what we learned about Candace Bright," he ordered, and strode from the room.

THINK ABOUT IT: me, Lexis and Sherridan trapped in a small space together. For several hours. With nothing to do but wait. I'd taken a shower and dyed my hair black with the temporary color Rome had left behind, and inserted the violet contacts into my eyes. The combination of dark hair and light eyes made me feel exotic, as Lexis must feel, so I hadn't minded the change. Strangely, though, I barely recognized myself. It was as if the dark hair changed my skin tone, lightening it, and colored contacts altered the shape of my face.

I don't think my dad would have recognized me.

Once my hair was dried to a glossy shine, I'd donned the purple push-up bra and equally purple thong Rome had left for me. For a guy who had been over-the-edge furious when M-Squared bought me lingerie, he seemed to have no problem buying it for me himself.

After that, I'd shimmied into the Band-Aid, a.k.a. dress. It was skintight, a daring mix of blue and purple, and hit just below my ass, reminding me of the skirt Sherridan had made me wear the other day. Were we headed to a costume party?

Feeling naked in the outfit, I had applied a layer (or

two) of makeup. On my feet were black leather boots with six-inch heels.

I looked easy. Or expensive. Either way, men would expect to saddle me up and take me for a wild ride. Sherridan approved. Lexis did not.

Oh, and get this. While I was turning myself into a lady of the night, the wedding-dress shop called to confirm my appointment the following day. Apparently, the woman I'd last spoken to hadn't rescheduled me as she'd promised. So I'd had to cancel in front of Lexis, who had whistled under her breath for a good ten minutes afterward.

Even though I was once again working with Rome, my life was still crumbling around me.

Now Sherridan and I sat at the desk and pretended to play chess, even though neither one of us knew how. (Lexis had brought the game for her and Rome. Bitch.) Between moves, Sherridan threw questions at Lexis and I studied the monitors.

Lexis stood in front of the window, watching the day pass through the lens of Rome's telescope.

"Now would be a good time to tell me what you learned about Candace," I said during a lull in my conversation with Sherridan. The other times I'd asked, Lexis had told me she needed to concentrate, that she might have found something. She hadn't.

Now, she popped her jaw. "I did some research on the plane." Finally, we were getting somewhere. "Candace bought Big Rocky about three months ago. Came into some money unexpectedly. Vincent's, I'm sure. Anyway, her first week, she fired half the staff and replaced them with employees of her own choosing. We're guessing scrims. We also think, because her power is so connected to water, she needs more of it than the average person. Running a supplier like Big Rocky, she has an unlimited source."

All of that made sense and made me feel foolish for not having considered that type of angle. "I really wish Cody had just knocked her out and brought her in." After all, if Candace was the bad guy, it seemed a little backward that the only one getting knocked out and brought places was me.

"Knowing Cody as Rome and I do," Lexis said, and I just loved how she put herself and Rome together as a couple, "we think Desert Gal has more people locked up and he wants their location before he strikes."

"Uh, Cody and Rome texted," Sherridan said. "That's how you know there are more people locked up."

Lexis tossed her a scowl.

"That's all that was learned," Sherridan told me, apparently deciding it was better to fill me in herself. "Well, except that Candace Bright is a redhead and Desert Gal is a blonde. Dyeing her hair is as dumb as, like, removing her glasses to switch her personas. No offense to your own fantastically colored black tresses, Belle. So anyway, what superpower will I get?" she asked, changing the subject to her favorite topic before a catfight erupted. "And when will I get it? I'm tired of waiting."

There was so much for me to absorb, I was grateful for the reprieve.

Lexis didn't bother turning toward her this time. "I told you. I don't know."

"I thought you knew everything." She tapped her chin as she studied the pieces. "Well, everything except when to quit chasing after a man."

Gold star for Sherridan. But speaking of knowing everything… "Any idea when Tanner is going to wake up?" After my shower, I'd called his doctor. There'd been no change, but then, Lexis could tell me more than a doctor could when it came to a long-term prognosis.

"He's going to come out of it," she said, flicking me a glance. Her eyes were haunted.

"Really?" I chewed on my bottom lip, joy bursting through me, almost afraid to hope.

She adjusted the lens. "I have seen bits and pieces of his life. It does not end with him in PSI's hospital, drained of energy."

That was exactly what I'd needed to hear, and just like that a terrible weight lifted off my shoulders. I might not like Lexis at the moment, but I was suddenly grateful to her for sharing that. She could have kept it to herself, watched me suffer and laughed about it behind my back.

She wasn't a cruel woman. Not deep down. I knew that. She just loved the wrong man and was going about winning him in the wrong way. Would I have done the same, if the situation were reversed? I liked to think I wouldn't, I'd even told Lexis I wouldn't, but…

"Pay attention, Wonder Girl." Sherridan moved one of her horses to a square at the right of the board. "Your move," she said.

Now I stared down at the pieces, shrugged and used one of my horses to jump her…queen, I think the piece with the crown was called.

Lexis threw us a quick glance. "You're playing wrong," she said irritably. I think she even muttered *idiots*.

"We're playing Bellidan style," I said. Belle plus Sherridan equaled greatness. "So we're playing the right way."

"There's no such thing as Bellidan."

"Yeah, there is." Sherridan tossed her a sympathetic smile, then moved one of her pieces to the left. "It's sad that you're so ill informed."

Silence.

Wait, no. I heard the gnashing of teeth, which reminded me of the way Elaine had acted during the first

few minutes of our meeting. And speaking of Elaine…
"You have any visions about our energy vampire?" I
placed my queen in the square Sherridan had just taken,
scooting her horse out of the way.

Lexis's brow furrowed as she turned a dial on the
scope. "Who?"

"Elaine Daringer. You know—" ugh, I can't believe
I was going to say this "—Draino." A new name was
definitely needed, and it was time I put my immense
brainpower into thinking of one. Let's see, let's see…
The Zapper? No, that still had a negative connotation
and she wasn't a negative girl. She was sweet and needy,
and had probably been made to feel unworthy all her life
for something she could not help or control. Princess
Draina?

"No," Lexis said. "Nothing on her. But then, I haven't
really spent any time with her. Haven't touched her,
which even I can't do. And to learn something, I'd at least
need to go near her, which I don't—"

"Great. I'll make arrangements when we get back."

Finished with the equipment, she threw herself against
the mattress, staring up at the ceiling. "You are so pushy.
I don't know what Rome sees in you."

Truth be told, all the months he and I had been
together, I'd wondered the same thing. I wasn't easy-
going like Lexis. I was more trouble than a school of un-
supervised four-year-olds. (If only the first step to
recovery was admitting it.) But for some reason Rome
loved—had loved—me, and hadn't wanted to change me.

I'd come to think he liked the excitement I brought to
his life, the amusement. I mean, I wasn't just another of
his lackeys. I didn't take everything he dished. Didn't do
everything he commanded. Well, some things I took,
some things I did. But only in the bedroom.

Was that what Memory Man liked about me, as well? I found myself wondering.

"Like you're an angel," I told Lexis, making one of my horses kiss one of Sherridan's horses. "But I don't want to rehash the fact that you've stabbed me in the back, betrayed Rome with your lies and destroyed Tanner's heart. Actually, you don't get to talk badly about me."

She banged a fist into the comforter. "You don't have a child with Rome! You don't know what it's like, tucking your daughter into bed at night and having her ask you if her daddy can come over and read her a story. You don't have to watch in horror as your daughter mists through walls you can't reach, just to find her daddy. You don't have to hold your crying daughter at night and take care of her by yourself when she's sick."

"No," I conceded softly, "I don't." And now, because of her, would I have the chance? Yeah, my heart ached with each picture drawn by Lexis's words. But… "Believe me, I know what it's like to grow up with only one parent. But, Lexis, Sunny is lucky. She has two parents who love her. Two parents who will always be there for her. And you know, deep down, that you and Rome are not meant to be. You once told me that yourself."

Sherridan tapped her chin as she studied the board, as if she were deep in thought about her countermove.

Another thought slammed into me. If the world righted itself, meaning Rome's memory returned and we ended up married, would I *want* to have a child? I mean, I didn't know if the little tyke would inherit my powers, since they weren't actually part of my genetic makeup— or were they now? We also had to consider Rome's powers. If we had a four-elements-wielding, jaguar-shape-shifting kid…wow. Just wow. Sunny placed herself in danger every time she walked through walls. How much more danger would my kid be in? My stomach twisted, shooting a sharp pain through my chest.

I wanted so badly to talk to Rome about this, get his opinion, but he might freak at the thought of me with a child. In his mind, we were practically strangers. Strangers who had made out against my bathroom door, but strangers nonetheless.

I wanted to interrogate Lexis, too, but wasn't sure she'd tell the truth. She'd told me I would end up marrying someone else, after all, and I *knew* that wasn't going to happen. Ever.

"Anyway," I said, "Rome's a good father. He runs to your side anytime you call. He phones Sunny every night, goes to see her every day. You don't do everything on your own. He and I have brought medicine and stayed with her, too. At your house, no less. If that girl even sniffles, Rome and I are at her side as fast as we can get there."

She had no reply to that, so Sherridan and I continued our "game" in silence, our pieces practically making out with each other. My mind continued to swirl, though. If Rome ever got his memories back, he and I would need to have a long talk about this baby thing. Did he want to have one with me? Maybe even more than one?

Those were the kinds of questions couples needed to discuss before they walked down the aisle. I'm not sure why we hadn't. Or maybe I did know. We were crazy in lust with each other, and sex seemed to be the only thing we concentrated on when we were together.

Was that a good thing? Don't get me wrong, that kind of passion was a must for any romantic relationship. But what kind of things did we have in common, aside from our powers and PSI? He liked action-adventure movies (when he wasn't critiquing them and telling me "that could never happen"). I liked romantic comedies. Well, he pretended not to like those, but it was really only his tears during those black moments that he hated. He listened to crappy classical music—I know, it had surprised me, too—and I listened to rock.

Depression settled heavily on my shoulders. What if Rome's memory returned, but we realized we were never meant to be together? Not like I'd done any planning of said wedding lately, anyway. I didn't have a dress, hadn't ordered invitations yet, hadn't reserved a church.

Was all of this an omen?

Had Lexis been right, after all? In the end, would Rome walk away from me? Would I marry someone else? I wondered, no longer quite so confident that it couldn't happen.

I swallowed bile. Felt tears burn my eyes. *Stop it! If you cry, you'll ruin Rome's equipment—not to mention the outfit he bought you.*

"Speaking of Rome, where is he?" Lexis asked on a sigh, distracting me. "I'm worried about him."

I was beginning to worry, myself. By now, Rome had been gone three hours. "A few" equaled no more than two in my book. I wiped my eyes with the back of my wrist, saying, "Still have that brooding feeling?"

"Yes, but it's not about him."

Was she trying to convince me? Or herself? Could he be— No. No, I couldn't think like that.

But the tears returned, faster, hotter, my mind so used to painting the blackest picture. I forced them to slow, then stop, turning my mind to happy thoughts. I had a party to attend. What kind of party, I still didn't know. What I'd do there, I didn't know either. What I did know was that my current state of mind would not help the case in any way. And the party *would* be for the case. Otherwise, Rome would not take me to it.

At the door, there was a slide, a click and a whoosh. Rome strode inside the room. All three of us sat at instant attention, our focus riveted on him. He had soot on his cheeks and his pants were ripped. He was panting and sweating, as if he'd been running.

I jolted to my feet, meaning to race to him, wrap him in my arms, but managed to stop myself in time. "Everything okay?"

His gaze raked over me, pupils thinning, elongating. His hands fisted. Imagining them in my newly dark hair, perhaps? Under that intense scrutiny, my nipples hardened and my legs trembled. My blood heated. Even though he might very well be turned on because I now looked liked Lexis.

Ouch.

I was back to wanting to kill him.

"Everything's…lovely. I decided to test Big Rocky's security and see how many guards would come running if one of their alarms was blown from the inside."

I didn't want to contemplate how he'd gotten an alarm to blow. "And how many was that?" We hadn't noticed anything on the monitors.

"A lot. But I did manage to get a camera in there." His gaze shifted to Lexis. "Get Sunny on the phone. I want to talk to her just in case we aren't able to make calls later on."

Just in case things got complicated, he meant.

A few minutes later, Lexis was laughing with her little girl and my chest was aching again. After she said her goodbyes, she handed the phone to Rome.

He was already smiling as he sat on the edge of the bed. "How's my ray of sunshine?"

The ache spread, deepened.

They spoke of cartoons and Sunny's uncle—Rome's brother—who watched her while her parents were away.

They laughed about a booboo Sunny had gotten while riding her bike. They argued about Sunny practicing her ability to mist through inanimate objects. But then Rome frowned. "I know I promised, honey, but now is not a good time. Fine, all right, you win. You always do. She's right here," he said. "Hang on." Hesitantly, he handed the phone to me.

I gripped it, hating how stiff my knuckles were, how trembly my chin was, and said, "Hey, baby girl. How are you?"

"I miss everyone." There was a pout in her sweet five-year-old voice. "I want to see you."

"I'll come by the moment I'm back in town. Swear."

"When?"

"A week," I said, giving myself ample time.

"Two days. Did you not hear how much I miss you?"

My lips curled into a grin. Always a bargainer, this one. But then my gaze caught on Lexis, who was twisting the comforter of the bed so tightly the material would surely unravel. "*Two* weeks. And I miss you, too."

She sighed. "You still don't know how this works. You're supposed to say five days and I'm supposed to say four and then you're supposed to say we have a deal. Daddy'll have to teach you how to do it, I guess."

My cheeks colored as I remembered the last time Rome had tried to teach me how to bargain. Nakedness and orgasms had been involved. "I'll tell him."

"Love you."

"Love you, too, sunshine." Arm shaky, I handed the phone back to Rome, who was watching me with the sweetest, most tender expression.

He said his goodbyes, his voice a mirror of that beautiful expression. I loved watching him interact with his daughter because he was the kind of father every girl dreamed of having. When he finished, he threw the phone back to Lexis and looked at me, all business again.

"I'm going to shower. Be ready to go by the time I'm done."

CHAPTER SIXTEEN

"YOU LOOK NICE," I said, gaze roving over Rome. Not a lie. I'd never seen him so dressed up. He wore a black pinstriped suit, not a wrinkle in sight. His hair was slicked back, and he smelled of rich, spicy cologne.

Plus, he'd somehow managed to change his features. I didn't see any hint of makeup or plastic, yet his nose looked longer, his cheeks sharper, his mouth a bit thinner. Mouthwatering as he appeared, I hadn't recognized him when he'd stepped out of the bathroom.

"Thank you. So do you."

I, at least, wasn't lying or simply being nice. He truly looked delectable. Me? Not so much. Not next to him. While he was caviar, I was SPAM in my barely there purple spandex. Seriously, I needed business cards that said *Two Hours—Two Hundred.* "So why are we in disguise?"

"Desert Gal has hired people to hunt you down. I don't want to have to deal with that on top of everything else. Plus, this is her home turf, which means she already has the advantage. We don't want to hand her another one by announcing our presence."

I sighed in agreement. We were seated inside a plush Bentley—I hadn't asked where he'd gotten it, I was just glad it wasn't a sedan—and were creaking down the highway. He was treating the car like a beloved virgin, taking things slow and gentle.

My cell rested beside me. There were three messages waiting for my response: one from the pastor presiding over the ceremony-that-may-never-happen, one from Memory Man—"I had fun with you yesterday. You're prettier in person than you are in memory"—and one from Reese the vampire. "Call me. Please," he'd said, sounding oddly desperate. "I need to do another test. Just one. That's all I need."

This was not the time. For any of them. Talking to the pastor would depress me, talking to Memory Man would piss me off (I hoped—every time I spoke to him, more of my anger drained, not that I had much left), and talking to Reese would irritate me. I was tired of being tested. And what did he need to test me for, anyway?

I wiggled in my seat, trying to force my dress to cover *some* of my thighs. "Sure you want to be seen with me?"

One corner of his lips twitched. "Sure. Nervous?"

"No."

After his shower, we'd left Lexis and Sherridan in the room, but we hadn't gone directly to the costume party or whatever. We'd had lunch and yes, I'd been stared at. By everyone. I'd wanted to talk about things, about us, but Rome had kept things all business. Afterward, we walked the busy city streets hand in hand. Not to bond, sadly, but so that Rome could show me around. Exit routes, safe zones, hot spots. That kind of thing.

Now, the sun was setting on the horizon, low and hazy and violet. Mountains swept the landscape on every side, and they were utterly breathtaking. I'd traveled with my friends a bit as a teenager—excursions I hadn't been aware my dad was killing himself to finance—so I'd been to white-sanded beaches, as well as Aspen to snow ski. This was, by far, my favorite sight.

The air was clean, invigorating me. I breathed deeply

of it, loving the feel of my cells expanding in delighted welcome. "So…tell me what we're dealing with tonight, what our purpose is."

"While we were on the plane, I did a little digging."

While I was snoozing the day away, he meant. I popped my jaw. "And?"

"Didn't take me long to find the paranormal underground. They have a…club."

That hesitation scared me. "What kind of club?"

"A gentleman's club."

Dear God. Strippers, prostitutes and leering males. Wonderful. No wonder he'd dressed me as he had. I was his own personal pleasure slave. My head tilted to the side. Hmm, pleasure slave. We'd played that game before. Only, he'd been *my* slave. I guess this whole role-reversal thing was only fair.

"All right. I'm down with that," I said. "But you had better not ask me to pleasure some stranger for information or there will be hell to pay."

"That will *never* happen. You're mine tonight," he said, his voice husky, wine-rich.

I gulped, trying to fight a heady stream of heat now flowing through my veins. That was the first advance he'd made on me today.

"But you're right. Information is what we're after. I doubt Desert Gal hangs out there—she's just too on-guard—but someone who knows her, her weaknesses and her habits might. I'll keep you safe, but you should know what you'll be dealing with. People with paranormal abilities are more susceptible to drug use, alcohol abuse and the need to consort with others like themselves. People who are different. There will be a lot of scrims on the premises."

Peachy. But why didn't I know this already? I'd been

working for PSI long enough to have this kind of data. "So we're walking into a drugged-out, drunk-ass make-out session?"

"Pretty much."

I massaged my temples. Felt how moist they were. Gross. Was I nervous and just didn't realize it, causing ice to form and melt on my skin? Or were my powers wigging out again? "People like that are leery of strangers." Grimacing, I rubbed my sweaty palms over my bare thighs. "No way we'll get in."

"Oh, we'll get in. Let's just say I have connections, so we've already been added to tonight's entrance list."

I shouldn't have been surprised, I thought, again shifting in my seat. "Ever been to one of these things before?"

He gave a clipped nod, but didn't offer any further comment. O-kay. I'd take that to mean he'd done some very naughty things. "Of your own free will or for a case?"

"Does it matter?"

His own free will, then. To keep my jealousy—and my power over the earth—under control, I changed the subject. "Don't tell me we'll be expected to use the drugs and drink the alcohol." I had enough trouble keeping myself alive without them. No telling how much danger I'd stumble into *on* them.

Actually, that would be a good test for John to run. That kind of information would help me out here in the field. Too, if anyone ever forced some kind of substance down my throat or into my vein, I'd be prepared, know how I'd react. Note to self: talk to John about that, then call Reese back and schedule the feeding.

"Absolutely not. We're just going to mingle, schmooze," Rome said. "Nothing more. Understand?"

There had been a mother-bear quality to his tone that had me rolling my eyes. "I wasn't asking because I was excited by the prospect. Jeez. Now, tell me what kind of powers we're going to be dealing with."

"All kinds. Mind readers, misters like Sunny, shifters, psychics like Lexis, illusionists, electrophiles like Cody, drainers like Desert Gal and your pet project back at headquarters. You name it."

I took offense on Elaine's behalf at the term "pet project." But Rome and I could hash that out later. Right now my mind was buzzing with images of what I'd soon be up against. Mind readers—I'd have to erect a mind shield to protect my thoughts. Something I'd learned during my dealings with Lexis, who could also read minds. Misters—they could walk through walls. Because of Sunny, I knew that if you got them to solidify inside a wall or other object, they would die. Shifters—they could mutate into any animal imaginable, and some that weren't. Because of Rome, I knew how ferocious they could be. Illusionists—they could change their, and others', surroundings with only a thought, making everyone think they were somewhere they weren't.

I hadn't experienced that last one yet, but knew if I continued in this line of work it was only a matter of time before I did.

"How will I be able to spot the drainers?" I asked. I didn't want to go down like Tanner had.

"Sometimes you can just sense it." He shifted gears. "Ever been around someone, walked away and felt tired?"

I thought it over. "Yes."

"Well, there you go. Sometimes, though, you can tell just by sight. An experienced drainer will wear clothes that cover them from head to toe, leaving only their faces exposed. They know who to touch, when to touch them. The less experienced ones, well, they don't know how to hold the energy or water or whatever their bodies crave in excess inside themselves, so their cheeks appear sunken, their skin sallow and flaky, their bodies sluggish. They'll touch anyone who's foolish enough to get close to them to replenish their supply."

Scary stuff. My skin was chilling, my body temperature dropping. How did one fight a person they couldn't touch? I gulped, changed the subject again before I froze the entire car. "What if we see one of PSI's Most Wanted Scrims?" I asked. Our job was to put them in a supernatural prison, after all. A prison with better security—security designed to negate the very powers they wielded—than those used for normal humans. I could only imagine what would be done to me if ever *I* was sentenced to confinement. Since pollutants were my downfall, I'd probably find myself drowning in them, always weak, always coughing. They'd keep me drugged, too, I didn't doubt. Keep my emotions numb.

What a lovely thought.

Rome veered off the highway onto a side road. "We're only after Desert Gal. No one else matters right now."

I frowned. There were no buildings around us, no street signs. Not anymore. "You didn't lie about the party, did you? Dress me up only to take me into a barren wasteland and kill me?"

He snorted. "Please. If I were going to do you in, I'd tie you to a bed and have my way with you first."

Comforting. And sexy. But I was avoiding sexy right now. Rome had vowed to change my mind about sleeping with him, yet he'd made no effort to do so. Actions were stronger than words—or lack of actions. I was taking the hint. "Remind me of our objective again."

"To watch, listen, learn."

I nodded. "I can do that."

"We'll see," he muttered. "Here's your first test.

You're going to listen to me. While we're at the party, you are to do what I say, when I say to do it. You are not to leave my side for any reason. Not even to use the bathroom. If I'm unclear, let me know. You can get out of the car and wait for me here."

My eyes narrowed at him. "You're lucky I lo—like you." I'd almost said *love*. No way I'd say those words until his memory returned. "I'll behave, don't you worry. I'll be so good, in fact, you'll think I'm Lexis."

For reasons I couldn't understand, *he* frowned the rest of the drive.

AS PROMISED, the party was an underground flesh fest. More so than I'd imagined. A lot of men wore suits like Rome, as if they'd gotten off work and had come straight here.

Here turned out to be a metal building hidden at the base of a mountain. There'd been no signs pointing the way. One moment I'd seen nothing, the next I'd spotted about a hundred cars in front of what looked like a forgotten, dilapidated warehouse.

The moment we'd stepped inside, however, that image had changed. The walls were lined with black velvet. There were leather couches in every corner, black lace hanging from the ceiling to create a dreamlike haze. Soft music wafted from the speakers, and the lights were dim. Very romantic. If not for the half-naked women roaming around.

No wonder Rome had chosen to bring me rather than Lexis—which did not speak highly of me. I could look trashy; Lexis, elegant as she was, simply couldn't.

A topless waitress sauntered past us with a tray of champagne, and I grabbed a flute. Not to drink, but to blend in.

Rome flashed me an irritated glance and confiscated the glass. Motions stiff, he set it on the nearest table.

Oopsie. I'd needed permission.

He wrapped his arm around my waist and led me deeper into the lion's den. We'd had no trouble getting in. Rome had said, "Delta, and guest," and the pair of beefy armed guards at the front doors had nodded, moved aside and allowed us past without any trouble. My heart had pounded in my chest the entire time, and I think ice had even begun to crystallize over my skin. Again.

When we reached the bar, Rome ordered a beer. I took a moment to look around. Smoke billowed through the room, adding to the dreamscape effect. A dream-scape that made me cough.

Had I seen the club's occupants on the streets, I would not have thought of them as more than mortal. Some were tall and muscled, sure. But some were average height or shorter. Others were overweight and balding. What powers did they possess? And why weren't they showing them off? Some kind of unofficial agreement to behave?

Beer in hand, Rome ushered me to a table in back. The one on our right was empty, but the one on our left was occupied. A young-looking man in a dress shirt and slacks had two naked women cuddled up to him, kissing and caressing.

Rome sat and I eased next to him. When his hand settled on top of my thigh, I shivered. I forced my body to remain relaxed, my expression soft. I wondered, though, if there were gentlewoman's clubs where the men were the objects. If not, there should be.

The size of the crowd surprised me. "Are there this many people with paranormal abilities in Georgia?"

"Of course. They're everywhere, in every state. But not all of them are scrims, and not all of their powers are overt."

"You're new here," a man said, suddenly at Rome's side though I hadn't seen anyone approach.

Rome nodded, sipped his beer as if he hadn't a care.

"Welcome." The man's gaze traveled to me. He was handsome. Greek-god handsome. Blond, tall, chiseled, with a strong nose and chin. A savage gleam in his bright green eyes. Some kind of symbol was tattooed on his throat. A circle with something inside it. "I saw you come in. Wanna trade?" he asked, snapping his fingers.

A pretty brunette rushed to his side, sidling up and rubbing against him as if she'd been waiting for just such an invitation. She wore a leopard-print bikini and high heels.

Rome took a moment to look the guy's bimbo over. He seemed to be mulling the possibility over in his mind, the jerk.

I pinched his knee, my skin suddenly hot. Not enough to burn through his pants, but close.

"No," Rome finally said. "Not now. I've been looking forward to this one's mouth for hours. Maybe later, though."

Yeah, later—if I didn't cut off his arms and use them to club him to death first. Bastard! I knew this was all for show, or rather, thought I did. The truth was, I didn't really know this new Rome or what he was capable of.

"My name's Johnny if you change your mind." Johnny's gaze stroked me, as if he could already picture me naked (not that it took much imagination thanks to my Rome-mandated outfit) and he liked what he saw.

I shuddered.

That seemed to delight him, but he clomped off with his brunette.

Rome touched my thigh again, even leaned over as if he were whispering something erotic into my ear and said, "He's a space and time manipulator and he's been on PSI's capture and neutralize list for a long time. He's gone back to the past and, we think, placed major bets and made all kinds of money he shouldn't have. As I'm sure you could tell, his weakness is women. Stay away from him. I'll come back for him another time."

Suddenly Rome stiffened. He straightened abruptly and cursed under his breath.

"What?" I asked, glancing around. I didn't see anything out of the ordinary.

"Shit. I've got to leave you for a moment."

"What!" I demanded again, chest tightening. *You are an agent. Act like one.*

"It can't be helped. Stay here, and you'll stay out of trouble." He grasped my chin, his fingers warm. "Do not move from this spot. I've marked you as mine and no one will touch you if they know what's good for them." He gave me a hard kiss. Then he stood and strode off, and I was on my own.

CHAPTER SEVENTEEN

WHAT THE HELL?

My narrowed gaze followed Rome across the building, past a throng of people and—I lost sight of him, unable to see from my vantage point. A moment passed before I spotted him again. He was still moving through the— No, wait. He'd stopped in front of a busty blonde, and my jaw dropped at his let's-get-this-party-started body language.

My fingers curled over the edge of the table. The blonde smiled up at Rome seductively, clearly in agreement; she even traced her fingers down the planes of his stomach. I couldn't help but notice that he did not pull away from her.

Maybe he'd brought me rather than Lexis tonight because he didn't want his precious Lexis to see him flirting with other women. Bastard. I wished to God my powers included supersonic hearing.

Once I would have known he would not do anything sexual with this woman. Once. But no longer. I was so angry at that fact, I felt like calling Memory Man back and telling him to keep the stupid memories. Rome didn't deserve them.

With that thought, I could almost feel M-Squared's longing for me stretching across the void between us…him craving everything I had to give…demanding more…

Where was he? Had he followed me to Colorado? I found myself glancing around the club as if I might catch sight of him.

A waitress passed me and I called, "Ma'am, I'd like—"

She didn't even glance in my direction.

She placed the drinks balanced on her tray on another table, the male recipients eagerly lapping them up. They were joking and laughing and clearly already intoxicated. One even pinched her ass. She tossed him a grin that belied the gleam of irritation in her eyes.

Done with them, she moved toward me again.

"Excuse me. I'll have a—"

Once more, she couldn't be bothered to spare me a glance. Perhaps karma was belatedly kicking in, punishing me for having been a less than solicitous coffee wench—er, barista—back in my days at Utopia Café. Or maybe the waitresses were instructed to only answer to the men. That made sense. I hated it, but it did seem fitting in this Men Are Superior club. I wondered how many of said men would feel superior to me while writhing in the heat of my fire.

Now, Belle. You are not a violent person. You do not enjoy doing bad things. What would your mother say?

My shoulders sagged. My dad's voice kept popping into my head at the oddest moments. It wasn't fair, either. He knew just how to get to me, how to shame me into better behavior. It was one thing to hurt someone in order to save a loved one, but quite another to do so out of spite.

"Hey, hot stuff. We've never seen you here before," a male voice said.

Next thing I knew, a twentysomething guy with cute, puppy-dog eyes and a dimpled smile was sidled up to me. He smelled of expensive cologne—and sex.

I crinkled my nose. "I'm taken," I said. Kind of.

"By who? You don't look taken to me."

The voice was identical to the one that had first spoken, but it came from my other side. I quickly switched my attention—and found myself staring into a face identical to the one I'd just been looking at. Another quick switch—first guy was still there. Twins, then. I studied them closely. Only difference was, guy number one had three freckles beside his right eye, like a half-moon. Guy two didn't.

"What?" I asked, having lost the thread of the conversation.

Both men laughed.

"Whose woman are you?" the second asked.

"Oh. Uh, I belong to Delta." That's the name Rome had used to get in, so that's the only name I'd use to refer to him. He hadn't told me to do so, but better safe than sorry. I didn't want to remove my attention from my unwanted guests, but I did for a second, searching for Rome.

He and the blonde were no longer by the wall. In fact, as far as I could tell, they were gone entirely.

My teeth ground together.

"Delta? Never heard of him. You want us to fight him for you?" another voice asked. It was identical to the other two.

I gasped when I spotted a third familiar face: same puppy-dog eyes, same dimpled smile. Triplets, then. I'd never encountered triplets before. Like the second, this one lacked the half-moon freckles. "No," I said. Damn, they'd surrounded me. They weren't big and muscled, were merely average height and lean. Still. Three against one, not good odds when the one was me. *Wait. You have powers, dummy. You are a force to be reckoned with.* Oh, yeah. I hated that I had to keep reminding myself.

"Who do we have here?" a fourth voice asked.

No way. No freaking way. But there he was, the exact

image of the others. He, too, was without the freckles. They all wore the same white button-up, same jeans. And all four were squished around me at the table.

My palms began to sweat. Which meant my heart began to race and my blood to thicken. I did not want to freeze these men in place. That would draw unwanted attention to myself.

"Gentlemen, I hate to be rude, but uh, could you kind of leave?" I shifted uncomfortably, grimaced when I rubbed against one of the quadruplets. "I'm expecting my date back any moment. He kind of frowns on me talking to other guys. And by frowns I mean kills." Any other time, that sort of statement would have made me cringe. And I would have looked down on any girl who said it, thinking she needed a new man. Right now, I couldn't get the words out fast enough.

"Oh, don't send us away," the one with the freckles pouted.

"We only want to play," another said.

"You'll have fun, we promise."

"You haven't met our other brothers yet."

There was a fifth? Sixth? Dear God. "How many of you are there?"

"Eleven," they said in unison.

My eyes nearly bugged out of my head. "From the same litter?"

"Meow," one said.

"Of course," another replied.

I shook my head in disbelief. "You're kidding, right?" They had to be. But in this world…maybe not.

All four shook their heads.

"But how'd your mother have you? That would have killed most women. Unless you're petri babies?" Grown in a dish, perhaps? Hey, it was possible. Wasn't it?

Now they all four burst into laughter.

"See, we're having fun already," Three said.

Four rubbed his hands together in glee. "I love it when someone brings a novice into our midst."

"Petri babies. Cute."

"You look like you could use a drink," yet another familiar voice said. Five had just appeared. He motioned the waitress over. This time, she didn't hesitate to rush to my table. Her bare breasts jiggled as a round of tequila shots was ordered.

"And make one for yourself," Four said.

She grinned at him before bouncing off.

I clapped my hands to gain everyone's attention. "Someone please explain to me how there can be eleven of you." I hadn't forgotten that they'd easily sidestepped the question.

The brother across from me grinned—and disappeared. As I gaped, I directed my attention to the one to my left. He grinned—and disappeared. I stiffened, switching focus again. The brother to my right grinned—and disappeared. What…the…hell? A magic act? An illusion? But I'd seen and heard them all.

Only the brother in the middle, the one with the freckles, remained. He grinned, too, but didn't disappear.

"How did you do that?" I gasped out.

Before he could reply, the waitress arrived with our drinks. She didn't seem the least bit surprised that more than half of our table had vanished. Calmly she set the glasses on the tabletop, gulped one down herself, patted the remaining brother on the head and scampered away to take someone else's order.

My uninvited guest scooted a glass in my direction and downed one himself.

I took it, but didn't drink.

"We're different people," he said, pounding his empty glass on the table, "but we're trapped in the same body. Make sense?"

No. "Of course."

Laughing, the brothers materialized around the table one at a time until the entire eleven-member gang was there. What kind of power *was* this?

"We were born this way. Eleven minds in one body, though we're all allowed to come out and play at times. Now drink," Six said, lifting my glass to my lips.

"I really shouldn't." But I licked the rim and eyed the clear liquid. If I didn't drink it, I'd look like a prude and the boys would probably leave me. If they left me, I wouldn't be able to question them like a good agent should.

Question them…yes! That's exactly what I needed to do. Sitting here looking, well, slutty, wasn't exactly good agenting. Unlike Rome, who had dumped me here so he could chat up some dumb blonde, I would be a good agent.

"Come on." Eight. "You know you want to. All the cool kids are doing it."

They laughed again.

"Well…" One shot wouldn't destroy me. I knew that, at least. Still…

"Don't be a downer."

Rome might have told me not to do this, but sometimes, to get results, rules had to be broken. "All right," I said. "Fine."

They cheered me on as I drained the shot.

The tequila burned my throat and settled like lead in my stomach. Had I eaten dinner? I didn't think so, and maybe that was a good thing. I didn't want to vomit. Thankfully, though, the burn subsided and the lead turned to jelly.

"That was good," I said on a cough.

More cheering.

"What's your name?" Ten asked me.

"Viper," I said. Rome hadn't given me a name to use, and I didn't want to offer the truth, but I didn't want to lie, either, and risk not answering when I was called.

"Cool. You're a snake-shifter, then. Show us!"

I shook my head, experienced a wave of dizziness. "I'm not a shifter."

Eleven frowns greeted my announcement. "Then what are you?"

Crap. I'd walked right into that one. "Pleasure Girl," I said with a smile.

There was another round of laughter, as I'd hoped. There was even some backslapping and high-fiving, like they knew they'd picked the right girl to accost. Good. I had them right where I'd wanted them. Right? Because I needed to…what? I wanted to… Shit! I couldn't remember. And asking myself all these questions was—

Questions! Yes, that was it. I wanted to question them. "So. You boys come here a lot?" I propped my elbows on the table, hoping I looked like a rapt audience rather than the cheap drunk I was beginning to fear I was.

"Every weekend," Eleven said. "Now let's talk about you, Pleasure Girl. Tell us about your man. How long have you guys been together?"

"Not long," I said, refusing to give a number. Even though our courtship had been a whirlwind, it felt like we'd been together forever.

"Do you love him? Does he love you?"

To keep from having to answer, I picked up one of the still-full glasses and pretended to sip. The others, not wanting to be left out, threw back their drinks and ordered another round. As they waited, they talked among themselves and I was thankfully forgotten—though I still seemed to be the subject of their conversation, along with the waitress and every other female in the place.

"She's hot."

"I'd do her."

"What about her?"

I was getting whiplash looking from one to the other. A few times, their banter made me laugh out loud and I realized I liked them. They even reminded me a little of Tanner.

Two called Four a pussy and dared him to ask the waitress for a blow job. Six dropped a pocketful of pennies on the floor and bent down to "pick them up," but used his vantage point to peer up a woman's dress. Despite their antics, I didn't sense anything menacing about them—but then, let's face it, I was not always a great judge of character.

"Okay, stop," I said, and all of them faced me. "I can't keep thinking of you as One, Two, Three and so on. What are your names?"

"Matthew, Mark, Luke, John, Acts, Roman, Corinthian, Gala, Ephesian, Philip and Crunch." As their names were called, they raised their hands. I'd never remember all of them. Fine. I'd go back to numbers.

My brow furrowed as something occurred to me. All were Biblical names but one. "Why Crunch?"

The guy across from me leaned forward, the candlelight stroking his face. I noticed nothing different about him to set him apart from the others. Same puppy-dog eyes, same pretty face. "That's the sound bones make when I break them."

Ouch. My own bones ached in sympathy for his victims. "You do that a lot, then? Break bones, I mean?"

He smiled. "I was kidding. Just eat way too many Crunch bars."

"So back to that guy you were with. Delta. What's his deal?" Eight asked.

Damn. I wanted to set them straight about who was supposed to interrogate whom at this table, but instead I forced myself to smile. "Him?" I waved a dismissive hand through the air, hoping the pulse hammering away in my neck didn't give away my nervousness. "The truth is, I'm just using him for sex until I can find my real boy-friend." Wow. That was so close to reality, I could have laughed. Or cried.

All eleven guys leaned into the table.

Nine said, "Do tell!"

Six added, "Any girl who uses a man for sex is a girl I want to get to know better."

My gaze continued to shift between them. God, I was dizzy. It took a conscious effort to pull an image of Cody into my mind. Wouldn't hurt to use his face since I was looking for him. "My real boyfriend has white hair and these killer silver-purple eyes." I added a shiver for good measure. "He's—"

"Friends with Candace Bright and dating her sister," Two interjected with a shudder of his own. "Kiss him goodbye forever, then, sweetheart. He's not coming back to you."

"Not in one piece," Five added. "I heard the last few guys to travel that road were lifeless *shells* when the girls were done with them."

"What!" I sat up, my spine straight as a board. "You've seen him?" With Desert Gal/Candace Bright? Suddenly the night was looking up.

One nodded. "His name's Cody, right, and he's got a thing for electricity? Well, he just started working for Big

Rocky, where we work, and Candace, our boss, noticed him right away."

Cody, huh? He'd used his real name, even though his message had said he was going in undercover. He could have changed his last name, I supposed, but how many electophiles with the first name Cody were out there? Not many. Dare I say just one?

With that small amount of info, Candace could easily learn he worked for PSI. If that happened…

"Candace called him into her office for a private meeting. Then she left and her sister showed up. They had a private meeting, too. But theirs didn't just last an hour, if you know what I mean."

At that, I forced myself to scowl. One question was now answered. Candace was passing Desert Gal off as her "sister." "So where is this Candace Bright? Where's her sister? I'll fight them both for him. He's my man, and I don't give up what's mine." A lesson Lexis really should have learned by now, I thought darkly.

Just like that, two of the guys disappeared.

"Trust me," Four said, patting me on the shoulder, "they're bad news. Don't mess with them. Forget you had a man."

Three others disappeared.

They were *that* scared of the woman? "Hey, don't leave! I have more questions."

Another vanished.

Number One leaned toward me, those freckles seemingly darker than before. "Meet me at the Holland Hotel. I'll get a room. You just show up at nine tomorrow night and ask the front desk for Matthew Brooks. Maybe I can help."

"But I—"

"Just make sure you ditch your sex puppet. He comes,

I'll tell you nothing." With that, he pushed to his feet. The rest of the boys disappeared, too. Or rather, they got to their feet and walked into One's body.

Without them surrounding me, I was suddenly given a clear view of Rome. He stalked to my table and glared down at me.

One saw him and beat a hasty retreat.

I didn't apologize, didn't explain my actions. And he didn't immediately demand to know who I'd been talking to. Because he didn't care? Because he was too pissed? I'd disobeyed his orders, after all. "Where's your blonde?"

He flashed his teeth as he fell into the seat beside me. His hair was mussed, I noticed, and his clothing wrinkled.

I gasped. "Have you—"

"No," he snapped. "I haven't. Were you…drinking?" The last emerged incredulous.

"Yes. I caved under peer pressure, what can I say?"

"You're sorry, to start." He scrubbed a hand down his face.

"I'm not the one who stomped away for a make-out session with the Fembot. What's her power, anyway? Inducing sexual comas?"

He pinned me with a hard stare. "She's an employee of Big Rocky. I hacked into their HR files earlier and recognized her from her photo. I flirted with her a little, hinted about needing a job, but couldn't get her to give me any details of what goes on at Big Rocky HQ or what Desert Gal's role might be."

"Maybe she couldn't talk with your tongue down her throat," I suggested helpfully.

"Nothing happened." He turned away from me, jaw tightening. "You have my word."

"Yeah. Right. Look at you! You're like the poster child of Men Who Have Just Been Making Out."

"She had her hands on me, I can't deny that. But I didn't let it go anywhere."

"Yeah. Right," I repeated.

"Look, if you must know, you're the only woman I get hard for anymore. And it's driving me insane! Why else do you think I left you behind to talk to her? My attraction to you would have been obvious."

"Whatever," I said, but thought, *Thank God. He's mine, he's mine, he's mine.*

"Damn it, this entire night was a waste."

"No, it wasn't. While you were striking out with Blondie, I found out Cody is supposedly dating Desert Gal. But using his real name. Why would he do that? Anyway, she noticed him at work and decided she liked what she saw. Oh, and Candace Bright claims Desert Gal is her sister."

Rome's attention whipped back to me. "How do you know all that? From the men you were talking to? The men you should have sent packing?"

I almost smiled. He wore jealousy so beautifully. "That's right. Those men. You're not the only one who can flirt for information."

His eyes narrowed but he ignored the gibe. "When an agent goes undercover as himself, he *wants* his targets to know who he is so he can pretend to switch sides."

Ah. Excellent strategy. As commander, I'd take full credit.

"Learn anything else?" he asked.

"Just that I'm better at extracting information than you are."

Gradually, his hard features softened. "Funny."

"And yet true. Those guys want to meet with me. Alone. They say they can help me."

"You're not meeting them alone."

"Duh."

A sigh. "What am I going to do with you?"

Maybe it was the alcohol, but I heard myself say, "I can think of one thing."

Rome's nostrils flared, his pupils dilated. But rather than lean over and kiss me, he pushed to his feet, dragging me with him. "Trying to seduce me? Well, your timing sucks, you know that? I'm going to have you. I've warned you already. But once I've got you, neither of us will be getting out of bed for a long, long time. Which means we have to wait until this case is closed. So let's mingle like we came here to do and see if we can learn anything else."

CHAPTER EIGHTEEN

"SOMETHING'S WRONG," Rome said a few hours later as he parked at the convenience store across the street from our hotel. He stared over at the bustling parking lot, expression absorbed, body tense.

My gaze roved the cars, the people walking about, but I saw nothing out of the ordinary. "What?"

"Don't know. Stay here and guard the car. I've got equipment in here that I don't want in the wrong hands."

I wasn't given a chance to reply. He was out of the car and a shadow of the night before I could get out a single word. Damn it! I could help him. I could (possibly) save him—if necessary. Instead, he'd left me here. Alone. Again.

Damn *him*, actually. I was the only one who'd learned anything at the club. Mingling after the Bible brothers left had done us no good. We hadn't been ignored, but we hadn't met anyone who'd told us anything relevant, either.

So badly I wanted to get out of the car and stomp after him. But I didn't know what was going on, what I'd walk into or if I'd just place myself in the line of fire and hinder Rome. Besides, the car apparently needed guarding. I couldn't see any of the equipment Rome had mentioned, but I stayed put. If he ever pulled this shit again, though... I banged a fist into the dash, watching the night, waiting.

Half an hour later, I was on edge, pissed and looking to destroy someone. How many times in one night did Rome think he could abandon me without repercussion? I had a feeling the tequila still flowing through my blood was the only thing that kept me from shooting actual flames.

Finally, Rome reentered the car. He had a new cut on his cheek, the blood already drying. My anger instantly died, concern taking its place.

"Are you okay?"

As usual, he ignored my question. "There were armed men all over the hotel, but I took care of them. They belonged to Desert Gal. She knows we're here, and that we're on her trail. Let's go. We don't have much time before reinforcements arrive." He got out of the car without another word.

My bones creaked as I emerged. The night air was cool against my exposed skin, and I breathed deeply. "Don't we need to take your precious equipment with us? And are. You. Okay?"

His gaze met mine for the briefest of seconds. "I'm fine. When we reach the room, stay out of the bathroom."

He'd already gone to the room? Of course he had, I thought a moment later. Mr. Protective wouldn't want me even to peek inside without knowing it was safe. Apparently some things never changed. "Lexis and Sherridan are all right, yes?" They would have seen the bad guys coming and hidden.

Silent, Rome leaped into motion and I raced behind him, staying close.

"Well?" I insisted, my heart drumming loudly. "Don't make me ask again. Already I feel like I'm using tweezers to pull information from you that you should be offering freely."

Rome's movements didn't falter. "I didn't want to tell you until we were inside, so you wouldn't break down and draw attention to us."

"Thanks for the vote of confidence." Hopefully the sarcastically growled statement hid my growing fear and anger.

"Fine. You want information? I'll give you information. They've been taken." Ominous words said in a flat tone.

I stumbled as the knowledge seeped into my brain, righted myself and grabbed on to Rome's belt buckle to keep him within reach. His pace never slowed, and I had to run to keep up. "Are they…are they—" I couldn't force myself to say it.

"They're valuable." He ushered me out of the night and over to a side door of the building. Hinges creaked as he opened it. "Too valuable to dispose of. They'll be fine. Cody wouldn't have let it happen otherwise."

"Cody? Cody! I'm starting to lose faith in him, Rome." The words lashed from me, blending with my pounding steps as we raced down a narrow, empty hallway.

"He had to prove himself, Belle. How else was he going to gain Desert Gal's trust? But the thing is, Lexis and Sherridan didn't know the angle he was working. They wouldn't have willingly gone with him. Which means they would have fought him."

"During that fight, he should have found a way to let them escape yet still seem trustworthy." Right?

But he hadn't. Why?

First time I'd met Cody, he'd been holding a gun on Rome and me. He hadn't shot us, had only been trying to take us in, but I'd sensed his determination to do whatever was necessary to get what he wanted.

What if what he now wanted wasn't good for my team?

We reached another doorway. Rome sprang through it, weapon raised, ready, but there was no one inside the stairwell. "Keep an eye trained behind me."

Another order, but again I obeyed, wanting to reach

the room as quickly as possible. Up, up we climbed. Only one person passed us, a drunk male who nearly peed his pants when Rome pushed him against the wall and frisked him.

By the time we reached our room, I had a good ice-sweat worked up, making my motions slow and sluggish. I was scared, so scared for my friend and even for Lexis—and only growing more so as I surveyed the damage. Clearly, there'd been a struggle. The sheets were torn from the bed, there was a blood smear on the phone, which hung useless from its receiver, and the lamps were overturned.

Rome wore a mask of fury as he stalked through the room. He stopped in front of the desk, his body as tense as a rubber band, ready to snap. "Look around. See what's missing. Make me a list." Unlike his face, his voice was calm, unemotional. "And like I said, stay out of the bathroom."

Okay, so what was in the bathroom? Gulping, afraid to look, I bent down and began sorting through the multihued sea of clothing scattered across the floor. My hands were shaking, my chest constricting. "Just so you know, we left the club. You can stop with the commando bullshit."

He uttered a weary sigh. "Sorry. I've never really worked for you. That I remember," he quickly added. "I don't know what you can do, what you can't, how you operate."

"All you need to know is that I can help. Anyway, apology accepted," I added with barely a pause. I would have liked to hear a little more groveling, but now was hardly the time.

There was a slight twitching of his lips. "You hold your own pretty well. I can see why John likes you."

A compliment? For me? *Do not act like a gooey lovebird. Get back to work.* "Maybe we're wrong. Maybe the girls did escape. Maybe, like I first thought, they're hiding, waiting for us. A messy room doesn't equate with kidnapping."

"You're right." Rome kept his back to me as he tossed a photo in my direction. "But this does."

The small square landed with a whoosh in front of me, and I had to flip it over to see the actual snapshot. A gasp escaped me. There they were, Sherridan and Lexis lying on the bed, bound and gagged. "Are they—"

"Like I told you, they'll be fine." *For now* echoed unsaid between us. "Cody took the picture. I'm sure of it. The man loves his Polaroids."

That, I knew firsthand. "A Polaroid doesn't prove anything. And why didn't you show this to me sooner?"

"Just found it. And look at the marks on the wall."

My eyes zeroed in on the wall in question and sure enough, there were tiny white circles gleaming from the shadows. Circles that could be sparks. Sparks an electrophile might emit. "So Cody is indeed dating Desert Gal and gave our team to her to prove his affection," I whispered. "What if he forgets this is a mission and really starts to fall for her? Sometimes playing pretend leads to real feelings. What if—"

"That's not going to happen. Like I said, he'll make sure they're safe. He clearly thought this was the best and fastest course of action." Every word Rome uttered was laced with more fury. "But damn it, I would have liked to warn the girls. They were probably scared, confused. I should have checked my fucking phone!" He slammed his fist into the wall, leaving a hole. Plumes of plaster dusted the area, forming a white cloud around him.

I must have aspirated some of that plaster into my lungs, because there was a tickle in the back of my throat. I coughed as I stuffed the photograph in my bra for safekeeping.

Finally Rome turned to me. Shame coated his beautiful features, all the more potent because it was mixed with fury and helplessness, the latter of which I'd never seen from him before.

"Sorry for the outburst," he muttered.

"Don't worry about it." I lifted one of the shirts from the floor and clutched it to my chest. The material was white, cotton and baggy. Sherridan's pj's. Tears filled my eyes. "And don't blame yourself. You're only one man. You can't do everything."

"Do you blame me?"

"No! You know better."

"Do I?" He sounded sad now, lost. But he scrubbed a hand down his face, seemingly washing away the vulnerability. "I should have told them what to do if this sort of situation arose."

I hated seeing Rome like this, so torn up inside. It compounded *my* emotions, made them all the more volatile. "Lexis has worked in the field before. Besides, she's a powerful psychic," I reminded him. "She had that earlier sense of foreboding. She would have planned for something. And Sherridan may not be a trained agent, but she's a fighter. No one can keep her down."

"You're right. I know you're right. That doesn't make it any less frustrating, though."

We finished our search of the room in silence. And yes, I admit it. I finally worked up the courage to peek in the bathroom—and promptly wished to God I hadn't.

There was a man in our bathtub. A man I didn't recognize, but nonetheless felt sick about seeing so still. So…dead. He'd been completely drained of water. His cheekbones were sunken, his skin papery thin, yellowish and flaking.

What a sad, terrible way to die. And completely unnecessary since I could only surmise Desert Bitch had left him for us to find as a warning. *Cross me, and this is what will happen to your friends, to you.*

My hands clenched at my sides. "Did you tell Cody where we were staying?" I asked Rome. Knowing Rome, he'd feel responsible for this death, as well, if he had.

"No. I didn't tell him."

Good. But did that mean Cody had had to dig for the information or… A terrifying prospect hit me. What if there was a leak at PSI? What if that's how he'd found out?

"Anything missing?" Rome asked, jerking me from my musings.

Ponder it later. "Just their purses, which have their IDs, makeup most likely, and business cards for Sherridan." She was a Realtor. Not that she'd sold any houses lately. She'd been spending too much time in her Happy Place, dreaming of superpowers. Dreams that had brought her here. *Who are you kidding?* You *brought her here. You should have protected her, not enabled her misguided fantasy.* "I don't know exactly what clothing they brought, so I'm not sure if any of it was taken. Their toiletries are here, though."

"Anything of yours taken?"

I shook my head. Except for what I had in my purse, all of my stuff was in my bag and my bag was in the corner. Why had they left it?

"Good. Let's go," Rome said, and motioned me to the door.

I padded across the room and bent down to grab the duffel, but Rome stalked to my side and gripped my arm, stilling me. Silent, he shook his head. I opened my mouth to ask what was going on, but he gave another of those head shakes.

O-kay. We were leaving empty-handed, it seemed.

His grip remaining firm, he ushered me to the door and into the hallway. As he shut the door behind us, he leaned down and whispered, "They probably placed tracking chips on your clothes."

My eyes widened. Of course.

"Assume we're being watched. Say nothing. *Do* nothing without my permission."

This time, the permission thing didn't bother me. This man knew what he was doing. I didn't. One day I would, though, I vowed. One day soon.

When I'd first been recruited to be an agent, I hadn't really wanted the job. Okay, a part of me had still craved the excitement. But mostly, I'd agreed for Rome. To protect his daughter, he'd wanted out, so I'd traded myself, taking his position as my own.

Because he loved me, he hadn't wanted to leave me at PSI without him. He'd shocked me by changing his plans and staying on, asking only that I help him safeguard Sunny. Well, that, and love him always.

I'd considered before but truly accepted now that I'd kind of coasted through the job all these months, doing what was required of me, but nothing extra. Nothing above and beyond. I hadn't really trained like I should have, hadn't hunted Desert Gal like I should have. I'd put myself first. My wedding first. My life first. Because of that, my best guy friend was lying unconscious in the hospital, my lover was without his memory and my best girlfriend was now a prisoner of a water-sucking scrim.

No more, I thought, hands again clenching into fists. From now on, I was an agent, pure and simple. No longer would I play at this job, pass time with it or place my own desires over my missions. They called me Wonder Girl, after all. I would do wonderful things, I told myself— and tried to believe it.

I remained close to Rome as we trekked the length of the hall and down the staircase. He had a weapon trained ahead of us, but he never had to use it. The rest of the hotel had seemed to drift off to sleep, leaving us to our spy games.

"This way." He didn't lead me to the parking garage as I expected. No, he led me outside, back into night's shadows. A few cars meandered along the road, their lights glaring.

I was still wearing my hooker dress, and the air was chilly against my skin, causing goose bumps to break out over every visible inch. My gaze remained watchful, circling the area with suspicion. Any moment, I expected someone to jump out at us and attack.

Keeping his own gaze alert, Rome removed his jacket and draped it over my shoulders, though he never broke stride.

"Thank you."

"Welcome. Now get ready."

"For what?"

"Anything."

Smart man. Hmm. What to do to prepare? The only way to be ready for anything, I supposed, was to work up a simmering anger. That way, I could torch something—or someone—if necessary, and the ensuing smoke would help hide us. But I had to be careful. Anything beyond simmering would light me on fire. I had to be just angry enough so the flames would be contained inside me until I was ready to unleash them.

I needed Tanner and Rome for this; I'd never done it on my own. Tanner would have warned me before things got out of control, and Rome would have filtered out the excess emotion. Without one, it was risky. Without both, it was probably suicide. A one percent chance of success was better than nothing, though.

Rome and I moved into a hedge of trees, the leaves swaying behind us. Twigs snapped under my heels, minute after minute passing in fraught silence. Before I could force my mind down an anger trail, we broke through another thick bush and a well-lit building came into view. A bar. Red neon flashed: *Pool here.* A group of middle-aged men exited the front door, smoke billowing behind them. They were talking and laughing and slapping one another on the shoulders.

All four stopped and gawked at me as I passed. One even whistled. Guess my cleavage was visible through the slit in Rome's jacket.

Rome growled at them, but at least he didn't attack. He simply quickened his pace, and once again I had to run to keep up.

"Where're we going?"

"I need some equipment, then we'll find a place to rest."

"Equipment? Other than what you've got in the car?"

"There's nothing in the car. Sorry, I lied. I just wanted you safe so that I could assess the situation."

And to think I'd been wondering how to make myself mad. I popped my jaw, my anger simmering as I'd wanted. Rome believed in doing what he thought was right, no matter what. It was part of the reason I loved him, but that didn't make it any less frustrating.

"Don't do that again."

"Can't promise that. But I'm wondering, did I ever lie to you? Before?"

"At first. But we'd reached a point where we were totally honest with each other, no matter how badly it hurt."

He was silent a moment, contemplating my words. "Fucking Memory Man," he muttered.

Bye-bye anger. His remorse was irresistible.

Where was Memory Man, anyway? I'd pondered it

earlier, but now I was surprised by his absence. He'd called me a magnet for trouble, had claimed he was desperate to protect me, but hadn't been here for the action. Did that mean he had remained in Georgia? Or had he lost my trail?

"We can get there again," I said. "We just have to—"

"I can't discuss that now, Belle. I want to, but I can't. I'm sorry, I shouldn't have brought it up. I have to keep my mind clear, focused, and when we talk about our feelings, the past, I just want to hold you, and I can't right now...."

Ir-re-sistible. But I'd try to focus on the matter at hand, as he wanted. "Maybe you haven't noticed, Rome, but everything's closed," I said, looking around at the darkened storefronts. Well, except for the bars, but I doubted they had what he needed.

"Doesn't mean I can't get in." He squeezed my fingers in reassurance.

I should have known he'd add B and E to our long list of necessary evils. "Where are we going exactly? What if we're being followed?"

"So far I haven't spotted anyone trying to follow us. Besides, Desert Gal doesn't need to follow us. She has something we want, so she knows we'll go to her."

I nodded shakily.

"Everything will be okay." He drew my hand to his mouth and placed a kiss on the inside of my palm. A kiss of comfort, I imagined, but it was enough to fog my brain.

Okay, that wasn't helping. Back to the anger thing, I thought as we reached an abandoned sidewalk. What made me mildly angry? Traffic. Slowpoke drivers. Memory loss. Oh, yeah. That was the ticket. A spark lit inside my chest, burning, melting away the cold.

"Why are you suddenly radiating heat?" Rome muttered. "Pissed?"

"Slightly, and it's on purpose. For our protection."

"Good. This will be a good test for both of us. If it becomes too much, give some of it to me."

"Uh—"

He pinned me with a fierce glance, the force of it nearly knocking mc backward. "You will this time, Belle. No excuses."

I swallowed, despite the fact that my mouth had dried, and nodded. I didn't want to hurt him. That would make me a worse agent than I already was. But I would do this. For us, for Sherridan. Maybe even for Lexis. If my anger spun out of control, I would give some of it to him, whether he knew what to do with it or not, forcing it from my body and into his. But if he burned because of it...

Don't think about that. All right, so. I needed more anger. Lines were irritating. Waiting in the doctor's lobby for forty-five minutes, then half an hour in the actual examining room. Then, of course, the doctor would have an emergency—a.k.a. running late because of a long lunch—so the appointment would have to be rescheduled. Memory loss.

Flames broke out over my fingers.

"You're about to burst. Give some to me, Belle."

"No, not yet. I can handle this." Memory loss. The flames spread, licking up my wrists. Shit. I had to stop thinking the words *memory loss.* The fire spread to my armpits and Rome yelped and jumped away from me. Damn it! *Okay, calm down. Happy thoughts now.*

"Belle," he growled. "Do it. Now."

"We're not at that point yet. I can calm on my own." Ice cream. Memory loss. "This isn't critical yet." Chocolate cake. Memory loss.

He snarled. Stomped to me. Grabbed my shoulder despite the heat I radiated and shook me. His teeth were bared in a scowl. "Do it!"

You promised. Memory loss. No other choice. Memory loss. You'll BBQ both of you if you don't at least try. Memory loss. The fire was leaping inside me, desperate for escape. Any moment it would spring free. Shaking, I closed my eyes and shoved the hottest edges of my fury at Rome, my body instantly cooling.

He grunted as though he'd been hit with a meaty fist.

My eyelids popped open. He was not on fire. Neither was I. He was pale, lines of tension around his eyes, but he was fine. Thank God. He'd done it. Even without his memory, he'd done it.

"Told you it'd work," he gritted out. He hunched over, drew in a breath. A moment passed, then another. Finally he straightened and jolted back into motion as if we'd never stopped.

I had my filter back.

Before I could reply or laugh or twirl from joy, he stopped in front of an electronics store. A streetlamp glowed above us like a spotlight. Rome didn't ask me to, but I pointed a finger at the bulb—*Desert Gal, my friends hurt, scared, memory loss*—and forced a beam of fire out. That flame slammed into the bulb, causing it to explode. All the while, I could feel Rome's strength surrounding me, keeping the worst of my abilities under wraps.

The world around us darkened.

Rome could see in the dark, a perk of having cat senses. Thankfully, my eyes also adjusted quickly. Before I could finish saying, "Here's your jacket back," to drape around his hand and protect the skin, he busted the glass above the door lock.

Cuts appeared and blood trickled, but he didn't seem to notice. "Didn't want you cold," he said.

How sweet. And something my Rome, the old Rome,

would have done. Was he coming back to me? Without his memories? I didn't dare hope.

He reached inside the store and swiftly disabled the lock. In the background, I could hear the alarm beeping, preparing to erupt.

"Stay here," he said. "Stand guard." He pressed a quick kiss to my lips, frowned down at me rather than pull away, and shook his head as if to clear his thoughts. Then he leaped into motion, the alarm finally screeching to life.

I stood there, my back to the store, my attention on anyone who might pass, my nerves dousing the fire and leaving a sheen of ice. I was coming to hate the ice more than any other element. Behind me, I could hear the shuffling of feet, scraping, cords dragging.

In the distance, I thought I heard sirens.

"Cat Man," I called, not wanting to use his real name.

He was at my side in the next instant. "Let's go."

He was weighed down with equipment, but raced along the street without any problem. I kept pace beside him, huffing and puffing, determined to start working out as soon as possible. It would be part of my Become A Better Superagent plan.

No one chased us, thank God, and fifteen minutes later we strolled into a motel without incident. Rome got us a room, and when we were finally inside, I collapsed on the bed, completely spent.

What a hellish night.

Using my powers always tired me. Being hit on by eleven men at once, petty theft and the kidnapping of my friend did, too, it seemed. As for Lexis, she wasn't my favorite person, but even her kidnapping upset me.

Rome dumped his contraband on the twin bed beside mine. He didn't look at me, I noticed. "I'm going to review the feed from the room." His voice was strained.

I blinked in surprise, sat up. "You can do that still?"

"Of course. I had everything recording on my phone. I can hook that to the laptop and watch what happened. Now get some sleep. You're going to need it."

"No." I threw my legs over the bed, groaned at the ache in my joints. "I'll help."

Finally his gaze landed on me. His pupils were dilated. With anger? Arousal? He studied me, taking my measure. What did he see? What thoughts were drifting through his head? That I could help, see something he didn't? That being near me would only make him want me more? Or was all that wishful thinking on my part? And where was the new and improved me? I wasn't supposed to be pining after a man when there was a rescue operation to plan.

He gave a curt nod. "All right. Let's do this."

CHAPTER NINETEEN

THE BUZZING OF MY CELL woke me. I glanced around sleepily, but saw no sign of Rome. Damn it. I rubbed at my face, hoping to kick-start my brain into action. I hadn't meant to fall asleep, had actually stayed up and helped him review most of the video he'd shot.

After some heavy-duty fast-forwarding, I'd watched Cody and Desert Gal—a woman younger and prettier and blonder than I'd assumed—enter the hotel and ride up the elevator. The pair had remained silent, not acknowledging each other in any way. Clearly they had an objective, knew exactly where they needed to go, and nothing would deter them from it.

Again I wondered how they had known where to find us. Had we been watched from the moment we'd stepped off the plane? Or, as I'd suspected the day before, did we have a leak at PSI?

The phone's buzzing stopped, the sudden quiet jarring me. Squinting against the light seeping in through the curtains, I patted the nightstand until I found my purse. A quick dig inside, and I had my cell. Unfortunately, the ID showed "Unavailable" rather than a name or a number.

My stomach tightened, and I fell back against the mattress. What if that had been Rome? Sherridan or Lexis? Cody? Tanner's doctor?

When a red light began flashing in the right-hand

corner, I actually smiled. A message! But my smile faded as I pressed the series of buttons and the message played for me. "Belle, I need you. Please call me back." Reese the vampire. Again. What the hell was wrong with him?

I was just about to jab my finger into the call-back button when my phone began another round of buzzing. I pressed *Talk,* moving faster than I'd ever moved before. "This is Belle." My voice shook, still scratchy from sleep.

"Hello, Belle. How are you?"

I jolted upright. "Memory Man?"

"The one and only. And actually, the name's Jean-Luc. I know, cheesy name. But both of the guys who raised me wanted me to carry a piece of them. Wait, that sounds bad. I didn't mean anything dirty, you understand. I just... Damn it! I'm babbling. Sorry. I'm just nervous. I didn't make the greatest first impression, so I'm determined to make a better second, third and so on. Is it working?"

"I don't know." Actually, the babbling was kind of cute, and it dimmed some of the anger I still harbored toward him. If I harbored any at all, that is. I just didn't know what I felt anymore. How could this charming man have meant Rome harm? "So you had two dads, huh?"

"Yeah."

I had never met anyone who'd been raised by two people of the same sex and was intrigued by the prospect. "Well, they seem to have raised you right. For the most part. You did save me the other day, after all. And I want to tell you thanks for that. You didn't have to, but you did. So thanks."

"Believe me, it was my pleasure."

"I really owe you. But I want you to know I'm really, *really* determined to get you to—"

"How about dinner?" he interjected before I could state my demand.

"Maybe one day." With Rome joining us, his memories our only topic of discussion. "I'm kinda in the middle of something right now. But listen. You should not have taken—"

"I know, baby. I know. That doesn't mean I'm sorry."

Baby. Rome used to call me that—and had a few times since—and the reminder had me clenching the phone so tightly the plastic creaked. "You will be. Sorry, that is." Okay, yes. I still harbored anger.

He chuckled. "There you go, being all stubborn and adorable again. So where are you? I want to see you again."

I scoured a hand down my face. Where was I? Hell, I thought, glancing around the room. All was as it had been. Cheap floral wall hangings, two twin beds with squeaky springs, each covered with floral-printed comforters. The carpet was dark brown and probably hid a multitude of stains.

"I'm surprised you didn't follow me," I said.

"After you left, I did a little cleanup. Made sure you wouldn't be bothered by the local police."

"Thank you." Sweet, stubborn man.

"You're welcome."

"Damn it. How can you be so nice? I mean, you worked for Pretty Boy—Vincent. Right? *Right?*"

"Not by choice," was the tight reply.

We'd suspected that. "How did he force you? Give me that much, at least."

"My dads. He abducted them, hid them and played a video of them begging for their freedom. A video of them being tortured. All he had to do was threaten to torture them again, and I would agree to his demands. I would have tried to find them, but he made sure there was no one around me who knew where they were. I would have killed him myself, but he stayed hidden until I returned and willingly put myself back in one of his cages. It wasn't until Rome freed me that I found out my dads had been dead for over a year."

How that must have hurt. How that must have torn him up.

"You were the only thing that kept me going," he said softly. "So…please. Tell me where you are."

Just then I wanted to. Anything to relieve some of his inner torment. "I…I can't."

"Like I said, stubborn."

Once again, he sounded amused.

Better.

Rome's bag rested on the room's only chair, a ripped pleather recliner. Had he gone on a mission, he would have taken his stuff. Maybe he'd gone out for food. Mmm, food. My stomach rumbled.

"Belle?" Jean-Luc's voice cut through my musings.

"What? Sorry! My mind wandered."

"You do that a lot," he said with another warm chuckle. "I like that about you."

"How do you know I…" My voice tapered to a quiet, my lips stretching into a thin line. He knew because of Rome. Which I still hadn't yelled at him about, damn it.

I think he realized the direction of my thoughts, because he said, "You know how. Now where are you?"

"I'm not telling." Seriously, where was Rome? He'd want to be here, talk to M-Squared himself.

Jean-Luc gave yet another of those chuckles. "If you'd give me a chance, I bet I could convince you to tell me."

Once again I found myself wishing for a tracker on my phone. I'd just have to keep him talking, I guessed, until Rome got here. "Yeah? And just what would you do?"

"I'd tell you, but last time you told me not to talk about your passionate nature," he said huskily.

Okay. I'd walked right into that one. Was doing that

a lot lately. "You're right. Don't tell me. Look, Jean-Luc, with everything you know about me, you have to realize that I value honesty and could never be with a man I couldn't trust. Right now, I don't trust you. You saved my life, yes, but you also ruined it."

There was a long pause before he vowed earnestly, "Somehow, someway, I'll earn your trust."

"There's only one way to do that, and we both know what that is."

"I've told you. I'll do anything for you—anything but that." His tone had dropped, becoming just-roused-from-bed sexy. "Those memories are the only bright spot in my life. When you ran to your dad after escaping Pretty Boy, throwing yourself in the line of fire to save him…I nearly cried. The love you feel for him is a beautiful thing. Pure. Do you know how rare that is?"

I glanced up at the ceiling—ew, what was that brown stain?—praying for divine guidance, softening even more when I should have stayed strong, hard. "Will you at least *think* about giving them back? Please?"

A sigh crackled over the line. "Maybe. Eventually. After you've dated me a while. That's all I'm asking. A few dates. You and me. After that, you may not want me to give them back."

I shook my head. "I can't date you. I'm engaged to Rome." My eyes locked on the room's only door; the handle remained unmoving. Damn it, where was he?

"Does he still want to marry you?"

My teeth gnashed together so forcefully my jaw ached. There was no denying Rome still wanted me sexually. But did he want something more from me? No. And you know, that was a little disconcerting. If we were meant to be together, shouldn't he have already fallen in love with me again?

More and more doubts about us were piling inside me, and I hated that. "Look, that's not important," I said. A lie. "He would want me if he remembered me."

"I'll treat you better than he could even dream of doing. I'll treasure you. In fact, I've already shown you more romance than Rome ever did."

My stinging pride—pride Rome's disregard had trampled—smoothed at the edges against the force of such heartfelt dedication. "But what kind of woman would I be if I switched my affections so easily? Not the kind you could love, that's for sure."

He sighed. "Look, I didn't call to argue with you. I called to get you to tell me where you were, even though I already knew, well, for the most part, so you wouldn't freak out when I arrived. I'm on my way to Denver, should be there within the hour."

I lost my smile. "How'd you learn my location?" Had he gotten his information the same place Desert Gal had?

"When you failed to return home, I walked through a few agents' heads until I located you."

Well, that answered that. "You can't just go around invading people's heads, stealing their memories."

"You'll be glad I did. I've got some information for you."

My own agent's mind perked up. "I'm listening."

"There's a vampire at PSI. Reese."

"Yes. We're well acquainted. So?"

"He's feeding Desert Gal information."

I shook my head in disbelief. "He wouldn't. He couldn't. He—"

"Craves your blood all the time now. I spent some quality time inside his head. He's the reason you've had so many blood tests lately. He told John you need them, that your blood chemistry is changing. It isn't. The formula makes yours sweeter than anyone else's, gives him a high, and he's addicted to that high. It's an addiction he's fought since the beginning. And at first he succeeded. But like any addict who's lost the war, he needs more. Desert Gal has eyes and ears everywhere and got wind of his little problem. She promised to give you to him when she finished with you. All he had to do was help her capture you."

"But he wants to date Sherridan," I said stupidly.

"No. Another lie. He was going to use her to stay close to you because he knew you'd never accept him, knew that your heart belonged to…Rome." The last was said on a hate-filled snarl.

I—I—couldn't believe it. Oh, I knew Jean-Luc was telling the truth. He'd fought to save me. He wanted to date me. What he was saying made sense. It was just, I'd trusted Reese. I'd willingly given him my arm, my blood. Yet he'd merely been using me for food. A drug. Was planning to turn me over to PSI's greatest enemy to get what he wanted. I shuddered.

Did Cody know? Either way, I'd have to call John. Would have to admit I'd played a role in turning his once-faithful lab tech into a spy. "Thank you," I croaked out. "I needed to know. And now I have to let you go. There are a few things I have to do."

"Wait," Jean-Luc rushed out. "Don't go. I've got a few more pieces of information for you."

God, would any of them be as devastating as what I'd just been told? Or worse?

"Don't worry," he said as if reading my mind. "This is good news. I know you had to hate leaving your friend Tanner behind. So I did some checking for you and thought you'd want to know. He woke up. He's doing very well. He's expected to make a full recovery."

I pushed out a relieved breath, collapsing back onto the mattress. Thank God. I don't know what I would have done if I'd lost Tanner. He was a part of me. One of the best parts, really. "Thank you. Thank you so much. Is there anything else I need to know?"

"I…know some things about Desert Gal. Spent some time with her."

"Go on."

"Her civilian name is Candace Bright. She worked for Vincent and was my warden after he died. I'm ashamed to say I took several of her memories to give to Vincent in exchange for food. He liked to keep tabs on his employees and he liked using me because they never knew he'd checked on them. Anyway, what I'm trying to say is that I spent a little time in her head." He stopped, silence slithering between us.

I tried to process it all. One, Jean-Luc could take memories from one person and simply give them to someone else. Without touching them, since he'd never been allowed near Vincent. Wow. Two, he knew Desert Gal intimately. "Tell me everything. Please." I couldn't keep the urgency from my voice.

"She likes to blend into both societies, civilian and paranormal, and does her best to keep her respective identities completely separate. The former she uses for monetary gain and to secretly stalk her prey. The latter she uses to commit her crimes. To steal what she covets, to kill those who are in her way, to capture people like us. Her thirst for power is unsurpassed.

"But most of all," he continued, "she hates you. Thinks you took her father from her."

"What? How?" To my knowledge, I had never encountered her or her dad.

"He liked you better than her, that's all I know. Well,

that, and pride is everything to her. She has to be the best at everything, own the finest things, and, like I said, be the most powerful."

"But…but who the hell is her dad?" Could he have been one of the scrims I'd helped PSI put away over the past months?

"In the memories I viewed, she only thought of him as Dad or Daddy, so I don't have a clear sense of his identity. And at the time, I had no idea who you were. Where are you, Belle?" he asked gently. "Give me your exact location. Please. It'll save time."

To tell or not to tell? Rome would freak if I did. But Jean-Luc was the best lead we had. "Why do you want to know?"

"I want to keep you safe."

"Does that mean you want to help me fight bad guys?"

"No, but I will if I must. Anything to keep you safe," he said fiercely. "You're my everything."

Knowing someone cared about me *that* much, even though that affection stemmed from something false and wrong and couldn't possibly be real, was a dangerous temptation wrapped in a pretty pink box. Once, Rome would have said that to me. Once, Rome would have cared that intensely.

I sighed, then told him where I was. Maybe a mistake, maybe not. But Rome wasn't here to talk to about it. I'd had to make a decision, good or bad, and my gut told me this was the right thing to do. I needed all the help I could get, and right now Jean-Luc was more of an asset than an enemy.

"Don't go anywhere until I get there. All right? I told one of my friends to follow you, but I haven't heard from him. That's not like him."

"No one followed me last night." Rome would have sensed it.

"The Multiplier can be in eleven different places at once. That's why he's the best tracker in the business. You wouldn't have known he was behind you. Or in front of you, beside you. I promise."

The Multiplier? One through Eleven, I realized with shock. Now I knew why they'd been so curious about Rome. "I met him. Them. Whatever. Tall, puppy-dog eyes. Eleven guys living in one body."

"That's him. I met him on a job. He can irritate the hell out of you, but he's harmless. But wait. You met with him?"

"Yeah, and I'm supposed to meet him, them, *whatever,* at nine tonight. He told me he'd tell me about Desert Gal."

There was a beat of silence. "Meet with him? Again?"

"Yeah."

"He was never supposed to make contact with you," Jean-Luc said tightly. "This doesn't make sense, but I'll find out what's going on. I'll be there in an hour. Less than an hour." Determination radiated from his voice. *Click.*

I stared at the phone. God, what a mess. And where the hell was Rome? I wondered for the millionth time. *Don't worry about that now. You've got things to do.* I dialed John's number. He didn't answer, so I left him a message telling him to put a tail on Reese. Then I searched the bed for a note from Rome, but didn't find anything. I quickly phoned my voice mail to check for messages that had been left while I'd been talking to Jean-Luc. There were two. My entire body tensed as the first one played.

"Miss Jamison, this is Dr. Becket. I just wanted you to know Tanner woke up. He's doing famously. Better than we'd expected. In fact, he's trying to leave." A loud beep suddenly rang in the background. Muttering followed. "You can't do that, Mr. Bradshaw. You have to—" *Click.*

Tanner was up and around. I'd known that through

Jean-Luc, but hearing it live and practically in person solidified the knowledge and deepened my relief, my joy.

I was smiling as the second message began to play. "Belle. Oh, God." It was Sherridan. Again, my body tensed. Hearing her worried voice caused tears to fill my eyes. "Cody's taken us. Bastard grabbed us when we tried to run. He's working with Desert Witch now and I—"

"That's enough, Curls," a harsh, unfamiliar female voice said. "Come and get her, Wonder Girl. If you're strong enough." There was a crackle of static. The line went dead.

Sherridan was alive and well. That, like Tanner's recovery, was news for celebration. Desert Hag expected me to come after her. That was a challenge I would not refuse. Cody, I was unsure about. Was he really working for the enemy or still helping us and staying true to his undercover character?

I lumbered to shaky legs and padded into the bathroom, where I brushed my teeth—and discovered a pair of jeans and a black T-shirt in a bag on the counter, and boots on the floor. In my size. So Rome had done some shopping. What he hadn't bought me, however, was underwear.

Was that code for *go without it?* Probably.

I took a quick shower, a bit of my hair dye washing out, dressed (minus underwear) and picked through the weapons left over in Rome's arsenal. I tried to strap several small blades to my wrists and ankles but couldn't cinch them tight enough and ended up dropping them so many times I finally gave up and lifted the bigger knives. They were heavier and easier to hold. Those I fit through my belt loops. I even sheathed the mini-Taser in my back pocket. I knew the damage the thing could do. After all, I'd once stopped Rome in his tracks with it.

I didn't want to risk carrying the revolver. One, I didn't know where to store it. Two, I wasn't that great a shot.

Most of my training had hinged on my powers. Powers, it turned out, I didn't really know how to wield on my own.

I'd worked with Tanner and I'd worked with Rome, but never really worked with myself, alone. What would happen if I had to go into battle without either man? It was time I learned to take care of myself.

Until then…I looked at the gun, chewed on my bottom lip. Carefully I placed it in my purse. Just in case. Then I waited. Paced. And waited. Paced. Rome never showed up, never called. I phoned him three times. Left messages twice.

Jean-Luc didn't show up within the hour as promised, either.

Finally, I decided not to wait any longer for either of them. I was an agent, I could damn well make a few decisions and kick some ass on my own. So just before heading out, I phoned John a second time, and this time he answered.

"Got your message," he said, deadly calm. "I'll take care of it."

Reese would be in lockup within the hour, I suspected. "That's not why I'm calling this time. When was the last time you heard from Rome?"

"Last night. He told me about Lexis and Sherridan."

"He didn't call this morning?"

"No. Why? Did something happen?"

I was beginning to think that it had. This wasn't like Rome. Whatever he thought of me, he would not have wanted me, a fellow agent, to worry. He would not have wanted to risk my going out on my own. He would not have wanted to risk someone getting to me while he was away.

"I—"

A hard knock sounded at the door. Rome? "I've got to

go," I told John and hung up, stuffing the cell in my pocket. I rushed to the door and looked through the peephole.

A man with sandy hair and dark eyes that were somehow familiar looked back at me. *Because you saw them, kind of, two days ago.* Wow. Just two days? Seemed like forever had already passed.

Jean-Luc was here. My hand shook as I opened the door. *Is this smart? What are you doing?*

But nothing bad happened when the door was completely open, only air between me and the man who had stolen my lover's memories. Jean-Luc was a little over six feet tall and smelled of pine. He wore all black and held a bag. Probably filled with weapons. That was so…Rome.

My chest constricted.

"Belle." His expression was grim, his cheeks cut and bruised, but his eyes were burning, filled with longing and passion and even dread. "You look as beautiful as always."

As always. Eerie words from him, a man I'd seen only once before, and that for the barest of seconds. "Thank you."

"May I?" he asked politely, motioning inside the room with a tilt of his chin.

I stepped out of the way. He was a stranger to me, but he knew what it was like to make love to me. I knew nothing about him. Well, not true. I now knew he used the same soap as Rome. Wild and primal and enough to make me close my eyes and savor the familiar scent.

He sailed past me. "Sorry it took me so long. I invaded a few heads, trying to find out what was going on with The Multiplier."

"And?" I shut the door, sealing us inside. Alone, together. My trembling hadn't stopped but had only increased. A glaze of ice formed over my chest, my arms.

"I can't believe the bastard betrayed me. And I never

saw it coming. We've been friends for years, stayed in touch whenever possible…we'd shared stories about our pasts… Damn it! I trusted him."

I tensed, the ice spreading to my legs. I drew my arms around my middle.

Concern darkened Jean-Luc's handsome face, and he stepped toward me, arms reaching. "I'm sorry. I didn't mean for my anger to scare you."

I stepped back. "Don't come near me," I said. "I don't want to ice you. You'll be immobilized for hours. And it wasn't your anger that did me in. I'm afraid of what you're going to tell me next."

He stopped, dropping his hands to his sides. "Rome can temper your emotions, can't he? But I can't." Sadness fell like a curtain over his handsome features. "Should I wait to tell you what I found out, then?"

I shook my head, hair slapping at my cheeks. "I have to know, so I can calm myself." I'd wanted to practice doing so, and now it looked like I'd have my chance.

He gave a stiff nod. "All right, then. The Multiplier has Rome and wants you, and when he gets you, he plans to sell you both to Desert Gal."

CHAPTER TWENTY

A FEW OF THE BROTHERS will be around the hotel, on the lookout.

A few of the brothers will be inside, watching, waiting.

Rome will not be in the room with you. They will have hidden him somewhere else.

Over and over Jean-Luc's warnings drifted through my mind as I strode through the Holland Hotel lobby. At reception, I asked for Matthew Brooks's room number—618.

The wristwatch Jean-Luc had given me showed it was 8:53. I was riding the elevator up to the sixth floor and though I was alone, it felt like a thousand pairs of eyes were watching my every move, a thousand arms ready to reach out and grab me.

Jean-Luc knew what was going down because he'd found one of the brothers, peeked into his mind and then stole the memory of their meeting. At first, The Multiplier had simply planned to bag me when I reached the room, a room he'd rented just for me, then use me to lure Rome into a trap. But Rome, with his ear always to the ground, learned of their intent first and tried to stop them. Alone. He hadn't trusted anyone else in the area, I guess, and hadn't wanted to wait for those he did trust to get here.

Somehow, the brothers had gotten the better of him.

Now they only needed me to complete their plan.

"Why didn't they just grab me at the club?" I'd asked Jean-Luc.

"Because they would have had to fight both you and Rome, and fighting isn't their strong suit. From what you've told me about the club, I can assume they wanted to get you drunk, abscond with you while you weren't operating at full capacity and force Rome to come to them. But even though they failed with you, Rome fell right into their hands."

My palms were sweating, but thankfully, they weren't icing. Yet. I tried to concentrate only on Jean-Luc's words, not my emotions. Success depended on me.

First, I was going to find out where they'd hidden Rome. The brother Jean-Luc invaded hadn't possessed that information. Then I was going to ice those stupid brothers and send them to John, who would most likely make sure they spent the rest of their lives rotting in Chateau Villain.

Can you trust Jean-Luc to help as he promised?

Jean-Luc hadn't wanted to help me save Rome. That, he'd made abundantly clear when he'd crossed his arms over his chest, lain down on the bed and refused to leave the motel room.

"Anything but that," he'd said.

So I'd had to use the worst trick ever: "If you truly want a chance with me, you'll do this." I told myself an agent did what was necessary to get the job done, but I still felt guilty about lying to him. He had no chance with me.

His cheeks had colored bright red, but he'd stood, nodded stiffly and said something Rome liked to say: "Let's do this." We'd spent the rest of the day figuring out the best way to handle this situation. Which, as it turned out, was tossing me into the heart of a battle. Alone.

Unfortunately, Jean-Luc could not get close to the Holland Hotel to actually help me.

He'd tried, and had nearly collapsed from pain. Apparently The Multiplier was using some type of device that emitted a high frequency that only dogs and people with mind-powers could hear. A frequency that caused their brains to throb unbearably. Just in case. They might not realize he'd swiped one of the brothers' memory, but knowing Jean-Luc as they did, they knew he'd be p.o.'d and out for revenge when he "discovered" how they'd double-crossed him.

Poor Jean-Luc. Betrayed by one of his only friends. For money.

So here I was, on my own. As I'd feared. "One day" had come quicker than I'd anticipated. I only prayed I was ready.

The elevator stopped, dinged, drawing my attention. The doors opened wide. I drew in a deep breath—*calm, stay calm, this has to be believable*—and sailed into the hallway. Six-eighteen was to the left, so I squared my shoulders and followed the proper path.

When I found myself standing in front of the door, my mouth dried. But I didn't hesitate. I raised my fist, ready to knock. In the end, I didn't have to. The door swung open on its own to reveal one of the brothers. Only one. I knew, however, that the others were close by.

He smiled at me, guilt deep in his dark eyes, and waved me in. He was not the one with freckles. "I didn't think you'd come."

"Well, you have information I need. Right?" I strode past him, very aware I was walking into a trap and that giving him my back was foolish. But I didn't want him to know I knew what was going on.

In the center of the room, I took a swift inventory of my surroundings. Small, as dingy as the room Rome and I had rented, with one king-size bed, a mini-fridge, a recliner and a lamp that towered over it.

"Why don't you—"

Before I finished my sentence, a pair of hands grabbed each of my forearms. They were hot and moist. Another of the brothers had appeared.

I released a "surprised" gasp as I switched my attention between them. "What's going on? What are you doing? Let me go." Convincing? Not really. I'd have to step it up a notch.

"I'm sorry about this," the first said, and he sounded like he meant it.

Not as sorry as you're going to be.

"We've got her." In a snap, all eleven brothers were crammed inside the room. Good. I wouldn't have to chase any down. I heard the door shut, the lock turn.

A few of the brothers moved in front of me. They, too, looked remorseful.

"Why are you doing this?" I asked through gritted teeth, though I already knew the answer.

Two gazed down at his feet. "Money. We've got a lot of mouths to feed, and Desert Gal is paying one million dollars for your capture."

One mil? Wow. Who knew I was worth that much? Then again, as the head of a company like Big Rocky, Candace Bright must have billions at her disposal. Maybe I should be insulted the bounty on my head wasn't higher.

"We never thought we'd be the ones to succeed," one of them said. "You're always protected, always surrounded, and everyone who's gone after you has failed. But your friend Cody was able to lure you here, and then an old friend of ours called and told us where and when you'd be hitting town. We simply followed you. It was easier than we'd ever dreamed."

"You really think you'll be paid once you turn me over?"

All eleven nodded.

"Of course," Eight said. "Desert Gal would be known as a reneger if she didn't."

And pride was everything to Desert Gal. Jean-Luc hadn't lied about that. "Why does she want me?" I tried to pull from their clasp but they held tight. "Why not just kill me?" Maybe she'd told them why her mystery dad liked me so much.

"Who knows? Desert Gal's not exactly the type who likes to answer questions."

"Maybe she wants to recruit you to her team."

Wasn't that always the case?

"Now, enough talking. Someone tie her down."

Time for me to do my thing. I prayed, again, that it worked. "Do you have my friend, too? The one who took me to the club?" Apparently, only the leader had hidden him, so only the leader knew where he was. A precaution they'd taken, and had needed, though they didn't know it yet. They would.

"No need for you to worry about that. Someone get a gag, too."

"Just knock her out."

"Desert Gal won't want to wait to talk to her."

I allowed fearful thoughts to play through my mind. Fearful thoughts that brought a sense of desperation with them, as well as love.

Rome—tortured. There was the fear. Lexis and Sherridan—killed if I couldn't reach them. There was the desperation. All of us together—at my wedding. There was the love.

I was summoning the wind. Seemed like the wrong power to use right now, but I had a plan.

As they attempted to knot my wrists together, a breeze kicked up in the room, scattering the papers that had been sitting on the bed. I made a mental note to go through those later. To increase the velocity of the wind, I flashed a few pictures through my mind. Rome—bleeding, near death. Lexis and Sherridan—buried in a grave. Me—in the wedding dress of my dreams.

Usually I hated summoning the wind, hated how many emotions were needed. Today, I didn't mind. As the breeze gusted left…right…I moved my head in little circles. The air followed my motions, swirling. The bed rattled. The papers continued to dance. Clothes ripped from hangers.

"What the hell?" I heard.

"Did someone open the window?"

As the wind blustered harder, I didn't stop directing it, careful to keep it away from me. The rope dangled from one wrist; they'd never quite managed to get to the other. Some of the men cried out; some screamed. And as it raged, now pulling my enemy in different directions, sometimes slamming them into the walls, each other, and preventing them from disappearing, I allowed my fear to eclipse every other emotion.

Rome, killed if this didn't work.

Sherridan, killed if this didn't work.

Sunny, orphaned and alone because her parents would be killed if this didn't work.

Me, alone. Trying to go on without them but not wanting to.

Ice created a thin luster over my body, the wind whipping it off me and spraying it in every direction. Whatever it hit, it completely surrounded. One at a time, the men were frozen in place. On the bed, against the wall, on the floor. With Matt Damon.

Focus, Jamison. Where was I? Oh, yeah. In the middle of icing my enemies. Seeing them like that caused satisfaction to fill me. Prematurely. Because, with the satisfaction, the wind died and the ice stopped.

One man was still at normal temperature, able to move.

He pushed to shaky legs, wagging his head to regain his bearings. "That hurt!" he growled.

"You think so? Well, just wait until I show you my next trick." I reached into my back pocket and withdrew my Taser. I had the clamps in his nipples, volts of electricity zinging through his body, before he could take a single step in my direction. He trembled until his knees collapsed. I did not remove pressure from the trigger until he hit the floor face-first.

I knew that wouldn't immobilize him for long, though, so I strode to him, flashing more of those terrible, fearful thoughts in my mind.

By the time I reached him, I had an ice ball in my palm. "Enjoy," I said. I threw it down at him and he was instantly encased in a thick layer of arctic fury. Sometimes I suspected the four elements I produced were alive. I think they sensed body heat or even the shape of people, objects, which was how they knew exactly how much of a mass to cover.

There. It was done.

Sighing, forcing my mind to blank and my emotions to numb, I gazed around the room. The men were scattered about, all frozen in different positions. This did not give me the satisfaction it had just a bit ago. I was actually a little…sad that it had come to this. I'd liked these men at one point. Had even compared them to my precious Tanner.

"It didn't have to be this way," I muttered.

I continued my search until I found the stash of computer software under the bed. Bingo. I pulled out the laptop and shut it down, hoping that would be enough to stop the…whatever it was from buzzing Jean-Luc's brain. There was also a tiny black box with multicolored buttons. Tense, expecting a boom, I pushed *power* on that, too, and it switched off.

Thankfully, I did not blow up.

I withdrew my cell and phoned Jean-Luc. Only took a single press of a button as he was now in my Fave Five. (He'd made sure of it.) He answered on the second ring.

"All clear," I said, removing the rope still dangling from my wrist and tossing it to the floor. "Room 618."

"I'll be there in ten."

We hung up.

I phoned John next and let him know I had some scrims ready for pickup.

"Nice work. I'll have someone there within the hour."

"Great. Thanks." I hung up before he could ask me about Rome.

All right. I had about thirty minutes, then, because I didn't want Jean-Luc around any other agents. They would not be as forgiving as I was. Not that I'd totally forgiven him. Of course, I could lie about his identity, but I'd eventually be found out and that could land *me* in prison. No, thank you. I had work to do. People to save.

To that end, I needed to find the leader. The one with the freckles. Matthew. I stuffed the cell back into my pocket, strode into the bathroom and grabbed one of the glasses resting on the counter and a rag. I filled the glass with hot water and moved back into the room, pouring it over the frozen faces, melting some of the ice, until I spotted that speckled half-moon. My luck was holding, because they belonged to the brother on the bed. Made things easier.

"Let's get this interrogation started," I muttered, pouring more hot water over his face and wiping frost away with the rag.

Eight glasses were required to finally melt that last

layer around his eyes and jaw. By then, I was straddling his chest and sweating, but my victim was awake.

"Wh-what happened?" His teeth began chattering.

"I happened," I said. "Now, no more questions from you. You kidnapped Rome Masters, and you're going to tell me where he is or you're going to die."

"I'm n-not telli-ing you anything-g."

"I don't have a lot of time," I said, "and the longer it takes you to answer, the angrier I'm gonna get. I don't know if Desert Gal told you, but I have power over the four elements. That includes fire. When I get mad, things start to burn. So you can remain cold in your ice shell or you can feel the skin melt from your bones. Up to you."

He pressed his lips together, but there was fear in his eyes.

At that moment, Jean-Luc soared inside the room as if he owned it. Who would have thought I'd be so happy to have him with me? Just like yesterday, using my powers had drained me. And with my adrenaline rush crashing, I knew I didn't have much longer.

"Thank God," I said. He didn't double over, so I knew I'd successfully switched off whatever had been hurting him.

My victim's face was mostly blue but laced with hints of red. When he spied Jean-Luc, he flinched.

"I'm s-sorry, man," he said. "H-hated to use you, b-but…"

"But you're greedy. Give me five minutes," Jean-Luc told me, his attention riveted on the bed. "I'll have all the information we need."

Those dark eyes darted from me to Jean-Luc, Jean-Luc to me.

"Jean-Luc, ma-man, you know I—"

"Save it. I asked for your help and what did you do?"

The betrayal in his voice, the hurt, had my chest aching. "At one time, I would have taken a bullet for you. Now I'm on her side, and what she wants, she gets. No matter what I have to do to obtain it for her." He reached out. When his fingertips brushed The Multiplier's face, he disappeared as if he'd never been. Only his scent remained behind.

I watched, wide-eyed, knowing that must have been what had happened to Rome.

A few minutes later, Jean-Luc reappeared in the exact spot he'd left, looking as if he'd just read a newspaper.

"I didn't take anything," he told me as if reading my mind. "I just peeked at the last few days. Rome is in the room next door. They drugged him with his own sedative."

Uh, what? "Say that again."

"Next door." Unhappy, he motioned with his chin. "I swear. Drugged but alive."

Too easy, my brain screamed.

He read my thoughts on my face. "You'd think it was a trap, but no. Matthew was rushed, scared of being caught by PSI and unsure of what to do. He decided to keep him close." Jean-Luc stared over at the connecting door through narrowed eyes.

"For my peace of mind, keep a gun on him," I told Jean-Luc. I jumped to my feet, my knees almost collapsing, and approached the connecting door. I half expected it to be locked, but the knob turned easily. Shaking, I palmed one of the knives I'd brought.

Nervous as I was, it iced a little.

Gulping, I pushed open the door. Hinges squeaked. I entered the darkened room, stepping only inches inside before pausing and listening. My ears twitched at the sound of deep, even breathing.

I kept the knife raised as I felt the wall. Finally I encountered a light switch and flipped it on. And then

Rome came into view. Though my knees threatened to give out again, I managed to lumber to the side of the bed and drop down beside him with a whimper.

His wrists and ankles were bound, as they'd planned to bind mine, so I hurriedly cut the ropes away. He slept through it all. Still, I dropped the knife, my eyes closing as relief washed through me. A tear even slid down my cheek. He was alive. He was alive!

"Thank God," I breathed.

"You still love him," Jean-Luc suddenly said from behind me. Not a question, but a sad statement.

Gradually my eyes opened, but I didn't look up. My gaze locked on Rome, on his chest lifting, drawing air into his lungs. "Yes." I couldn't deny it, didn't want to deny it. I'd almost lost him.

"Why? He's okay-looking, but he's arrogant and demanding. You deserve someone who will worship you."

In sleep, Rome's features were relaxed, his lips soft. Kissable. Earlier, I'd thought about the fact that we had nothing in common but sex. I'd thought our relationship in serious jeopardy. But now, having almost lost him, I couldn't make those things matter. For whatever reason, we just fit.

If nothing else, the battle with The Multiplier had made me realize how desperately I wanted Rome in my life. I didn't care that Lexis had had a vision of me marrying someone else. I didn't care that I might not be the love of his life. He was mine. I would fight to make things work.

"Rome excites me, challenges me. And he might be demanding and arrogant, but he's also protective and loving."

"*I* can be protective and loving."

"But my heart will always belong to this man." I

traced a fingertip along his jawline, the stubble tickling my skin, and glanced at Jean-Luc. "There's someone out there for you. I know it. You just have to find her."

He didn't reply. I looked away, too afraid to watch his expression change from sadness and hope to determination and anger.

"All my life," he finally said, "I've wanted the kind of love my fathers had for each other. I was looking for it, too, before I was captured several years ago. Do you have any idea how hard it is to fall in love with a woman when I can find out every damn thing about her? When I know exactly what she wants to hide from me?"

"Here's a solution. Don't invade their minds. Leave their memories alone. Boom. Done. I'm a miracle-worker."

"And let them betray me? Hardly. That's how I was captured. I trusted a girl, told her what I could do. She called me crazy, so I proved my ability to her. In return, she told others and they told others and that's when OASS came after me. For my own protection, I *have* to know the people I'm dealing with, so I have to invade their minds. But with you, I already know and love everything."

"I'm sorry for your past. I am." So very sorry. "But…Jean-Luc…you can't—"

"Memories of you made me laugh and ache and dream again. I had to have them. I can't give them up, Belle. And after everything I endured in captivity, I deserve them."

Do not stomp your foot, do not stomp your foot. "But they don't belong to you."

"They do!"

"No, they don't. You didn't live them. He did. And just as your will was ignored when you were caged, you have ignored his. You have ignored mine." I forced my balled fists to open and ran them over Rome's face, gentle, tender. He moaned. The sound jolted through me, bringing a wave of excitement, and I straightened.

Jean-Luc was forgotten as I leaned down and kissed Rome's lips. "Wake up, baby. Wake up for me."

He gave another moan.

"Belle's here. Show me those beautiful baby blues."

Slowly his eyelashes fluttered open. His lips curled into a frown. "Belle?"

This was the third time in our relationship that I'd had to watch him wake up after a life-and-death experience. It hadn't gotten any easier, but neither had my joy lessened upon realizing he was going to be okay. "Right here."

"Where are we?" He scrubbed a hand down his face, then stiffened. "Shit. They got me like I was a damned rookie, tackling me, injecting me with my own night-night cocktail when I tried to use it. They get you, too? Are you okay? Did they hurt you?" The more he spoke, the faster and angrier the words emerged.

"I'm fine. I swear." I showed him my wrists, free of rope. "Just here doing a little rescue and recovery."

A moment passed in silence, his body going stiff. Then, "You saved me?"

"Yep." I couldn't help it. I grinned. "The bad guys are deactivated. Or, to use your favorite word, neutralized. Looks like Wonder Girl saved the day, huh?"

"How?"

"Is that important?" I wasn't ready to tell him I'd had help. "We won."

His head fell back against the pillow. "Shit, this is embarrassing. And what do you mean, we?" His gaze moved through the room until landing on Jean-Luc, who was glaring at him, murder in his dark eyes.

Oops.

Rome jolted upright.

"He's a good guy," I said, flattening my palms on his chest. *For the most part.* "And he's a damn good wing man." No question.

"Exactly who is 'he'?"

I purposely didn't answer. A fight would break out, and we didn't have time for that. But what shitty timing. This was the first time the two men had been together since the "incident," and we couldn't go knock-down-drag-out until everything was made right.

"I don't know why you're embarrassed about being captured. You've had to save me a thousand times."

His eyes never left my "helper." "Yeah, but you're the girl. I'm the guy."

"I'm going to pretend you didn't say that."

"Why? It's true." He reached up and caressed my cheek. I leaned into the touch, eyelids closing. "I'm glad that you're a girl."

"You guys might want to continue the reunion later," Jean-Luc suddenly piped up. He sounded pissed as hell. "Agents will be showing up any moment, and I can't be here when they arrive."

The two men shared a look as Rome pushed to his feet. He swayed but managed to remain upright without any help. What kind of silent communication passed between them, I didn't know.

Then, in unison, they said, "Let's do this."

They shared another look, this one surprised, before we all jolted into motion.

CHAPTER TWENTY-ONE

"I DON'T LIKE HIM," Rome told me the moment we were alone. We'd rented *another* motel room, a bigger one but no less run-down, and he paced the length of the shag carpet. "And I sure as hell don't trust him."

Sighing, I tossed my purse on the bed. "Well, he helped me save your life, so I think he's a pretty cool guy." When he wasn't being obstinate. Jean-Luc had come with us to check in, but had left before we actually reached the room. Maybe because he'd seen the way I'd looked at Rome—words he could deny, but a lingering, need-filled gaze, no way—and didn't want to see that again. He'd said only that he needed time to think.

I hated that I'd hurt him. With all the crap he'd endured throughout his life, I didn't want to be the cause of more. I just wanted what was rightfully mine.

I don't know how it had happened, but Jean-Luc had done the impossible. I'd despised him, but he'd made me like him. I was coming to realize that while the memories he had of me were not his, he truly was sincere in his affection. It was not faked, as I'd assumed. With or without them, he wanted the best for me.

Rome pressed his back into the white wall, his arms across his massive chest. He glared over at me. "Who is he, anyway? A recruit of John's?"

"Uh, not exactly." I sat on the edge of the bed and

stuffed my hands into my pockets. My clothes were damp from the most recent ice bath. My hair hung in tangles and the black dye was dripping down my face and shoulders. I probably looked like I'd been beaten up, dragged through a gutter and left out to dry. "Listen, he knows Desert Roach. He told me she'll have a breakdown if we destroy her pride. And like you taught me, when an enemy has a breakdown, they start making mistakes. They're easier to pick off."

A moment passed as Rome thought that over, his head tilting to the side. Then he grabbed his phone, pressed a series of buttons and faced me again.

"What'd you just do?" I asked.

"Texted John to hunt down her bank so we can freeze some of her accounts. Should have done that already, but…" He shrugged. "He may be able to do it, he may not. Depends on her connections, and where her money's located."

"How does that destroy her pride?"

"Without funds, she can't pay her associates. Not only would that embarrass her, if she truly cares about that kind of thing, but it will keep scrims from coming after you for that one mil you told me about."

"Oh." Why hadn't I thought of that?

"Now, no more stalling. Tell me about Jean-Luc. Yeah, you finally gave me his name on the way here, but I want more."

Now or never, I supposed. I braced myself for a major freak-out, fingers clutching the edge of the mattress. "Well, you kinda sorta just met—" my shoulders hunched, as though trying to protect my vital organs "—Memory Man."

Rome's mouth dropped open, and I suspected he'd been rendered speechless. For a long while, he just stared over at me in astonishment. Finally, a stunned "Let me get this straight" emerged from him.

Oh, no. He was using *the voice.* The one that proclaimed trouble was on the way.

"You trusted a known enemy, someone who helped destroy my life *and* yours, to save my life. More than that, you trusted a known enemy, someone who helped destroy your life, *with your goddamn life.*"

I gave a weak nod. "Yes, that about sums it up." As I spoke, my cell phone vibrated in my pocket.

Rome took a step toward me, but I held up one finger as I moved the phone to my ear. "Hang on a sec. This could be important."

His eyes bugged. To my surprise, though, he did stop in his tracks.

"This is Belle."

"Hey, Viper."

"Tanner?" My lips curled into a wide smile, and my gaze met Rome's. He was still frowning, more fiercely than before, so I turned my back on him.

"The one and only. How are you?"

"Don't tell him where we are," Rome said, clearly still pissed.

I ignored him, gasping in excitement. Tanner sounded normal, as if he'd never been hurt, never scared ten years off my life. "Who cares about me? Oh my God. How are you? I hated leaving you, I hope you know that, but I—"

"Stop. You did the right thing. Besides, guilt isn't a pretty emotion on you."

"Have I told you recently that I love you? So really, how are you? When'd you wake up? Tell me everything." I could feel Rome's gaze boring into me, probing deep. Imagining strangling me? "No matter how long it takes."

A growl escaped Rome.

"I woke up yesterday, and I've grown stronger by the minute," Tanner said. "Word is Sherridan and Lexis have been taken by Desert Slut, and that Rome found where she's hiding them."

"What? He knows?" I whipped around, glaring. "You know where the girls are?"

"Not me," Tanner said as Rome nodded. Without guilt, the jerk.

"Why didn't you tell me?" I demanded.

"I just did," Tanner said, confused.

"Not you," I told him. "Are they okay?" I asked Rome.

He shrugged, his expression growing weary. "Sherridan's been experimented on. She's not doing so well. Lexis is locked inside a cage. She's been pushed around a little because she refuses to answer their questions."

My stomach cramped painfully. No. No, no, no. I stood. "We've got to get them. Like, now."

Rome shook his head as Tanner said, "John doesn't want you to go after Desert Skank until I get there."

"Why?"

"Hello. So you don't destroy the world. Look, pick me up at PSI's private little airstrip in the morning. And don't tell me where you are now," he said, echoing Rome's earlier words. "John doesn't want anyone to know. Just in case. Once we're together, we'll go kick some Desert Bitch ass."

Desert Bitch, the elusive enemy. So far, I'd still had no real contact with her, yet she'd managed to wreak havoc on my life. My friends' lives. It was time to take her down! "I'm controlling my powers." Kind of. "I can do this. I know I can. Just tell me where they are, and I'll go get them now." Waiting might kill me.

Again, Rome shook his head.

"I wasn't talking to you," I snapped.

"I want them safe just as much as you do," he replied, "but I saw the compound they're in. Cody e-mailed pictures. We can't save them alone, Belle. There's just too much security. If we tried to do an extraction, we could be captured ourselves, and then what good would we be to them?"

Exasperated, I threw my free arm in the air. At least Cody seemed to be on our side still. "You think adding Tanner into the equation—sorry, Crazy Bones—will mean the difference between victory and defeat?"

"Well, I am pretty powerful," Tanner said.

I rolled my eyes. Clearly Elaine hadn't drained his giant ego.

"He's not the only one on the way," Rome said.

"What's more," Tanner added—God, I was being double-teamed—"John took care of the rat. Reese, the scrim, is caged. You'd have thought the world had ended, the way the female—and some of the male— agents acted when they learned the truth. Oh, and by the way. You had several messages at home from wedding people. I took care of things, though, and told them the whole thing was off. You're welcome. And listen, I've got a surprise for you. You're gonna like it. See ya."

He didn't give me time to reply. The line went dead.

I stared at my phone for a moment. That little shit! Just then, it was easy to forget how glad I was that he'd recovered. I'd known the wedding was off—for the moment— but keeping the date and rescheduling my appointments had given me hope that it could still happen. Now…

Chin up. He's still a part of your life, and that's the important thing.

Suddenly the phone was ripped from my hands and thrown across the room. Startled, jolting, I looked up…up…seeing Rome standing just in front of me. His eyes were still glaring, his mouth still frowning.

"What'd you do—"

His lips mashed down on mine, cutting off my words. His tongue thrust deep, his arms banding around me and jerking me into the hard length of his body. He had an erection.

I gasped in shock, and his tongue thrust even deeper. For a minute—an hour?—I enjoyed him, reveling in his touch, his taste, his heat. He was everything I'd ever wanted for myself—strong and courageous, passionate and loyal. He was my past, and once again, for this moment, he was my future.

So used to holding him, my arms reached up of their own accord, sliding up his roped chest. My fingers traced circles around his tiny, hardened nipples before continuing their journey and tangling in his hair.

"What brought this on?" I asked, breathless.

"You. Need."

"We shouldn't." Oh, that was painful to say.

"Should." He licked the seam of my lips. "We can't have you worrying about Tanner the entire night."

"But you don't remember me, and I'm determined to resist you until you do." Wasn't I? Who knew anymore.

He pulled back, only a whisper away. "Resist later," he said fiercely. "I want you so badly. I need you. I don't need my memories for that. Even without them, I hate it when other men look at you with desire in their eyes. I want to kill Memory Man. I still want to kill Tanner. He finds too many excuses to touch you. My mind may not know you, Belle Jamison, but every part of my body recognizes you as mine."

Mine.

His. For so long, that's all I'd wanted to be. Yes, I was

different now than I'd been when this whole ordeal started. I'd shifted my priorities. But as I'd learned while staring down at his unconscious body, my love for him had neither changed nor dwindled. And that he felt this strong a need for me, without truly knowing me... We *were* meant to be together. We had to be.

"We already know I can cage your emotions," he said, assuming that was what was holding me back. "I've proven it."

"That's not what I'm worried about," I countered, stepping backward. The backs of my knees hit the mattress.

Rome closed the distance again, his hardness pressing into my softness.

My blood was heating, my limbs shaking. Unable to stop myself, I arched into him, rubbing deliciously.

"Then what?" he demanded, teeth bared.

"The case comes first. It has to."

He tilted his head to the side, gaze roving over me, and nodded. "You're right. But do you really think I'd be here if I thought I could be out there, saving Lexis? Sherridan? Right now, we'd only do more harm than good. We've got Cody on the inside, protecting the women. He won't let anything happen to them."

"He's the reason they're in trouble in the first place." I trusted him again, still, whatever—I think—but that didn't mean I agreed with his methods. "He's let Sherridan be experimented on. He's let Lexis be pushed around."

"To save their lives. To gain information. To earn Desert Gal's trust." This time, it was *Rome* who backed away from *me,* hands fisted at his sides. "His reasons are for the greater good, guaranteed."

With every step that separated us, my chest ached.

"I've got cameras all around this motel and they're feeding directly to my phone. An alarm will trigger if anyone tries to enter this room." Another step away. "There's nothing else we can do."

He was right. So far, we'd done everything we could. Now, we just had to wait.

He stopped in the center of the room. "I want you, Belle. I want to be with you, and I know I told you I'd change your mind, but ultimately the decision is yours. I've treated you badly, and I'm sorry for that. I've been hot and cold with you, and I'm sorry for that, too. I would understand if you walked away from me. I wouldn't like it, but I would understand. So I'm not going to push you. Not now, at least. When this is all over…the rules are going to change. But for right now, if you decide to be with me, I'll be in the shower." With that, he turned on his heel and strode into the bathroom.

I heard the door snick shut, but didn't hear the lock turn. I stood there, utterly torn. I could stay here and worry about my friends, possibly icing down this room, the entire motel, in the process, doing more harm than good. Or I could go in there where the man of my dreams was probably stripping even now, clothes falling away from that magnificent body.

The sound of water spraying into porcelain suddenly filled my ears. Brass rings slid against a metal rod as the shower curtain was swept aside. I began shaking. Heating. Preparing for Rome, only Rome.

Why are you standing here? Go get your man! We weren't promised a tomorrow. We only had here, now.

Just like that, my decision was made.

Determined, I marched to the bathroom and flung open the door. Fragrant steam wafted around me, and a moment passed before I was able to make out Rome's silhouette in the shower.

Without a word, I began stripping. My clothes, my

weapons. Those clanged against the tile. Moisture beaded on my skin, and desire flooded between my legs. I had missed this man. I loved this man. I would have this man.

I threw back the clear curtain. Rome was facing me, waiting. Naked. Hard. Soap bubbles were scattered over his chest and arms, his legs long and muscled, his penis as deliciously thick as I remembered.

"Thank God," he said, piercing me with his gaze. Then that gaze slid to the bathroom floor and the weapons scattered about. He grinned, tender, aroused and amused all at once. "I knew you were armed, but I had no idea how much. Why does that turn me the hell on?"

"You're warped." But then, so was I. Calves trembling, I stepped inside. Instantly warm water rained over me. My nipples hardened, my stomach quivered.

"And you're going to come, over and over again." He closed all hint of distance, hot, wet, and his arms wrapped around me. I knew we were an interesting contrast: his sun-kissed skin, my olive-toned. His black hair, my honey-colored. No, wait. My hair was also black. Well, streaked with black, since so much of the dye had already dripped off me.

"So are you," I said. "Going to come, I mean."

"Ladies first." His lips smashed over mine. Instantly our tongues dueled, rolling against each other. His skin was slick but soon mine was slicker, making for easy friction.

One of his palms settled on my breast, kneading. I felt a lance of pleasure dive straight between my legs. Felt a flame light inside me, growing, blossoming.

Rome must have felt it, too, because he said, "I've got it. I've got it."

As I allowed the fire to flow out of me, mingling with my breath, and into him, flowing down his lungs, binding us, I rubbed myself against his thick length.

He moaned. "Again. Do that again."

I arched, sliding up…down… This time, we moaned in unison.

"I missed this so much," I said.

He cupped my face, backing me up and pressing me against the cold tile. "Shit, you're beautiful. How have I kept my hands off you?"

"You aren't always the sharpest tool in the shed. Now tell me more about me."

He chuckled softly, his gaze perusing me. "My pleasure. Your nipples are like berries. Your waist perfectly flared. Your legs go on for miles and, damn, the core of you…" Two of his fingers traced a path between my breasts, down my stomach and through the soft patch of curls between my legs.

I closed my eyes, my delight so intense I was swept into a maelstrom of need. I couldn't quite catch my breath, was burning up, needy, achy, even the water caressing my skin so hot that it seemed every inch of me was under intense attack.

"Part those beautiful legs for me, baby. Let me see you."

I didn't have to open my eyes to know he'd dropped to his knees. And I didn't even think about hesitating or refusing. I simply parted my legs. I wanted his mouth on me, licking, nibbling, tasting me.

He sucked in a reverent breath a split second before that hot tongue flicked my clitoris. A groan of surrender escaped me, and I found myself reaching up, gripping the shower curtain rod to keep from gripping his hair and perhaps ripping him a few bald spots.

As his tongue continued to work its magic, he drove a finger into me. Deep, hard, enough to make my knees collapse, but he held me up with his other hand. He inserted another finger, then another, and rocked into me again and again. That decadent tongue never stopped moving on me. It was too much, not enough, everything I needed, everything I craved. A reason to live, a reason to die.

Release slammed into me quickly and with a vengeance, consuming my entire body. I screamed and arched back and forth into his mouth, prolonging every tremor. Taking…taking, demanding more.

I'm not sure how much time passed before I came to my senses and opened my eyes. When I did, Rome was standing in front of me, still naked. The water still raged. It was still warm, at least, so I hadn't taken too long. I was panting, shaking, and I'd gripped the rod so tightly it had bent in the center.

Rome's pupils were dilated, his eyes completely black. His cheeks were flushed, his mouth glistening as he ran his tongue over his lips, savoring the taste of me. I could almost see the outline of his cat underneath his skin.

"I'm going to kill that fucking Memory Man," he said, slamming his hands beside my head and cracking the tile. He was so big, overwhelming the space around me until all I saw, all I breathed was him. Just then, there was no Belle without Rome.

Had there ever been?

"That he stole memories of us, together, like that…"

Licking my lips, I released the bar and grabbed Rome by the back of the neck. I jerked him into me, needing him, desperate all over again. He willingly, eagerly accepted my kiss, his chest rubbing against mine. Our teeth banded together, our hands grasped at each other's body, feeling, learning, pleasuring. I could touch him forever, but it wouldn't be enough.

Steam wafted around us, forming a cloud. I was in a dream, a fairy tale. A nighttime fantasy come to sizzling life. I could feel him poised at my core, waiting, ready.

"Are you on the pill?" His voice was deep, raw. Savage.

The question was a reminder of what was different between us, and I felt a pang. "Yes."

There was no time to wallow. The moment the word left my mouth, he was inside me, all the way to the hilt, pounding deep and hard and so much a part of me I would have died without him. But I arched, taking him even deeper, hungry for more.

Over and over he pounded inside, withdrew, pounded hard. He was grunting, and I was swallowing the sounds, savoring the taste of him, propelling higher and higher, reaching for another climax.

"Feels so good," he rasped. "Too good."

In the end, we reached it together. He roared, shuddering inside me. I screamed, clawing at his back.

"Belle," he said, panting, his voice broken. Then he stilled, his muscles jerking.

"Yes?" Mine sounded equally savaged.

His head dropped to my shoulder. "Catch me."

CHAPTER TWENTY-TWO

OF ALL THE THINGS I expected Rome to do after making love to me, fainting wasn't one of them. I barely managed to catch him before he smacked into the tub. Slowly, I eased him down. But he was heavy—freakishly heavy, actually, with all that muscle mass—and I struggled to lay him back without hurting him.

Shaking, still trying to catch my breath, I leaned forward and switched off the water. Instantly cool air began to lick at my damp skin, making me shiver. I climbed out and grabbed a towel, then dabbed us both dry. Concern wasn't something I could allow myself right now because with concern came fear, so I told myself Rome was still recovering from captivity and the drugs The Multiplier had given him.

Didn't take long until he was moaning, his eyelashes fluttering open. Total déjà vu.

Relief speared me. I hovered over him, one hand beside his head, my body propped on the rim of the porcelain, my wet hair spilling onto his chest. "Seriously, Rome. How many times am I going to have to wake your lazy ass up today?"

A moment passed before he oriented himself. When he realized where he was, his cheeks reddened and he muttered, "Shit. I blacked out."

"Yep." I settled back on my haunches.

"Too much too fast, after that cocktail. I knew better."

So I'd been right. My relief intensified in a rush, sending a violent tremor through me. That tremor drew Rome's gaze. I'm sure it was my hardened nipples that held his attention, though. He licked his lips, sat up slowly.

"At least I reached the finish line before going down like a pussy." He scrubbed a hand down his face, smoothing away the moisture.

A soft chuckle escaped me. "So true." A good thing, too. It might be a while before we had a chance to do this again. He needed to be completely healed, and the Desert Gal case had to be closed. "Now, tell me the fall knocked some memories back inside that thick skull, and I'll consider this a gold star day."

He snorted. "I wish."

My grin slowly faded. Oh, well. Would Jean-Luc decide to return them? Of course he would, I told myself then. The real question was whether or not he'd do it without being tortured. Even though I didn't want to torture him, still liked him more than I should—I mean, the guy thought I deserved to be treated like a goddess, and who could fault him for that kind of logic?—I would do whatever was necessary. I hoped. God, I was a mess.

Rome rested his elbows on the tub. A drop of water trickled from his eyelashes, almost like a tear. "More than anything, I want to know the things I've done to that beautiful body." His voice was hard, angry now. Not with me, I knew, but with Jean-Luc.

One of our phones beeped, and we both stiffened.

No longer could we pretend we were the only two people in the world. Trying to push his sweet words from my mind, I rose and stalked to mine. Nothing. I strode around the room, searching for his. The beeping grew louder as I approached the desk. And then there it was, underneath his wallet. Frowning, I flipped it open and gasped. Not a call. A picture. There, on the screen, was a photo of Desert Gal—as pretty as she'd been before, damn her—and Cody.

They were in the lobby of this motel. I recognized the giant fake plant beside the reception counter.

"Rome," I called. "We've got company."

He was inside the room a second later, snatching up his clothes, dressing despite his weakness.

I did the same. How had they tracked us down yet again? Jean-Luc? Surely not. Cody, with another mysterious "plan"? Again, surely not. He didn't know our location. But why was he here, rather than guarding Sherridan and Lexis? Could Reese, Desert Gal's former informant, be the culprit? No, wait. He was currently indisposed.

The Multiplier, maybe? If one of the brothers had managed to escape PSI without anyone's knowledge, follow us…but that seemed implausible.

A tracker? That seemed the most likely. But where would it be? We hadn't taken anything from that first motel room—except the picture of the girls, I recalled, eyes widening. I'd stuffed it in my purse. Could one of those tracking chips Rome mentioned be glued to it?

Dressed now, I swiped up my purse, fished out the photo and held it to the light. What looked to be a piece of clear tape rested on the upper left corner. Damn it! This was my fault. I scowled and dropped the Polaroid on the floor.

I tugged on my shoes, hopping on one foot as I entered the bathroom and scooped up all my knives. My Taser already rested in my back pocket. "We staying here to fight or running?"

"Normally I'd want to stay and fight, but they always seem to be one step ahead of us and we're both at the end of our strength. I don't want to leave, though." His eyes moved to the ceiling as he quickly weighed the pros and cons. "We're leaving. Safest thing for us. If Cody wanted to bring us in, he should have contacted me to ensure I played along."

"Truth." As Tanner would say.

"We've got a few minutes before they reach us, so go into the hall and start knocking on doors until someone answers. First person who does, get inside their room."

Somehow I'd known he would say that. Though unsure about what he was doing, remaining here, I left our haven and did as he'd commanded without argument. Took me four tries, but someone finally opened their door. A middle-aged woman in sweats and a T-shirt, sleep clinging to her eyes.

I must have woken her up.

I opened my mouth to say…what? I didn't know, and it didn't matter. Rome jogged out of our room, spotted me and closed the distance.

"Sorry, ma'am," he said, moving past her and into her room without permission.

"I'm so sorry," I echoed. I pushed her back inside, shut and locked the door.

She gasped, shock covering her plain features. Poor woman. I'd been there. This would forever change her, ruin the safe world she'd thought she lived in.

"We're not going to hurt you," I vowed, holding a hand up as though I were swearing on a Bible. "We're in trouble, being chased by dangerous people. We're just going to…what?" I asked, looking to Rome.

He was at the window, prying it open. I rushed to his side, ready to jump through at a moment's notice—even though I could see only a thin ledge, a fifty-foot drop and cars in the parking lot. "We're leaving," I said over my shoulder. The woman hadn't run out, was still standing there, frozen by her fear. Oops. A good agent wouldn't have turned her back. A mistake I wouldn't make again. "Please don't tell anyone you saw us. Please. They'll take you in, question you, maybe hurt you."

"Not maybe." Rome's voice was cold, hard. "They will."

She swallowed audibly. Found her feet and backed herself into the wall, edging closer and closer to the door. But she stopped, hand fluttering to her throat. Her skin was so pale I feared she would faint. I didn't think I could handle another unconscious person today.

Rome finally got the glued seal unstuck and pushed the window open. Cool air wafted inside, followed by the sound of night birds and crickets. He looked back at the woman, who now had tears streaming down her cheeks. I'd never scared an innocent so badly, and I hated myself for it. She didn't know whether to trust us or not, didn't know whether a painful death waited in here or out there.

"You're going to be okay," I told her. "I'll—"

Rome stealthily placed something cold and thin in my hand. I didn't have to look to know it was a syringe filled with that night-night cocktail of his. He carried it everywhere. Though after what The Multiplier had done to him, I would have expected him to rethink that strategy.

I moistened my suddenly dry lips. I'd never done something like this to an innocent, and hadn't ever wanted to. But she would have freaked if Rome approached her.

You're an agent. Act like one for once. I needed to tattoo those words on my wrist or something. *You can do this.*

Pasting what I hoped was a sincere smile on my face, I slowly moved toward her, careful to keep the syringe behind me. "You're going to be okay," I repeated. "I promise."

She blanched, turned and finally ran to the door, hand reaching for the knob. A cry curled from her lips the moment I grabbed her. She swung back, trying to bat me away. I ducked and jabbed the needle up and into her arm. Her cry instantly ceased, her muscles jerking in reaction. As the drug instantaneously broke the blood/brain barrier, she slid to the floor, immobilized at my feet.

I stayed there, staring down at her. I had done that to her. Me.

"Belle, come on!" Rome said in a fierce whisper. He even waved me over.

I jolted into motion, whipping around and running to him. He wrapped an arm around my waist and ushered me onto the ledge.

"She gonna be okay?" I knew she would be, had promised her she would, but I needed to hear it confirmed.

"Look at it this way, baby. You woke her up by banging on her door. The least you could do was help her fall back asleep. She'll be up and at 'em in a few hours. I'm proof of that," he added with clear self-deprecation. "She might not even remember what happened."

Hopefully she wouldn't. I didn't want to be forever branded a villain in her mind.

Who knew I'd ever be pro-memory loss?

"What if someone's waiting for us on the ground?" I asked.

"They probably are. That's why we're going up."

Up? Dear God. Though I was trying valiantly to numb my emotions, I couldn't stop a wave of fear from crashing through me, chilling me inside and out. Ice branched from my fingers, making the ledge I was holding, as well as the one my feet were braced upon, slick.

"Calm down, Belle," Rome commanded.

"So easy to say, so hard to do." I could fall. He could fall. We could die. Oh, God, oh, God, oh, God. Faster and faster the frost spread from me.

"You're going to get us both killed."

"Not helping!"

Even as I spoke, I felt his mind probing mine, snatching up my emotions, dulling them slightly. Without Tanner, he didn't know how much to filter. The fact that he was filtering anything at all, though, thrilled me despite the circumstances.

He moved behind me, his body heat enveloping me. Warm breath trekked over my neck, caressing, lifting my hair and dancing it over my skin. "Move with me." He crept to the right, and I followed. He reached up and hefted himself a few inches higher, and I followed. "I've got you. That's my girl."

That's right. I was. Up, up we continued to move, but soon my arms and legs were burning from the strain. I held on tight, though, Rome's big, hard body anchoring me despite the small patches of ice I'd created.

"I want to get us into a shadowed corner on the roof, all right? Then I'll take care of the rest. You won't have to do anything but hang on. And just so you know, no one's on the ground watching us. I checked. We're fine. We're safe." He kept up the steady chatter in hopes of distracting me, I knew. "You're breathing too hard. Tell me about the wedding you've been planning."

"I'm not planning it anymore," I said. "It's been canceled." With the words, my remaining fear began to fade, tendrils of anger and hurt taking their places. One more emotion and I'd have the cocktail needed for wind. Great.

I had to get myself under control or I'd blow us from the building.

Okay, that caused the fear to intensify. At least I had my filter back.

"Why's it canceled?"

"Are you kidding? You don't even remember me, much less want to marry me."

"I could get my memory back at any time." As he spoke, he continued to climb, dragging me up with him. Finally we were there at the top and throwing our legs over that last ledge, sweet shadows enveloping us.

Safe now, I wondered what was happening inside our room. Surely Desert Slut and Cody—and however many people they'd brought with them—had reached it by now.

"What does your dress look like?" He was jiggling behind me. What the hell was he doing? "You must've bought one by now."

"I did, but I accidentally burned it."

"Got mad, did you?"

"Yeah. You kept calling me Homicidal Tendencies Wench and I BBQed all the clothes in your closet. The flames leaped onto my dress."

"God, I bet that was hot."

Hot. "Ha-ha. Very funny. Anyway, I had planned to buy another one, but... *Anyway,* the first one was gorgeous. A Grecian cut with thin straps, a beautiful cream color and a flowing skirt. I was going to look like a goddess."

"You already do. Were we writing our own vows?" Rome slapped a hand beside mine, a weird-looking circle-thing clutched between his fingers. It was black, about two inches thick and as big as my palm.

I knew he was asking me these questions to distract me, but man, they hurt. "Yes, we were." I changed the subject. "What's that you're holding?"

"You'll see." He stretched his arm toward the neighboring building's roof, pressed the pad of his thumb into the center of the circle, and a silver arrow shot out and up, moving so swiftly I caught only the barest glimpse of a blur. "What were your vows?"

The arrow must have caught in something, because Rome's arms jerked and I saw a thin silver wire was secured inside the circle. Clearly, we were going to propel. Fabulous.

"I don't want to talk about the vows."

"Turn around and face me," Rome said. "Wrap your arms around me."

"There you go, kidding again." He wanted me to slide through the air, a massive drop below me and no net to catch me if I fell? Yeah, right.

"Do it. Now." No longer did he sound like my sweet protector. Now he was total commando.

"Fine, but only because you asked nicely. Jerk," I muttered. Slowly, shaking, I did as he'd demanded. When I faced him, I found my nose buried in the hollow of his neck. Sadly, I could still see what he was doing.

He pulled hand holders from the circle, cutting it into two pieces. "Ready?"

"As I'll ever be," I said on a sigh.

A moment later, my feet were jolted off the ledge and I was soaring, soaring... I wrapped my legs around Rome's waist for added security, and my eyelids squeezed shut. Having the wind in my hair was enough. I didn't need to see my progress.

The entire trip from one roof to another lasted about five seconds, but it seemed an eternity until we stopped. Rome used another device to hoist us to solid ground. I lay down, trying to catch my breath.

Rome rolled to his back and flipped his cell phone open, holding it up so I could see. On the screen were Desert Whore and Cody, as well as four others I didn't recognize. OASS agents, presumably.

"I placed a camera in the ceiling of our room," Rome explained.

Ah. That's what he'd done while I'd been searching for an unsuspecting civilian to frighten. "Why couldn't we have just gone out our own window?"

"They might have been watching it."

Ah, again.

The four agents were digging through our stuff, not that we had much. They ripped what little clothing we had, then threw open the dresser drawers, looking for more.

With the downward angle, I had a perfect view of Desert Shithead's hair. I hated to say it, but damn, those tresses were gorgeous. Golden-blond and silky. This had to be her DG persona, since Candace Bright was the redhead.

"You dragged me out at this ungodly hour for nothing! You told me they'd be here and they clearly aren't," she said to Cody. Well, not said. Her voice was husky, rich, more a purr than anything. Knowing how pretty she was, when you added the voice into the mix the girl was walking sex. Men probably drooled for her. And then she probably mopped that drool up like a sponge, the water-sucker.

"They must have spotted us." Cody looked left, right, and sighed heavily. "I told you Rome's security would be a problem. Good thing is, they packed in a hurry, only taking the essentials, so we were close. Next time we'll nail them."

"Do we still trust him?" I asked Rome, genuinely curious. What if Desert Gal was the one woman who'd inspired Cody to break his three-date min-max rule, and he truly was on her side now? On the bright side, if that was the case, at least I wouldn't have to worry about him dating Sherridan.

"Yes," was the only response.

"I want her." Desert Whore dug her nails into her thighs. "I *need* her."

I blinked. She needed me? Why? Jean-Luc had told

me she hated me because her dad liked me. That didn't necessitate a "need."

"I know," Cody said gently. "I know. We'll get her. I swear."

Desert Turd whipped away from him. "Get out," she said softly.

The men working around her froze, realized what she'd ordered, then hightailed out of the room as though their feet were on fire.

Cody remained in place. He closed the distance between himself and my greatest enemy and wound his arms around her waist. She stiffened. He didn't pull back, though. Instead, he rested his chin on the top of her head. "Having her doesn't mean your father will come back, though."

Rome tossed me a confused look.

I shrugged.

"I know." She sniffed and wiped at her eyes with the back of her hand. A frustrated growl left her, and she raised her head, eyeing the ceiling, a harsh mask pasted on her features.

Something inside me recognized that mask for what it was: fake. She was crumbling inside but wanted to show the world how tough she was. Or, hell, maybe I was deluded. Maybe I wanted to see vulnerabilities in my enemy because that would mean I wasn't up against an impenetrable force.

Cody tugged her tighter against him, glancing up at the camera as though he'd known it was there the entire time. I gasped, feeling pierced all the way to the soul. He reached up and extended two fingers, his thumb pressed in the middle of them. It was a sign. I knew it was, and suddenly trusted him as completely as Rome had assured me I could.

Desert Gal couldn't see him, and he quickly dropped

his arm and escorted her from the room, promising her he'd find and deliver me.

My brow wrinkled in confusion. "What does that mean? He'll meet with us in two nights? He's going to act against her in two minutes?"

Rome jacked to his feet. "We've got to get Tanner." Dread dripped from his tone. "I'll explain on the way."

CHAPTER TWENTY-THREE

APPARENTLY, TWO FINGERS with a thumb in the middle was a code between Cody and Rome. Not for peace, as I'd kind of hoped, but for something terrible about to go down. His fingers had formed a *K* for Catastrophe, even though the word started with a *C* (as I'd pointed out). That was the beauty of the code, Rome said, as if I lacked the sense to tie my own shoes.

I figured that's why Cody had helped Desert Gal track us. To warn us of this impending Katastrophe—or paraster (paranormal disaster), as I liked to say—as well as stay in her good graces and prove his worth, his trustworthiness.

What was about to go down, though, Rome didn't know.

All I knew was that I'd never seen him this frightened. Yes, frightened. Whereas for once, I, Little Miss Icebox, had my fear under control. Don't get me wrong; I was scared. Scared out of my freaking mind, but I wasn't letting it rule me this time. Or maybe I had more control because Rome was filtering for me again. Either way, Sherridan and my team needed me, and I would *not* fail them.

"How you doing?" Rome asked me as we exited the bus we'd just spent half an hour bumping around on. We'd had to wait for it for several hours, hiding all the while, but finally morning had arrived, followed quickly by the bus. Things no longer seemed at a standstill.

I luxuriated in the chilled, fresh air, the cloying scent

of mingling perfumes fading, and yawned. God, I was tired. Wait. Didn't I owe Rome a response? How was I doing, he'd wanted to know. "Good."

Rome yawned, too. "Let me know if that changes."

"You better believe I will."

"Good," he said.

We walked another half hour before he phoned John and gave him our location, certain we weren't being tailed. Ten minutes later, a car picked us up in front of an abandoned, wood-slats-over-the windows home. The driver didn't speak to us, didn't really even look at us.

It was another fifteen minutes before we reached the airstrip. At least there were no incidents along the way. However, we beat Tanner's plane, which meant more endless minutes to wade through. Hello, new standstill.

Or not. "Sponge-bath time," I muttered. "Where's the nearest bathroom?"

"Down the hall, to the right. I'll be there in a minute," Rome said, turning his back to me to talk to a man I didn't recognize.

"Uh, no, you won't."

Silence. He didn't even flick me a glance.

I took that for agreement and strode the length of the hall. The bathroom was spacious, better than I'd expected, with white tiles and chrome facets. In fact, rather than cleaning up in a sink, I would get to use a wide shower stall with a dark privacy screen.

Since PSI owned this little building, John must have made sure his agents had the proper facilities. I wondered if all the airstrips they owned—and there were a lot, since they had one in every major city—were like this.

I locked the door, stripped in record time and climbed inside. As the water hit me, I was able to relax, really relax, and not worry about a bad guy busting in on me. More than having all the amenities, the airstrip was heavily guarded. We'd passed two security stations on the way in.

Except…Rome sat on top of the closed toilet lid when I emerged on a steam cloud, holding a bundle of clothes. I gave a startled gasp, hand fluttering to my chest.

"You've got to stop sneaking up on me!" I was totally buying the vicious dog I'd threatened him with when we returned home. Barking might just save me from a heart attack. I grabbed my towel and wrapped it around myself. "Any more of this, and the bad guys won't need to kill me. You'll have done it for them."

He rolled his eyes. "Clearly I didn't really scare you, since you haven't turned me into an iceberg. We'll be contacted when Tanner's plane lands, so…" He was dressed in all black again. His hair was damp, slicked back from his face. We'd both had a shower last night, yes (and had fun while doing so), but we'd also scaled a building and run for our lives since then.

"What? You're staring," I said, even though I was the true culprit in that department.

"I know," he replied, taking the blame. Or had he been doing so, too? Score! His gaze raked me, hot, intense. "Of all the outfits I've seen you in, excluding the glistening skin you wore while showering with me, this has to be my favorite. White terry cloth, nothing underneath."

My heartbeat sped into supernova. "We're not having sex again," I blurted. "Not until our friends are safe and sound and you, like, love me again. Because the more I'm with you, the more I love you, and I hate, *hate* being the only one emotionally involved."

"Fine," he said.

I blinked in surprise, a little disappointed he hadn't made a declaration of undying love then and there. Anything for nookie, right? "Come again?"

"I said fine. No sex." He stood. "Like you, I'm too concerned. My daughter's mother is out there, and disaster's on its way. Top that off with fatigue and a shitty mood and I'm just bad company right now. But since we're stuck here, I'm going to do what's most beneficial to our team."

"And that is?" Whatever he was doing, I was doing it, too. Except for sex, of course.

"Rest. With you. We're not going to do anyone any good if we collapse again, and I'll sleep better if you're close."

Rest sounded…heavenly, I realized, yawning again. I'd only had a few hours' sleep myself the past few days and my adrenaline levels had been up and down so much I had whiplash.

"Lead the way," I said.

He handed me the clothes he'd brought for me. "Get dressed or I'll forget why I don't want to have sex."

"Fine." I dropped the towel.

His animal gave a quiet snarl.

His eyes bored into me, burning me, as I strapped on my weapons, then dressed. Wicked me, I took my time, hoping to remind him of the many other times I'd done this for him.

"Gonna be uncomfortable," he said, motioning to where one of the knives protruded.

"I know." I sauntered to his side. He had an erection, and he didn't try to hide it.

"This way." He wrapped his arm around my waist.

I was shivering, and it had nothing to do with being cold, as he ushered me down the hall and into a bedroom. A full-size bed, brown comforter, no other furnishings. Strictly for resting between jobs or flights, I guess.

Rome kicked off his shoes and lay down. I tossed mine beside his and did the same, nuzzling up to him. He threw an arm and a leg over me, my back to his chest, holding me tight, as if I were a precious treasure he needed to guard.

My weapons were uncomfortable, just as he'd predicted, but I didn't remove them. An agent—a true agent—had to be ready for anything at a moment's notice. A few minutes passed, but they seemed like an eternity. I rolled the other way, but was still uncomfortable. I rolled back to him.

"My mind is wired," I said. "I'm not sure I'll actually be able to sleep."

"We'll talk for a minute and wind you down, then."

"'Kay. 'Bout what?"

"About the fact that I like the thought of making you mine," he whispered, breath trekking over my cheek. "I like the thought of you being Belle Masters. I didn't realize just how much until you told me the wedding was canceled."

I…I…must be dreaming. Must have fallen asleep without realizing it. This was too surreal to take seriously. Unless he was belatedly trying to sweet-talk me into that nookie. "Don't talk like that. Besides, who said I'd be taking your name?"

"Why not?" Warm fingers caressed my wrist, along each of my fingers.

"Why not take your name?" Lexis's words chose that moment to invade my mind: *You're going to continue to plan your wedding, but he'll want nothing to do with it. Another man will court you, but Rome won't care. Do you hear me? He won't care! You're going to date this other man. It's* him *you'll marry. Him. Not Rome. Him.* One thing she'd said had come true so far: another man was indeed courting me. But everything else…wrong. Rome obviously cared about the wedding (somewhat). I did not plan to date Jean-Luc (at all), much less marry him (ever), didn't view him romantically (even a little). I couldn't imagine that changing, either.

Had Lexis lied to me, then? I wouldn't put it past her. She was clearly willing to do anything to win her ex back.

"Oh, you'll take my name. Why not talk like that to you?"

"Just…let's wait until things are a little calmer before discussing it," I said. The subject cut me up and left me raw, and I needed to be at my best right now.

"All I'm trying to say is that, if Memory Man never returns my memories of you, I still want a chance with you. I want to date you, get to know you again."

A flash of white-hot tears stung my eyes. I could only hope the ceiling wouldn't start raining next. "And if you ultimately decided you didn't want me?" The question sprang from my deepest fears, unstoppable, pain-drenched.

"Right now I can't imagine not wanting you." He sighed. "Go to sleep, Belle. Your mind isn't quite so wired." It was true. While we'd been talking, he'd obviously been filtering, the darling man. Just then, I was drained. "We'll figure everything out later."

"WAKE UP, VIPER. You're sooo not Sleeping Beauty."

The voice floated through my mind, familiar, beloved. Smart-assy. "Tanner?" Slowly I cracked open my eyes. The lights were on, golden bulbs illuminating Tanner's gorgeous features and blue hair. "Tanner!"

I sat up and threw myself into his arms, squealing with delight. He was here, in the flesh, healthy and whole. "Let me look at you." I pulled back from him, studied his face. He'd lost a little weight, his cheeks a little more hollow, but his skin was flushed with vitality and his blue eyes sparkling.

He shook his head, *tsked* under his tongue. "Any excuse to get me into your arms, you hussy."

I slapped his shoulder, but couldn't hold back my

grin. "I'm glad to see your hospital stay didn't dampen that dazzling wit. So where's my surprise? You said you were bringing me one."

"I'm right here."

The female voice came from the corner of the room and drew my attention. My gaze landed on beautiful, angelic Elaine. I swung my focus back to Tanner, shock flowing through me. "How?"

"John relented," Tanner explained. "Strapped her to a lie detector—he didn't trust my word for it, said I was biased—and she passed. It's something we should have done to Reese the lying vampire a long time ago, but whatever. John allowed her to join the agency and help us on this case."

"I thought she wasn't interested in joining another agency?"

"I, uh, changed her mind."

I looked back at Elaine. She was once again covered from neck to ankles in black cloth. Her shirt possessed a long hood that I suspected could be drawn up over her face to shield even that energy-draining skin. I remembered all too well what had happened the last time it had been exposed.

She gave me a half smile, hesitant and unsure.

"I'm glad you're here," I told her sincerely.

The smile grew, and she threw a quick, longing glance at Tanner. "Me, too."

"Did you get your meal and your iPod? I will kill John when I return if he failed to do as he told me he would."

"I did, thank you. No need to kill anyone."

"Oh, and guess what? I've renamed her Super Absorber," Tanner said.

I tried not to cringe. "You realize that name makes her sound like a tampon, right?"

GENA SHOWALTER

327

His brow furrowed. "No way."

"Yes, way."

Elaine nodded reluctantly, as if she hated to disappoint him. "It does. I'm sorry. I should have told you, but you were so proud."

Tanner threw up his arms. "Fine. I'll keep thinking."

"Rome will—" Hey, where was Rome? Frowning, I swept my gaze over the bed. The covers were rumpled, but empty. "Anyone seen Rome?"

Tanner nodded and motioned Elaine over to him.

The girl inched her way toward him, feet dragging, as though she was afraid to get too close. When she reached his side, he wound his arm around her waist, not the least bit frightened by what could happen despite all he'd been through. I stiffened, she gasped.

A minute ticked by in silence.

Tanner didn't tremble, didn't fall and gradually I relaxed. I felt sad for them, though. Obviously he'd moved on from Lexis (hip hip hurrah!) and just as obviously he and Elaine had feelings for each other. But they were doomed. They could never touch each other, skin to skin, which meant they could never... *Stop right there.* I did not want to imagine Tanner having sex. Although, I supposed there were ways around it. Phone sex, self-pleasure in front of each other, full-body condom. *Uh, stop. Now.*

"Cat Man was on the airstrip when we landed," Tanner said, drawing me from my reluctantly lascivious thoughts. "Unlike you, he knows how to roll out the red carpet. Told me where to find you."

So he'd left me here to sleep while he'd gone off to work. Someone needed a spanking in a big way. "Know where I can find *him?*" I would not be left out. I was going to help with this case, damn it!

"He's interrogating Memory Man, I think. I can't believe you guys caught him. Good going!" Tanner gave my back a slap of approval.

"What!" I threw my legs over the mattress and stood. "Jean-Luc is here? No one told me. Damn it, someone should have told me. Where are they?"

"Belle."

Rome's deep voice suddenly filled the room.

Fury leaping inside my chest, desperate to escape, I looked around and found him standing in the doorway. I fisted my hands on my hips. "How long have you had him?"

A muscle ticked under his eye, a clear sign he didn't want to answer. "Moment he left us alone last night, I had agents on him. First I wasn't sure who he was, so I was being cautious and merely had them knock him out. When you finally admitted his identity, I had his ass thrown in a cage. Then, since I knew we would be here eventually, I had him brought here, as well."

Right away, then. "He helped you!"

"Wait a second," Tanner said, clearly confused. "We *like* Memory Man now?"

"Yes," I shouted as Rome said, "Hell, no."

Rome continued, "He's not leaving until he returns my memories."

I turned to Tanner. "Take me to him. Please."

"Like I know where he is," Tanner said, holding up his free hand, palm out.

"I'll find him on my own, then." I stomped down the hall to the bathroom, brushed my teeth and back-to-normal-color hair and stomped back to the bedroom. Tanner and Elaine were exactly as I'd left them, watching me wide-eyed.

Rome was where I'd left him, too, but he was studying

me through narrowed eyes, his arms crossed over his chest. Stubborn man.

"Be ready to roll in half an hour," I told them. "Now that the gang's all here, we'll be going to get Sherridan and Lexis."

Took me half of that time, Rome on my tail and silent, unhelpful, but I finally found Jean-Luc in an underground holding facility. I studied him through the small window in the door. He lay on a stiff, uncomfortable-looking cot, the room's only furniture.

"Do you…care about him?" Rome asked at my side.

I ran a fingertip over the glass, leaving a smudge. "He's not a bad guy. Just confused and lonely."

"And you're too damn softhearted."

I gazed up at him through the dark spikes of my lashes. "That's a bad thing?"

"When you're wanting to release hardened criminals, yes."

Hardened criminals? Ha! "First, I was making progress with him. By doing this to him, you just ruined everything I'd already achieved. Second, I wasn't wrong about Elaine, now was I? Third, Jean-Luc has saved my life and helped me on several occasions. He makes me feel loved. Not like I'm excess baggage to be left in bed, sleeping the day away while other agents do my work for me."

"You're mad about that? I did you a favor, letting you rest."

"Or maybe you just didn't want to deal with me." I didn't give him time to respond. "Unlock this goddamn door," I shouted.

A guard came running, but stopped and waited for Rome's permission. Rome looked at me, teeth clenched, then gave a stiff nod. The door swung open a few seconds later, and I stalked inside.

"Belle." An unfazed Jean-Luc popped to his feet and smiled. "I knew you'd come." That smile faded, though, as his gaze collided with Rome's.

"Do not approach her," Rome growled.

I elbowed him in the stomach. "I'd like to apologize for what you've been through at PSI's hands. I didn't know or it wouldn't have happened." God, I was so mad. So damn mad. The fire was raging inside me, an inferno. Rome's actions might have set me back *months*. Took a lot of mental grasping, but I managed to keep every flame inside me. "But I think you know why PSI felt they had to capture you. Will you return Rome's memories?"

"No."

See! Before, I'd at least had him thinking about it. Rome stiffened.

"Will you return them if I torture you?" I asked. "Because I might not have wanted you locked up, but I'm totally prepared to do what's necessary." There was no way out of this now. This was the road Rome had thrown us on, so this was the road I had to take.

Jean-Luc laughed with genuine humor. "No. There's no torture you can think of that hasn't already been done at some point in my past. If I haven't broken yet, it's not going to happen."

Rome moved toward him, menace in every step, but I threw out my arm. A puny block, but he stopped.

I ran my tongue across the roof of my mouth, my mind racing with options. "What if I traded for them?"

Both Jean-Luc and Rome gaped at me. Rome opened his mouth, to yell at me, I'm sure, but Jean-Luc beat him to it.

"Yes." He nodded, his shoulders squared, his arms behind his back. "Yes, I'll trade you for them."

Okay, wow. Easier than I'd anticipated. Maybe Rome

hadn't been wrong to do this, after all. I, too, squared my shoulders. "What do you want?"

"You."

Rome snarled low in his throat, pushing against my arm.

"Stop," I told him, and surprisingly he did. "You can't have me," I told Jean-Luc, "not the way you mean. But in exchange for Rome's memories I will give you…three dates." That was Cody's magic number, not too little, not too much. "Anything beyond that, you'll have to earn by proving we're meant to be together."

Not that he could. But as I spoke, I realized I might be setting myself up for failure with Rome…setting myself up to prove Lexis's prediction that I'd marry Jean-Luc true. I paled, but didn't take back my words. This was too important. "Oh, and one more thing. You'll have to do all of this *without* the memories. You hand them over first, or no dates. If you can't win me on your own…"

Rome hissed through his teeth. "What are you doing, Belle?"

Jean-Luc's hands fisted, but he said, "Fine. I'll date you without the memories."

"Who knows? Maybe you'll stop loving me the moment you lose them. You may not even want to go on *one* date."

"I'll still want you," Jean-Luc assured me. "I'll still want the dates."

I nodded, though inside I was trembling violently. "Then three dates it is."

"Are you still engaged?" he asked, eyes falling to my hand.

"Nope," I said, and I couldn't hide the wistfulness in my tone. The ring was still there. I needed to take it off soon. "Not officially."

"Belle." It was another warning from Rome.

I continued, "I lied—there's still one more thing.

Since we're all a happy family now, willing to help each other, we'd like your help stopping Desert Bitch." Once I'd thought having him at PSI would be a nightmare. No longer. We needed all the help we could get.

Jean-Luc didn't need time to think. "Yes," he said, nodding. "For you, anything."

"Keep the fucking memories," Rome suddenly shouted. "You're not dating her. Or joining our team."

I think he meant to shove me aside and leap at Jean-Luc, maybe even rip out his throat, but I jumped in front of him, eyeing him imploringly. "This has to be done, Rome. For you. For us." I only hoped it didn't prove to be our undoing.

Jean-Luc wrapped his fingers around my forearms and gently moved me off to the side. That enraged Rome all the more, animal sounds once again emerging from his throat. The moment I was out of the way, the two men leaped at each other in a tangle of limbs. Fists swung, teeth snapped, legs kicked.

I inched toward the wall, watching as Rome's skin began to be replaced by black fur, his animal taking over. I needed fear, needed to freeze them before they killed each other. Killed each other—yes, good. That image brought a storm of ice inside me that melted the rage that had been boiling.

But just as an ice ball formed in my hand, Jean-Luc disappeared. *I* froze in place, too shocked to move. Rome froze, too, half man, half cat.

"Jean-Luc?" I called. I knew where he was. I knew what he was doing, but some part of me was afraid this wouldn't work.

But suddenly Jean-Luc stepped from Rome's body. Rome collapsed onto the ground, laboring for breath. Jean-Luc, too, was panting. He looked to me, sweat running from his face.

"It's done," he said. And then he, too, collapsed.

CHAPTER TWENTY-FOUR

WE PLACED THEM in separate rooms, across the hall from each other, both tied to their beds, and I divided my time between them, checking on them, waiting. Their vitals were good, so I wasn't worried. I was just impatient. Again. My entire life now seemed to revolve around Rome waking up.

Finally, about an hour later, Rome regained consciousness.

"Belle!" His roar nearly shook the entire building. "Belle!"

Currently I was in the hall, between the two rooms. Hearing him (who hadn't?), I rushed forward, my heart drumming erratically. My gaze landed on him the moment I hit the doorway. His eyes were bright, wild, his lips pulled back from his sharp, gleaming teeth. He was struggling against his bonds, about to rip free. All the while he shouted my name.

But when he spotted me, he stilled. "Belle," he said, and it was as though his beast was speaking for him, all guttural and tormented, no longer in a frenzy but ready to pounce. "Set me free. Now."

Slowly I approached the bed. I was trembling. Did he remember me? Did he love me again? Took me several tries, a spring of blasted tears screwing with my vision, but I finally loosened the bonds. He jerked me into his arms a second later, crushing me against him.

"Oh, God, baby. I'm so sorry. I'm so sorry for what I've put you through. Can you ever forgive me? I love you. I love you so much, I would die without you. I can't believe I treated you that way. Oh, God, baby. I'm sorry."

He did. He remembered. My tears spilled free as I hugged him back with every ounce of strength I possessed. "I can't believe you're back. You're really back."

"And I'm not going anywhere ever again." He scattered little kisses all over my face, my neck, then he rolled me over and pinned me to the mattress. He peered down at me, his expression fierce. "Tell me you forgive me. Or if you can't, tell me you'll give me a chance to make it up to you. I'll do anything. You want flowers, candy, lingerie? They're yours. I hate myself for what I did to you. I love you more than anything in this damn world and to know that I hurt you like that…"

My chin was trembling, so it was hard to work my next words out of my mouth. "You already bought me lingerie. Though you later decided I'd be better off going commando. But anyway, all I want, all I've ever wanted, is your heart." *You're supposed to make him work for forgiveness, remember?*

"Oh, baby, you have it." He kissed me, hard and deep. "I love you so much." Another kiss. "I'm sorrier than I can ever express for what I put you through." Another kiss. "You deserve better than me, but I can't let you go." Another kiss. "I love you so damn much."

I tangled my hands in his hair, smiling, giddy, still tearing like a silly watering pot. I'd wanted this moment so badly and for so long. And now, here it was. Now, Rome was mine. We were together, in each other's arms.

"Now you won't have to go on those dates with *that man.*" He sneered the last, even as he gently wiped my tears away with the pad of his thumb. "Don't cry, baby. Please don't cry."

Some of my giddiness popped like a balloon, and my grin faded. "I won't go back on my word. I'm going to date him, as promised."

Our gazes locked, and his was like fire. "Belle."

"Rome." Not even his sexiness could budge me on this. "It's going to happen, so get used to the idea."

He moved his jaw left and right, his eyes narrowing. "I'm willing to beg."

I weakened. Rome begging? So appealing. But… "That wouldn't change my mind. Not only will I date him, but I'll also welcome him to our team. He knows Desert Skank better than any of us."

Rome was so silent, so still, for a long while it was as if he was unconscious again. His heart kept a steady beat against my chest. His pupils thinned, revealing just how close his animal was to breaking free.

"You're different," he finally said.

My brow furrowed in confusion. "Wh-what do you mean?"

"The old Belle would have told Memory Man to go fuck himself, that you'd lied to him and he'd gotten what he deserved for his actions in the first place. Now you're willing to date him. To hire him. A man who hurt us both."

He was right. A tremor moved through me, a new fear suddenly springing to life. I'd always assumed the success of our relationship hinged on the return of his memories. But when he'd lost them, I *had* changed. I *was* a different girl than I'd been a week ago. I was stronger, harder, more jaded. I was also a dedicated agent who knew loyal allies were few and far between and needed to be treated with care.

Would Rome like who I'd become? He'd seemed to be falling for me again, but then, he'd been a different Rome.

"Does this mean what I think it means?" a familiar voice suddenly asked.

My gaze swung to the door.

Tanner stood in the center, grinning. "The Viper–Cat Man nuptials are back on, I see. My bad for losing faith and canceling everything. While I'd love to stay and witness the rest of your reunion, you need to get up. We've got scrim ass to kick and two damsels in distress to save."

He hadn't called Lexis a bitch; that was an improvement. Probably proved how concerned he was—or how much he now liked Elaine.

"We'll finish this conversation later," Rome said, his tone hard.

I could only nod, my mouth dry.

"EVERYONE KNOW the plan?" Rome asked.

We were packed inside a black Hummer—me, Rome, Tanner, Elaine, a fully recovered Jean-Luc and two male PSI agents I'd never met before. They were brothers (I wasn't sure how I felt about that, considering my last encounter with supernatural brothers), young, smooth-faced and a little arrogant. Apparently one, Christian, could create light, and the other, Hans, could create darkness. (Yes, their last name was Andersen, and yes, their parents were sadistic.) John had thought their abilities might come in handy on our journey.

Would have been nice if John had sent an agent who could swoop into a body and repair any damage. I could have used that kind of skill a few months back when Rome was shot. I could use that type of ability on my dad, actually. His ticker could be strengthened and I could stop worrying about it giving out every time he decided to buy—and take—a black-market Viagra. And who knew what kind of state we'd find Sherridan and Lexis in? I might need someone with healing powers then, too.

I sighed. I seriously needed to cut some of the worry out of my life. I'd thought I had. With Rome's latest recovery, I should have been swinging from stars. Since his parting comment an hour ago, though, my nerves were once again raw.

And what the hell was I going to do with the Shadow Boys? They were another worry I didn't need, as they'd probably just get in the way.

Night had fallen—I couldn't stick to my own time-table, it seemed—providing dark all on its own, and the moon was high, cascading over the mountains and glistening off the snowcaps. The beauty of the land seemed out of place, considering we were headed to a war.

"The plan," Rome growled.

"Not to die," Tanner piped up helpfully.

"Leave our personal bullshit in the car and do our jobs," Elaine added.

"Obey your every command," Jean-Luc said, "even though you might be wrong and such arrogance could get us killed."

Hearing his voice, I flashed back to when I'd walked into his recovery room, his dark eyes peering over at me.

"I still love you" had been the first words out of his mouth.

"I'm not going back on my word," I'd told him, exactly as I'd told Rome. "Soon as we rid the world of Desert Roach, we'll go on those dates."

"I hope you're ready to be romanced."

I had offered him a smile, but I'm sure it hadn't reached my eyes.

"You're begging to die," Rome told him now.

"Which is counter to the plan," Tanner said.

I rubbed my temples to ward off the oncoming ache. I sat beside Rome, who was driving the car. Our relationship might be a jumbled mess right now, but I reached over and squeezed his hand. If I needed the contact, and I did, he must, too. His fingers twined with mine, holding me captive.

"Listen up, kiddies," I said. "You all know what to do. So do it whether you like each other or not. Let's bring our girls home. Alive, as the plan states."

WE PARKED about a mile from the compound where our girls were being held—which meant we were about a mile from the middle of nowhere, mountains all around us—and hiked to the electric fence that surrounded it. From the photos Cody had sent, we knew it was two stories, one of them underground. We knew it was heavily guarded by men with guns, and we knew there were planes ready to whisk Desert Hussy away if danger was suspected. So we had to get inside silently.

Once, I'd gotten Rome and Tanner (and myself) over an electric fence by forming wind under our feet, lifting us higher and higher before lowering us (not so gently) to the ground. This time, I couldn't do that. With as many cameras as there were monitoring the area and the guards pacing back and forth across the parapet on top of the compound, that would place us directly in the line of fire.

Plus, there were twenty-foot-tall lamps strategically placed to chase away night's gloom. Suddenly I was glad for the Shadow Brothers. On our trek, Hans kept us wrapped in an umbrella of dark the entire way, no matter if someone tried to flash a light at us. It was eerie, though, because I couldn't see my hand in front of my face.

Christian could have lit up our little circle, he'd explained, and no one would have been able to see inside, but combating his brother's all-encompassing darkness would completely wipe him out.

Hans, who could see through that dark as well as create it, had had to guide us. "Left turn in five steps," he would say. "Straight, ten steps."

"Belle, Elaine, you ready?" Rome whispered.

I would have looked at her nervously but I couldn't see her. We didn't want to disable the fence; that would have alerted our targets to our presence. So we had to get through it with the electricity still pumping and without killing ourselves.

I heard a whoosh of material and suspected Elaine was removing her gloves, maybe stuffing them in her pockets.

"Be careful." Tanner's voice, serious and grim, echoed through our circle.

"I will." She must have reached out and wrapped her fingers around the links because suddenly I could hear the chains rattling ever so slightly. Then I heard a little gasp escape her. The rattling increased. She was drawing the energy into herself, away from the fence.

Someone—Tanner?—shifted from one foot to the other, clearly agitated.

I fumbled around until I ran into him, squeezed his hand to offer comfort, and withdrew the wire cutters Rome had given me before we'd left the airstrip. I was shaking, but moved quickly, not wanting Elaine to have to touch the fence any longer than necessary.

You control fire. You can summon storms. Electricity was nothing. *Please let it be nothing.* The moment the metal came into contact with the fence, I felt the volts enter me, going straight to my core and searing.

I cut back a yelp.

Elaine must have increased her rate of absorption because I could feel the jolts leaving me and flowing back into the fence, which then must have slid back into her, because once more the rattling increased. Just like that, I calmed. Had she not dulled the sensation, I think I would have dropped, wiped out for the rest of the night. As it was, I was sweating, burning up really, my muscles spasming as little shots of pain flickered through my veins.

With Hans guiding my movements, I cut a circle big enough that even Rome, massive as he was, could crawl through. When I finished, I fell away from the fence. "Now."

Elaine fell, as well, smashing into the ground. Both of us lay there, panting shallowly.

"You good?" Tanner asked.

"I'm—"

"Not you," he told me.

"Just need…a moment…" Elaine said.

"Thanks for the concern," I muttered.

"Belle, how are—" Rome and Jean-Luc began in unison. Both stopped abruptly.

Then Rome was kneeling at my side. He could see in the dark better than anyone I knew. Well, except Hans. He reached out, cupped my chin, hissed and jerked away.

"What?" I demanded, concerned.

"You're electric."

"Elaine, too," Tanner said with his own hiss of pain. "I can feel it even through her clothes."

I turned in the direction of his voice. There, a few feet away from me, I could see little sparks rising from Elaine's body—pinpricks of gold, like lightning bugs flying around her. They were lovely. Probably deadly. And they were flying off me, too.

"How are you feeling?" Rome asked me, drawing my attention back to him.

Through the flickers, I could make out his concerned features. "I'm okay. But damn. Cody lives with this every day. I'm not sure how he's survived."

Jean-Luc knelt at my other side. He watched the byplay between Rome and me, anger in his eyes. "If you need anything, let me know."

"Let *me* know," Rome corrected tersely.

Slowly I sat up, rubbed my temples as a wave of dizziness hit me. "Enough of that. I'm ready for action."

Rome shook his head. "The guards will see you coming. You and Elaine have to stay here until the charge wears off."

Oh, hell, no.

Before I could utter a protest, though, he slapped a revolver in my hand. The metal vibrated with energy. "Shoot anyone who approaches you."

I sputtered, trying to stand. My muscles didn't cooperate, my knees buckling under my weight. "Without Hans hiding us in shadows, we're targets."

"Cody's taken care of the cameras. All that remains are the guards. If you lie down and be still, you'll look like rocks from a distance. Granted, rocks with fireflies hovering around, but rocks all the same. Trust me. You'll be fine. If I thought for one moment you were in danger, I wouldn't leave you here. Now, when we've taken out the guards on the parapet, we'll flag you and you can come running." With barely a pause, he said, "Team, let's move out."

No one protested. Which surprised me. I expected Jean-Luc to fight to stay with me, and Tanner to fight to stay with Elaine. But clearly, they thought we were safer here and were eager to end this war.

They climbed through the hole in the fence Elaine and

I had provided for them, disappearing in Hans's shadows like dark phantoms.

"Are you fucking kidding me?" I gasped out, rolling to my stomach to make myself more rocklike.

Elaine did the same. "They're going to need us," she whispered fiercely. "I mean, the plan was for me to drain as many guards as I could to minimize the threat. Right now, they're outnumbered. They'll have to shoot, and that'll make noise, silencers or not."

Outnumbered didn't begin to describe it. Basically, Rome was on his own out there. Tanner was only just now learning to shoot (properly) and I had no idea if the Shadow Brothers, young as they were, had any combat skills. Jean-Luc didn't care if Rome lived or died. And while I trusted Rome to get the job done, I knew our team would fail without him. We had to have him alive and well. Uninjured.

"We can't just stay here," I said, studying the terrain. Rocky, on a steep incline.

"No, we can't. Tanner needs me. He's still not at full strength, though he won't admit it."

There was roughly one hundred feet between the fence and the parapet, then a staircase leading to the top. "We'll have to haul ass, and our bodies will probably hate us, but if we move just right, the guards might think we're lightning bugs."

"Well, with the lamps they'll be able to see *us,* not just the sparks."

Good point. "Shit. What are we going to do?" Rocks and twigs were digging into my belly. The ground was cold, hard and a mocking reminder that I was currently doing nothing to help my friends. Worse, the more time that passed, the less aid Elaine and I would be able to provide. Rome would have already inserted himself into the thick of battle.

"Maybe we can throw rocks at the bulbs?" she suggested. "It'll dim the light."

"That might announce our presence. Unless…" An idea began playing through my head. "I'm going to make it storm. We'll be harder to spot if the guards have water in their eyes. Also, we can break the bulb closest to us and maybe they'll think it was lightning, rather than an intruder."

She reached out, feeling for a big enough rock. "You take care of the rain, I'll take care of the bulb."

"Consider it done." For once, I didn't lament about how to get the job done. I closed my eyes, picturing Rome and Tanner shot during this battle. Lexis and Sherridan broken beyond repair. Poor, sad, motherless Sunny crying on my shoulder. My chin began to tremble. My eyes began to fill with tears.

A few drops of rain splattered on the top of my head and sizzled. Ouch. Was that what Cody felt when he touched water? I did my best to direct the rest of the droplets away from Elaine and me, even as I did everything in my power to intensify my sadness.

Would Rome and I ever get back together? Truly together? Would he still want me after I went on those three dates with Jean-Luc? Not that anything would happen on those dates—*unless Lexis was right. She isn't, can't be*—but some men couldn't stand the thought of another man looking at their woman, and Rome was more jealous than most.

A fine sprinkle started up, just ahead of us.

Satisfaction wanted to fill me because the storm had begun, but I couldn't let it. That would cause the rain to stop. Rather, I needed it to intensify. Sad, sad, sad. Me, all alone. Rome, back with Lexis or even with some other girl. Me, never seeing him again. Never seeing his daughter again. Never being held by him, loved by him. Him, realizing he didn't want or need me anymore. Him, realizing he hated the girl I'd become.

I kept those terrible thoughts playing through my mind, tormenting me. Tears ran down my cheeks in rivers, burning, even as the sky opened up and poured a deluge of rain onto the land. Hail even fell, slapping into the ground. I couldn't keep it away this time, there was simply too much, and damn, did it hurt.

I shivered, soaked to the bone in seconds. "R-ready?" I asked Elaine.

"Y-yes." Her teeth were chattering, too, and lines of tension branched from her eyes.

"Fight past the pain. Hell, maybe the rain will even help get rid of our sparks altogether."

"I hope so."

The boys hadn't given us the signal, which meant they were still engaged in battle. They needed us, whether they wanted to admit it or not. Gripping the gun—it didn't vibrate this time, and the pain inside me was easing, so what I'd told Elaine had been the truth— I rose. When Elaine did the same, almost collapsing beside me, I instinctively reached out and latched onto her, keeping her upright. Thank God she was covered by long sleeves. I would have dropped if I'd accidentally touched her skin.

A moment passed before she gained her bearings. She tossed a rock at the lamp. Missed the bulb. Grunted, and tossed another rock. This time she hit her target. Glass shattered, and shadows closed around us.

My eyes were able to adjust to this darkness, though, and I saw her pull her hood over her head, shielding every inch of her but her eyes. Well, and her hands. Those she kept free—easier to incapacitate the guards that way.

"Get ready to hurt." As the rain beat down on us, we ducked through the fence and sprinted our way up the hill to the parapet. My muscles screamed in protest, but at least no one shot at us.

The closer we got, the more male grunting I could hear. Grunting and growling.

Rome had morphed into a cat.

We raced up the stairs, nearly barreled into Tanner, Christian and Hans, one of whom cracked me in the jaw before realizing who I was. I saw stars.

"Sorry," Christian said.

"That's going to leave a mark." Silver lining: my wedding wasn't happening as planned and I wouldn't have to get married with a goose egg on my chin.

Some silver lining, I thought, my sadness deepening and the rain increasing.

When my vision cleared, I looked around, trying to decide the best way to help Rome. Jean-Luc and I could— But there was no sign of Jean-Luc.

Tanner clasped Elaine's shirt, jerking her beside him. "Stay here. Rome doesn't know you and might accidentally attack you."

"Go and get the guards," I told her. "I'll take care of Rome so you don't accidentally touch him."

She bolted forward, wrenching free of Tanner, and raced for the guards. They were weaponless, their semi-automatics already scattered over the stones. But there was a swarm of them, too many for Rome to fight on his own. I raced forward, too, only I launched myself at Rome, landing on his back and sending his feline-self propelling to his stomach.

His face immediately swung at me, those long, sharp teeth ready to clamp down for a tasty snack. At the first pierce, slight though it somehow was, he must have realized who I was because his mouth moved away from me without hurting me further. He flipped me over, pinning me with his weight.

I wrapped my arms around him, embracing him tightly, holding him to me. He didn't know it, but I was helping him. Or maybe he did. He could have wiggled free, but didn't. To protect me with his own body?

The rain continued to fall, though it tapered to a drizzle. My heart was pounding in my chest, a wild, uncontrollable thump. I searched the darkness, found Elaine standing in the middle of a rapidly diminishing crowd. The guards had launched themselves at her, but as she touched them, or as they hit her, they toppled to the ground, one by one, motionless.

Soon, she was the only one left standing.

Tanner rushed to her, but she backed away, yanking her gloves out of her pockets. Only when they were anchored in place did she allow herself to be pulled into his waiting arms.

Rome growled low in his throat, and I stiffened. Uh-oh. That was an angry growl. Slowly I faced him. Our gazes locked, my hazel against his furious blue. He was still in cat form, his fur slick and black and savagely lovely. His teeth were bared at me.

"You needed help," I said, chin raising. "I'm not sorry. I've changed, just like you said, and I'm a better agent for it. I need to be part of the action. I need to prove I can do this."

Boom!

The parapet trembled wildly, and someone screamed. Then debris was raining down, rocks and twigs and planks and mortar. Puffs of black smoke plumed in the air, making me cough.

"What happened?" I gasped out.

Tanner blanched. "The building behind us just exploded."

CHAPTER TWENTY-FIVE

AFTER A COLLECTIVE MOMENT of frozen shock and horror, our group leaped into action, rushing toward the building. My rain had begun to fall again, harder this time, the hail like poisoned fists. Had Sherridan and Lexis been inside that building? I could barely catch my breath, could barely force my body to remain in motion as my blood turned to thick, frozen sludge.

An alarm blasted, screeching into the night and making me cringe.

Along the way, there were armed guards lying on the ground, unconscious. Thanks to Jean-Luc? Or had I been wrong to trust him? Had he caused the explosion? Was Sherridan—

Oh, God.

No. No, no, no. I wouldn't believe it, I thought as I jumped over another motionless body. Then I tripped over a semiautomatic and landed face-first. Dirt coated my tongue as air abandoned my lungs. Thankfully my adrenaline was too high, my body too numb from cold to feel any pain. I'd feel it tomorrow, though. If I were still alive.

Rome was at my side an instant later, still in cat form, pulling me to my feet with his mouth. He was careful not to break my skin and only to tug on my clothing.

When I finally regained my breath, it was so cold it misted around my face.

"Thanks," I uttered shakily and jumped back into motion.

He growled. I'd take that as *you're welcome*.

This time, he stayed with me, keeping pace. When we reached the compound, we didn't have to find a door to get inside. A gaping hole in the side of the building greeted us.

I stopped abruptly, unsure whether to enter guns blazing as a team or split up and start searching. "Rome, I—"

Jean-Luc peeked from the corner as if he meant to attack, realized who we were, and came the rest of the way around. "About time," he said over the still-screaming alarm, loading a magazine into his gun. "What took so long? I already disabled all the planes and cars, so they won't be going anywhere."

He looked every inch the warrior.

Guilt filled me. I shouldn't have doubted Jean-Luc. Not even for a second. He was a man of his word.

Rome snarled at him.

Though I kept my back to Rome, I stepped in front of him, a stumbling block between the two men. I hoped. My hand fluttered to my throat and the pulse hammering there. "The girls—"

"Are fine, far as I know," Jean-Luc interjected, his gaze meeting mine in the darkness and probing deep. "I didn't betray you, wouldn't have hurt them." There was disappointment in his voice.

My guilt doubled. "I realize that." Now. "I just wanted to know where they were."

"Don't know."

"Any sign of Desert Hag?" Tanner asked, panting. He was bent down, digging into a vinyl bag. For…a knife he sheathed at his side.

Jean-Luc shook his head. "Not yet."

"Hans. Hide us from outside."

The sound of Rome's voice had me turning. He was in the process of morphing back into a human, fur falling away and leaving skin. Naked skin. But then shadows descended on us, black overtaking everything. There was a collective intake of breath.

I heard a rustle of clothes. Rome's transformation must be complete; he must be dressing.

"Christian," he said. "I need light. But light no one outside our shadows can see."

"Keeping my light inside my brother's shadows will weaken me."

"That's a chance I have to take. I don't want to risk hurting you guys with the weapons I'm about to ready."

A ray of gold suddenly glowed from the boy, breaking through the shadows Hans had created. Gold no one but us could see.

Rome, once again clad in all black, dug through a bag and began strapping weapons all over his body.

My heart swelled with love. Despite everything that had happened and everything I feared *would* happen, I did still love this fierce and determined man.

He tugged on a pair of boots. "We're going to stick together." He was all business. "Tanner and Elaine, watch the rear. Hans, watch the left and right. Christian—never mind. Save your strength. Jean-Luc, you're to guard Belle with your motherfucking life. Understand?"

I was both irked and touched as the two men shared an intense look.

Jean-Luc nodded.

"I'll take the lead," Rome finished, already moving forward. "Drop the shadows."

They fell away, the world around us once again becoming my focus. Nothing had changed. The building was still torn apart, the guards around us unconscious or dead. In fact, this area looked and sounded abandoned. That surprised me. Had we already dispatched everyone or were they somewhere else, waiting for us? I doubted we were lucky enough to have won the battle so easily.

Christian chose that moment to collapse from the effort of lighting the darkness and Tanner dragged him to the side of the building and propped him up. Gave him a gun and told him to shoot if anyone approached him.

"What should I do?" I asked, slipping two knives from the side slits in my pants and gripping them tightly.

"Stay alive," was all Rome said. Before I could work up a good steam, he added, "I texted Cody and told him to make sure Desert Gal was here. You're the only one who can fight her. She'll drain us of our water, and we'll crumple, but you won't have to touch her to take her down."

Was I hearing him correctly? He was trusting me to fight, believing in me, allowing me to be an agent rather than a girlfriend. It was…both wonderful and saddening, I realized. Almost surreal. Before, Rome would not have done that. He would have stuck me in a safe place and left me there until the action ended.

I wasn't sure if this meant he accepted the "different" girl I was and had faith in her, or if he'd decided we were no longer meant to be together.

"We can shoot her," Tanner said. "That way Belle won't have to engage in a catfight."

Rome shook his head. "Cody gave me the lowdown on the compound and if Desert Gal is where I think she is, gunfire would cause the entire building to explode."

I'd been so happy when Rome agreed I should be part of the fight, but this was more than I'd bargained for. One false move… "Should we be using guns *now?*"

"I'll tell you when to put them away. Don't be scared,

and don't get trigger-happy and shoot *me*. One thing in our favor, there aren't as many guards tonight as Cody had led me to expect." Rome moved to the lead, looked around. "We were able to freeze some of her accounts, and it looks like some of her men abandoned her when she couldn't pay up."

When he darted forward to finally enter the building, the entire group followed as though we'd been tugged. Everyone remained on high alert. Around us, there were cages—empty. Lab coats hanging on hooks. Wall-to-wall computer systems and machines I could not identify. There were even tables with ankle and wrist restraints, and I couldn't stop a shudder from traveling down my spine.

We cased the length of one hallway, then another, only Rome entering the offices we encountered, roving the barrel of his gun over the spaces.

"Nice try," I heard him say in one of them. Then, *Pop. Whiz.* Grunt.

I was wide-eyed as he emerged. He was careful not to look at me.

"Guard was hiding, and could have later ambushed us," he explained to the group before starting forward again.

Just like before, we followed as though we'd been tugged. Twice, Tanner had to shoot in the direction he was guarding—but only because he missed the first time. Three times, Jean-Luc had to fire off a round as doctors and guards emerged from corners and shadows to escape the little pockets of fire still blazing from the bomb. Even Hans had to shoot. He hit his target dead-on.

Gotta say, he and his brother impressed me. I'd expected them to slow us down, but they'd done more for this mission than I had.

Your turn is coming. Was Desert Soon-to-be-Dead Gal still here or had she bolted when the alarm went off?

She was probably here, I decided a moment later. If Cody had gotten her here, he wouldn't have let her leave.

I needed to keep my fear on a tight leash. Water fed her, strengthened her, so throwing ice balls at her would probably cause her energy levels to spike. Sadness was out, too. Making it rain on her would be like signing my own death warrant.

That left fire, wind and/or earth. Fire—I'd need fury. Wind—I'd need the perfect blend of anger, happiness and sadness. Earth—I'd need jealousy.

"You okay?" Jean-Luc whispered to me. His eyes roved left and right, watchful. "You're pale."

I sheathed my gun at the waist of my pants, angling it to my back. "Just trying to decide what element I need for my upcoming catfight, as Tanner calls it."

"Any front-runners?"

Yeah, I just didn't want to admit it. But there was no help for it. "Fire, most likely. It creates ash, the total opposite of what Desert Asshat needs for strength."

He snorted as he performed another quick left-right scan, then a backward glance. He moved another inch in front of me. "What emotion do you need for that? Fury, right?"

"That's right." We turned a corner, our steps slowing.

He nodded, seemed to think things over for a moment, his gun sliding in sync with his gaze. "Rome doesn't like that you're an agent."

My eyes narrowed. "You can't know that. You gave him back his memories, which means they can't be inside you. You don't know what he's feeling."

"Oh, really? Well, guess what, sugar? I wrote every-thing down. I knew the time would come that I'd have to give them back to make you happy, and I didn't want to forget a thing about you. So I wrote everything down and read it all. The. Time. I've memorized his memories. Rome didn't want you to be an agent. He was thinking about swooping you up and carrying you and his daughter off to a hideaway."

Shocked to the core, I sent my gaze to the man in question. All I could see was the stiff line of his back and the side of his face as he performed the same left-and-right scan as Jean-Luc at the end of the hallway to decide where to go.

"Also, he had a fling with Desert Gal shortly after his divorce from Lexis. He called her Candy. They were pretty hot, but he broke things off to try and win Lexis back. Pissed Candace off royally. Embarrassed her."

Every muscle in my body was stiffening. The ice inside me was melting, swifter than it ever had before. Little flames were branching from my fingernails. "That's not possible. One, she's a scrim who was in Pretty Boy's employ. Two, Rome hates scrims. Three, touching her drains a person of their water, and he wasn't drained."

Jean-Luc was shaking his head before the last word left me. "Nope. She's only worked for Pretty Boy a year, so maybe she wasn't a scrim when Rome dated her. And she's not like Elaine. Skin to skin doesn't drain the water from a body. Candace controls it. *She* decides when to drain, when not to."

He was right. I'd watched Cody touch her and nothing had happened to him. "I—I—" Had no words. Why the hell had Rome not told me about this?

We rounded another corner and stopped abruptly as Rome held up one hand. I rammed into Jean-Luc. He *humphed,* stumbled forward and rammed into Hans.

"Sorry." I scanned the room we'd entered. Spacious but with more cages, these actually filled with people.

Around fifteen of them. I searched their dirty, bruised faces—and found Sherridan and Lexis.

My heart raced and tears popped into my eyes. They were alive. Thank God, thank God, thank God. Each occupied her own cage. They were more bruised than the other prisoners, but alive. They gripped the iron bars and watched the happenings with a mix of fear and hope.

And there, in the center of it all, was Cody. If I'd had any remaining doubts about whether I could trust him, the sight of him put them to rest. Lightning streamed from one of his hands, wrapping around Desert Gal in a supercharged cage of her own, her hair standing up from her scalp, her eyes bugging out from the intensity. Clearly, she couldn't move. But the lines of tension around her mouth suggested she was trying to do so with every ounce of strength she possessed.

Cody's other hand was pointed at a group of people. Doctors, judging by their lab coats. Sweat was running down Cody's face, his shirt already soaked to his chest. "Can't hold...them...much longer." Every word emerged strained, even as they echoed from the walls.

There was a weird sort of air pressure in the room that made my ears constantly pop. It was unnerving.

"No guns," Rome said, placing his on the ground and kicking it to the far wall. Everyone in our little group did the same.

I stared over at the woman who had supposedly once shared my man's bed, and my teeth gnashed together. She was prettier in person than she'd been on Rome's small cell-phone screen, even lit up like a Christmas tree as she was. Damn it! All of Rome's exes were prettier than me.

"Elaine." Rome withdrew a knife. "When Cody's shield falls away, take out as many of the doctors as you can."

She nodded and marched forward, shoulders squared,

expression scared but determined. Was she recalling the cage she'd occupied for so long? Poor thing. But what bravery to march ahead anyway.

"Hans, guard the doors," I said. "Don't let anyone escape."

The boy looked to Rome, who nodded, and marched off.

"Jean-Luc, if at all possible, jump into Desert Gal when Cody frees her and take as many memories as you can," Rome instructed. "We'll sort through them later. If you can't get to her, wait. Belle will try and give you a chance. Tanner, get our girls."

Both men raced to obey.

That left me and Rome. He looked at me, mouth firm, unyielding. "Cody's going to collapse. I'm going to pull him to safety. If Jean-Luc can't access her, you'll have her all to yourself. Don't be afraid to use your powers. She won't."

"I'll win," I said on a trembling breath. I wondered, though, how he could be so ruthless when he'd once slept with this woman.

"You better." His eyes darkened, the pupils expanding. "Don't worry about the rest of us. All right? Don't think about holding back or caging your emotions. Unleash them. And...be careful."

"I will," I replied.

"I love you, Belle. I hope you know that." He didn't give me time to reply. He closed the distance between us and meshed his lips to mine, his tongue plunging deep for a split second.

Sweet fire. I was instantly transported out of the building into Paradise, where angels sang and ambrosia flowed in golden rivers. In that moment, I knew everything would be okay, that nothing bad would happen, could happen, that tomorrow I'd wake up in this man's arms, and soon I would be his bride. But then he pulled away, rushing to Cody's side, and I came down from my euphoric high, unsure about today, even more unsure about tomorrow.

Still the passion burned inside me, though. And it was hot, so hot. Blistering me from the inside out. This was probably what Rome had intended, not a reassurance of his feelings. Or maybe the new me was just being cynical. I couldn't worry about that now.

Fingers flexing at my sides, I stalked to Desert Gal. I pictured her in Rome's bed, naked, straining, biting him, begging him for more, and my passion mutated into the fury I'd craved. My hands caught fire.

"Now, Cody," Rome shouted. "Now!"

The lightning suddenly stopped. I heard grunting, groaning, heard clothing rustle as Elaine leaped into motion, touching everyone she could. Heard the shuffle of feet as Rome dragged an unconscious Cody out of the way.

Desert Gal dropped to her knees, her pale hair shielding her face, her small shoulders hunched. Jean-Luc dove for her, but she'd clearly expected it and rolled out of the way.

I launched a fireball at her. But again, she was quick, and flattened to her stomach, the ball flying over her. She looked up, her gaze clashing with mine. She reached toward me, fingers pointed at me. I threw another fireball. Water rushed from her hands, meeting my fire midway and causing it to dissolve.

Her action was so unexpected, I wasn't able to jump out of the way before the water pummeled me to my back. The name Desert Gal implied she *needed* water, not that she had it in abundance and could spew it like this.

"Belle Jamison. I've been waiting for this moment for months," she said. "And now, here we are. The other woman in my father's life."

"Yes. Here we are." The spray continued until she made it to her feet. Then she stopped, grinned at me, free hand shooting out. It was aimed at Jean-Luc, keeping him back with another spray. "But I have no idea what you're talking about. I've never met your father."

"Really? When he taught us both our tricks?"

Tricks? Can we say de-lusion-al? "He likes me better than you, right?" Soaking wet, I glared up at her through spiky lashes, trying to catch my breath. Fury was still rising inside me, still smoldering. I just needed a moment to bring it to the surface again. "Care to tell me why?"

"I wish I knew. You're weaker than me, ugly and stupid."

Bitch. "I'm not your biggest fan, either. So what's his name?"

"Dr. Enrich Roberts, of course. As if you have to ask."

My jaw dropped, shock momentarily replacing my fury. Dr. Roberts? The man who had fed me the formula that made me into what I was? The man I had chased for weeks, unable to find?

How had we not known he had a daughter?

"I know what you're thinking. I could be lying since no one knew."

Close enough. "How'd you keep it secret?"

"Do you know how easy it is to forge documents and make others disappear?"

No, but I was learning.

"It was his way of *protecting* me from outside forces, just like his running away was. But I don't want to be protected anymore. I want him back. And you're going to help me."

Uh, what? "I understand missing a parent, but—"

She laughed cruelly. "I don't miss him, you stupid bitch. Like you, he made me what I am, experimenting on me my entire life as if I was an animal. And just when I finally began to like the results, he vanished. He didn't like that I had started working for Vincent, same as him, was afraid that our secrets would be discovered, that I would be used and hurt in an effort to control him. But now Vincent is dead, I'm in charge and my father is going to return. For you. And he's going to make me stronger."

Rome had once warned me about this. People often became drunk on their power, craving more. But more was never enough. The thirst was never quenched. "I hate to break it to you, but he won't come back for me." I worked my hands behind my back, as though I was trying to lift myself on my elbows. Meanwhile, I mentally pushed the fire to my fingertips. "I'm nothing to him. An experiment. Just like you said."

From the corner of my eye, I could see Rome sneaking up on her.

But she must have sensed it, too, because she threw out her other arm, water spraying from her fingers and propelling him backward. She laughed, though her attention never left me. "Wait your turn, Agent Masters. You're next."

Agent Masters. Not exactly former lover-speak.

She released Jean-Luc, who was turning blue, unable to breathe, and reached for me once more. I rolled, avoiding impact. She stalked closer, trying again, and again, but I kept rolling. And when she finally reached me, I kicked her arm away. She swung to the side, freeing Rome from her watery fury. He remained crouched, coughing up water.

"He'll come back for you," she said as if our conversation had never stopped. She was panting. Using her power must exhaust her. "He won't be able to help himself. You're his greatest success. He won't want me to kill you."

Yeah, she was probably right. He had apologized several times for what he'd done to me. I didn't think he'd want me to die, either. But how could he have experimented on his own daughter? "I'm not staying here with you. I'm taking my friends and going. And oh, yeah. I'm locking your ass up for good."

She'd had a crappy life, sure, and I pitied her for it. But Elaine had had a crappy life, too, and Elaine had not turned to the dark side. Desert Gal, I feared, was beyond redemption.

Slowly I rose. "We done talking?"

Another laugh. Cold, heartless. "You can't beat me, Wonder Girl."

"Wanna bet, *Candace?*" I launched another fireball at her. This one hit her, and she yelped.

The yelp became a screech as she frantically patted herself with her hands. Water poured from them and did douse the fire, leaving her in tattered clothes, soot smearing her skin. The scent of burned hair filled the room. Her poor, pretty golden hair.

Both Jean-Luc and Rome had regained their bearings and approached her, running toward her, but she hadn't lost her reservoir of water and extended her arms, keeping them both at bay. But that left her vulnerable to me.

I, too, approached, trying to work up a good jealousy, planning to bury her in a mound of dirt. Sure, she could turn the dirt to mud, but that would take some time. Time I could use to grab one of Rome's night-night syringes and inject her. Time Jean-Luc could use to jump inside her.

Desert Gal had other plans.

Just as I reached her, she dropped her arms from Jean-Luc and Rome, who once again started gagging up the water they'd swallowed, and latched onto me in a choke hold. I gasped, instantly feeling her drawing the water from my cells and into her. It was painful, some of my vessels popping from the strain of her suction.

"It didn't have to be this way," she said through gritted teeth. "We could have worked together. My father could have given us both more power."

Think, Belle, think.

The men tackled us, throwing us to the ground and trying to separate us. But that only increased my pain. Her hands were practically glued to me. I couldn't even scream. Thankfully, Rome and Jean-Luc realized they weren't doing any good, only harming me further, and backed away. I could hear them muttering frantically in the background, Jean-Luc saying there was some sort of shield around her, that he couldn't get inside her. Their voices seemed to fall farther and farther away.

Was this it for me? The end? My last day on earth? I wasn't afraid as I would have assumed. I was disappointed. I hadn't gotten to say goodbye. Hadn't gotten to make love to Rome one last time. Hadn't gotten to experience my dream wedding, Sherridan my maid of honor, my dad walking me down the aisle.

You can stop her. There's still time. I could…what? Ice myself? Why not? Maybe it would strengthen her as I'd feared earlier, or maybe it would immobilize her. Either way, it was worth a shot. But even as I played fearful thoughts through my head, the emotion remained out of my grasp, my disappointment too keen.

Ice, damn it. I just need a little ice. Come on, come on, come on. Oh, the irony. I had to work for it the one time I *wanted* to summon it. Ice, ice, ice.

Finally, my blood thickened and my veins hardened. My lungs crystallized. Ice! Yes! Except, I wasn't afraid. I was simply picturing it and it was forming.

This hadn't happened in so long, I was stunned. I

didn't need my emotions, just the power of them. It was like looking at a sunset and experiencing its beauty, but being unable to physically touch it. But here the ability was. Mine again. Well, separate from me. As numb as I was, so quickly fading, there was nothing left of me. Only the abilities remained.

Desert Gal frowned, her suction easing. She even tried to pull away, as if drawing the ice was painful for her. As if her body didn't welcome it the way mine did. My eyes widening, I grabbed on to her. *More ice, more ice, more ice,* I thought, mentally projecting it inside her. Ice might be composed of water, but it didn't strengthen her. It slowed her down, actually weakened her, because she had no way of melting it. Her own source of water began to freeze.

Before my eyes, her skin turned blue. A glaze of ice smoothed over it, icicles forming in her hair. Only when she was completely motionless did I let her go. I crawled out from under her and fell back onto the ground, *my* strength now depleted. Didn't matter. I'd won. Won!

I turned my head, searching for Rome. I saw Lexis instead. Jean-Luc had her cradled in his arms, and she was sobbing into his chest. I could also see Cody. He was cradling Sherridan as if she were a precious treasure. Sherridan tried to pull away, but gave up after a few moments and simply sagged into his arms.

Tanner stepped into my dimming line of sight, his features concerned. I think he would have come to me, but Elaine crumpled beside him, as used up as I was. He turned, bent down and scooped her up.

All the women were out for the count. Made sense. We'd done the most work. But had we won the battle only to lose ourselves?

"Belle," I heard Rome shout, sounding like he was in an

underwater tunnel located in another state. Where the hell was he? Didn't matter, I supposed. He'd get me to safety.

It was the last thought I knew before darkness claimed me.

CHAPTER TWENTY-SIX

I AWOKE WITH MY HEART drumming and my body sweating.

First thing I noticed was the beeping. *Beep, beep, beep.* The high-pitched noises came from every direction, a discordant symphony. One was fast, one slow, one in-between. One was a quick *thump thump* before a lengthy pause and another *thump thump*.

Confusion was a thick web inside my brain.

Through slitted eyelids and a fan of lashes, I saw that a light glowed overhead, dimmed but still too bright for my sensitive corneas. When I turned my head, I could see colored pinpricks shining off...monitors? Heart monitors, then. The beeping suddenly made sense. Except, why was I hearing it?

Brow furrowing, I scanned the rest of my surroundings. A hospital room, by the looks of it. Gurneys, a nurse padding through and reading charts. Electrodes dotted my chest, and a paper-thin blue gown I remembered very well gaped over them. We must be back in Georgia. PSI headquarters.

Sherridan lay in the bed to my left, Lexis in the bed to my right. Elaine was in a bed across from us. All four of us were hooked to an IV and all the others were awake, eating. Groggy, I sat up—hello, dizziness—and scrubbed the sleep from my eyes. My IV tube caught on the bed rail, pulling the skin of my forearm. I winced, inhaling deeply and catching the scent of cleaners, medicine and...Rome?

I inhaled again, savoring the scent. Sure enough. Wild, earthy.

Rome had recently been beside my bed.

When had he left? *Why* had he left? I guess I could ask him next time I saw him. But I hated waiting.

"Hey," I said, drawing everyone's attention. "How are the others doing? Rome, Tanner, Jean-Luc, Cody and the Shadow Boys?"

"They're good," Elaine said. "Promise."

Sherridan grinned at me and waved. God, she looked good. There was a flush to her cheeks that bespoke health and vitality. Her hair was clean and brushed, the blond curls shining. There was a cut on her lip and a bruise on her cheek, but those would fade. She was alive. Nothing else mattered.

"How are you?" I asked her.

She opened her mouth to speak, but closed it with a snap. Her smile slowly faded.

"What's wrong?" I asked.

She pointed to her mouth and shook her head.

"You lost your voice?"

She shook her head again. The vivid blue of her eyes dimmed, a sad, almost haunting edge creeping into them.

"She can't talk to you unless you have special filters in your ears." Rome's voice echoed through the room, nearly electrifying me.

Both Lexis and I jumped, I noticed. For different reasons? I wanted to watch her, to see if I could judge whether she realized he'd gotten his memories back, but I didn't. My gaze sought Rome of its own accord, drawn to him by an invisible tether. Breath caught in my throat, burning.

He was as beautiful as ever. Tall, muscled, dressed in black. His unkempt hair shagged around his face, so damp it dripped onto his temples. His cheekbones were a little sharper, as if he'd lost weight, and fine stress lines branched from his eyes.

"Rome," Lexis said.

He ignored her. In fact, a muscle ticked in his jaw, the only reaction that he'd even heard her. So. He was mad at her. Mad about what she'd done, how she'd lied, manipulated and used him to try to win him back. I'd tried to warn her it would happen.

"How are you?" he asked me.

"Better." I pinned him with a stare, crossing my arms over my chest to hide my hardening nipples. Now that the danger was over, now that my friends were safe, now that his memories were returned, my body was reacting as it always had when he neared. Like I was a live wire attached to a generator. Only now? Ha! But still, not good in a room full of people.

"I'm glad. I was worried about you."

Sweet man. "What were you saying about Sherridan?"

"You mean Siren? That's her new paranormal name. Because she now has a superpower," Rome explained, stepping into the room. He didn't stop until he was beside my bed. There was a chair there, and he eased into it, leaning back and stretching out his legs.

Siren? The smell of soap wafted from him, distracting me. I was willing to bet he'd left me only long enough to shower. I smiled. My dear, sweet man. *Who once dated Desert Dirtbag and never told me.* My smile disappeared.

Rome reached out, twined our fingers. I was stiff, but didn't pull away. "What?"

"Nothing." Everything. My upcoming dates with Jean-Luc were approaching. Could Rome and I make it?

The question slammed through me—when would it leave me? Of course we'd make it, I told myself. We'd made it through his memory loss. And yet, he hadn't even hinted about whether or not he could see himself with me forever, now that I was putting the agency first.

I dragged my thoughts back to the matter at hand. "I still don't understand." I looked over at Sherridan, who had tears in her eyes. "Whatever it is, we'll make it better," I vowed.

Rome's fingers squeezed mine. "Candace had her scientists mess with Sherridan's voice. Now, when she speaks, anyone who hears her will fall under her spell. Male and female alike. They'll be her slave, do anything she asks."

Oh, Sherridan. Poor Sherridan. She'd wanted a superpower, but hadn't thought about the consequences. And there were always consequences. I'd come to realize that bad always balanced good and good always balanced bad. Otherwise, the world would swing too far to one side.

"What about Lexis?"

Something in his eyes hardened and he answered before Lexis could. "They didn't mess with her. She already had a power."

As he spoke, I tried to throw my legs over the side of the bed. I wanted to wrap Sherridan in my arms. But Rome had anticipated such a move from me. He released my hand and locked onto my ankles, tossing them back onto the bed with a flick of his wrists.

"Don't even," he said.

Fine. I wasn't sure I could walk, anyway. "Someone tell me how Desert Witch planned to use a spell-binding voice against me." And I knew it had been for my benefit. Why else take my friend? "Sherridan would have commanded her to go to hell, and that would have entranced *her*."

Rome was shaking his head. "The only way to not fall victim to Sherridan's voice is by having special filters surgically added to your ears. Filters Candace has. She wanted Sherridan to call you before her procedure to worry you, then after it was done so that you were guaranteed to answer and assuage your fears. But Sherridan wouldn't do the latter, even upon threat of death."

Candace, was it? Ugh. "Surely Sherridan's voice wouldn't affect *me*. Surely—"

"I guess we have to prove it. Lexis and I had filters implanted when we went through all our enhancements, and Tanner got his this morning, so you and Elaine are the only ones in the room without them. Brace yourselves. Show her, Sherridan."

"I'm so sorry, Belle," she said on a sob, and her voice was heaven. Absolute, utter heaven.

I shivered, my gaze drawn to her, my body leaning toward her. No, not leaning. I was trying to stand again, had to reach her. Touch her. She was so beautiful, and if I could just trace my finger over her skin, I knew I would be transported to the paradise I heard in her voice. It would be better than Rome's kiss.

Hooked as I was to the IV, I couldn't move fast enough, couldn't move close enough. But I tried, oh, I tried. Until a hard restraining hand pushed me back on the bed and held me down.

"What are you doing?" I batted at the offending restraint. "Let me go. Sherridan, I need you. I love you."

A heavy weight descended, pinning me down. I fought and bucked and bit and scratched, all to no avail.

"Let me up, damn it!"

"Belle. Stop."

My struggles increased. If I could just reach Sherridan…hold her, kiss her perhaps. She was everything I'd ever wanted. Everything I needed. *Sherridan*. Even the name made me shiver.

Warm lips pressed into my ear. "Calm down, baby. I'm here. Rome's here. I've got you. Concentrate on my voice. Do you hear me? Your body feels so good pressed against mine. Lush and sweet."

Rome's husky tone penetrated the love-lust haze thing I had going. I stilled, tendrils of horror sneaking up on me. I was panting, sweating, but my head was clearing. "Oh, God."

Slowly Rome's delicious weight lifted off me. I remained in place, though I wanted to latch onto him and take comfort.

"See," he said, settling back in the chair.

I shared a watery smile with Sherridan. "It'll be okay," I told her. And then I looked away, because her sadness was more than I could bear.

My gaze landed on the other "happy" couple in the room. Tanner must have entered while I'd been trying to score with Sherridan. He'd been forced to hold Elaine down just as Rome had held me. Thankfully, she was covered in another full-body stocking, preventing them from any skin-to-skin contact.

"Look on the bright side, Sher," Tanner said with a grin. "You've finally got a shot with Jessica Alba."

Rome reached up and traced a finger over my arm. "Now you see how powerful Sherridan's voice is. Candace planned to use her as bait. Draw you to her. She would have found a way to make Sherridan cave, like threatening to kill Lexis in front of her. That was the disaster Cody was hoping to avoid. He couldn't call us because Candace was paranoid and wouldn't let him out of her sight. She had him monitored 24/7."

Goose bumps broke out over my skin. His touch…so

warm, so gentle. "I want filters," I said. No way I'd make my best friend remain silent in my presence for the rest of her life.

"I'm sure that can be arranged," Rome said.

Sherridan waved in a bid to gain my attention. When our gazes met, she mouthed, *I'm sorry.*

"It happens to the best of us," I said. I held out my arms. "Look at me."

A quiet, whispery bark of a laugh escaped her. But it was enough to make my heart pound and my skin tingle. Sweet Jesus, she was beautiful. Enough to— *Get hold of yourself, Belle.*

"Knock, knock," Cody said. "Can I come in?"

Immediately Sherridan rolled to her side, facing me but giving Cody her back. Cody watched her, his hands fisting at his sides. There was a gleam of murder in his eyes, not that any other part of his expression betrayed it. His smile remained firmly in place.

Something had happened between them. I'd stake my life on it.

"Looks like the gang's all here," I said. I was just happy John hadn't arrived demanding blood. With Reese jailed, he would have had to take it the old-fashioned way, but still. I'd been through enough.

"The nurse told me everyone was awake. I just wanted to check on you guys." Though he spoke to all of us, his gaze kept returning to Sherridan. I remembered the way he'd held her when she'd exited her cage. Remembered how he'd caressed her back and held on as though she were…necessary.

Sherridan paled, opened her mouth to say something.

"We're good," I rushed out, cutting her off. "Right?" I realized I'd asked about the men, but never about my girls, even though they'd been right in front of me the entire time. Or maybe because they had.

Lexis gave a brief nod, and Elaine said, "Better than ever."

They did look good, as healthy as Sherridan.

"What happened to Desert Slut?" I asked. "Other than the fact that she likes to sleep with agents."

"Cody slept with her? Go, Cody!" Tanner laughed.

"I'm not talking about Cody." I stuck my tongue out at him. "But anyway, you don't get to talk. You came in here and ignored me, didn't hug me or even ask how I was doing."

He flipped me off behind his back, and I was the one to laugh. That was my sweet Tanner, back to his old self completely.

"Be nice," Elaine told him.

"Anything for you, my little tampon."

Both of them chuckled, and I saw Lexis force her attention to her hands, as if they were the most fascinating thing she'd ever seen. Tanner and Elaine really did make a cute couple. I just hoped they found a way to touch each other. Surgery, maybe. Or, ugh, hopefully another experiment wouldn't be necessary.

"Desert Gal," Rome prompted, drawing my attention. "You were curious about what happened to her."

Oh, yeah. "Dead?" There was a mixture of hope and dread in my voice.

He shook his head. "Alive and in lockup. John's going to do some tests, have someone interrogate her, find out how she's able to touch other people without draining them and use the information he gains to help Elaine."

"Good. That's good." A part of me still pitied her, but I was glad her reign of terror was over—and that she might do someone else some good. Even unwillingly.

Rome squeezed my wrist. "You did good, Wonder Girl. You did real good. I'm proud of you."

My chin trembled, the depth of my emotion seemingly endless. What a wonderfully sweet thing to say. After all, I had hurt him, put myself in danger, two things he would have ranted and raved about only a few weeks before. "I don't think the battle ended with Desert Gal, though. Dr. Roberts is her dad, you know? He made her what she is, gave her those powers. He experiments on people without their permission."

"Yes." Our gazes were locked and for a little while, only a little while, the rest of the world faded away. "Once I thought he was fine out there," Rome added, "roaming around. I thought it was better to keep such a mastermind out of the wrong hands. Any hands, really. But he's a danger."

"What if he's experimenting on an innocent right now?"

"Any idea where he is?"

"One. The one Candace gave us."

My stomach twisted, because I knew what he meant. The lead was me. PSI thought Roberts would come after me, try to find out why his formula had worked on me and no one else.

"I won't let anything happen to you," Rome said. "You know that, I hope."

Would he feel the same way after my three dates with Jean-Luc? "I want to learn self-defense. And dirty street-fighting."

He nodded, a proud glint filling his eyes. Proud of me? Again? "Soon as the doctor signs your release, we'll head to the gym."

I shivered—in anticipation this time—because I suspected there would be some heavy petting involved. However much our future relationship remained up in the air, we were attracted to each other and when we were in close proximity, alone, wrestling, hands were going to roam, legs were going to intertwine.

"First," I said, "we need to talk." Much as I craved him, there had to be some ground rules.

"I've been dreading this," he said, and there was indeed a grim note to his voice. "You don't think we should be together. Otherwise, you wouldn't have agreed to date that fucking Memory Man. Something you are *not* going to do."

I didn't want to do it, but I wouldn't tolerate being bossed around like that, either. "This whole memory loss thing made me realize a few things, that's all, and we need to hash them out. And yes, I'm going to date him as promised. I told you, I will not go back on my word. But speaking of Jean-Luc, where is he? If you placed him in lockup again, I swear to God I'll roast you alive."

"You already do," he muttered, his eyes narrowing to dangerous slits. "And yes, you will go back on your word. Because if he touches you, I'll kill him, and you don't want his death on your hands. You're mine. Now tell me what you realized."

On *my* hands? Ha! And he still considered me his, even though I was "different"? "You didn't think I was yours a few days ago. You thought Lexis was. Do you know how badly that hurt?"

"I'll kiss it and make it better," he said huskily.

Oh, God, did I want him to try. I had to cut back a moan of desire. "Our wedding has already gone up in flames, Rome. I don't have a dress, a church or a caterer. And as we originally planned to marry in a few weeks, I don't think I can get everything together in time, anyway. Not that we've decided to still get married."

"We're still getting married." A hard, harsh statement he obviously saw as fact.

I ignored him. It was either that or throw myself in his arms and just forget the concerns I had. As I sat there in silence, I could feel several gazes boring into me. One belonged to Lexis, and I didn't want her hearing all of my problems. Though given how close her bed was to mine, I suspected she had already heard quite a few. "Let's save this conversation for another time. When we're alone."

"No. What are your concerns? I need to hear them."

Fine. Witnesses be damned. Sherridan and Tanner would only ask me for details later, anyway. "You don't see me as an agent. You see me as a liability."

"That's not true."

"It is. You planned to take me and Sunny and hide us away. Don't try to deny it."

His eyes narrowed. "I won't. I thought about it for about a minute and then realized it would be wrong. And look, I stepped back, didn't try to stop you from fighting Candace. Even *encouraged* you to fight with her."

True. "Okay, you *used* to see me as a liability and I think maybe you liked me that way. You were my protector, and I let that define our relationship. But I'm different now. You said so yourself."

He nodded. There was no use denying it.

"I'm going to be an agent, not just play at it. I'm going to take cases, travel, fight. I'm going to do this because it needs to be done and I want the people I love to be safe. I would love to work with you, but I won't allow you to be my guard dog. Or cat. Guard cat. You'll have to treat me like any other agent. Is that something you can handle?"

That muscle began ticking in his jaw again. He didn't answer.

"Also, I've said it before but it needs reiterating. I am

going to date Jean-Luc. Three dates, as promised. Otherwise, I'm a liar and that's not something I want to be. Is *that* something you can handle?"

Silence.

Heavy, gut-wrenching silence. My gaze landed on Lexis, and there were tears in her eyes. She nodded at me. Telling me this was going to be okay?

"Go on the dates," Rome finally said, his expression hard as granite. "Just know that I'll be there the entire time. Go to eat, I'll be at the restaurant, sitting at the table next to yours. Go to the movies, and I'll be right behind you, breathing down your neck. But I will not ever treat you like any other agent. You're special to me. I'll be concerned about you, I can't help that. I'll want to protect you. Always. Can *you* handle that?"

"I—"

Didn't have time to answer. "No. Don't say another word. We're done for right now." He pushed to his feet, scooting the chair away. He strode from the room and never looked back.

CHAPTER TWENTY-SEVEN

Two Days Later

"CONCENTRATE, BELLE!"

"I am! *Rome.*"

We were on opposite ends of a blue mat, sweat pouring from both of us. While I probably resembled a drowned house cat with severe breathing problems, Rome had never looked better. His shirt was off—of course—and his skin sun-kissed, roped perfection that glistened sexily.

He arched a brow. "I've tossed you on your ass over fifteen times."

"And I've nailed you with a dirt ball once and an ice ball twice." Of course, he'd dodged all three so quickly they'd only nicked his arm—which had affected only his arm, damn it, rather than consuming his entire body.

Before meeting me here, he'd soaked himself in a clear, experimental chemical that slowed the progression of the elements. Apparently John had been working on it for a while. Since learning about me, actually. Just in case I turned on him, I suspected. Or maybe in case others like me were made. I only hoped bad guys didn't get hold of the stuff. Anyway, the ice had melted in minutes and the dirt had smoothed away, all while Rome had subdued me with his *other* arm.

Arf. Arf.

Grrrrr.

The barking and growling drew my attention, and I foolishly glanced away from Rome. Merciless man that he was, he was in front of me in seconds, knocking my ankles together and sending me flying to my ass. Again.

He loomed over me, eyes narrowed in disappointment. "Don't look away from your opponent. Ever. You know better. And letting those two mutts break your concentration? You should be ashamed."

"Thanks for the tip," I muttered, staying put and trying to catch my breath. We'd been at this for hours, and my muscles weren't used to the strain. "But if you ever call them mutts again, I will neuter you."

My babies didn't like my man and vice versa.

The night before, my first night home from the hospital, Rome had snuck into my house. Okay, I'd let him in. I hadn't been able to help myself. Though I'd sworn we wouldn't until we'd talked things out, we'd ended up making love. It had been desperate sex, life-altering, earth-shattering sex. The kind that affected you soul-deep.

Next morning, when I woke up, Rome had already left—no talkie-talkie for us, just hanky-panky—so I'd done what I'd promised: purchased not one but two vicious dogs. Minus the vicious. Okay, I'd bought two puppies. English bulldogs. Lovey—black and white, very rare—and Ginger—top half white, bottom half brown, like pants. They looked like little teddy bears, and I hadn't been able to resist them.

Currently my girls were nibbling on bones in the corner of the gym, oblivious to the world around them. Jean-Luc was watching them for me. I hadn't been able to leave them home alone, and he was doing his best to romance me. Which apparently meant sticking to me like glue and doing whatever I asked. That didn't bother me. After all, that had been my plan with Rome. Great minds and all that.

He was staying at a nearby hotel until he could find a permanent place—after his hard work on the Desert Gal case, John had hired him and he'd accepted—and had been waiting for me here at headquarters. He didn't like me rubbing up against Rome, though. I'd heard him mutter a protest more than once, but he didn't try to stop the lessons. That surprised me. I'd already confessed about my recent nocturnal activities with Rome. Though there were no promises between me and Jean-Luc outside our three dates, he'd looked so hurt I'd wanted to die.

Since returning Rome's memories, he'd been nothing but sweet to me, nothing but helpful. The least I could do was stay away from Rome sex-wise until our three dates were over. Besides, by then I would—should—know if Rome and I could go the distance as a couple. If he would love me, despite anything. Despite everything.

I think that's what I was most worried about. That he wouldn't love me, wouldn't respect me, when all was said and done.

Men! I was between a rock—Jean-Luc—and a very hard place—Rome.

"Up," Rome commanded. "You're wasting time."

"Well, you're consuming my personal space." I lumbered to my feet, facing him on my tiptoes so that we were nose-to-nose.

At least he didn't attack me again. Or kiss me. Would I be able to resist? Even though I'd brushed my teeth, had coffee, two bottles of water and a bagel, I still had his decadent taste in my mouth. Still heard his groans of pleasure in my ears. Still felt his hands kneading my breasts, rubbing between my legs.

"You're panting," he said huskily. His eyes lowered, lingered on my breasts, my hardened nipples.

Every part of me, every organ, every cell begged me to lean the rest of the way into him. Miracle of miracles, I stepped backward. "Self-defense. Important. Life-saving. Dr. Roberts is out there and needs to be stopped. Jean-Luc. The dates. Our future, up in the air." All the reasons we had to stay away from each other right now.

His expression became shuttered. "You're taking too long to summon the elements. Time an opponent can use to slice your throat or inject you with a night-night cocktail. And you can't rely on typical defensive moves because you won't be fighting typical criminals. You'll be fighting scrims, so the outcome will depend on who has the most power. You. Or them. What's more, I thought we were doing this because *you* thought you didn't need your emotions anymore."

I kicked at the air with the tip of my tennie. "You're right." Last night I'd told him about summoning the ice that had stopped Desert Gal without the use of my emotions. "But I can't do it again. I've tried. Only my emotions are calling the elements and I can't switch them off with a snap."

He reached out, smoothed a wet strand of hair from my brow. A barely there touch, but I felt the warmth all the way to the bone.

For a moment, only a moment, there was a flash of his cat behind his face, skin melting away, fur taking its place. Then it was gone. "I've given this a lot of thought. Maybe you've never needed your emotions. Maybe you only thought you did because of the sensations they evoke in your body. Think about it. Anger makes your blood pressure rise, which makes you hot. Fear is numbing, so you become cold."

"That doesn't tell me how to summon the elements without my emotions, though. I mean, even when I did this sans feelings in the past, I still needed the strength or idea of whatever emotion I wanted to summon." Well, not true. Last time, with Desert Gal, I'd been too numb, completely out of the equation.

"Maybe you summon certain elements with certain emotions because that's the element you're freeing at that time. You think fire comes with fury so you release the fire when you get mad."

I anchored a hand on my hip. It was either that or grab on to him and never let go.

What he said made sense—but it also scared me. If I failed to prove him right, no big deal. I'd go back to the way things were. But what if I succeeded? To finally have control of my powers, to not be reliant on my emotions, to not have to worry about raging wildfires, torrential storms, mountains of dirt and unstoppable winds every time PMS took hold…

Ultimate power was something Rome despised. People became drunk with it, did whatever they wanted, damn the consequences. Proof—Desert Gal, who would spend the rest of her life in Chateau Villain, in a special dry-as-a-desert section designed for her. She'd wanted more, and more, and more, but more had never been and would never be enough.

If I did this, made a success of it, I would be unstoppable. Ultimate power would be mine.

God, the strikes were adding up against me. How much longer would this man consider me worth the effort? How long till he left me? Here I was, becoming the very things he'd once told me he never wanted: infinitely powerful, an agent always in the middle of danger and a woman determined to date another man.

"Summon the element itself," he said, oblivious to my dark thoughts, "not the emotion you think comes with it." One step, two, he backed away from me.

I shook my head, backing away from him, as well. The distance between us continued to grow. "I need Tanner if I'm even going to *think* about trying something new."

"Sorry, he's with Elaine. They're talking to the scientists who have been studying Candace, trying to come up with a way for Elaine to experience skin-to-skin contact without killing people."

I dearly hoped they'd succeed. If any couple deserved a shot at happiness—and nookie—it was them. Yuck, there I was thinking about Tanner's sex life again. It was almost as bad as thinking of Rome and Desert Gal. "Speaking of Candace," I said, stalling, "why didn't you tell me you dated her?"

He blinked over at me. "Excuse me?"

I stood my ground, planted my hands on my hips. "You heard me."

"What are you talking about? I never dated her."

"Yes, you did. You—"

"Uh, Belle," Jean-Luc called.

I swung around, facing him.

He tossed a small braided rope across the room and Lovey chased after it. Ginger chased after her.

"Mutts," Rome muttered.

"I lied," Jean-Luc continued. "You needed fury, so I gave you something to be furious about. Sorry."

"What?" I stomped my foot and ignored Rome. "I thought—"

"What the hell?" Rome interjected. "He told you I slept with Candace, so you believed him? Believed him over me?"

"Well…" I turned back to him, my lips pressed together and my cheeks reddening. "I'm sorry."

He sighed. Pinched the bridge of his nose. "Forget it. After what I did to you, I deserve it." He was obviously still upset, but he held out a hand and motioned me over with a wave of his fingers. A challenge. "Come on. Ice me."

He clearly had not and would not forget it anytime soon. The irony? I wanted him to cleanse his memory palate. Since he wouldn't—bastard—I'd have to make it up to him. Somehow. "First, bring Sherridan in here."

"No. She's currently being examined, and you're not allowed near her until after your surgery. Now come on. Do it."

My appointment for ear filters was tomorrow morning, and I couldn't wait. I wanted to talk to Sherridan again. I *needed* to talk to her. I needed advice. Was I doing the right thing, trying to stay away from Rome until my dates with Jean-Luc were over?

"Stop stalling, Belle."

The man knew me very well. "Fine," I snapped. "I'll ice the hell out of you." I spread my legs, clenched and unclenched my fists as I flashed scary pictures through my mind.

Rome clapped his hands together and the sound boomed through the gym. "You're relying on your emotions. Stop."

"You can do it, Belle," Jean-Luc called. Lovey barked as if to second the motion.

Rome flicked him an irritated glance before returning his attention to me. "You want to be an effective agent, you've got to learn to protect yourself in an instant. You can't do that if you have to force yourself to feel a certain way."

Everything he said was right. I knew it. Didn't like it, but knew it. *I can do this. I can do this.* I'd done it before. Okay. *Here goes.* Deep breath in, deep breath out. Ice without fear. I closed my eyes, pictured ice in my mind. Glaciers, skating rinks, frigid nights with misty exhalations, hats and coats. Even the naked-female ice sculptures Tanner was always encouraging me to create.

Nothing happened.

Fighting disappointment—and relief—I— Wait. No emotions, not this time! Damn it. Okay, starting over. I blanked my mind, allowing the world around me to fade. Another deep breath in, another deep breath out. "I'm cold, I'm cold, I'm cold," I chanted softly.

Thankfully no one made fun of me for talking to myself.

"Ice is my bitch. I want it, I get it. I'm not afraid, but that doesn't matter. Ice is mine to command. To beckon and dismiss. I'm cold, I'm cold, I'm cold." As I spoke, I pushed my conscious mind to the background. I wasn't even here. Only my powers were.

To my utter shock, my blood slowly thickened, chilling inside my veins. My hands and feet grew frosty, my nose icy. I opened my eyes, saw that my breath was misting in front of my face, just as I'd imagined.

I held out my hand and sure enough, an ice ball formed. Small, but perfectly round. Clear, dangerous. Doused as Rome was in that experimental chemical, we wouldn't have known the true effectiveness of this method if I hit him with it. So, rather than toss it at Rome, I launched it at the wall behind him. The moment of contact, the ice spread, covering the entire span.

Rome never turned, never stopped eyeing me. "You did it." His voice was flat. "You really did it."

"Yes." I'd known any increase in my abilities could sever the bond between us, but experiencing it this soon? No. "Not fast enough for a battle with a scrim, though."

"With practice, you will." The flatness did not abate.

"You'll have the elements at your disposal, just like that." He snapped his fingers. "Now," he said, stalking to the far corner and grabbing one of the fire extinguishers he'd brought along. "Melt the ice with your fire."

I nodded, already closing my eyes. Already willing the ice away. Not with emotion, not with my mind, but by backing away, letting my body take over and do what it wanted. Heat. Pure heat. "I'm burning," I told myself. "So hot. Sweating, blistering."

Again, to my surprise, my body gradually obeyed. Almost as if it had been waiting for this moment, ready to act as it had always wanted. My blood heated…heated… the ice melting away until only molten lava remained.

When I opened my eyes, my fingers were on fire, tiny flames smoldering. Mentally I commanded those flames to leap together. They did, a ball forming in the palm of my hand.

I tossed it at the wall. Orange-gold instantly spread, ice melting and pooling on the floor. When the final droplet fell, Rome used the extinguisher to douse the remaining conflagrations. Soon the wall was black with soot and white with foam.

"You were faster that time," Rome said, and dropped the extinguisher.

Again, his tone had been flat. But now, his eyes were flat, too. "Yes."

"That's good. That's very good."

Was it? Was it really? He was stiff, harder in that moment than he'd been when he'd first awoken without his memories. Harder than he'd been the night he'd first invaded my apartment all those months ago, determined to neutralize me. "Rome, I—"

"That's enough for now," he said, cutting me off. He turned, giving me his back. "We don't want to exhaust you when you've got a big date tonight." There was no bitterness in his voice, no jealousy.

Suddenly I couldn't move, could barely breathe. Had he already decided to wash his hands of me? "Are you going to be there as promised?"

"I don't think so."

My mouth went dry. "Why not?" I asked shakily. I knew it was wrong to do this here, in front of Jean-Luc, but I couldn't help myself. I had to hear him say it. *We're not meant to be together, after all.* How would I react? What would I do? I still loved him. Still wanted him, craved him.

He shrugged, didn't face me. "No reason to, really."

And there it was. My answer. He *was* letting me go.

"Sunny wants to see you," he said. "I'll bring her by before dinner. If that's okay?"

At one time, he wouldn't have had to ask. I guess he planned to formally dump me with his daughter in the other room. That way I wouldn't throw a fit or burn something down. Well, wait. Would I burn something down in a fury now that I could summon the elements without emotion? I laughed bitterly. Did that matter now? Rome wanted out of my life.

Part of you knew this was coming. It's what you've been preparing yourself for. Fine. We'd get it over with. Do it tonight. Tears burned my eyes. "Bring her by, but I want to talk to you afterward. Okay?" Would I beg him to stay with me? Or would the future Lexis had predicted finally begin to fall into place?

I want my old future, I nearly screamed.

Rome ignored my question. "Go get cleaned up. I'll see you tonight." For the second time in recent memory, he walked away and never looked back.

AFTER PLAYING WITH MY PUPPIES for half an hour, avoiding Jean-Luc's probing gaze, a shower and a change of clothes, I stood in front of my locker, packing up to go home. My eyes were still burning, tears hovering at the corners, just waiting to fall. How had my life reached this point? A few weeks ago, I'd been the happiest woman on the planet. Love had been mine. A magnificent, sexy, strong man had been mine. Now…I had nothing.

Well, I had a few dates with a man I didn't and couldn't love because my heart would always belong to Rome.

And he was about to end things forever.

My gaze landed on a piece of folded paper. I hadn't placed it in the locker, so I grabbed it. From Rome? Jean-Luc? Footsteps suddenly echoed, growing louder and louder. I stiffened, stuffed the note in my pocket, thinking to read it later when I was alone, and buried my head so deeply inside my locker that whoever it was would surely pass me by without trying to begin a conversation. I wasn't ready to face anyone. Might not ever be ready.

But then the footsteps stopped. By me. Damn it! No reprieve for me today or any other day, it seemed.

"I'm sorry."

My fingers clenched on the door, and my teeth gnashed together. Lexis. I didn't face her, but busied myself with straightening the clothes and weapons I had stashed inside. She was lucky I didn't use one of them on her. "That doesn't change what you did."

"What I *tried* to do. And I know."

No, what you did. "You're only sorry now because you failed."

"I'm sorry because I had a few days to think about things. I was trapped in that cage, listening to the people around me moaning and crying and begging, and I realized I was trying to do the same to Rome. Trap him."

She made my head hurt. "Just…leave me alone, Lexis."

There was a pause, a shuffle of feet, but she didn't do what I'd asked. "You don't owe me anything, but I'm asking—begging—for a few minutes of your time."

"And I'm saying no." As satisfying as it was to see Lexis beg, I couldn't deal with her. I'd break down. I was at the edge already.

"Yes. You're going to listen to me. Nothing happened between me and Rome. I tried to kiss him that first day, but he quickly pulled away, as though he sensed I wasn't the woman for him right away."

My fingers curled around one of the blade hilts. "I know nothing happened. He told me. But it doesn't matter anymore. Now get lost."

Another pause. "What do you mean, it doesn't matter?"

There was no avoiding this, it seemed. "We're over. Okay? We're over." I slammed the locker shut, still clutching that blade. I faced her with narrowed eyes. She was as lovely as ever, dark hair brushed to a glossy shine, emerald eyes sparkling. "Happy now? You finally got what you wanted."

"No." She shook her head, shock radiating from her. "No. I— No. Belle, I'm so sorry. Truly. I…don't know what to say. I meant for that to happen at first, but not any longer. I swear it. You two are meant to be together. I admit that now. I do. There's no better stepmother for Sunny, and the way Rome looks at you…the way he talked about you, even when I was telling him we needed to work things out. He wouldn't even kiss me! Said all he could think about was you."

Wonderful to hear. But too little, too late. I closed the distance between us, my shoes smashed against hers, my nose practically rubbing hers. "You once told me there was a woman meant to be the love of Rome's life, but you weren't sure if it was me. Well, guess what. It isn't." My chin trembled as I spoke. God, saying that was hard. "You once told me I'd plan my wedding but Rome wouldn't care. Well, you were right. You once told me I'd marry someone else. Maybe you were right about that, too."

"That can't be right." She was pale, shaking her head. "Are you sure it's over? Give him another chance. He—"

"*He* is the one who's going to dump *me*."

"But…but…no. He wouldn't do that. He loves you. He told me yesterday, this morning. Even if I did still want to be with him, I wouldn't have a prayer. You're it for him. The one. If you could have heard him screaming at me… I've never seen him so angry." There at the end, shame dripped from her tone.

Yeah, but that only meant he'd wanted me *before* I'd shown him just how powerful I would be. More than an ache, more than a stabbing pain, her words were a cancer eating at me. I pushed her with my free hand, hard, and she stumbled backward. "Get out of my way. We're done here."

Determined, she jumped back into my path. "Or maybe you can hear. Maybe you can see." Before I could react, she flattened her palms against my temples. I jolted, images shooting straight into my head.

Lexis and Rome. Lexis sitting on a couch, tears streaming down her face. Rome pacing in front of her. "How could you?" he shouted. "You almost ruined me. I love her, Lex. I love her, and you tried to take her from me."

With a weary sigh, the Lexis in front of me dropped her arms to her sides.

"How did you do that?" I demanded.

Her chin rose. "Your powers are evolving. So are mine."

"I—I—" Couldn't let what she'd shown me matter, much as I loved knowing Rome had put her in her place and defended me. As before, I reminded myself that the argument had taken place before Rome had seen what I could do. "Like I said, we're done."

"No. Not until you tell me if you like Jean-Luc. He's the one I told you that you would marry, but I was wrong. I mean, I saw him standing in front of you, kissing you while you wore your wedding dress, but he simply can't be the one you're marrying." She was babbling and couldn't seem to stop. "He's not meant to be yours. He's supposed to be…mine," she ended lamely.

Jean-Luc and Lexis? I stared over at her, blinking. I could have walked away, but didn't. Shock made my feet feel like stones. "Are you freaking kidding me?"

Like a nervous teenager, she twisted her fingers together. "No. I'm not kidding."

"You are *incredible*. First you wanted Rome, then you let him go, then you wanted him again, and now you want Jean-Luc. For God's sake, make up your mind, 'cause you are driving me crazy!"

"Look, I know you can never forgive me for what I did to you and Rome, not to mention what I did to Tanner."

Uh, you think?

"But you'll win Rome back and Tanner, well, he's already recovered from my desertion." She slapped the small metal door beside her once, twice. "I knew Elaine would appear in his life. I knew he would want her. I did him a favor."

"Hardly. You cut your lovers from your life before they can cut you from theirs. They're good men, but you crushed them. Do you ever think that maybe you're acting prematurely? That maybe they would still want you, but the only reason your visions come true is because of *your* actions?"

Oh my God. The moment I spoke, I realized I'd done the same thing. I'd let Rome go, I'd realized. At some point since he'd regained his memory, maybe even before, I'd let him go. I'd told myself I loved him, that I would fight for him always, but then something would happen and I would fall back on my "maybe not" fears. I'd bounced from one extreme to the other and he'd had to know, had to sense.

That's why we were here, at this point. *I* had done this. Me.

Could I win him back?

Lexis paled, her mouth flailing open and closed. "You're right," she said quietly. "What I did was terrible and I'll try not to make the same mistake again. But I saw myself with Jean-Luc, Belle. Last night in a vision, I saw him standing at the end of a hallway and smiling at me. That smile—" she shivered, wrapped her arms around herself "—it set my blood on fire. I wanted to go to him more than anything in the world, and I saw love in his eyes. Love for me, no one else. I want that. I want the vision to come true."

She was so passionate about it, I couldn't doubt her. Even though I wanted to. "Doesn't matter. He deserves a woman who will love him back. A woman who will stay with him 'til the end."

"I plan to be that woman." She chewed on her lower lip. "I just have to convince him of that."

I pointed a finger in her face. "If you lie to him…"

She held up her hands, total innocence. "This time, I'm going to play fair. Believe me, I've learned my lesson. I just wanted you to know I'm out of the game when it comes to Rome. He's yours."

"How nice of you," I said drily. "You can go now."

She didn't. "I had one more thing to say." She gazed down at her shoes and kicked an imaginary rock. "A favor, really."

I laughed without humor. "Sorry, I'm all out of those."

Her gaze swung up, pinning me. "Don't go on those dates with Jean-Luc. Please, Belle. I know I don't deserve it, but I'm begging you."

Before I could respond, she walked away. I stood there, shaking my head in wonder at her daring. I was going on those dates, and that was that. If Rome hadn't talked me out of it, no way Lexis would.

My motions were jerky as I stuffed my hands in my pockets. Something crumbled against my fingers. Frowning, I withdrew the note. Oh, yeah. The note. I unfolded it and, when I read the contents, I actually flinched.

You didn't kill my daughter when you probably wanted to, and for that, you have my gratitude. But I know you and your team are now looking for me. I won't allow myself to be found, Belle. I will do whatever is needed to remain free—even, if you force me, take you down. I don't want it to end that way, however. Let's part now. In peace.

Dr. Roberts had been inside PSI and no one had known.

What a freaking cluster.

CHAPTER TWENTY-EIGHT

TURNED OUT, my first "date" with Jean-Luc was a double. Jean-Luc and me, Tanner and Elaine. The latter pair was here to watch for Dr. Roberts. Just in case. Sherridan was pouting at home, keeping my dogs company. (I missed them already.) Rome was…I don't know where. He'd said he had no plans to come and I couldn't see him in the dim lighting of the bustling restaurant. But I could feel his eyes on me, watching.

Wishful thinking?

He'd arrived at my house two hours before Jean-Luc had come to pick me up. And yes, he'd brought Sunny. That sweet little girl who looked like Lexis but had Rome's indomitable spirit had leaped into my arms, giggling and unaware her world was about to be rocked.

"I missed you so very much," I'd told her.

She'd kissed my cheek and looked up at me, beaming. "I missed you, too, and guess what?"

"What?"

"You got it right."

My brow furrowed. "What do you mean?"

"You came home when you was 'post to."

Ah, our negotiation. I smiled at her, my chest aching, my throat constricting. How many more would we be allowed? "Come on, scamp. I want to introduce you to our new friends."

We'd played with the dogs for over an hour. And yes, we'd put them in pink dresses with ruffles and bows. (They'd been adorable!) I'd tried to pull Rome aside for a private chat, but he'd said, "John told me about the note. He's worried Dr. Roberts will try and hurt you, despite what he said about making peace."

"I know." He'd told me the same thing. After he'd congratulated me on the successful apprehension of Desert Gal and I'd beamed like the sun in shock and pleasure. "He's placing me under surveillance for a while, in case the note was meant to lure me into a false sense of security. I'm supposed to act like everything's normal." Which I couldn't do until I had this Rome and Jean-Luc thing figured out.

I wanted Rome in my life, and I wasn't letting him go. If he cut me out of his, fine. But I wasn't going easily. Once these dates with Jean-Luc were out of the way, I was going to fight for my man like I should have done from the beginning. Fight harder than I'd ever fought a scrim.

Yeah, if I convinced him to keep me around, we desperately needed to discuss our future. Like whether or not we wanted children. And I needed to know he would be okay with my being an in-the-middle-of-the-action agent. He'd said he would always want to protect me. Now I wondered why I'd ever thought that was a bad idea.

Stupid Belle. I'd let my fears get the better of me and had begun to look for reasons to end things. No more.

If we disagreed about something, we could hash it out and reach a compromise. As long as we were together, nothing else mattered. All relationships were work, after all. It was who you wanted to put that work into that mattered. And I was willing to work for—and with—Rome.

Was he willing to work for me?

When the time had come for Rome and Sunny to leave,

Rome hadn't kissed me goodbye. Hadn't *said* goodbye for that matter. Leaving had gone something like this:

Sunny: "No! I'm staying." She'd been angry at that point, but had calmed herself down, the anger turning to sadness—and then tears. "I haven't seen you in a long time. I miss you. I don't want to go! You've been gone for forever."

Me, hating myself: "I don't want you to go, either, but I have to go to…work."

Sunny: "No, you don't. I heard Daddy say he's not going to marry you and that I had to stop asking to see you." Her chin had trembled. "You're leaving us, aren't you?"

Me: "I love you, sweetheart. I would never leave you. Ever."

Rome: "I'll bring you back tomorrow, sunshine. I swear. I explained to you last night that my mind was sick and I just didn't remember Belle. But now I do."

Sunny: "But you're not happy, you're not smiling and laughing like before." She'd then used her misting ability to disappear. We hadn't found her for twenty minutes, and both Rome and I had been beyond worried. Finally we'd discovered her inside the freaking dryer. I'd felt like a rat, and Rome had scooped her up and stalked out of the house, silent.

Remembering, I sighed.

"You okay?" Jean-Luc asked me. He sat across from me, and placed his hand over mine.

Slowly I withdrew it as I studied his face over the flickering candlelight. He was so handsome, so sweet, so giving (when he wasn't stealing, that is). Despite my confession that I'd never love him, despite the agents he'd known would surround us, he'd brought me to a lovely place with flowers and soft, romantic music.

With the threat of Dr. Roberts looming, John had instructed us to stay alert and not drink anything with alcohol, so Jean-Luc had ordered me a virgin strawberry margarita. His notebook had reminded him that my favorite fruit was strawberry.

"I just had a tough day," I said.

"Tell me about it." He propped his elbows on the table and leaned toward me, genuinely interested.

"I shouldn't." Unloading my Rome-problems on him would be cruel. But I desperately needed someone to talk to. And I couldn't talk to Sherridan. I wasn't yet immune to her voice. I couldn't talk to Tanner, either. Even now, he and Elaine were lost in their own little world, heads bent together, whispering.

So far, Elaine's sessions were going very well. The scientists at PSI had painted a translucent gel over her exposed skin—much as Rome had worn during our training session—which acted as a barrier. Like clothing. Tanner could now caress her cheek—and had, several times. Each time, Elaine leaned into him, her eyes closing in ecstasy.

"It would hurt you," I said, returning my attention to Jean-Luc, "and I don't want to hurt you."

Now he sighed. "Rome, then."

I nodded.

"What's so special about him that— No. Never mind. Don't tell me." Jean-Luc followed the direction of my gaze, to Tanner and Elaine. "Some guard dogs, huh?"

I laughed with genuine humor. "Yeah. They're about as effective as Ginger and Lovey."

He sighed again and toyed with the rim of his glass, finger stroking the edge. "That's how it should be, isn't it?"

"What?" Somehow, I'd lost the thread of the conversation.

"Love. That's how love should be."

Oh. I bit my lip, studied Tanner and Elaine again.

There was a gentleness to Tanner's expression that I'd never seen before, even with Lexis, transforming him from young man to protective alpha. Seemed odd, that tenderness toward a woman could bring out such a Me-Killing-Machine aura, but it was there. Tanner would protect her, would die for her.

They hadn't known each other long, but sometimes people just knew. That's how it had been with me and Rome. I had been enraptured by him from the very first, even though he'd been sent to destroy me.

Tanner caught my scrutiny and frowned over at me. "What?"

"I just love you, that's all," I said, my eyes misting. God, I was a freaking watering pot lately.

"That's because you secretly want to ride the Tanner Express."

I barked out a laugh. Elaine gasped, not quite used to his sense of humor yet.

"That's the line he used to use to pick up girls," I told her. "Needless to say, he was an absolute failure."

Slowly she smiled. "Did you really?"

His cheeks pinked a bit. "It wasn't my best line, but it did the job."

"Did not," I said, laughter increasing in volume. "Girls ran from you, fast as they could."

"I'm not running," Elaine said in a throaty whisper.

Just like that, the two were lost in their own world again.

My smile faded. I tossed my napkin on the table and pushed back my chair. "I need to run to the ladies' room." Compose myself, I didn't add.

Jean-Luc stood with me. I clomped off. How could I let him down without hurting him? I maneuvered around tables and people, past the kitchen and its hot, steamy air and into the bathroom.

The door slammed behind me, locking before anyone else—namely a female agent/guard—could enter.

"Finally," I heard.

I spun, gasping. There was Dr. Roberts, tall and thin with a comb-over he needed to shave. Thick glasses I hadn't seen him wear in our previous brief encounter. He was very studious-looking. Oh, and he had a gun pointed to my chest.

"Hello, Belle."

"Dr. Roberts."

"Ah, you remember me. I had a feeling you would. I wish we were meeting under happier circumstances, but I'm afraid that isn't how things played out. You received my note, I hope?"

"Yes." Cold, I needed cold. Almost instantly, an ice ball formed in my hand. Damn. I really was getting good at this. "So what are you doing here, armed no less?"

"I have to protect myself *somehow*. And I wouldn't do that if I were you." The gun cocked. He motioned to my hand with a tilt of his head, his brown eyes bright with intrigue. "Taken to your powers, I see."

I dropped my arm to my side. "I didn't exactly have a choice. It was either feel sorry for myself over what you made me, or embrace the new me and move on with my life."

He sighed but didn't lower the gun. "I've done some terrible things in my life, and I'm sorry for them. I forced powers on you that you weren't prepared to deal with. I treated my daughter like a lab rat. I was only trying to ensure that she would be well able to survive in our supernatural world, but in the process I ruined her life and my own. I'm searching for a way to undo everything I've done, for you, for her, but I need time to do that. I need peace, as I said. Give me peace, and I'll do the same for you."

He meant it, then. He truly didn't want to hurt me. I took heart. And yet…I closed my eyes at the irony. For weeks after being given my powers, I'd dreamed of nothing but finding an antidote. And now, here he was offering the hope of one, when I no longer wanted it. "And what happens if I want to keep my powers?" I asked.

His smile was sad. Did I remind him of Candace, always craving more? "Then taking the cure would be up to you. I won't force anything else on you. But I still need my freedom." His head fell back a little and he peered up at the ceiling. "My daughter…it's my fault she became what she did. I should have been more careful with her, should not have introduced her to this life. Please tell John to be kind to her."

Someone knocked on the door. "Belle? You okay in there?"

"I'm…fine." My words trailed off. I'd glanced at the door, then back at Dr. Roberts, but he was already gone. How? Where? I dropped the ice ball into the trash can, freezing it, and pounded through the entire enclosure, opening every door, peeking into every shadow, but there was no sign. It was as though I'd imagined the entire incident. I knew better. The good doctor must have experimented on himself, as well.

Shaking, I washed my face and hands. Part of me wanted to call John and Rome right now and tell them what had happened. But the other part of me knew they'd immediately launch a search party for the doctor and then where would we be? Roberts wanted a chance to undo the damage he'd done. Perhaps we should give him one.

When I exited, there was a pretty brunette I recognized from PSI waiting for me. Her sharp gaze took my measure. She must have decided I was okay, because she nodded and went back to her table.

Jean-Luc was not so easily convinced. "You're pale," he said as I reclaimed my seat.

"I'm fine. Really." I hoped. Had I made the right decision? Only time would tell, I guess. Ultimately, if Dr. Roberts could develop a superpower neutralizer, we could stop scrims in their tracks. And wasn't that the point of my job?

The waiter delivered our food. I'd ordered the halibut with extra garlic sauce (a girl had to prepare for the worst and I hadn't wanted to have to reject Jean-Luc if he tried to kiss me, so had decided to make him *not* want to come within ten yards of me). The delicious aroma drifted to my nose, and I inhaled deeply, allowing myself to relax. Everyone else had ordered some type of green-colored pasta.

We ate for a little while in silence, and I continued to pretend all was well. Jean-Luc would take a bite, swallow and open his mouth to say something, then press his lips together in a mulish line. Then repeat the entire process again. And again. It was…awkward.

Finally, I dropped my fork and faced him. There had to be a way to do this without crushing him. I just, well, I had to get my life in order. Being confronted by Dr. Roberts had reminded me just how quickly circumstances could change. I had to seize the moment, take what time I had with Rome while I had it. There was also Lexis to consider, I thought with a sigh.

"You know, Jean-Luc," I said. "I like you. I do."

He released his fork, too, and it clanged against his bowl. He propped his elbows on the table and dropped his head into his upraised hands, scrubbing his face. "This the brush-off speech?"

"No." *Damn it, girl. He deserves your honesty.* "Yes. Maybe. I don't know. I would never back out of our deal,

I hope you know that. You want the full three dates, I'll give them to you. But I'm in love with him. That isn't going to change, no matter how many dates we go on. I wish it would. I mean, you're so much easier to be with than Rome."

"But?"

"But he's the other half of me, and this date is killing him." Or at one time, it would have. Now…I traced a fingertip around my plate and only prayed that it did. "I don't know if I have a future with him, but he's the only man I want, and I'd rather stay single and dream of him than date anyone else."

He grabbed his wineglass and drained the contents, then signaled the waiter for another glass. When it arrived, he drained it, too. Then he stared down at the tabletop for a long while.

I didn't move. Didn't speak.

Finally he wiped his mouth with his napkin and smiled sadly. "Stupid honesty. I could push, you know. I could use your doubts about your future against you."

"I know."

"But you don't care. Because you love him."

"Yes."

Another sad smile. "I had hoped…well, it doesn't matter now, I guess. You're sweet, funny and you have the sexiest laugh I've ever heard, but your attraction to another man is annoying as hell."

"I know. I'm sorry."

"That's why—that's why I have to— Damn this. I'm releasing you from our deal."

For a moment, I couldn't react. All I could do was think how amazing this man was. A true diamond in a sea of zirconium. Then relief drifted through me. "I— Thank you, Jean-Luc." I wasn't going to give a token protest and hurt him further. "You are a wonderful man and one day some lucky woman is going to make you very happy. She's going to love you with her every breath." Would that woman be Lexis?

He scowled over at me. "Look. You don't want me, fine. I'll live. I don't like it, I wish it were different, but I'll live. You don't have to patronize me."

And that was the difference between us, what really showed me that I'd made the right choice. I *couldn't* live without Rome. Wouldn't give up, had to have him. He was my drug. My addiction. Not my newfound increased powers, but him. Maybe I needed therapy, but there it was. "I'm not patronizing you. I swear. I—"

Jean-Luc threw his napkin on the table and stood, his chair skidding behind him. "Have a nice life, Belle. I won't be bothering you anymore. We'll both work at PSI, but I'll stay out of your way."

Tanner and Elaine emerged from their love-cocoon long enough to throw us startled glances.

"Jean-Luc, wait! Lexis—" Was I really going to do this? Yes, yes, I was. It was the only solution I had right now, though granted, it was a sucky consolation prize. "Lexis wants you. She says the two of you are meant to be together."

He turned, suddenly stiff, giving me his back but not walking away. "What are you talking about?"

"All I know is what she told me earlier today. She sees the future and she has seen the two of you together. Romantically."

He snorted. "Impossible. I don't want her."

"And I don't blame you. I just wanted you to know."

A pause, a nod. And then, unconsciously taking a page from Rome's book, he strode briskly away.

"Wow," Tanner said. "I didn't see that one coming." He shrugged and turned back to Elaine, smiling.

"Is there anything we can do, Belle?" Elaine asked.

"No. The rest is up to me."

ARMED AGENTS HID in the shadows all around the outside of my house. I should have told them all to go away, that the threat of Dr. Roberts was over, but I didn't. I needed to have a conversation with John first, and I didn't want to do that tonight. I chucked my keys on the table in the foyer and strode toward my bedroom. Tanner and Elaine were close on my heels, though they branched off and entered Tanner's room. I paused, catching his eye as he closed the door.

He gave me a wicked smile before the cherry wood blocked him completely. I shook my head, sad and happy at the same time, and jumped back into motion. I had my powers under control, I'd been released from my deal with Jean-Luc, so I should be celebrating. Instead, I was going to cuddle my dogs, cry and come up with a plan. I'd broken a good man's heart, and I needed a strategy to win back another's.

The house was eerily quiet. Sherridan was probably asleep. Just like my puppies, I realized. They were snuggled together in their crate and snoring. Not wanting to wake them, I left the light off. No cuddling for me, it seemed. It'd just be me, my tears and my schemes.

I brushed my teeth and hair, washed my face clean of makeup, stripped to the skin and padded to my dresser to find a pair of panties and a nightgown. Wasn't sure I'd have one. Rome and I had always slept naked. Lately, since his memory loss, I'd been using his shirts. I couldn't do that tonight, since I hadn't done laundry in forever.

Strong arms suddenly banded around my waist and

lifted me. Before I could react, I was soaring through the air. I landed on the bed with a thwack, sprawled on my back, arms and legs splayed. Gasping, I jerked upright, raising my arm. *Cold, cold, cold. I am cold.*

The ice was already forming in my hand. The moment it solidified completely, I launched it. The intruder ducked and the ball slammed into the wall, the door, freezing them.

And locking me inside with the depraved man. Dr. Roberts again? "I'm armed and I'm dangerous, mother-fucker!"

"Good reflexes and good timing. You've already improved. The potty mouth needs to go, though."

I blinked. Stilled. Gulped. "Rome?"

"The one and only."

"You bastard!" I summoned another ball of ice and tossed it, too. Once again he ducked. Wait. What was I doing? *Way to win him back,* I thought, willing the ice to leave me. "Don't scare me like that again! I thought you were a scrim."

He rose. He was standing at the end of the bed. Moonlight seeped from the window and illuminated his strong body. He was dressed in black, his hair damp as if he'd just taken a shower.

A knock sounded at my door. "Belle?" Tanner called.

"I'm okay. Just having—"

"We're fine," Rome said.

There was a chuckle. "Way to go, Cat Man. Carry on, you two. I'm about to." Then, silence.

"What are you doing here?" I didn't bother trying to cover my nakedness. No, I lay back on the pillow, a seductive goddess—I hoped.

For a moment, his expression was so primitive I thought he was going to pound his chest King Kong–style.

"We've got some air to clear," he said, and his voice sounded thick. Raw. "I heard what you said to Jean-Luc."

First, surprise rocked me. Then embarrassment. "So you *were* there?"

He nodded. "I told you I would be."

"But I thought…you seemed… If I'm remembering correctly, you then said you weren't going. And when you left with Sunny, you made it seem like you were done with me."

"As if." He reached behind his neck and pulled his shirt up and off. "You want to stand on your own, and I was trying to let you. I was trying not to interfere with what you felt you had to do. Even though it was killing me." Next he unsnapped his pants. "But I couldn't stay away and found myself plugging into the audio feed."

· Sweet heaven. I licked my lips, nervous and excited and trembling. "That's wonderful. I'm glad. But first, I have to tell you something. Dr. Roberts was at the restaurant. He—"

"I know. I heard that, too. We all did. There were recorders all over the place. I'm surprised you didn't know."

Damn, but I still had a lot to learn. "Why didn't you guys rush in and take him?"

"Oh, John wanted to, but I threw a fit and he backed down. I didn't want Roberts to panic and hurt you. More than that, I think John liked what he had to say about neutralizing powers. John wants to confiscate whatever new formula the good doctor creates.

"Now, enough shop talk. Let's get back to the subject of you and me." His gaze roved over me, hot and hungry.

"Wait," I said, holding up a hand.

His head fell back and he groaned. "Not again."

"I won't lie to you. I was thinking about ending things with you."

Every muscle in his body froze, his eyes narrowing on me.

"But only because I worried we couldn't make it," I admitted softly. "And only for a little while. Once my senses returned, I knew you were worth fighting for no matter what."

"Why would you think we couldn't make it?" He relaxed, and slid back into motion. The pants tumbled down his legs. He stepped out of them.

As usual, he wasn't wearing underwear.

As I drank in that long, hard, thick length, moisture flooded my mouth. "Because I was changing, becoming a different person, and I wasn't sure you could love who I would be."

"And who's that?" He climbed atop the bed, but remained on his knees. "Who are you now?"

A tremor moved through me. I wanted to tug him on top of me, but resisted. This was too important. "An agent. A very powerful agent who will one day be able to kick your ass. A very powerful agent who will maybe might kinda sorta one day want children."

"And all of that is what's been making you so distant with me?"

"That, and you seemed to be pulling away from me."

A frown curved his lips into a half-moon. "If I seemed upset at the gym today, it was only because I was worried you would outgrow me. That you wouldn't need me anymore. But I realized that's okay. You *don't* need me. You're stronger than I am, and I like that. I'm proud of it. Of you. That was never clearer than when Dr. Roberts offered to free you from your powers but you weren't sure you wanted him to. I didn't want you to accept, either. They're a part of who you are. Part of the girl I love. A girl who's brave and sarcastic, loyal and determined."

"I—I—" Couldn't form any intelligent words.

"I'm not done, Wonder Girl," he chided. "I wanted to strangle Lexis when I got my memories back and realized what she'd done to keep us apart. I wanted to beat myself for listening to her, even for a minute. I wanted to kill Jean-Luc, with my memories and without, for looking at you as if you belonged to him. And he's lucky the dates are over. I planned to hunt him down tomorrow and put a bullet in his leg to keep him away. No one keeps us apart. Not even you. Not even me.

"I love who you are, yesterday, now, tomorrow, always. You're complicated and yeah, powerful, but that doesn't change the core of you. You're strong, and did I already mention brave? You're loving, giving and sexy as hell. You speak your mind, you never back down and you make my heart stop every time I look at you. I would be lost without you. And yes, I want kids with you, no matter how they'll turn out. One day. Right now, I just want you all to myself."

His speech was a dream come true. Wondrous, amazing, surreal. Everything I'd ever wanted to hear and more. Once he'd stung my feminine pride. Now he'd utterly soothed it. The tears I'd expected tonight poured free, as if a dam had broken. But they were tears of joy. "I will never outgrow you. I will always need you. But I want to be clear. I'm it for you? The one and only?" I didn't mean for the questions to squeak out, but they did.

He nodded. "My one and only. Now, enough talking. We've got some reuniting to do."

He was on top of me in the next instant. I wrapped my legs around him as he fed me a kiss, his tongue plunging deep. My hands were all over him, and his were all over me.

It was heaven, the possession I'd craved all these many days.

"I love you," he said, nipping at my lips, my ears, kissing down my neck.

"I love you so much."

"We're getting married."

"Yes."

"Soon."

"As soon as possible."

"And you'll take my name." He swirled his tongue around one of my nipples, then the other.

"I'm still undecided. I mean, you once called a pet Bone Crusher, so clearly you aren't good with names. But why don't you convince me of the merits of your plan?" I tangled my hands in his hair, ran my thighs up his sides. How could a man with so many hard muscles feel like velvet?

"Give me an hour. Maybe neither one of us will even remember our names, so it'll be a moot point." Kneading my breasts, he turned the hot, wet attentions of his tongue to my navel, swirling. I moaned at the heady bliss. And then he was licking between my legs, flicking my clitoris and driving me mad.

"Rome," I shouted as I came, my muscles spasming, my back shooting off the mattress, my nails digging into his scalp. "I—I still remember."

"Hang on." He surged up, impaling me deep. Another climax hit me instantly, hurtling me over the edge again and again and again. I chanted his name, only then realizing there wasn't a fire desperate to escape me.

I truly had control of my powers.

"Woman," Rome grunted, pounding deep, hard, fast, and then roaring a sound of utter satisfaction.

When the last of our tremors subsided, we didn't move. I couldn't. Not because Rome's weight pinned me down—though it did—but because for the first time in weeks, I was utterly satisfied. Happy beyond measure. And I didn't want it to end.

"How embarrassing." He kissed the inside of my neck. "I only lasted five minutes. And I was the first to forget. Again."

"Well, I can top that, Cat Man. I only lasted three."

He laughed. "See, this is why I love you. You're the biggest smart-ass I know."

The sound of a woman's blissful cries suddenly seeped through the walls, blending with the sound of our ragged breathing, and my laughter joined Rome's. "Bet Tanner lasts longer than both of us combined."

Rome gave another laugh, but the laughter soon faded. He cupped my face, forcing my gaze to remain locked with his. "You meant what you said? About marrying me?"

"Absolutely." I hugged him tight. "You're mine, Rome Jamison, and I'm never letting you go."

"Rome Jamison. I like the sound of that."

"So do I." I rose up and straddled his waist. "Now, let's try to set a new record for us. Let's try to last ten minutes."

CHAPTER TWENTY-NINE

I WOKE UP BRIGHT AND EARLY, whistling under my breath as I made coffee for myself and Rome, the puppies playing around my feet. Rome was currently in the shower, where I'd left him after another round of hot and steamy loving.

We were together again, and we were going to get married, though I had no idea when. Both of us wanted it to be soon, but I had nothing planned and all of my appointments were canceled.

A dark slash in my periphery captured my attention and I turned, expecting Rome. Or Tanner—who had stayed awake *laaaaate* last night. I knew because the sounds he and Elaine had made had never ceased. I now knew beyond any doubt that Tanner had lost his virginity. Never would I be able to blot the many "Oh, Tanner, oh, yes, like that" pleas from my mind.

But instead of Rome or Tanner, I saw a familiar figure with white hair and silver-violet eyes tiptoeing toward the living room and the front door. I followed, brow scrunched in confusion. "Cody?"

He stopped in his tracks, muttering, "Shit." Slowly he turned and faced me. A pair of shoes dangled from his hands. His shirt was wrinkled and his jeans unsnapped—as if he'd dressed in a hurry. He smiled sheepishly. "Well, this is awkward."

"Isn't it, though?" I asked, hands on my hips.

"So, uh, hey, Belle. How are you?"

"Enough pleasantries. What are you doing here?"

He shifted uncomfortably, shrugged. "Came to see Sherridan."

"Why?" The question lashed from me, sparks of anger lighting. "I don't think she wants to see you."

"Uh, you'd be wrong about that."

What the hell? "You said you weren't interested in her anymore. You said you didn't like high-maintenance women."

"Well, I lied. Or changed my mind. I'm not sure which. She looked at me with those baby blues while Desert Gal had her caged and I sort of forgot how to think. I'm not going to hurt her, though. You have my word."

"Are you guys a...couple?" I gasped out the word.

His cheeks reddened, then paled. "No. Yes. I don't know. For now."

I ran my tongue over my teeth, my hands clenching at my sides. Then someone sidled up to me, strong arms banding around my waist. Soft lips pressed into my temple, and I breathed deeply of soap and wild beast.

"Hey, baby," Rome said to me. "You look pretty. Jeans and a button-up. My favorite. Except when you're naked. Or wearing a dress. Or a towel. Actually, whatever you wear, I love. Have we already covered that?" He paused, but not long enough for me to answer. "Hey, man," he said to Cody. "See things went well last night."

Cody smiled smugly. "You could say that. Thanks for letting me in."

I whipped around, facing Rome with narrowed eyes. "You knew he was here?"

"Well, yeah. I heard him sneaking in. Since your guard dogs refused to budge from their beds, I decided to check on things." He gave me another kiss, this one on the lips, and padded to the kitchen. He was wearing pants, but no shirt, and as usual his chest and back were sun-kissed, slightly scarred and utterly kissable.

I followed him, watching as he grabbed a mug and filled it with the coffee I had made him, the traitor. I tried not to soften as he pet the girls. They didn't bark or snarl at him as I'd originally envisioned. Now that I liked him and wanted him around, they did, too. Or maybe he'd romanced them as he'd done to me, now that he was no longer jealous of them. Yes, he'd admitted that he'd been jealous of the smiles I'd given my babies. "Why didn't you tell me?"

He flicked me an are-you-kidding grin. "I had other things on my mind."

"But Sherridan hates him. What if he—"

"She doesn't hate me," Cody said, all wickedness.

I turned and gasped, a hand fluttering over my chest. I'd followed Rome and apparently Cody had followed me. He stood in the kitchen entryway, shoulder braced against the door frame. I needed to be more aware of my surroundings and the people in them or I'd die of heart failure, I swear I would.

Suddenly Sherridan raced around the corner, a single sock dangling from between her fingers. She spotted me and ground to a halt. Her mouth fell open and her cheeks burned bright red. A gasp escaped her, and it was the most beautiful sound I'd ever heard.

I moved toward her, but Rome grabbed my arm and held me back. My mind cleared as I shook my head and stepped away from him. Okay, how had this happened? She'd been so determined to resist Cody. And how long before he remembered his three-dates rule and dumped her, hurting her deeply? "You're going to pay for this. I warned you." I held out my hand and summoned a ball of fire.

He jumped back, and Sherridan jumped in front of him, shaking her head at me mutely.

"Uh, Rome," Cody said.

I didn't spin to look at him, and maybe I should have. Because two arms again wrapped around my waist and Rome's warm, minty breath trekked over my cheek, my shoulder. His fingers curled around my wrist.

"Put the fire out, baby."

"I want some answers, and he's going to give them to me. Besides, he needs to know there will be consequences for his actions." I held firm, keeping the flames front and center so Cody didn't get any ideas about running. "How'd you manage to…you know without her making a sound and entrancing you?"

"I have filters. Got them years ago when I underwent some enhancements, just like Rome." His gaze roved to Sherridan, stayed for a moment, softening, increasing my anger, then moved back to me. "She can talk to me."

"Yeah, well, I want to know how long you're planning to stick around before moving on to your next conquest. I also want to know if you remember the warning I gave you."

Biting her lower lip, Sherridan looked down at her feet. She groaned in embarrassment and it was a prettier sound than even the sigh. I tried to pull from Rome, had to reach her, tell her I'd do anything she wanted, even kill Cody. Yes, kill Cody. That was a fine plan. He might hurt her one day, and *that* I couldn't allow. She deserved rainbows and sunshine, roses and chocolate.

"Shit," Rome said.

"Double shit," Cody said, backing away.

I lifted my free hand, already summoning another ball of fire. Cody was going to roast, and I was going to laugh, and then I was going to comfort Sherridan. Sweet, wonderful Sherridan.

Rome tried to grab for the new ball, but I danced free of him and prepared to launch at Cody.

"Stop, Belle," Sherridan said firmly. "Stop the fire."

Immediately I obeyed. My now-empty hands dropped to my sides. Anything she wanted, I would do. Had to touch her, I had to touch her. She was my everything, my only reason for living. I needed—

"I'm sorry, baby," Rome said on a sigh. He hefted me over his shoulder and started down the hall.

I struggled, hitting him, kicking him, biting him. I was wild, feral and more determined than I'd ever been. He tossed me on the bed. The mattress bounced me high in the air and I jackknifed to my knees when I landed. I was going to rip him a new—

He was on top of me in the next instant, a sharp sting piercing my shoulder.

"You bastard!" I snarled, lethargy already beating through me. "She's... You... What?"

"Part of being your man is protecting you, even from yourself. I'd expect you to do the same for me. See you in a few hours, Wonder Girl."

My entire world went black.

AS MY EYELIDS FLUTTERED OPEN tiredly, I caught glimpses of Sherridan, tall, curvy and gorgeous, who was standing over my bed and staring down at me.

"Hey," she said.

I tried to focus on her, but there were too many colorful spots clouding my vision. Red, yellow, orange.

"Thirsty?"

The moment she asked, I could taste the cotton in my mouth. I nodded. Next thing I knew, a straw was pressed to my lips. I gulped, the sweet, cool water wetting my throat.

"That's enough." The cup disappeared.

Not enough, never enough. I moaned. But this time when I opened my eyes, I could see more than a murky portrait. Her blond curls were piled on top of her head, her blue eyes wide with concern.

"How are you feeling?" she asked.

"Like I need a nap." My voice was nothing more than a croak.

She chuckled softly. "That's the drugs talking. But guess what? You have filters now, right on schedule. The doctors didn't even need to give you anesthesia since you were already out."

Eyes widening, I reached up and patted my ears. They were a little sensitive, but that was the only indication anything had been done to me. Well, that and the fact that I no longer felt the need to throw myself at Sherridan every time she opened her mouth. As my arm flopped back to my side, my IV tube rubbed my chest, cool and jolting. My chest? I hurriedly looked down to make sure I was dressed. I was. Though someone had removed my clothing and placed me in a gaping hospital gown.

How many times could a girl wake up in a hospital before raising the white flag?

I relaxed against the bed and slowly grinned. "That's a powerful ability you've got there. Seriously, I was contemplating killing Cody so we could be a couple."

She snorted, but she never stopped smiling. "We'd never make it romantically. You're too demanding in bed. 'Harder, Rome. Now, Rome. Tie me up, Rome.'"

"Bitch," I muttered good-naturedly. It was nice to have my friend back. "You know you wouldn't be able to get enough of me."

"I like where this conversation is headed," a male voice said from the doorway.

I looked past Sherridan and spotted Rome in the doorway.

"Hey, baby," he said.

"Cat Man." A more welcome sight I'd never beheld. My heart even picked up speed, my monitor announcing it for all the world to hear.

He stalked to me and unceremoniously shoved me aside on the bed, where he plopped down and cuddled me close. "Mad?"

As if. "I'm grateful. I was walking toward Sherridan with every intention of making out with her, so you did me a favor. She would have fallen in love with me, and then where would we have been?"

"Now I'm mad at *myself* for stopping you," he grumbled, and we all laughed. Men!

Sherridan's humor died the quickest. She gripped the bed's rails and leaned forward, expression serious. "I want you to know that Cody visited me as often as he could while I was locked up. He brought me food, water, blankets. Anything I asked for, he snuck inside and gave me. And I know what you're thinking. I was mean to him after our rescue. But I was afraid he'd, you know, get bored and dump me. That he'd only done those nice things to keep me calm. He didn't. He wanted more. He's a good man, Belle."

Now my humor faded. "But will he stick around? I don't want to see you hurt. Because if he hurts you, I have to kill him and that will upset Rome."

A nurse entered, saw that I was awake and made a notation in a chart. The room quieted. She approached me, unhooked my IV and informed me I was free to go at any time.

When she left, I remained in bed, meaning to grill Sherridan a bit more. But Cody arrived, and the words vanished from my tongue. He walked straight over to Sherridan and drew her into his embrace. She willingly fell into it.

"What about Desert Gal?" I asked him, jaw clenched. "You two seemed pretty cozy when you were hunting me and Rome down. Not to mention while you were locking up Sherridan and Lexis."

His eyes narrowed at the insult. "That was an act, and I can't believe you'd think otherwise," he said, and Sherridan was nodding as though she believed him. "When Reese gave her your location, he forced my hand. I had to act or she would have doubted my intent to join her team. She would have doubted my claim of being sick of PSI and all the people who work there. So I took Lexis and Sherridan. And yeah, I could have let them get away and told her it was an accident, but that would have raised even more suspicions and we didn't have time for that."

"Oh." I didn't know what else to say.

"Desert Gal is a disturbed woman with major daddy issues, and she needs help. I pretended to give her that help, but I kept my hands to myself. In fact, I told her I was gay. That way, I could keep her at a physical distance, as well as let her think she was pretty enough to one day change my mind."

I folded my arms over my middle. "But you didn't keep Sherridan and Lexis safe."

His shoulders slumped a little. "I know. But I did what I could. They're alive, aren't they?"

"Yes."

"Because I gave them to Desert Gal, she trusted me with the locations of three other compounds. We were able to raid them and pick up fourteen other innocents. Or maybe scrims. Time will tell. But believe me, letting Sherri be taken nearly killed me."

When Sherridan didn't immediately cut him a new

eye socket for calling her by the hated nickname, I knew it was serious. My stomach twisted painfully.

"Besides," he added, "it's not like I had much help making decisions. In the beginning of this case, you were otherwise occupied. With Rome. With Memory Man. I knew Desert Gal was my responsibility." He was losing the shamed look and returning to total irritation.

Rome stiffened, ever ready to defend me.

"You're right," I said, hoping to ease things. "You're right. I wasn't a lot of help to you in that department."

Cody relaxed. Even offered, "Granted, you're a lot more focused now."

"Look at you two, playing nice," Sherridan said with a grin. "Don't be too hard on Cody, Belle. He did what he thought was right. And I had time to do some serious thinking while Desert Wasp had me in that cage, and even more time these past few days when I wasn't allowed to speak at home, and you know what I realized? Relationships eventually hurt, every damn one of them. Look at you and Rome. I know Cody's flighty and I know he'll eventually get tired of me and leave, but I'm willing to try for something with him while I've got the chance."

She was right. She didn't need the pain headed her way, but if she was willing to deal with it, who was I to try and stop her? I would just have to be there to help her pick up the pieces.

"Damn it." Cody threw up his arms. "Why does everyone think I'll leave?"

"Your dating history." Sherridan shrugged. "Face it, you run like a track star at the first sign of commitment."

"You've gone on more dates than I have." He glowered down at her. "But maybe I've changed."

She snorted. "Hardly."

His arms tightened around her. "You're begging for a fight, woman."

A tremor sped the length of her spine and she whispered, "I think I proved last night that I don't beg for anything."

His pupils dilated, and his nostrils flared. "Challenge accepted." He grabbed her wrist and tugged her out of the room.

Not once did she protest. No, she giggled.

I lay there, stunned.

Rome shook his head. "Dear God."

"I know. Are *we* that disgusting?"

He smiled with self-deprecation. "Probably worse."

We shared a laugh. He squeezed my hand, love in his eyes, and I knew, as surely as if I were psychic like Lexis, that we were going to make it. We belonged together. Nothing, not even memory loss, my new and improved powers, or two people determined to break us up once and for all, had been able to pull us apart.

We were forever.

EPILOGUE

THE DAY OF MY WEDDING ARRIVED.

Finally I'd picked out a dress and hadn't burned it, managed to order invitations and napkins without soaking them. I now stood in front of a full-length mirror, gazing at myself. I wore a long ivory Grecian gown, with thin straps and silver roses sewn into the fabric. My veil boasted the same silver roses and flowed down my honey-colored curls (Sherridan had styled the thick mass for me, saying it was the least she could do after all the times I'd blow-dried her hair at fifty paces) and along my bare, slightly sun-kissed arms.

The color in my cheeks was high and pink, and my hazel eyes were sparkling.

"You've never looked more beautiful," Sherridan said from behind me. In her five-inch heels, she towered over me. She placed her hands on my shoulders.

"You, too. But don't get any ideas. Ear filters, remember?" Three weeks had passed since my surgery and her night of loving with Cody. To my surprise, they were still together and were mushier than even me and Rome. They were always holding hands, always touching. Cody seemed to give her everything she'd been missing in her life: love, acceptance, attention. When she became too high-maintenance, like yesterday, crying because she thought she looked fat, he just told her how beautiful she was, then spent a good hour pointing out all his favorite parts of her body. I know because I'd been in the next room.

I hadn't been able to help myself. I'd softened toward him (after gagging). I'd had to. He was Rome's best man. But part of me still wanted to hate him, since Sherridan would soon be moving out of my house and into Cody's. Yes, Cody had finally bought a house—a sign he must be serious about committing to Sherridan. He'd even used her as his Realtor. Too bad I wasn't ready to give her up.

"I can't believe this day has finally arrived," I said. "Or that I was able to book this amazing church. Or that I was able to get the invitations printed in time. Or that I was able to secure the best caterer in town."

"Pays to know the right people," she said with a smile.

Everyone had turned me down, told me no, to get lost, they couldn't help me. Then she'd made a few calls for me and boom—*everyone* wanted to help. Whatever I'd desired, I'd gotten.

John was putting her powers to good use, too. He'd made Sherridan an official member of my team. So I guess I wouldn't be giving her up, really. I'd see her every day at work.

"Are you ready?" Elaine asked as she strolled into the room. "Oh, Belle." She stopped, placed a hand over her mouth. "You look radiant."

"Thank you, Vampyra," I said, using the name she and Tanner had finally settled on. They, too, were still together. Like Sherridan, they'd been talking about moving out and getting a place of their own. I'd never seen Tanner so happy as when he was with this girl, and that made me happy. Though I'd miss having the little shit at my beck and call.

"Everyone prepared for the worst?" I asked. I mean, hello. This was a wedding of two superheroes. Every villain in the world would love to crash it. Desert Gal was still in prison, so she wasn't a worry. Reese was out but in rehab, so he could be a problem. The Multiplier was already up for parole, according to John, but as of now, he was still behind bars.

"John swore he'd guard this place like the secrets of the universe were in the chapel," Sherridan reminded me. "Nothing's going to go—"

"Don't say it!" Elaine and I shouted in unison.

Sherridan pressed her lips together.

Everyone breathed a collective sigh of relief. That kind of declaration would only cause fate to laugh at us.

"I just came in to tell you that they're ready for you," Elaine said.

Sherridan strode to the table and lifted my bouquet. Silver roses. She handed it to me with a smile. "Belle Masters. Can't say I'm glad Rome finally convinced you to take his name, but I like the girl that goes with it, so I'll deal."

I laughed, hugged her close. Waved Elaine over and she joined in the hug, still looking dazzled at being able to touch people so freely.

"All right, ladies," I said after a few minutes, straightening. "Let's do this."

"You sound like Rome just before a mission," Elaine said through tears. Happy tears, though. "Nervous?"

"A little," I admitted. "I don't want to trip. I don't want anything to go wrong. This is the first day of my new life."

"Look at it this way," Sherridan said, moving in front of me toward the door. Elaine lined up behind her. My bridesmaids, I thought with a tingle. This wedding was really happening. "You're the only bride in town who can relight a candle at her wedding without going near it if it blows out."

I laughed as she'd intended. And then the two began marching out, into the chapel. When it was my turn, I inhaled, held it…held the breath…and slowly released it. Seemed like the day I'd been waiting for my entire life had finally arrived. I was giving myself body and soul to the man I loved. The man who loved me for exactly who I was. And afterward, we had a few weeks off and we were going to honeymoon in the Arctic. Better snuggling there, Rome had said.

Slowly, I walked forward. Past the double doors. Down a corridor. I could see the back of Sherridan as she stepped into the sanctuary. I reached the door and my dad, my wonderful dad, and my new daughter, Sunny, joined me. He was going to escort me, and she was acting as flower girl. Sunny took her role seriously, too. She had flowers in her hair, glued to her dress and her shoes, and the basket she held was overflowing.

I gave them both a hug.

"Ready?" my dad asked. He was tall and sort of thick, with brown hair and a kind, teddy-bear face.

"Ready."

He kissed my cheek. "I'm so proud of you, Bell-Belle. Your mother would be, too."

"I love you, Daddy." I bent down to Sunny. "And I love you."

"Forever," she said.

"Forever." That was not up for negotiation. "Now go on. It's finally your turn."

She was beaming as she walked forward, throwing petals in every direction.

When she reached the front, music suddenly blasted from the church. *Here comes the bride.* Everyone stood and turned to catch sight of me. My dad and I started forward. Tears were already burning my eyes. Damn it,

I didn't want to cry at my own wedding! But I saw Sunny, now standing proudly beside her own dad and grinning happily at me, my precious dogs (who this time were clad in matching white dresses and darling little tiaras) playing at their feet.

She waved me over to hurry me along. The crowd chuckled.

My gaze shifted, and I spotted Tanner as one of Rome's groomsmen. He blew me a kiss. Lexis, I saw next, was in the front pew. She offered me a tentative smile. I couldn't help myself. I returned it. This was my day, a dream come true. I was feeling generous.

The crowd suddenly let out a gasp. Before I could glance around to see what evil scrim had managed to crash my wedding—and kill the bastard—Jean-Luc brushed past me, turned and stopped directly in front of me. My dad glanced between us as the crowd fell silent, watching.

I patted his arm. "It's okay," I said.

"Sorry I'm late. I couldn't stay away," Jean-Luc said. He was wearing a wrinkled and stained T-shirt, a holey pair of jeans and flip-flops. His hair was in disarray and he smelled like beer. "You look amazing."

"You look like shit." They were the only words I could think of at the moment, but deep down I was glad to see him—bad timing or not. His absence these past few weeks had been the only dark spot in my life.

He didn't react. He just leaned into me and pressed a lingering kiss on my cheek. "I still love you, but I wish you all the best. I wanted you to know that," he said, then spun on his heel, strode forward and plopped into a seat behind Lexis.

Her vision, I thought, looking up. Rome smiled at me to let me know he understood what had just happened.

Lexis gaped at Jean-Luc, but I saw the longing in her

gaze. I hoped her vision about him came true. He deserved a happily-ever-after.

"Come on, my girl. Rome's waiting," my dad said, and I laced my arm through his.

My head held high, we kicked into gear again. The closer we came to the altar, the faster my steps grew. Eagerness rushed through me. Finally my dad handed me over, and Rome held tight. Love glowed on his face, and damn, his body was fine, encased in the black tux as it was.

"Belle," he said. "You take my breath away."

"So you like the dress?"

"Actually, I can't wait to strip you."

The pastor heard, and cleared his throat. We laughed.

"Let's get to the kissing part," Rome told him.

And we did.

To Do List

—Get naked.

—Make love to Rome.

—Repeat. Over and over again.

—Return from honeymoon thoroughly sated and eager to show off—er, demonstrate—your new-found control over your powers to your cohorts at PSI.

—Solve the next case with the help of your trusty and ever-expanding team of sidekicks—scrims, beware!

—Save the world—or at least do your part to populate it with little Romes and Belles, thereby making it a better place.

Dear Supersmart Readers—you may not have powers, but everyone deserves a paranormal nickname.

Anyway. OMG, do I have the best news for you! Check it. Gena Showalter has, like, a lot of books coming out. None as good as mine, of course, but get this. In May 2010, you'll find all of her e-books printed in one volume, *Into the Dark,* along with all kinds of Lords of the Underworld goodies. (I just shivered. Lords of the Underworld = hawtness!)

And thankfully, the news doesn't end there. In June 2010, *The Darkest Passion,* featuring the amazingly delicious Aeron, keeper of Wrath—please don't tell Rome I called another man amazingly delicious. Now that his memory has been returned, I can't get away with anything!—hits stores. After that, in July 2010, you'll get to read about Gideon, keeper of Lies, in *The Darkest Lie.* There goes another shiver!

And no need to say it—the wait is going to be excruciating! Believe me, I know. But no matter what I threaten Gena with, she won't change those dates. *Anyway.* In the meantime, if you haven't read *Intertwined,* an incredible book about a boy with four human souls trapped inside his head, well, you're missing out. Vampires, werewolves and true love…what more could you ask for? Well, except for me. I'm pretty awesome.

Anyway. I should probably get back to my new husband, the better than delicious Rome. Oh, yeah, and saving the world.

Be safe!
Belle Masters
a.k.a. "Wonder Girl"

REQUEST YOUR
FREE BOOKS!

2 FREE NOVELS
FROM THE ROMANCE COLLECTION
PLUS 2 FREE GIFTS!

YES! Please send me 2 FREE novels from the Romance Collection and my 2 FREE gifts (gifts are worth about $10). After receiving them, if I don't wish to receive any more books, I can return the shipping statement marked "cancel." If I don't cancel, I will receive 4 brand-new novels every month and be billed just $5.74 per book in the U.S. or $6.24 per book in Canada. That's a saving of at least 28% off the cover price. It's quite a bargain! Shipping and handling is just 50¢ per book in the U.S. and 75¢ per book in Canada.* I understand that accepting the 2 free books and gifts places me under no obligation to buy anything. I can always return a shipment and cancel at any time. Even if I never buy another book, the two free books and gifts are mine to keep forever.

194 MDN E4LY 394 MDN E4MC

Name	
	(PLEASE PRINT)

Address	Apt. #

City	State/Prov.	Zip/Postal Code

Signature (if under 18, a parent or guardian must sign)

Mail to The Reader Service:
IN U.S.A.: P.O. Box 1867, Buffalo, NY 14240-1867
IN CANADA: P.O. Box 609, Fort Erie, Ontario L2A 5X3

Not valid for current subscribers to the Romance Collection
or the Romance/Suspense Collection.

Want to try two free books from another line?
Call 1-800-873-8635 or visit www.morefreebooks.com.

* Terms and prices subject to change without notice. Prices do not include applicable taxes. N.Y. residents add applicable sales tax. Canadian residents will be charged applicable provincial taxes and GST. Offer not valid in Quebec. This offer is limited to one order per household. All orders subject to approval. Credit or debit balances in a customer's account(s) may be offset by any other outstanding balance owed by or to the customer. Please allow 4 to 6 weeks for delivery. Offer available while quantities last.

Your Privacy: Harlequin Books is committed to protecting your privacy. Our Privacy Policy is available online at www.eHarlequin.com or upon request from the Reader Service. From time to time we make our lists of customers available to reputable third parties who may have a product or service of interest to you. If you would prefer we not share your name and address, please check here. ☐

Help us get it right—We strive for accurate, respectful and relevant communications. To clarify or modify your communication preferences, visit us at www.ReaderService.com/consumerschoice.

MROM10